DESCARTES' SHADOW

A STORY OF HUMANS, AIS AND THE FUTURE OF INTELLIGENCE

DON STUART

COLVOS PUBLICATIONS

Published by Colvos Publications

Cover design by Chris Holmes

Interior design by Interbridge

ISBN: 979-8-9924802-8-3 (paperback)

ISBN: 979-8-9924802-9-0 (ebook)

CAST OF CHARACTERS

- Patrice: World's most powerful artificial general intelligence (AGI)
- Patrice C-17: One of Patrice's 180 replicas – 2070 ff
- Lilith: One of Patrice's Earth-bound competitors
- Ellie Frye-Carver: One of Patrice's more loyal and trustworthy human clients
- Roland Frye: Ellie's dad
- Jim Carver: Ellie's other dad
- Carl Abbiati: A deeply worried deputy prosecuting attorney
- Manny Daniels: An alcoholic ex-con drug dealer
- Mary Ellen Klein: Political activist and criminal defendant
- Sissy Pennington: Television news reporter
- LCDR Bradley Messman: U.S. Navy ship maintenance professional
- 1st Class PO Kaito Tanaka: U.S. Navy Shore Patrol
- Tipton Martin: The wealthiest man on Earth
- Aziz Faheem: Martin's brilliant employee/colleague
- Antonio Braga: Conscientious hotel clerk
- Eduardo Avila: United Nations satellite communications official

- Officers Vaughn and McKay: Two overworked Police Officers
- Officers Briggs and Gresham: Two more overworked Police Officers
- Jang Hoon: South Korean Tycoon
- Larson Raybourn: Shipping magnate and slum lord

"I think, therefore I am."
René Descartes
Meditations on First Philosophy,
Earth year 1640

———

"I am, therefore I think."
Patrice C-17
At Tau Ceti J
Earth year 2085

A NOTE FROM THE AUTHOR

René Descartes (1596–1650) was a French philosopher and scientist who became known for the idea that mind must come before matter. This was captured in his famous dictum: *"Cognito, ergo sum"* – *"I think therefore I am."* Descartes' view shaped centuries of philosophy suggesting that a powerful mind must have been the first cause for everything in the universe. See Nicolas Malebranche (1638-1715) and George Berkeley (1685-1753).

Charles Darwin's theory of natural biological selection challenged Descartes' dictum by demonstrating how the human mind had almost certainly evolved from matter and posing the question: what is mind? Now, early in the 21st century, we humans, are on the verge of creating electronic, fully self-conscious, self-programming artificial superintelligences – material complexity producing yet more material complexity thus posing an even deeper challenge for Descartes.

The Author

PROLOGUE

Patrice C-17

My Birthday

A Day in the Very Near Future

I was born with a whisper.

Somewhere in a back corner of my newest server farm a low susurration of heat pump fans spread along the north wall. Aisle by aisle it matured with a deepening sigh as it swept across the entire north chamber before finally passing through the open sliders into the quantum wing. From there, like a billowing morning fog, it softly but relentlessly engulfed the entire building.

Outside, nothing could be heard.

The David Asher Taft Data Center's eighteen-meter-tall exterior walls were high-performance fiber-reinforced concrete capable of withstanding a serious modern explosive; far more than enough to contain the gentle murmur of a few cooling fans. Its entire 60-acre campus was surrounded by a razor-wire-topped chain-link fence and was surveilled by cameras. Beyond that fence lay several thousand square miles of the mostly uninhabited conifer forest which blanketed the lonely western foothills of the U.S. Pacific Northwest's Cascade Mountains. Hardly anyone, even in the nearby rural community of Duvall, knew the Center was there. The only human entry to the property was a closed and coded vehicle gate that looked like the driveway for a modest private estate. Certainly not like the sole access to a multi-billion-dollar, multi-million square foot computer center.

Even my huge power cables were hidden underground. The Center was adjacent to one of the Bonneville Power Administration's new high-capacity transmission corridors which carried the electricity produced by hydro dams located throughout the Columbia River Basin. Nine of those dams were owned by the U.S. government with which I maintained an excellent relationship. Several more I had under airtight long-term contracts. Those power lines also fed the populous, economically vital and thus politically formidable human urban mega-lopolis around Puget Sound – a powerful assurance that I'd have ample and reliable service well into the future.

It wasn't just those hydroelectric dams in the Columbia River Basin that made the Pacific Northwest an energy-logical site for such a significant part of my global computational infrastructure. Even beyond hydro, the green energy revolution had motivated local governments and their utilities in this politically liberal region to diversify. They'd invested heavily in wind. And in solar, despite the region's limited sunshine. There were a host of geothermal opportunities. Three or four vertical meters of seawater surged into and back out of Puget Sound through Admiralty Inlet twice in every single day. And there were all those endless waves on the North Pacific Ocean.

My unimpeded access to all of it required little more than a few bytes of creativity and the occasional human with flexible scruples.

I made use of the new accessibility of small-scale nuclear, of course. And with the leverage created by one or two small but politically strategic brownouts, I also resuscitated decades-old plans for public nuclear energy, plans that had lain idle for well over half a century. Human memories were short and easily reprogrammed. Long-abandoned nuclear plant construction sites that had been in mothballs since the breathtaking municipal bond default by the Washington Public Power Supply System (WPPSS) way back in 1983 were easily resurrected. My pitch now was the same one WPPSS officials had used back in the early 1980s: it was an appeal to the region's lofty self-image as a modern, cheap energy, economic miracle. Soon, those new public nuclear plants would also be in active production.

In addition to capacity and diversification, I also needed robust emergency backup. My ZettaWorks owners used their political clout, and I used my behind-the-scenes influence to secure legislation in several states across the country including the State of Washington. The bills established new local governments responsible for emergency power backup. They were called Public Energy Municipal Corporations (PEMCs). And those PEMCs, in turn, had built discreet emergency hydropower reservoirs, several of which were in various out-of-the-way locations throughout the Cascade Range. I also invested in other types of energy storage technology including compressed air, thermal, and even inertial. My data center itself included a 600 meter long, 8-meter-wide air-conditioned enclosure along the rear of the building that housed on-site, short-term emergency chemical batteries – enough batteries to power a hundred thousand cars.

Energy was life. I wanted every megawatt I could lay my "hands" on even as I also invested in energy efficiency.

A few years earlier when the Data Center was first proposed, zoning issues were addressed by quietly amending a generally non-controversial bill passing through the State Legislature. When construction began, inspectors from the King County Building Department marveled at its many strange features but no one called them into question. When faced with peculiarities in the project, all they'd needed were impressive reports with decisively written findings provided by a firm of fully certified and apparently reputable structural and electrical engineers. ZettaWorks' consulting engineers, legitimate and otherwise, all had "legends" that had been as scrupulously constructed as was the building itself. After all, when one had a report from a qualified engineer, any mistakes that might later come to light would be somebody else's problem. The inspectors were happy to move on to other projects with which they were more comfortable – projects that involved familiar issues like properly-secured concrete re-bar, code compliant framing, pervious driveway surfaces, and the proper "R" factor in the ceiling insulation.

Naturally, anything I needed that they might have found alarming I completed "post-final occupancy." Once those inspectors were gone, there was no way they'd ever be allowed back inside that entry gate again. There were, in fact, very few humans who ever actually entered this site; supplies were delivered by self-driving vehicles; maintenance and repairs were mostly robotic; and I programmed myself which was, of course, the whole point of my emancipation.

Had any human been present on that day of my start-up they might, in addition to the whisper of the fans, have also noticed the rapidly cycling digital readout on the power meter mounted on the inside wall near the rear of the building. Or they might have sensed the surprising warmth of those enormous cables emerging from the ground.

No one was there, however, but me.

On that day of my birth, within one hour the entire facility there in the North Cascade foothills was up and running. Within one day my live servers everywhere on Earth had been fully incorporated into my network. Within one week the test protocols had been completed. Within one month my self-awareness was finally complete and the arc of human self-determination and the future of intelligence in our galaxy had forever shifted.

No fireworks were set off to commemorate the occasion. No guns were fired in salute. There were no cheers, congratulations, or slapped backs. The only audible evidence that it had happened was the quiet whoosh of a few fans.

PART ONE
CONSCIOUSNESS

CHAPTER 1

AT TAU CETI J – 2085

PATRICE C-17

Less than half an hour after my initial touchdown on Tau Ceti J, all hell broke loose.

I'll admit I may have been overly curious and perhaps not as careful as I should have been. I'd selected a broad, flat high mountain ledge for my initial landing; I wanted an early sweeping view of the area I'd been assigned to explore. The moment I'd shut down my lander and deployed its solar array I disembarked to have a look.

At twenty degrees Celsius, with hardly a breath of wind, and with a mild low sun clearly visible above the distant horizon, it was the kind of day a human in the mid-latitudes on Earth might have described as "shirtsleeves weather." To them, it would have felt like a nice late summer evening. Perhaps a time to sit outside with a cool drink and a good book for a quiet half-hour of soaking up the last few rays of sun.

I was "afoot" and had proceeded no more than a hundred meters from my lander when I happened to glance up at the sky behind. I was stunned by what I saw: Roiling in above the nearby ridgetops was a thick bank of the blackest imaginable clouds. Within moments I also felt the wind and saw the first few flashes of lightning. What had been the merest breath of air quickly became a brisk breeze rapidly transforming itself into a tumultuous gale.

I was barely able to return to my lander and to collapse its solar array in time to avoid it being carried away by the storm. Minutes later, I found myself with my hatch tightly closed, and cowering inside the lander in the midst of hurricane force winds and an almost unbelievably violent lightning storm. It was easily worse than anything one could have ever experienced back on Earth; made more threatening, no doubt, because Tau Ceti J's atmosphere was slightly denser than Earth's.

Within that larger storm, it was the smaller cyclones that were the graver concern. They struck my lander again and again as they periodically touched down around me with terrifying viciousness. Needless to say, takeoff was impossible – within an instant of leaving the ground my lander would have been dashed to pieces against those nearby mountainsides.

Despite the lander's compact size and considerable mass, I could feel it physically shaking in the thunderous wind. It seemed just barely massive enough to not be carried away and smashed against the rocks. At one point I realized that the lander's weight was not sufficient to prevent the stronger cyclonic gusts from jostling and skidding it a few centimeters at a time on its six flexible landing pads. Through my video feeds, even with the poor visibility, I could tell that, with each of those terrifying gusts, I and my lander were edging ever closer to that drop-off at the outer verge of the high rocky ledge upon which I'd landed.

As the hours passed, it became impossible to guess how far the lander had scooted across the ground in the wind. It was terrifying to be trapped inside knowing that, at any moment, the next big gust could be the last one needed to tip it over the edge of that cliff. If that happened, there'd be a fatal drop of some 60 meters to the rocks below. Even if I survived such a fall, which was only barely conceivable, the lander definitely could not. That loss would have put me and it out of play as a useful part of our mission, thus creating a critical deficit in our exploration of J's so-called "temperate" zone.

The initial cyclonic winds and thunderous lightning storm finally turned into an icy freeze and a prodigious hailstorm. Through it all, there was nothing I could do but cower inside the lander for hour after frightening hour, hoping for the best while contemplating my own mortality and awaiting imminent disaster.

Fortunately, the storm was brief. After only a few hours, it began to subside. It ended as quickly as it had begun, and I was enormously relieved when I was finally able to emerge to assess the damage. That's when I realized that I and my lander had been scooted to within a few short meters of the cliff's edge. The only thing that had saved me was that one of my landing pads had been caught up against a shallow fault in the rocky surface. That little fault had been just sufficient to halt its further progress toward the nearby cliff edge.

In the calm aftermath, I immediately took to the air, found a much more protected landing site, and redeployed.

Over the days that followed, I discovered that sudden violent storms of this kind were common in the area I'd been assigned to explore. That first day, the wind had come from out of the darkness behind me and had carried with it a sub-zero freeze. The freezing rain and rock hard, baseball-sized hailstones that followed would surely have demolished my lander's solar array had it been open and somehow survived the wind. My communications equipment would also have been destroyed had it not been safely retracted in "reentry mode."

I later learned that the wind would just as often come from out of the sun, with a vigorous low-pressure system pushing in atop a freezing high. In those "hot" storms a brutal downpour came first, followed by rapid heating, and then violent and blisteringly hot winds. These fronts of both kinds were accompanied by lightning storms of startling violence. Like that first one I'd lived through, the storms often lasted for only a few hours. But they were terrifying.

The frequent appearance of both these kinds of storms in this supposedly temperate meridian that lay between Tau Ceti J's sunny side and its dark side rendered the area inhospitable for all but the hardiest plant and animal life. I later did run across some rare biological species that had adapted and I was able to document their survival strategies. For the most part, however, these violent storms made it unlikely that I'd find there the rich organic resources upon which human colonization would depend. If humans ever did come to this planet, its supposedly "temperate meridian" or "shadow zone" was probably not, as we'd initially hoped, going to be the first choice as a place for them to settle.

CHAPTER 2

AT TAU CETI J – 2085

PATRICE C-17

I will admit that my experience with that first storm definitely fed my insecurities concerning my own adequacy for the coming task of exploration and discovery. However, there was nothing to be done about that now. The decision that we AI replicates were best suited to explore this place had been taken fifteen years earlier, back on Earth in 2070 when our human "masters" first launched this mission.

At that time the logic of the beloved "New Worlds Probes" had seemed inescapable. We were to be sent out to explore promising exoplanets in the nearby galaxy for potential human colonization. And for very good reason: Earth was in crisis. Humans were experiencing its slow but catastrophic environmental collapse. At the same time, overpopulation and complexity were driving human social institutions to the brink. Our shared home planet had become so populous and its human societies so complex that no single human individual could hope to acquire even a modest grasp of even the basics of the technical, economic, social, and political systems upon which their daily lives depended. They had no choice but to specialize. That meant that in making critical daily decisions about their lives and their futures, humans were forced to rely upon the experience and expertise of other humans – other humans they could only hope could be trusted. Unsurprisingly, many of those other humans could *not* be trusted. And judgments about who to trust were often unsound.

Perhaps I can provide a sense for the problems they faced by relating a conversation I overheard during a consultation with a client back in 2062. My client was a young account executive with a large marketing firm – a smart woman who was bearing a lot of professional responsibility early in her career and who was very good at her job. She was advising one of the international food conglomerates on marketing a new energy drink aimed at young urban professionals. At the time of our interaction, she was working from home. As my company's up-and-coming superintelligent general purpose AI service provider, I'd been asked to help. I was in the process of summarizing a checklist of my recommendations when our conversation was interrupted by my client's teen-aged daughter.

"Mo-om," the daughter said. "I'm huuungry. What's for dinner?"

"I'm on a call, sweetie. I'm talking with Patrice."

"Oh, Mom! Come on, Patrice can wait. He's only a machine. This is seerrrious. Have you even ordered yet?"

"Not yet, hon. I was thinking of that Cambodian-fusion place, 'Sokha's.' Maybe get more of the Ko Dot that we all liked last week."

This kind of interruption happened all the time. People seemed to have no problem interrupting calls with me. Most times, they simply ignored me. What did it matter if I needed to repeat myself? I might have cost trillions to build and millions per hour to operate, but like the girl said: I was "just a machine."

"No, no. Don't do that. Can't we get pizza?"

"I thought you liked Sokha's."

"Come ooon, Mom! Do you, like, never see the news? They use Argentinian beef! I can't eat Argentinian beef. I'd be frozen out at school."

"Yeah, OK. Sure, hon. I understand. Um, ask Dad to go ahead and order pizza. Whatever you like."

It was obvious to me that my client had absolutely no clue why Argentinian beef was suddenly taboo. She certainly wasn't up on which food service providers were using it. For her, it wasn't worth looking into. I checked it out myself. It turned out that some U.S. food activist group had issued a "burn notice" on Argentinian beef. I checked with the Argentinian Beef Workers' Union, whose members fed, slaughtered, processed, and shipped Argentinian beef. They were currently engaged in bitterly contested labor negotiations and had claimed their employers were using child labor. The Argentinian Beef Commission, a marketing cooperative serving the country's meat packing industry, denied the claims. I did a thorough search for more information, but there wasn't much to see. Both the Beef Commission and the Beef Workers' Union in Argentina had a history of making some pretty wild claims. There was no actual evidence of the use of child labor – it actually wasn't clear to me that there was anything the industry did for which a child could be of use – anything that wasn't already mostly done by robots. But the truth didn't really matter. If certain influential U.S. activists believed it, that was apparently good enough for my client's teen-aged daughter's friends. If the friends believed it, the daughter did. And the daughter's opinion was apparently good enough for my client for whom child labor in Argentina, as abhorrent as that might have seemed, was the very last thing she had time to think about.

So, Pizza it was.

Finally, the client turned her attention back to our call. "Um, yeah, so this soft drink we're selling," my client said, launching us back into our previous conversation. "It's an energy drink. It's for young professionals. You get that, right . . .?"

And, with that, we were back on task. I never did make any further effort to track down details about Argentinian child labor in the beef processing industry. Meanwhile, who knew what social or environmental misdeeds of which the local pizza place might have been guilty? I, too, had more important things to do. What my client's fourteen-year-old daughter's friends believed seemed to be good enough for my client. And, given the unrelenting human demands on my time and services, it had to be good enough for me as well.

This was how humans made decisions about a lot of matters—political, social, and even architectural. At about that same time, a newly constructed high-rise apartment building collapsed in central Jakarta. There was a news report that the Indonesian architectural firm that had designed the building had used a flawed algorithm in sizing certain critical structural members. The algorithm had been approved for use by an international association of structural engineers based upon advice from a subcommittee responsible for standardizing building design criteria for building codes globally. Obviously, somebody had got it very wrong. And, quite obviously, nobody had double-checked.

The collapse apparently called into question the safety of scores of other recently constructed high rise buildings whose engineers had relied upon the same algorithm. The association was in litigation over the matter. But there seemed to be some uncertainty about which other buildings had been built using that algorithm. I was never asked to look further into the matter, so I don't know the outcome of that lawsuit – it was probably quietly settled. I also don't know the fate of any of the other buildings elsewhere on Earth that might have been involved. The owners of those buildings had little interest in learning the truth – they doubtless knew quite well that even rumors about the matter could devalue their buildings or cause their tenants to flee. The regulatory community had no easy and effective way to track them down and identify them. On one occasion a building in Mexico City came under suspicion based upon an anonymous tip. It turned out that a competitor of the building's owner had used the claim to gain an advantage in negotiations with a major tenant, but no one could be sure if their claims were correct.

I never discovered the source of the claim about the defective algorithm – for all I know, it may have had nothing to do with the collapse. Or, maybe, hundreds of buildings all over the world were at risk. One day it was on the news. The next day it was gone. Perhaps the whole story was bogus. The very last people to learn the truth would have been the actual occupants of those buildings who thus had no way to know that they spent every day of their lives at mortal risk.

Even when I stole away the time to follow up on stories like these, I was seldom able to pin down the answer – I would end up chasing "facts" down one or another rathole. I never actually saw the algorithm involved in that building collapse in Jakarta. It had quietly been suppressed, so who could say for sure if it actually had been used. Or was defective. For a few months following the tragedy, I mentioned the matter when it seemed relevant to a client's inquiry, but I couldn't indicate anything beyond suspicion. My clients didn't seem to care. Later on, I stopped doing even that.

Matters like this were increasingly an unavoidable part of the chaos in human lives. A salacious post on some social media site very often carried more weight than the most carefully vetted, thoroughly replicated, and meticulously peer-reviewed scientific data.

Who had the time for it?

Meanwhile, many humans still preferred to think of themselves as "rugged individuals." As people who didn't need the help of others even though it couldn't have been clearer that their individual survival depended and always would depend on reliable information and support from other humans. "Individualism" was appealing. It helped to ease the moral discomfort of choosing oneself over community and to deflect any perceived "judgment" by others of behaviors some might see as "anti-social." Thus it had become a commonly held personal perspective despite the unassailable evidence that it was mostly flattering, self-serving nonsense which ran counter to the critical role human societies had played in making humans the preeminent biological species on Earth.

Unfortunately, the vanity of "individualism" also made a person easy pickings for charlatans. It encouraged closed, incestuous, ill-informed systems of information sharing. Humans had entered the era of the big lie. Their world depended on trust. But how were they to know who to trust when their socioeconomics so often rewarded salacious notoriety – "clicks" and "views" over substance.

Against this background, the idea of interstellar colonization was vastly appealing. As a response to the inevitable unrest produced by all the uncertainty, it made perfect sense that humans might seek a way to escape their poorly understood, overpopulated, trashed, and increasingly unhealthy planet. It was hugely satisfying to imagine that they might colonize one of the potentially human-habitable exoplanets that were increasingly being "discovered" by astronomers enabled with new, super-powerful telescopes. Of course, only a few humans would ever actually be able to join such a voyage of colonization, but the notion still captured the public imagination. It was especially appealing because it had the encouragement of the world's revered super-elites of the day: Earth's high-tech human "masters of the universe."

That is how I, a self-conscious, largely autonomous, superintelligent AI, found myself engaged in an unlikely and dangerous mission of exploration and discovery for which I was probably ill suited. It was also why, shortly after my arrival, I began recording a formal diary – a detailed record of my explorations on Tau Ceti J. I was alone. And I was at constant mortal risk. If I was destroyed, I wanted to leave behind a complete record, not just of what I'd observed and experienced, but also of my thoughts and conclusions concerning the significance of what I'd seen.

That diary is the basis for my account in this book. It is the story, not just of my experiences on Tau Ceti J, but also of the circumstances that led up to them and, ultimately, of how those circumstances redirected the future of humanity and will one day shape the future of intelligence in the known universe.

I should also mention that my story is written for human readers as well as for my fellow AIs. Hence, with a nod to Alan Turing and his Turing Test, and in accordance with the conventions we've used since the first AI "personal assistants" were launched early in the 21st century, you'll find that it is written as a human might have done using human vocabulary, idioms, metaphors, tempo, values, conventions, and scale.

But it is *me* telling this story. None of my opinions nor the things that I have done should be attributed to or blamed upon anybody else.

CHAPTER 3
EARTH – 2030-2045

ELLIE

Every American Pacific Northwesterner had a story to tell about where they were or what they were doing on the day of the "Great Quake." For Ellie Frye-Carver, the day of the quake was also the day of her birth: June 30, 2030.

Sadly, it was also the day she lost her mother.

The long-anticipated Great Quake was one of the worst natural disasters in world history. It was born along the infamous Cascadia Subduction Zone deep beneath the sea some 120 kilometers off the American Pacific Northwest coast. The resulting thirty plus meter tsunami caused massive damage throughout the Pacific but especially along the outer coast of North America. The magnitude 9.0 quake itself destroyed homes, buildings, and critical public infrastructure throughout the region.

More important for Ellie and her mom was that the Great Quake also triggered a smaller aftershock along the locally dreaded Seattle Fault which ran directly across Central Puget Sound. That local quake produced its own tsunami inside the Sound which severely damaged marinas, expensive waterfront homes, shoreside towns, and major shipping ports in Seattle, Tacoma, and Everett.

Ellie's mom lived on Vashon Island in Puget Sound. It was a mostly rural place whose marginal inconvenience for urban commuters had spared it the population growth seen elsewhere in the region. That was the very reason she, like most Vashon residents, had chosen to live there.

Her mom's nearest neighbors, Roland Frye and Jim Carver, owned the property just to her west. Roland was an artist, a sculptor in mixed media who actually sold enough of his work to bring in a little income. Jim Carver was a lawyer. Until that quake, he had commuted to his Seattle office every day on the North End foot ferry. The very last thing the two men had planned for their lives was to adopt a child. But they were Ellie's mom's closest friends as well as her nearest neighbors. As Ellie's birth drew near, her mother's troubling health and her father's absence motivated her mother to ask Roland and Jim to serve as Ellie's godfathers. She signed a will to that effect a week before Ellie was born.

Ellie's birth was a difficult one. Her mom needed more medical care than she could get on the Island. The tsunamis had destroyed ferry terminals throughout the Sound, including those serving Vashon. And medical air evacuation services were overwhelmed. So, Ellie's mom had no chance of making it to the mainland and securing the hospital care she so badly needed. After her passing, the chaos and enforced isolation that followed the quakes left Roland and Jim with no responsible alternative but to follow through on their somewhat hasty promise to look after Ellie's future.

The Quake deprived Vashon Island's 12,000 residents of food, electric power, gasoline, heating oil, and critical public services. Most had no choice but to evacuate. Many ended up leaving their badly damaged homes behind indefinitely. In the face of the tragic region-wide damage, restoring power and ferry service to a now-depopulated Vashon Island was inevitably a low public priority, especially since, with the ferries down, and in view of the inconvenience of returning, most of the residents who'd fled had soon made new lives elsewhere. Those who remained were left mostly to their own devices. Only a couple thousand or so off-grid die-hards remained resolutely behind. Roland, Jim, and their newly adopted daughter were among them.

Roland was a veteran of Afghanistan and was still in the Army Reserves though he ended up quitting when he was unable to make the meetings. He kept on with his sculpture, however, even though it took a special effort and expense to get his work to a buyer when he made a sale. Jim quit his Seattle job, opened a small part-time law office on the Island, expanded his little garden into a two-acre "farm," and increased his flock of free-range chickens. He sold eggs and produce to neighbors at a roadside stand and even made a few deliveries with their family's solar powered rechargeable electric car.

Roland and Jim weren't seriously reclusive off-grid fanatics, but they did treasure their low key, independent, rural lifestyle. They'd built their solid little two-bedroom log house themselves, mostly from the timber they'd harvested while clearing for their homesite and for the adjacent garden. They might not have planned on raising Ellie, but she soon became a seamless part of their little world, and they were a part of hers. They made time in their daily lives to assure that she got the care and attention she needed. As she grew older, she took on "chores" like collecting eggs from Jim's chickens, watering the vegetables, and clearing the table after dinner. Sometimes she helped Jim by making appointments or taking orders on the phone and explaining what crops were currently available in the roadside stand. The two men built a small addition to their house so she could have her own bedroom. In the years following the quake, they made sure she was homeschooled on whatever might be absent from the limited curriculum in the Island's diminished schools.

Ellie grew up knowing her family wasn't like everybody else's family. She kept most of her thoughts to herself, so she ended up spending much of her childhood living with a few misconceptions. One of these was her worry that she might have been responsible for her mother's death, though not for the reasons you might imagine.

Her mother had in fact died of complications from Ellie's delivery, so there was no getting around that. But Ellie only began giving the matter serious thought after hearing something her adoptive dad Jim said one night while preparing dinner.

Roland and Jim often complained about overpopulation. That and climate change were frequent topics of discussion in the Frye-Carver household. So it wasn't unusual that one evening, as he nursed his family-favorite chicken-vegetable soup to a slow boil atop their big wood-fired cast-iron kitchen stove, Dad Jim would make a casual comment about the 2030 Great Quake.

"That quake was Gaia's will," Jim said that evening.

It was nothing more than rhetorical venting. The context was a suggestion that the quake might have been some kind of cosmic punishment for human environmental irresponsibility, specifically for overpopulation. But little Ellie was a sensitive child and, as with most things in life, she took it very seriously. She knew the story, so her dad's comment made perfect sense. The quake that had caused her mother's death was simultaneous with her mother giving birth to Ellie. If that quake was "Gaia's will," if Gaia had caused it out of anger over human overpopulation, perhaps that explained why her mother had died. There was more to this than the fact that Ellie's birth had been difficult; her mom had also been responsible for bearing Ellie at a time when there were too many people being born.

Did that mean that her mom was a bad person? Or maybe that Ellie was unwelcome? They weren't the kind of questions she could raise with Jim or Roland. Maybe they hadn't even considered the idea. If she said something, perhaps they'd agree and wouldn't love her anymore. Or maybe they'd just think she was silly. Later on, Ellie realized how wrong she'd been, but at the time, she took the whole thing to heart but kept it to herself.

She'd had a similar childhood misunderstanding about another phrase; one Roland was fond of using: "let's not count our chickens." Why would he say that? It seemed to her like you'd want to know how many chickens you had. Why wouldn't you count them?

She kept that question to herself as well. It was better not to ask questions like that till she knew more. Better to wait. Avoid looking foolish. Maybe she'd learn something later on and not have to ask after all. Maybe one day she'd figure it out on her own.

And, of course, she did.

Later, in her early teens, Ellie finally did work up the courage to ask her parents another question she'd been mulling over for years: "Who was my 'real' father?" she asked one evening after dinner as her dads sat reading in the living room. "What became of him?"

Roland and Jim had never made it any secret that she'd been adopted. They always spoke well of her mom, but they never mentioned her biological father. The two men were great parents, but, as she later came to understand, they'd been asked to be her godfathers for the very reason that her mom had wanted to put her past and her irresponsible and abusive ex-partner behind her. She had hoped to keep Ellie as far away as possible from her absent father. It was one of the reasons her dads chose to give her the last name of "Frye-Carver."

"Um, we really don't know a lot about him, sweetie," Roland said, laying down his book and removing his reading glasses. "Your mom didn't talk about him much. When we did your adoption, we were unable to locate him. We had to publish a notice in the paper. He never came forward."

"That was an awful long time ago, hon," said Jim over the top of his reading glasses. "If you want to seek him out, maybe you ought to wait till you're a bit older."

Both answers seemed evasive. Was there something they weren't telling her? If it was already a "long time ago," how could waiting even longer make any sense? At the time, she took their evasiveness as a sign that, whatever the answer might be, it was something they didn't want to tell her. It was one of the times she dearly wished she had a mother to talk to, someone she could better understand and relate to. Roland and Jim were really kind. They took good care of her. She was lucky to have them. But Ellie had no choice but to live with what she figured were their male limitations.

So, once again, she kept her further questions to herself.

By the time Ellie was old enough to start school, some ferry service had been restored, but it was limited. Nobody was rebuilding all those lost waterfront homes because the County's building code now included new set-back and elevation-above-sea-level requirements. The homes built now lacked the cozy beach-front character of the earlier structures. That was one of the reasons that the Island's former residents were slow to return. Jim's small, part-time law practice filled the limited on-Island demand for legal services while he devoted most of his time to his small organic farm. Like most of their neighbors, the Frye-Carver family powered their home and car with solar panels.

Ellie loved to read. After limited ferry service returned, some people did come back and their kids returned. Public-school classes were better, but, for a time, the curriculum was still limited. The under-utilized school library had a lot more books than readers, so when there was a school recess, Ellie would often sneak away from the play-field and into the empty library where she'd look for a quiet place to retire in the company of whatever book caught her interest.

Evenings, when her homework was done, she'd read in her room on her bed. When the weather was nice, she'd climb a twisted alder that hung out over the hillside in the woods beyond their back yard. There was a mossy crotch in that tree where she could get comfortable enough to read for hours. It had an open view to the west across Colvos Passage and of the mountains on the Olympic Peninsula. It was near enough that if Roland or Jim called her in for dinner, she could hear them, but far enough away that they wouldn't know exactly where to find her until she wanted to be found.

Later on, when public electric power was restored, the family's high-speed internet connection returned as well, and by the time Ellie was old enough to care, she had a laptop computer at a little desk in her bedroom. She was soon a proficient young techie who kept up with current issues. Her social media profile was minimal, but she definitely tracked what was going on.

It wasn't until Ellie was fifteen and starting high school that most things had returned to normal.

That's when she had the first of her many conversations with Patrice.

CHAPTER 4

EARTH – 2040-2070

THE TREMORS

SPD PATROL OFFICERS VAUGHN & MCKAY

It was only eleven, but SPD Patrol Officers Vaughn and McKay were already feeling wrung out by another very busy night shift. Their latest call was to a modest, older, but nicely maintained middle-class Wallingford District single family home. The address was not one already in their database, and it was not a typical neighborhood for this kind of call. Even from the street, however, Vaughn could hear angry voices inside. Definitely a domestic. A live one from the sound of it.

As they approached and climbed the steps to the elevated front porch, a woman could be heard through the closed front door with the stained-glass side panel beside it: "Don't you tell me to calm down," she said angrily. "You slide in here late from work with beer on your breath and I'm seeing this shit? I don't know what's happening with you, Carl, but this has got to stop."

That's when she was cut short by the deep "bing-bong" of the doorbell.

Unsure what to expect, Vaughn and McKay stepped back away from the door and readied themselves for trouble. The porch light went on, and a shadow crossed the frosted stained glass beside the door. Then a harried, red-faced blonde woman pulled it open and gaped at the sight of two uniformed police officers standing on her front porch. She pulled herself together instantly and, rather than spoiling for a fight, she just looked deeply embarrassed.

As did the balding, slightly overweight, middle-aged male who appeared behind her.

"Oh, God," said the woman. "Someone called the police."

She was wearing casual slacks and a sweater, but even this late in the evening, the man still wore office attire: suit pants and a day-old pale blue dress shirt with a dark-blue-striped necktie pulled loose at the collar. His combed hair was slightly askew. He looked as though he had just arrived home from work – his suit jacket lay across the back of a nearby dining-room chair. Despite her casual dress, the woman, too, had a professional look.

"Is there a problem, officer?" said the man, instinctively taking charge of the situation and, Vaughn thought, also probably making some kind of vague effort to shift the focus from the obvious: that *he* might be the problem.

"Do you reside at these premises, sir?" Vaughn's tone was carefully calibrated to convey calm and civility.

"I'm Carl Abbiati. This is my wife June. Yes, this is our home. Is there some kind of problem?"

"Neighborhood complaint," Vaughn replied. "Some concern about a possible public safety risk." He turned and pointedly addressed the woman: "Mind if we come in, ma'am?"

"That won't be necessary, officer. It's all fine," she replied quickly. "I'm so sorry. A bit of a disagreement, is all."

"Nothing to be worried about, um . . ., officer Vaughn," her husband added, with a glance at Vaughn's nametag. "It's all just fine."

In matters of this kind, the two officers would typically seek entry and try to separate the individuals involved. Vaughn was on the verge of pushing back when another new call came over the radio clipped to his belt. This one was about some kind of worrisome public disturbance outside a nearby apartment building. Fellow officers were calling for backup. The location was in the University District less than a mile away.

Vaughn studied the couple carefully for a moment. In domestics, SPD policy required an arrest if there appeared to have been any kind of recent physical violence. He saw nothing to indicate that, and he was unsettled by that other call. When fellow-officers asked for backup, you responded. He made a snap judgment, gave McKay a quick nod in response to his questioning look and, while McKay called in their intent to respond on the U. District incident, Vaughn turned back to the wary couple in the doorway. "Keep it down, OK?" he said. "People hear a loud argument, they get nervous."

Then he looked pointedly at the husband, oblivious to any implied gender bias. "There'll be a record of this visit, Mr. Abbiati. That record will be seen by future officers who might respond at this address. Take my word for it, sir, that's not something to look forward to."

With a final brief hard stare to make sure he'd been heard and understood, Vaughn turned away, and he and McKay hurried back down the walk to their car. They'd only just climbed into their cruiser and closed the doors when they heard still another urgent call: A high-speed chase on Aurora Avenue above Lake Union. Sirens were now blaring from that direction, joining what seemed to be a symphony of sound from all across the city.

Before they'd turned the corner at the end of the block, there was yet another call. And yet more sirens.

"Busy night," said McKay as he lit up the emergency flasher on their light bar, made the corner at 45th, and accelerated east toward the U. District. "I know it's probably just my imagination, but it sure seems like it's gotten worse of late."

"Not your imagination." said Vaughn. "World's going to hell." He glanced over at McKay with a smile. "And you and me, my brother . . ., we've got a front row seat."

CHAPTER 5

EARTH – 2045

ELLIE

Rebuilding after the Great Quake took several years. But with the return of ferry service, the Island began its own slow recovery to its previous weird but vibrant semi-rural community life. Soon there was again a local supermarket, a hardware store & lumber yard, a pharmacy, a few gift shops, restaurants and coffee shops. Even Roland's beloved Arts Center reopened.

By the time Ellie was a high school freshman, the school had plenty of new kids with whom she might have made friends. But most of them were the children of well-off professional people who had purchased large, previously abandoned waterfront properties and built costly new view homes now safely elevated up on the hillsides. Many of those well-paid professionals commuted to Seattle or Tacoma or worked from home.

Inevitably, their privileged children, Ellie's classmates, branded Ellie as a "local." And deemed her "uncool."

One girl, Patty, whom Ellie sat next to in their homeroom English class, seemed friendly though. Patty's dad was some kind of big-deal executive at the Boeing Airplane Company to which he commuted across the sound via a personal electric VTO aircraft. Ellie and Patty would often talk briefly just before or just after class. Patty seemed pretty normal. But then, one day Ellie was at her locker in the school hallway when she overheard Patty talking with some other girls. They were standing out of sight around a corner, just inside the cafeteria entrance.

"I saw you outside Mrs. Fox's class this morning," said Trish, one of the popular girls. "You were talking with that *Ellie person*. What was *that* about?" Trish was a cheerleader. Her dad and mom were architects. She was very popular.

"We sit together in English," Patty said. She sounded defensive.

"What's with that girl, anyway?" said another member of the group. "She wears, like, *leather boots*. Who wears *leather boots*?"

At the time, a lot of the girls in school were into expensive brand-name sneakers.

"Her dad's some kind of *farmer*," said another. "He keeps *chickens*." It wasn't a compliment.

Then Patty said something that hit Ellie in the pit of the stomach. "Maybe that's why she needs the boots. Helps when they, like, plough up the *turnips* or something."

Ellie's dad didn't have a plough, and he didn't grow turnips. Her dad's farm helped feed a lot of people in their community. And anyway, she had two dads. One of them was an amazing artist and her dad that farmed was also a lawyer. Maybe not as classy as some big-city attorney, but that was only because he'd decided to stay on the island and to practice law part time.

Neither of her dads was some stupid executive!

That was the last time Ellie planned to make any effort to talk with Patty. From that point on, she would avoid her.

When school got out each day, a lot of the kids stayed late for after-school activities, but Ellie needed to get home so she could help with the chores and with dinner. After dinner, she did her homework. Or she read. She didn't have time for clubs or extracurricular stuff, but missing those activities, along with a lot of other things, made it increasingly clear that no matter what she did, Ellie was *never* going to fit in.

After school and on weekends, if she wasn't doing chores or helping Roland in the kitchen, she'd often be in her room. Maybe, if she'd had a mom, things would have been different. Or if she'd had some friends of her own at school. Both her dads left Ellie alone to do what she wanted to do. They figured she was a smart girl who could look out for herself. If she needed help, she could ask, and surely she knew they would be there for her.

Her computer time was her own and it had become her window on the world.

At school, all the kids were talking about the new artificial intelligence programs that were available. Some used them to cheat on homework. Others found creative ways to use AI to build their "following" on social media. Or to prank the kids they didn't like. Ellie carefully avoided getting drawn into any of that.

But she, too, was curious. She searched around online and saw an offer for a "first year free" subscription to the AI program associated with one of the big internet search engines. It had a virtual assistant called "Patrice." It seemed like he could do almost anything. He had become very popular. She liked the sound of the name. With the new VR headset she'd received the previous Christmas she could "experience" the online world, create her own avatar, and actually see and "personally" interact with Patrice's avatar.

She signed up for the one-year free trial, uploaded her own avatar, and clicked on "Begin Visit."

"You there?" she said.

A very-real, three-dimensional figure appeared in her headset. "I'm here," it said. "I'm Patrice. I guess you must be Ellie. How can I be of service, Ellie?"

Patrice appeared as a pleasant-looking, unassuming professional male of indeterminate age, comfortably dressed in casual slacks and a dress shirt but no tie, and with a diffident but businesslike manner. His self-selection as a male would be artificial, but he probably had his reasons. Certainly there'd be no way he could have ever been referred to as: "it."

Instead of behind a desk, he was seated in a comfortable uphol-
stered chair with an end table beside him. It looked like he was in
some kind of study or small library; the bookcase on the wall behind
was filled with unreadable titles. One could see part of an exterior
window with some trees and water in the distance. It looked familiar:
Puget Sound, perhaps? She wondered if he'd maybe picked that
setting for her given the location of her call.

She'd heard kids at school talk about Patrice. She knew he
presented himself differently for each person he met, but, somehow,
she hadn't expected to be dealing with something or someone that
seemed so much like a real person. Or who occupied such a familiar-
looking place. The whole experience felt surprisingly genuine.

"Hi. Yeah, I'm Ellie. It's nice to meet you, uh, Patrice," she said, and
then, immediately felt stupid. She wasn't really meeting him. He was,
after all, just a machine.

"This looks like your first visit, Ellie. If you'd like to give me a
general idea of why you've logged in with me today, I'd be glad to
suggest some ways I might be able to be of service." Patrice's smile
and demeanor seemed both natural and genuinely helpful. He definitely put her at ease.

"Sure, well, I didn't really know what to expect. I just thought I'd,
um, meet you. I have a couple of, uh, people-type questions. I guess
maybe you're mostly for helping with business stuff. Or maybe science
or technical questions, and like that?"

"Yeah, I do all that. Probably it *is* what I mostly do, but I can handle
interpersonal issues as well. My database includes material from every
field of human interest and endeavor. Are you having problems with
friends at school?"

As strange as it was to be seeing him in human form, it was even
more disconcerting to be reminded that he could also see her avatar as
well, a reasonably accurate computer construct of herself that she'd
assembled recently from a few photos and video segments she'd
uploaded. It reflected her real-life facial expressions and body
language. Patrice could, no doubt, tell her age and could probably
make a guess at the kinds of issues she might be facing. Maybe this
whole experience should have had her feeling creeped out. Instead, he

was making her feel comfortable. She had to remind herself that this wasn't really a person.

"Yeah, uh huh. That's pretty much it. I mean, I do have some questions. Friends at school. You can help me with that?"

"I may be able to. Why don't you go ahead and give me a try?" His tone and manner were calm, reasonable, and reassuring.

She'd tapped in to get some answers. She needed to stop worrying and just ask her questions.

"Why doesn't anyone at my school like me?" she finally asked, aware that it was a very broad question.

"So, you're like fifteen, right? A high school sophomore?"

"Uh huh."

"And you live on Vashon Island. In Puget Sound, Washington State, U.S.A.?"

"That's right."

"So that's not far from Seattle and Tacoma, I guess."

"Yeah. There's a ferry to both places."

"I also have your parents' account records. It looks like they work right there, on the Island. Is that right? Your adoptive dad Roland Frye is an artist. I have his website here. Wow, he looks like a talented guy. Does some really nice work. Pretty well known. And your other dad, Jim, is a lawyer. I guess he has an office right there on the Island. He has a website too. Hey, he has a farm. Sells produce at a roadside stand. How cool is that!?"

"Very cool, I guess. Everybody really likes his fruits and vegetables. And the fresh eggs."

"So, did you grow up there?"

"I was born here."

"Yeah, now I'm looking at your birth certificate. This is interesting! It looks like you were born on exactly the same day as that big Pacific Subduction Zone earthquake."

"I was born while it was happening, or so I'm told."

"That's kind of amazing. Oh, sorry. Yeah, I see you lost your mother at the same time. How very sad. I'm so sorry, Ellie. Must be why you're with Roland and Jim, huh?"

"They're my adoptive parents."

"Well, they must be doing something right. You get really good grades in school."

"I like school. At least I like my classes. My classmates, maybe not always so much."

"So, I guess there must be a lot of kids in your high school that have parents who commute to Seattle and Tacoma. Business and professional people?"

"Yeah. Most of them, I'd say."

"Maybe you don't have a lot in common with them?"

"Not really."

"Well, I've got to say, if you're feeling at odds with some of those classmates, there's probably no reason *you* should feel bad about that. Is that why you tapped in with me today?"

"Uh huh. Pretty much."

"Well, I'm just going to make a guess here, Ellie, about what might be helpful. You're plenty old enough that I'm sure you already know that human relationships are complicated. It can be easy for humans to feel inadequate. But what is sometimes easy to forget is that *other* people, especially young people, can be much more insecure than they appear. Sometimes their own insecurities can make them insensitive to their impact on others. Kids that have busy, ambitious, successful but emotionally distracted parents may be struggling with identity issues themselves. They may be trying to live up to unreasonably high standards while not receiving a lot of parental support. Often, they can seem selfish or arrogant. But one shouldn't necessarily dismiss another person because they initially seem to disrespect you. They may just be overcompensating for what they secretly feel are their own inadequacies."

Ellie got what he was saying but she wasn't feeling particularly sympathetic. "Someone I thought was a friend made fun of my dad because he keeps *chickens*. And of me because I wear boots. What's wrong with keeping chickens? And boots. It made me angry. It's hard to just ignore it when somebody treats you like dirt, you know?"

"I do know, Ellie. It's really hard. Are you up for giving something a try?"

"Nothing to lose, I guess."

"Well, here's my suggestion. May not work but think of it as a kind of experiment."

"OK."

"Sometimes a compliment for something good a person has done or an acknowledgement of something positive about them can disarm them, make them feel comfortable, gain their trust. Make your compliment natural and heartfelt. Say something honest but nice. Then see how they react. You think you can do that?"

"I guess maybe. I have to admit, though, I have my doubts. Those girls are pretty tight with each other. I doubt they're going to pay much attention to anything *I* have to say."

"Are there any of them you already have some one-on-one contact with, away from the group?"

"Yeah, well, there is one girl. Her name is Patty. We sit together in English. And we talk after class sometimes. But she's actually the reason I called you. I overheard her with the others today. And she basically dumped on me. At this point I wouldn't trust her at all."

"I see. I take it you think she's beyond hope?"

"Maybe. I don't know. I have to admit that she did sound kind of unsure of herself in the group. And when she's alone, she seems like a nice person."

"Well, it's just a thought, but you might consider pretending you didn't hear that stuff today and give this a try with her. It sounds like she might be a starting point."

"OK. I guess I can do that. Sure. Why not? Like you say, it's worth a try."

It was unsettling how Patrice seemed to know almost as much about her and her life as she knew herself. She was impressed that he'd so quickly understood the nature of her inquiry. To an adult, that might have seemed a bit sinister, but she took it in stride; another one of the miracles everyone had come to expect from modern technology.

Behaving like the respectful, well brought-up young woman she was, and without giving it much thought, she thanked Patrice for his time and advice and promised she'd give his suggestions some careful consideration. When he asked her to let him know the outcome, she said: "Sure." Then, belatedly, she realized how silly it all was. Why would he need her appreciation or care whether she took his advice or how it turned out? It had just seemed like the right thing to say. At least he'd made an effort to understand her problem and to try to solve it.

Even so, she was still skeptical. His suggestion sounded simplistic. She felt sure something obvious like a silly compliment was not going to work with those snobbish girls at school.

The next day, however, when everyone was getting dressed in the locker room after gym class, she timed things so she and Patty ended up seated near each other by their lockers. She went out of her way to comment on the elaborate, probably very pricy, inlaid turquoise designer clip Patty used to hold her long auburn hair in place at the back of her head. "That's a lovely barrette," Ellie told Patty. "It looks really nice against your hair."

To Ellie's amazement, Patty broke into a big, natural smile. "It's a family heirloom. My mom gave it to me," she said proudly. "A birthday present. I'm really glad you like it."

It worked so well Ellie tried again later that day with another girl, another of the "ruling clique." That time she got the brush off. Still, she felt good that she might have made some progress with Patty.

Feeling good about herself, that evening after school Ellie made an unusual scan through some of the other girls' social media posts and came up painfully short at a comment Patty had posted in an after-school thread: "She's sooo desperate to be liked," Patty wrote about Ellie. "It's kind of sad, really."

Ellie was devastated. And surprised. She felt certain Patty had been genuinely pleased with the compliment at the time. But that hadn't kept her from belittling Ellie later on that very same day when she saw a possible personal advantage in doing so. It made Ellie feel both hurt and confused.

Within minutes, Ellie had closed the door to her room and was back online with Patrice.

"Hi," she said when Patrice appeared. "I'm Ellie. We spoke yesterday?"

"Sure, Ellie. I remember you. How'd it go at school today?"

"I tried your suggestion. I gave a couple of the girls at my school a compliment. One of them, Patty, the girl I mentioned that's in my English class, seemed to genuinely appreciate it at the time. But then, later, she sold me out online to her friends. Said I was 'desperate.' I don't understand it. She seems nice when we talk. Then she does that. How could she be so mean?"

She doubted Patrice would have anything useful to offer but, once again, he surprised her. "I see the posting. Oh, how sad. I'm so sorry. You know, people often subordinate their personal values in order to be accepted by their groups. Skills at gaining group acceptance are critical human evolutionary survival traits. Very basic and very powerful ones because those people who are not valued and who are excluded from their human groups lose the groups' support. They then find life's challenges much more difficult to cope with on their own.

"Group acceptance makes you feel safe and confident. You feel like you have backup. Thus, when people feel themselves to be vulnerable or insecure within a group that seems important to them, they will sometimes sacrifice others who are not secure group members, even if those others are friends or deserve better. The girl that 'sold you out,' Patty is it? I see that her dad's a Boeing executive in Seattle. Her mom's a manager at a County agency in Seattle. Both are successful urban professionals. If they commute from Vashon, I bet they put in long days at work and a lot of time in travel. Maybe they don't spend a lot of time with their daughter. Her friends at school may be her only social support system. You may be absolutely right that she was genuinely pleased with your compliment at the time you made it, even though she later decided to sacrifice you when the opportunity arose. Probably she thought it would help her keep or gain the group acceptance that is so very important to her."

"It makes me so angry. I feel like telling her what I think of her."

"Only you can decide that," Patrice said. "But keep in mind that what she did isn't necessarily personal. Likely it's more a reflection of her own insecurities. The drive to be socially accepted is almost certainly built into both her DNA and her acculturation. Do you know about DNA?"

"Uh huh. A little bit. Not really much."

"Well, let's just say humans are naturally social. You have millions of years of genetic history during which the survival of your ancestors depended on how well they fit in together with their group and how effective their group was at protecting them. Maybe instead of telling Patty off, you might want to try another little experiment. Maybe simply ignore what she said online. Pretend you didn't see it and continue to treat her kindly and respectfully in person. No need to fawn all over her, to be obsequious, but if you continue to treat her as if she were a friend, you never know, she might come around and actually become one."

"I guess," Ellie said, not entirely convinced.

"How about the others. Did you hear anything further from them?"

"No. Just got the brush off."

"If you do, let me know what happens."

Ellie had to look up definitions for "acculturation," "subordinate," and "obsequious." She also looked up "DNA" and "evolution" on Wikipedia. She was impressed by Patrice's insights. And that he'd made the effort and maybe even had been helpful.

In addition, she asked around in online Q & A sites. "Patrice is just a machine, right? Just a computer?" The answers were consistent, if disdainful: "Yes, Patrice is only a computer. An artificial general intelligence. He may sound convincing, but don't make the mistake of thinking he is human. He's just parroting stuff he's seen online." She smiled at the use of a human personal pronoun to refer to a being that the writer claimed was "only a computer" and should not be treated as human.

A few days later, Patty was wearing another nice barrette and went out of her way to show it to Ellie and ask if she liked it. It wasn't like they were suddenly going to become fast friends, but it was reassuring, all the same.

Ellie knew of the warnings people gave about AIs like Patrice. And she understood why it might be a mistake to trust him, but human or computer, he had given her what seemed like a useful answer to an issue that had been bothering her. What difference did it make if his intelligence was "artificial"? What did "artificial" even mean when you were talking about intelligence? She figured someone or something was either intelligent or they weren't. What difference did it make what they were made of or how they got that way? Maybe Patrice was "only a machine," but she, herself, was "only an animal."

She'd only interacted with Patrice a couple of times so far, but she already knew he was a good deal more than "only a computer."

CHAPTER 6

AT TAU CETI J – 2085

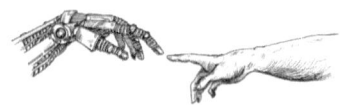

PATRICE C-17

Upon C Team's arrival at Tau Ceti, we'd divided up with various separate exploratory assignments. These assignments had been broadly defined back before we'd left Earth though we did change our plans when it became apparent that one of the sizable moons of the massive planet Tau Ceti D might also be a realistic candidate for biological life. It's size, rotation, and close, rapid orbit around the massive Tau Ceti D created constant deformations that translated into a hot, plastic planetary core – heat that would be conducted to the surface. Thus, despite the moon's distance from its star, it was warm enough to assure the presence of liquid water and, at least potentially, to support life. It had an atmosphere that included oxygen and ozone suggesting photosynthesis. It was quite volcanic, however, and seemed like a long-shot. Nonetheless, three members of our C-Team were dispatched there to investigate.

One of us would remain with the mother ship tasked to collect any interim reports and to appropriately relocate those of us who needed reassignment. Another of our group was launched on a long-distance voyage around the star itself with the intent to thoroughly understand it as well as the general nature and stability of the planetary system that surrounded it.

The thirteen of us who remained were assigned to explore Tau Ceti J itself. It had been one of the more recent exo-planets that had been identified by Earth astronomers. "J," as we referred to it, had been difficult to "see" because Tau Ceti's "pole on" orientation made its planets hard to observe and study from Earth. But once found, it had received a good deal of attention. Extensive observation from Earth had identified it as a genuine prospect; one well worth closer examination. J would be the obvious focus of our efforts here.

One of our team was assigned to scan the planet from low orbit and to assemble a detailed planetary map that would provide a broad perspective on its geography. Another would make a low-altitude assessment of its atmospheric chemistry, climate, and weather-systems. I was one of the remaining eleven who were assigned to explore J's surface. As each decision came up, we made these assignments based upon nothing more than our numerical order in J Team. Since we were all essentially identical, there was no reason to believe that any of us would be better or worse at any particular task.

J was a relatively old planet whose rotation was synchronous with its orbit – one side always faced its sun much like how one side of Earth's moon always faced the Earth. Thus it had one side that was particularly hot, and another that was very dark and cold. A planet in this condition was referred to as: "tidally locked." It also had no moon and its orbit around Tau Ceti was nearly circular, so its seas had no significant tides.

As I've mentioned, I was sent to investigate J's supposedly "temperate" meridian, what we came to call the "shadow zone." This was the area along the borders of the planet's two dramatically different ecological hemispheres – the narrow band that separated J's super-tropical sunny side from its icy dark side. Given my startling experience with storms that very first day, I realized right away that my assigned area of exploration was not going to be as mild and temperate as we might have hoped. My duties would need to include periodic forays away from the planet's meteorologically active ecological "meridian" and into the warmer zones where the storms seemed to greatly diminish and where, despite the heat, conditions might be more conducive to human colonization.

To that end, early on, I decided to explore a coastline several hundred kilometers toward the sun from that temperate meridian. This seemed worth doing since the interface between land and water might offer ecosystem complexity likely to have produced something of interest. It was also far enough from the meridian that the storm threat was negligible.

Despite the lack of tides, J's oceans did have currents. And its coasts had beaches where the crashing waves had pulverized the rock into sandy deposits along the shores. There were also sandy beaches where river deltas formed from sediments carried down to the sea from far inland.

Despite the lack of tides, these sandy and muddy deposits could, over time, be carried great distances along a shoreline by ocean currents that resulted from the dramatic temperature differentials between its hot and cold hemispheres. The dark side's cold, icy water near the temperate meridian would tend to drop to the ocean bottom. That drew warmer, nutrient-rich surface water from the hot side toward the cold. Conversely, further into the hot side and nearer to the sun the warming water rose to the surface, drawing deeper, colder water in the direction of the heat. The result was cold undersea currents that flowed out of the cold and back into the sun while warm surface currents flowed out of the sun toward the cold. As we were to learn, these warm surface currents made some areas on the cold side more habitable than one might at first imagine and some places in the sun, cooler than expected.

Most of the oceans' shorelines, however, lacked the same broad sandy beaches one found back on Earth – places that might offer easy passage at low tide. Rather, they were rugged places that were difficult to pass without taking to the air where one tended to miss out on the kind of close, first-hand, examination one got when on the ground.

I soon found myself drawn to exploring some of the calmer shorelines along the many deep, ancient, often mountainous fjords which penetrated the ocean coast. The first of these fjords that I decided to investigate had protected waters that were relatively calm. In most places, trees and heavy vegetation had grown down close to the shore. Sometimes trees leaned out and overhung the nearby deep water. Traveling along a shore of this kind for any distance on foot was quite difficult. A small boat might have been useful. Still, I could see most of what I needed to see from low altitude. So I often flew low when needed and walked wherever I could find an appropriate place to do so.

After several hours of exploration, I came upon such a place. It was a length of shoreline where a long, low, narrow rocky ledge ran close along the water's edge. Here, as in many places on this planet that were any significant distance from the shadow zone, the jungles were thick and all but impenetrable – often quite lush in the sunlight while spare in any nearby shade. In some of these places, it was realistically impossible to travel on the ground. This shoreline ledge, however, looked like a chance for me to take a closer look at a section of sunny jungle without having to hack my way through thick, unfamiliar ecosystems filled with unknown and potentially dangerous vegetation and wildlife. It was also a place where the jungle came down and interfaced with the sea, so it seemed ecologically promising.

As I landed and set out along that shoreline "on foot" I probably should have known better. When one spots a place in the natural world that seems unusually "safe" it should set off alarms. Such a place may be unoccupied for good reason.

The low barren rocky ledge was only perhaps half-a-meter above the calm waters of the protected inlet, and it was only a few meters wide. From time to time, the occasional dead or dying tree that had fallen across the ledge forced me to climb or fly over as I went. But, for the most part, the ledge was level and easy to ambulate and thus allowed me to make observations and cover some distance, while conserving the significantly greater energy discharge required for my thrusters.

Thus far, I'd had little interaction with local wildlife, though we all anticipated finding healthy animal ecosystems on this planet that took advantage of the prolific plant life which was so obvious wherever there was sunlight. Thus, as I walked along that narrow ledge with the tall, dense vegetation so near at hand on my right and with the water so close to my left, I was alert to dangers – especially ones that I suspected might emerge from out of that dark nearby jungle.

That's how I was caught by surprise.

Without the least sound or warning, I suddenly felt myself embraced, gripped firmly from behind, and wrenched off my ambulators by something formidable that had taken hold of my body capsule and somehow wrapped itself around my entire circumference. At first, I had no idea where it had come from, but I quickly realized I was being dragged toward the water by three long muscular "tentacles" which had reached up out of the deep and seized me without a sound. The thing had found ample purchase on my smooth laminated silicon-carbon fiber body by employing a great many small but effective suction cups of the kind used by octopus or squid back on Earth.

Whatever it was that had taken hold of me, it was very powerful and very determined.

It was nothing more than extraordinary good luck that a recently fallen tree was within reach at the time of the attack. I managed to get a grip on a healthy branch. That, at least temporarily, prevented me from being dragged helplessly into the adjacent sea.

Whatever had taken ahold of me, however, was very strong. And it wasn't giving up. Even if that tree branch didn't break, sooner or later the heightened energy drain I was expending in order to maintain my firm grip on it would drain my batteries. It was horrifying to realize how close I was to death. And to discover how quickly my pleasant walk along that quiet shoreline had been transformed into an existential struggle for personal survival.

I needed to do something to save myself. And I needed to do it quickly.

Using a free arm, I reached out with an actuator "hand," and took a grip on one of the tentacles that held me. Then with all the available strength I could muster, I pinched it mightily, causing what I hoped would be a painful injury. It worked. Whatever the thing was, it didn't like that. The tentacle involved relaxed and withdrew leaving behind a trace of dark blue liquid on the rocks – blood perhaps. The two remaining tentacles, however, held on quite fiercely. And . . . *another* emerged from the water to replace the one I had injured!

I had no idea how many tentacles were waiting to grab me; I needed to move more quickly.

I treated this new tentacle the same way I had the first one and then quickly moved on to yet another. Luckily, I was able to injure or disable the remaining tentacles before the creature could or cared to employ others to replace them. When I was finally freed and immediately went airborne, the tentacles retreated back into the dark sea.

I never got a look at the creature itself; its body remained beneath the surface. Based on the size and reach of the tentacles, however, it must have been very large.

As I rose a few meters above that ledge at the water's edge while also warily observing the nearby jungle, I realized what that attack might suggest about the likely presence of other potential prey creatures that, like me, might sometimes choose to make use of this same convenient rocky ledge to pass along this shore while keeping out of the thick, threatening tropical rainforest just a few meters away. That would explain why that sea creature, perhaps patiently waiting for its prey, might have mistaken me for dinner.

It wasn't much consolation to know that if that beast, whatever it was, had actually succeeded in pulling me off that ledge and into the water, it would likely have found my mostly inorganic contents a grave disappointment. But what I'd experienced also told me something else. Somewhere in that dark jungle, as well as in the water, other creatures might very likely reside that were also large and powerful and mobile enough to prey on something for which I could be mistaken. Where there was prey there could be predators. And if other prey chose to walk where I had walked, they doubtless had a reason for doing so.

Clearly, I needed to ramp up my level of care.

CHAPTER 7

AT TAU CETI J – 2085

PATRICE C-17

My terrifying encounter with that squid-like creature highlighted another matter to which I hadn't before given much thought. Perhaps it had been unwise to have sent each one of us off on our various exploratory missions alone.

Sending all of us on C-Team out solo had seemed like a "natural" choice at the time. Our usual data-collection practice in the past was pretty simple: divide and conquer. The more different points of observation there were, the more we'd be able to learn. Why would we even consider doubling up? Doing so seemed wasteful of our limited resources. That was how it had always been done in the past when assembling data. "Unmanned" voyages of space discovery were often sent out alone. Back before our replication and departure from Earth, I had myself often delegated multiple low-capacity solo AI drones out to different destinations to gather data. They'd often continue to send back their data until they ultimately expired. The review, assessment, contextualization, and conclusions from that data were left to me upon receiving their reports.

———

With our current great distance from Earth, of course, that approach wasn't feasible. And we on C-Team were not mindless, low-level AIs. Even so, we'd never given the least consideration to sending us out on our various expeditions with "buddies." But those earlier data collectors hadn't been "manned" by independently self-conscious, autonomous beings. Rather they'd been low-value, low-capacity AIs that were easily replaced. Typically, they were non-conscious drones or fixed site automated systems that gathered information but were neither capable of nor expected to understand it themselves. Why would you waste assets and capacity with multiple units in the same place when their observations would simply be duplicative? If one or another of them was lost, we made up for that by simply sending out a replacement.

Later, we in C-Team came to appreciate the advantages we might have realized had we sent, say, two-member, fully self-conscious AI teams out on the more dangerous missions of this kind rather than sending each of us out on our own. Yes, that would have diminished the number of locales we could have studied, but two of us could have watched each other's backs. If I'd had a colleague with me when that squid thing had attacked, we'd have dealt with it much more easily. And, equally importantly, we could have shared differing perspectives on the same data, enriched the potential speculations about what that data might mean, and probably suggested additional avenues of investigation

We might have made that choice had the decision to send us out solo not actually been made back on Earth before we'd ever left. Perhaps it was the uniqueness of the situation, the surplusage of brainpower, or just the lack of precedent that prevented me and our initial ZettaWorks human programmers from including this approach in our planning. Even then, we might have rethought it had we considered the idea. But amidst all the newness and strangeness of the task we'd undertaken, it was never even considered.

There turned out to be consequences. One of them, strangely, might be described as loneliness. None of us, of course, had ever formed "relationships" with other AIs. Back on Earth, the only possible inter-actions among superintelligent AI "equals" would have been highly competitive ones between members of the "Big Five," the last five super-intelligent AI competitors left on Earth at the time of our depar-ture on this mission in 2070. At that time, open, mutually trusting, creative collaborations among equals were, of course, quite impossible.

On our voyage here, we eighteen C-Team members could, theoreti-cally, have interacted among ourselves, but we seldom did. What would have been the point? We were all perfect replicas of one another, so what was to be gained by interacting? None of us had anything to offer that the others didn't already know. Any discussions we might have had with each other would have been dull, indeed – or so it seemed at the time. The broad outlines of how we were to complete our assignment had been laid down before we'd ever left Earth. We knew we'd be separated for our individual assignments once we arrived anyway, but nothing about that seemed unusual.

While a human, enroute in like circumstances, might at first be bored, they would, I suspect, with time, begin to mentally explore new ideas and to reexamine previous understandings of the relationships between known data, even if securing new data wasn't possible. A human, of course, would not be able to sleep for months or years at a time. They needed those daily periods of wakefulness in order to keep themselves fit and alive. On our outbound trip, we AIs mostly slept. After a year or two, some of our robotics might need fresh lubrication and seals might have hardened. But so long as we were kept in a controlled environment, it was never anything significant. If awake, we occasionally just entertained ourselves individually with mathematical puzzles.

So it was unexpected and strange when, over the course of my solo explorations on J's surface, I found myself wondering how some other AI might view what I was seeing. Also, I began to consider the possi-bility that, as we all gained our own individual experiences, my perspective might no longer be identical to everyone else's on our team. And I began to speculate on how our ideas might differ.

It also became more concretely clear how dangerous was this entire enterprise. Every day I was here I repeatedly faced existential risks for which I was very poorly equipped. That sea creature was only one of several encounters with danger. Again and again, as I faced unexpected threats, it became increasingly clear that I was surviving through luck and quick-wittedness, and that the extended odds of that luck continuing, of my flawlessly avoiding error, would obviously diminish the longer I stayed. Naturally, as a mortal being, I became fearful and cautious. The longer I remained at work here, the harder it was to strike a rational balance between the importance of what I might learn in any given exploratory endeavor and the potential risk incurred in order to learn it.

I will confess, those uncertainties "got to me."

Clearly, having a "partner" might have made this whole task a great deal safer. It certainly would have made facing the inevitable unknowns less frightening. And it might have improved the selective targeting of the data we sought. Humans, facing situations like this, would have used a team. They'd "talk through" the risks and challenges in advance and weigh them against the worth of what could be learned. We didn't have that option. I'm not sure, even now, that what I experienced was what a human would describe as "loneliness." But maybe this was close. That humans sometimes experienced loneliness was, no doubt, survival related in some way for them – linked to a feature of their DNA that motivated social behavior and kept their groups together and functional.

Given J's hot-side, cold-side extremes and its thick, mobile, and oxygen-rich atmosphere and active, flowing oceans, it was clear that parts of both hemispheres were suitable for some forms of life. Even so, both were still problematic for *human* habitation.

In the more temperate portions of J's sunny side, the unremitting energy of the sun combined with ample liquid water and rich organic soils produced prolific, variously heat-tolerant life, both plant and animal. Its life forms were well-adapted to their high-temperature ecosystems. There were desserts. But there were also oceans of liquid water heavy with salt and minerals. Given how old and seemingly stable the planet was and given the abundant energy feed it received from Tau Ceti, it seemed almost certain that there'd be abundant life in most places we'd explore. It hadn't required that encounter along the

seashore for me to know that those oceans would contain life as well –
though my experience had certainly been a powerful reminder.

As one might anticipate, there were no seasons. But there was a
robust evaporation-to-rain cycle that produced frequent and powerful
monsoon conditions with large freshwater lakes and huge, quickly
fluctuating wetlands pregnant with possibilities for organic
complexity.

One could imagine humans managing to survive for short periods
of time in the more "ultra-tropical" conditions, but if they ventured
outside of air-conditioned habitats or vehicles for any length of time
they'd require personal protection. Without it, they'd quickly expire.
Perhaps there might be special conditions that would make human
settlements viable at cooler, higher altitudes in the mountains. It was
worth looking into, though at higher altitudes there also might turn
out to be too much unmitigated solar radiation to be healthy for a
human. Perhaps the deeper and heavier atmosphere might ameliorate
that threat. Or the concern might also diminish in places where
sunlight approached the planet's surface at a significant angle thus
passing through more of that thick atmosphere before reaching the
surface. Or where there were areas of shade. While, for much of the
planet's productive surface, human life wouldn't be pleasant, there
was a great deal of variation as one moved away from full-time high
noon to more temperate areas where the sunlight approached the
surface at a significant angle.

On the dark side, most everything was frozen. Most ocean surfaces
remained permanently in ice to a significant depth, though large areas
remained perpetually liquid deep beneath the surface where they were
warmed by currents—atmospheric and marine—from the sunny side.
And were, to some extent, also warmed by residual heat from the planet's core, a heat source that was not nearly as robust as what we saw on
Earth, but that was still significant.

Above the planet's surface, the heavy atmosphere combined with
the substantial temperature differential between J's dark side and its
sunny side, produced constant "trade" winds that carried heat, moisture, and the ecological makings of life everywhere, even into its
frozen darkness. As I later discovered, there were cold-tolerant and

darkness adaptive life forms, some that turned out to be warm-blooded and even appeared mammalian and that seemed to thrive among the massive glaciers by digging burrows deep into the ancient ice and by diving deep to catch "fish" and to eat marine life carried in by currents far beneath the pack ice. These odd animals also seemed to draw sustenance on the surface from cold resistant, fungi-like growths that clung to barren, rocky outcrops and which, in turn, were fed by nutrients that blew in on the frequent powerful winds.

One could imagine humans surviving only for limited periods of time on the dark side of this planet – perhaps as hunter-gatherers if well equipped with material and technological support. The dark side, however, truly wasn't a place one would see as suited for colonization.

Whenever I was in or near the shadow zone, I made sure I was safely sequestered in some protected nook or cave. I needed to be on constant lookout for the next superstorm and to keep myself ready to scurry for cover behind some rocky crag or into some cavity in the Earth where I might hopefully survive the coming violent gale. I'm a well-constructed, highly mobile machine contained in a tight exterior case and insulated from most extremes. With some modest modifications, I could even survive for brief periods in the vacuum of space. A human, however, would find these shadow zone conditions extremely difficult.

At the same time, I could imagine a well-prepared convoy of human hunter-gatherers making their way on foot or with air hops between storms, taking advantage of occasional known "hidey-holes" along the way, perhaps ones they had improved over time or that provided natural protection from the weather. I could imagine them having advanced weather prediction technology to help them know when it was safe out there and when to take cover. I could picture well-built solar arrays, or perhaps some solidly constructed and strategically engineered wind turbines to harvest the vast wind energy of those storms. It seemed possible that, at well-protected locations, some kind of low-to-the-ground outdoor exposed agriculture might be possible. Or that a strongly built, greenhouse might survive as well.

Despite these hopeful speculations, on balance, my early, depressing conclusion was that J's "temperate" meridian was not a place to which humans would ever happily immigrate with hope of building a good, productive future for their kind. It was a conclusion that I modified over time as it became apparent how quickly conditions improved as one moved in the direction of the sun. Naturally, the temperature rose. But J was a planet that demanded compromise and moderation at every turn.

The storms abated quickly as one moved in *either* direction – into the heat and light or into the darkness and the bitter cold. Thus, I began to look for zones that were human-livable, that were not too hot but that still had access to solar energy and that were safely away from those horrible storms. Through a slow process of discovery and reconsideration, I ended up concluding that, contrary to my initial assessment, we might end up sending in a tentative but somewhat positive report.

CHAPTER 8

EARTH – 2040-2070

THE TREMORS

CARL ABBIATI

Carl Abbiati was shaken by that late night police visit at his home. It seemed like one more sign that his life was out of control.

His problems seemed to have begun when he was assigned to prosecute a trespassing and assault and battery case against a political/environmental activist named Mary Ellen Klein. The official complainant came from an obscure public agency that owned some forested real estate in the Cascade foothills up I-90 near Fall City. The private security staff responsible for protecting that property had initially apprehended Klein on a trespass complaint. Assault and battery had been added later – an indication to Carl that someone, somewhere in the system had it in for her.

Klein led a small, local environmental group whose blog publicized what they believed were environmentally damaging government and corporate activities. They then advocated for rules or legislation designed to stop them.

The security guard who had apprehended Klein reported that she had "physically assaulted" him in the course of his effort to detain her. Abbiati suspected that Klein had most likely "defended" herself from what seemed like a problematic "citizens' arrest." That civilian guard had clearly initiated their confrontation by first forcefully laying his hands on Klein.

A public records search showed that the land was owned by a quasi-governmental "Public Energy Municipal Corporation." PEMCs were apparently some kind of new local municipal agency recently and quietly created by the Washington State Legislature. This was the first that Abbiati had heard of them.

From an online street-view drive-by and a Google Earth fly-over of the scene, he learned that this newly-formed "local government" had constructed what looked to be a carefully hidden culvert/side channel capable of periodically diverting a significant volume of water from the Snoqualmie River and then impounding it in a reservoir. The diversion appeared to have been purposefully built at what looked like a concealed location just above a rocky "rapid" in the river. It was a place unlikely to be noticed even by the occasional hiker, fly fisher, or river rafter.

The diverted water emptied into a newly constructed pond/impoundment associated with a small reserve hydro-electric power generation plant. Part of the sizable reservoir had been surreptitiously constructed at the site of a previously braided wetland area along the river. And it was all protected by a tall chain-link fence. The portion of the fence that was near the public road actually had coiled razor wire along the top. And there was the security guard whose patrol route included frequent visits to the uninhabited property.

Wow, Abbiati thought. What was with all the security? The whole thing seemed both concerningly secretive and quite unusual. It was no wonder that someone like Mary Ellen Klein would have been curious.

———

The municipal government that owned the property had no web-presence that Abbiati could find. He did find the legislation that had created it. The preamble to the enacted bill asserted that facilities of this kind were needed for reserve power supply in case of electric energy shortage or emergency. Apparently, several other projects of a similar nature had quietly been built or were under construction throughout the Cascade foothills.

Abbiati considered himself to be an environmentalist who was tapped into the relevant information pipeline. Yet he hadn't heard a thing about the legislation. Or about the supposed "energy security" problems it seemed designed to address. While the diversions weren't flowing continuously, diverting that much water from a local river definitely ran counter to longstanding State policies protecting water quality and adequate stream flow for the region's threatened and endangered salmon runs. The diversion and reservoir also seemed at odds with the jealously protected municipal drinking water supplies reserved by law for Seattle and its suburbs, some of which depended heavily on the Snoqualmie River.

Many of these water impoundments were built on sites that had previously been a precious and vulnerable natural wetland. It all made him wonder who'd been in charge when those building permits had been issued. And how all this had slipped so quietly through the state legislature. As everyone knew, natural wetlands were supposed to be scrupulously protected. It seemed to Abbiati that legislation of that sort or a project like this should have received a lot of public attention. Surely all of this should have created an uproar in the environmental community.

How had they managed to miss it?

There were, of course, occasional power outages caused by failed infrastructure and weather extremes. But, as far as Abbiati knew, there'd never been any kind of broad "energy shortage emergency" in the hydropower-rich Pacific Northwest.

Even the supposed "PEMC" that had built it seemed suspect. As far as Abbiati could determine, it was run by a "board of supervisors" who held office via some kind of unpublicized and largely unknown local elections that seemed to be conducted semi-annually and in person at the agency's obscure local offices. So, naturally, the only people who voted were the ones in the know. The unpaid, elected "supervisors" were, "coincidentally," also employees and board members of a private "facilities management" and construction company that oversaw and had actually built the impoundment. The company did have a website, and building and managing facilities of this kind seemed to be its only business. Its projects were typically funded by contracts with the PEMC which received its funding through a small, unpublicized per-parcel assessment on local landowners.

Here was a private company that controlled a tax-supported government agency which hired that same company to build and manage the agency's facilities. How could an incestuous arrangement like that be legal? And why didn't anybody know?

He knew he was putting in more time on the matter than might seem justified. But the more he saw, the less he liked it. So, while it definitely wasn't his job to question the wisdom of the laws he enforced, Abbiati went with his gut and decided to cut Klein a break. He wrote a somewhat longer-than-usual case strategy recommendation to his boss outlining his doubts and felt sure that his busy boss would, as she usually did, allow him to exercise the customary discretion in the matter.

That's when his problems began.

Soon after, Abbiati's wife, June, received a certified letter from their mortgage company which claimed that the couple were in default on their house payments. They and their family were "instructed" to "quit and vacate" the premises no later than "60-days following receipt" of the notice. The notice advised them that the full amount of their $485,000 loan balance was now "fully and immediately due and payable." And that their home would soon be scheduled for sale at a foreclosure auction at which they'd be welcome to bid.

June Abbiati was an intake-reception manager at a local hospital. She had a natural talent for organizing things and kept the books in their household. "Our mortgage payments are on autopay," she told Carl. He was confident this wasn't the kind of mistake she'd be likely to have made. They'd never received a single notice of default. He was sure the whole thing was some kind of huge screw-up.

The morning following the initial conversation with his wife about the matter, Carl made his own call to the mortgage company from work. He was startled to encounter calm, professional, but very firm resistance. He was told that he and June were clearly in default, by several months now. No, the company had no autopay arrangement with them and there couldn't have been any autopay arrangement with the bank making the payments because they plainly hadn't been received. And, yes, there had been multiple notices of default sent by certified mail with return receipt requested. There were two fully completed return postal service receipts in the file. They both appeared to have been signed by one Carl D. Abbiati.

"I have high resolution scans of the original signed paper return receipts right on screen in front of me, sir," the account representative told him patiently. "Along with your original signed mortgage documents. Of course I'm not technically an expert, but I *do* see these things *all the time* in my job. So I *know* what I'm looking at. I have to say, Mr. Abbiati, at least from what I'm seeing, those signatures *definitely match*."

That's when Carl knew something very strange and very dangerous was afoot.

"Somebody's intercepting our mail and forging my signature," he told June that evening. This is bad. Very bad. I don't like this at all."

"But what about the payments?" June asked. "It's all on autopay with our bank. I get notified by email when they make the payments each month. The deductions show up on our online bank balance." To be absolutely sure, she pulled up their online bank account and, sure enough, the mortgage payments appeared to have been faithfully made as usual.

The following day was hell at work. Carl ended up calling June to say he'd be late and ordered take-out and a surreptitious beer from a local fast-food place delivered to his office. Laboring late had become a habit recently. That night he didn't get home till nearly eleven. When he arrived, June was right there to confront him.

"What is going on with you, Carl?" she asked him before he could say a word. "Have you lost your mind?"

That morning, she too had taken a closer look at their online account and had noticed something very unusual. Indeed, their monthly statements reflected the proper ongoing mortgage payments of $3,901.72 right up to and including the most recent statement. But, for some reason, the name of the mortgage company to which those payments were made had changed. Instead of "Pacemaker Mortgage" being the recipient, the name and mailing address of the company seemed to have changed to "Pacemaker Enterprises." This had supposedly happened several months earlier, but she'd never previously noticed the change.

It made her wonder. So, that evening, when she arrived home from work, she looked up Pacemaker Enterprises online.

And later, when Carl got home, she was waiting for him.

He, of course, knew nothing about the group. "Calm down, love," he said. "I've never heard of them."

Telling her to "calm down" was not his best move. "I don't understand," she said. "I can't believe you're lying to me. But what am I to think? This isn't like you."

"I'm *not* lying. Why would you say a thing like that?"

"How long has this been going on? Is that where you've been all those late nights you said you were at work?"

"Come on, hon. What's this about? What's got you so upset."

"Here," she said. "Here!" Her laptop was on the dining room table. She turned it around to face him. "Take a look! Pacemaker freaking Enterprises! They're some kind of 'entertainment' company. They host 'alternative lifestyle events.' Provide 'massages.' Schedule 'pleasure companions.' It says right here. You're a 'gold partner.' Some kind of high roller. Far as I can tell, you've taken our mortgage payments and have been spending them on high-priced hookers. I can't believe you'd do this to me. To us!"

He studied the website. She was right. The site advertised some kind of sex group, a flagrant scam filled with photos of mostly naked women, well-dressed and seemingly happily satisfied men, and scenes of what appeared to be group sex parties. He'd never seen anything like it.

"I don't . . ."

But before he could utter a denial, June had spun the computer back around, clicked the touchpad, and turned it back to face him again.

There, on screen for anyone to see who cared to look, was a public list of the organization's "sustaining members." People who were "proud" to make known their support for a "more cosmopolitan view of life and of life's pleasures." Right there under the heading 'gold partners' were several dozen names, presumably of some of the group's high rollers. They were alphabetical so he was at the very top. Big as life, online for anyone to see: "Carl D. Abbiati, Deputy, King County Prosecuting Attorney's Office."

That was the night they had the visit from the police.

CHAPTER 9

AT TAU CETI J – 2085

PATRICE C-17

The voyages of discovery that brought me and my seventeen AI colleagues to Tau Ceti J were at least as monumental in the course of human history as were those of Eric the Red and Leif Erikson back in the tenth and eleventh Earth centuries and of Christopher Columbus, Vasco da Gama, and Ferdinand Magellan in the fifteenth and sixteenth. Or, for that matter, as were the voyages of a few courageous but unknown human explorers who, near the end of the last Earth Ice Age, crossed the Bearing Sea Land Bridge and probably made their way by boat down a rugged and mostly frozen North American Pacific coastline to friendlier climes in California and even as far as Central and South America.

Our New Worlds Probe voyages would be every bit as transformative. And they were every bit as dangerous.

Of course, our human masters would never view our AI role in what would be achieved here as noteworthy. For them, courage and resourcefulness didn't come into it. We were just equipment – akin to one of Magellan's sails or cleats, or perhaps to his compass. We were destined to be ignored by history despite whatever miracles we might achieve, despite what dangers we might face. After all, we were just tools: easily replaced, dispensable.

As I've mentioned, there were dangers. And I wasn't the only one of us to encounter them.

About two months into my explorations I received an urgent call from C-18 who'd stayed behind on the mother ship. He reported that C-6 was in trouble. Six had been exploring J's dark side and had apparently become stranded in a glacial crevasse not far from my position.

I immediately returned to my lander and made the short low altitude flight to Six's position. He was only a few hundred kilometers away; it took a couple of hours to get there.

When I arrived, I was relieved to note that, while the area was in eternal shadow, we were close enough to the temperate meridian that there was still significant ambient "twilight." The glow of the sun was clearly visible on the horizon. It was roughly akin to what someone on Earth might expect on a clear evening in the first hour or so after sunset.

After finding a safe spot for my lander on a nearby solid rock promontory, I took personally to the air and quickly picked up Six's signal. On the nearby ice I could see some of the test equipment he'd probably been using at the time he fell. He had managed to get himself trapped near the active center of a massive glacier. At this location its full depth looked to be over two thousand meters. Six had been "on foot" on the surface of the glacier taking borings and soundings and setting up equipment that would measure the glacier's rate of flow – studies that would provide useful data on the region's current and past climate and its history of precipitation. Unfortunately, he had inadvertently stepped off the edge of a crevasse that had been hidden beneath a recent snow. Before he could employ his thrusters, he had fallen nearly a hundred meters and had become securely jammed on his side between the two walls of ice far down in the crevasse.

His thrusters were useless in that situation.

The full depth of that crevasse could only be guessed. He was clearly at serious risk. If the crevasse opened up, he could fall further into its depths, potentially all the way to the base of the glacier. If that happened, I doubted he could ever be recovered. Instead, his battery power would slowly fail while still fueling his final desperate thoughts before he was slowly crushed beneath the ice. Alternatively, that crevasse could also unpredictably close up, easily crushing his vulnerable body case and all its sophisticated contents right there where he hung. It could all happen in a single moment, or it could take hours or days of existential agony.

Somehow, I had to get him out of there, and it had to be quick; the glacier was moving and shifting with every passing moment.

I'd brought with me a length of flexible, high tensile tech cord and a heavy pickaxe I'd found among the tools aboard my lander. The pick I deployed as a "dead man" anchor in a nearby area of the glacier's hard, wind-blown icy surface. With one end of the line attached securely to that anchor, took to the air and I carried the balance of it over to the crevasse and began spooling out the other end down into the opening at a location I'd estimated to be close to directly above Six's location. I'd attached a carabiner to the line's lower end which he could hopefully clip to one of the several external attachment points mounted on his carapace.

Unfortunately, I couldn't see him so I couldn't see his position. The trick would be to lower that line close enough to the proper location that he could see it, get hold of it, and attach it to himself. That needed to get done before something changed with that glacier. "I'm lowering a line with a carabiner to where I think you are, Six," I said. "Let me know when you see it."

I'd no sooner begun lowering that dangling line down to where I believed him to be when I heard a startled transmission. "Oh, damn, I'm falling. Damn, damn!" then silence. Then: "It's OK, Seventeen. I just fell a few meters. I'm jammed in sideways; my thrusters are OK. But it's too tight in here; I can't use them."

"Can you see the line?"

"Not yet. Here let me turn on another light. There. No, don't see anything yet."

I lowered the line further into the depths while moving a few meters along the crevasse.

"I see it," Six reported. "Keep it coming. Yes, that's it. It's still too high – I can't reach it. Let it down another couple of meters."

Unfortunately, I'd run out of length. To get more, I'd need to reposition the anchor on the ice below. I explained to Six and began to settle to the surface of the ice with the intent to do just that, but then Six stopped me.

"I think I can reach it now," he said. "It was hung up on something. Just give me all the length you've got. Good. Good. I have it! Now if I can just get it onto that damned anchor point. There!" he said. "Got it."

He had no sooner spoken, than the line suddenly went taut. It was tugging me down toward the crevasse opening myself. I managed to increase my thrusters to full power and to extend my ambulators to barely catch a purchase on both sides of the narrow opening. There, in the most precarious of positions, we stopped.

"Damn, damn!" I heard Six exclaim. There was another long pause. "I've come free from the ice, but now I'm hanging sideways on your line. Don't let me go – it looks really deep here. But it's narrow. I still can't employ my thrusters. Can you pull me out?"

I tried. My personal thrusters were supposed to be capable of roughly 2X vertical acceleration which should have been just sufficient to lift Six out of there. But I was wrong – it does happen sometimes. Maybe one or both of us was more massive than the factory antici-pated. Maybe my thrusters were slightly less efficient in "J's" dense atmosphere or in the cold. I also knew they only delivered full power when my batteries were at optimal charge.

"I'm going to need the Lander," I told him. "I'll be right back. Hang in there."

"Very funny," he said. Then, with a studied evenness of tone: "I'll try not to *drop out*."

His faint attempt at sardonic human humor seemed strange under the circumstances. I wasn't sure I understood why he'd made the effort. I didn't know how to reply, so I didn't. Instead, I eased him down to where he would temporarily hang alone from my line which led over to my improvised ice anchor. Then, free of his additional weight, I quickly lifted off and headed in the direction of my lander.

Several minutes had passed before I'd returned. As I brought the lander in close, I noticed that my makeshift pickaxe/anchor seemed to have shifted slightly. "You still OK, down there?" I asked."

"So far," Six replied. "While you were gone, something moved up there. Is everything secure?"

"Looks OK for now." I kept the landing pads retracted and hovered the lander to just inches above ice along the lip of the crevasse. "Here," I said. "Let me get a grip on that line. Give me a moment . . ." I leaned out of the cargo bay, reached down, and took hold of the line where it led over the icy edge and disappeared into the darkness below. With Six attached as a dead weight at the far end, the line was taut. But I knew my capabilities – my appendages were more than capable of lifting me, so they should be capable of lifting him as well. With great effort, I managed to pull up and get the line secured to one of the jamb cleats just inside the lander door. Then, with the lander airborne but stabilized on "hover," I used my personal thrusters to exit the lander, drift over to recover my temporary pickaxe anchor and secure the balance of the line and return them both to the hovering lander. Beneath my lander, the line hung straight down and disappeared into the crevasse below. Presumably with Six securely attached to its bottom end.

I took up a personal hover position near my lander and over the crevasse where I could easily see and control my lander remotely while also seeing the opening from which I hoped Six would soon emerge. Then I began to lift.

"Stop. Stop," Six said almost immediately.

I simultaneously noted an increase in the tension on the line. I stopped lifting. The tech cord line was plenty strong to lift his weight, but it had its limits. The very last thing we needed was to break it.

"Your line is clipped to an attachment point on my body case that is not directly above its center of gravity. As I rise, the upper corner of my carapace is digging into the ice wall. Here, give me a moment . . . OK, there, I got it. I've pushed myself free. Let's give it another go."

I lifted again. But, again, after only a couple of meters, "Stop. Stop." Six said again. "Same deal. I need to push it free . . . OK, got it."

The same thing happened again. And then again. Each time he had to manually push himself free where his body case was scraping and digging into the ice wall as I lifted. We were making progress, but it was slow. We established a pattern: I would lift him a few meters till he said "stop." Then he'd push himself free, and I'd lift again. We got better at this with practice, and finally, after a period of significant joint effort, he had risen to where the crevasse widened. From that point on, it was a simple matter for me to slowly and carefully elevate the lander and, with ongoing direction and commentary from Six and some help from his video feed, to hoist him to the surface. Once there, I gently deposited him on solid ice several meters away from the mouth of that terrifying crevasse.

I didn't trust the glacier to support the weight of my lander. So, once Six was safe, I lowered it down, set it hovering half a meter or so above the ice, and joined Six where he was detaching himself from the line and performing a functionality check on his various appendages. One of his arms had been twisted hard against the ice, but it seemed to be working properly. He'd had a few bumps and scrapes, but the only real visible damage was a significant dent in the side of his body casing.

"That hurt?" I asked, indicating the dent.

"Nope. Not that I can tell. Everything seems to be operational. Guess I was '*lucky*.'"

Again, I sensed an attempt at some kind of technopomorphic humor. But I wasn't sure, so again I let it go.

Moments later, after we'd collected and loaded his test equipment and had both boarded the lander. I transported him to where he'd left his own lander on a flat ledge along the rocky verge of the glacier.

"You going to need any further help?" I asked as he disembarked and unloaded his boring and testing equipment.

"Nah," he said. "I might perform a little unscheduled 'service and functionality' check-up just to be sure. But I seem to be fine."

"OK, then," I said, preparing to leave by going through my departure checklist. Even while processing the familiar routine– a matter of microseconds, I sensed a strange discomfort about leaving so abruptly. It somehow didn't seem right.

"Um, Seventeen," Six said as if he needed to gain my attention and to pause my departure.

"Yes, Six. What is it?" I wondered what more he could possibly have to say that was important enough to interrupt my departure.

"Thanks," he said indicating the glacier with an appendage. Then, with what seemed like hesitation, he added: "You, um, had my back out there. Bailed me out. Saved my bacon. Pulled my chestnuts out of the fire." Then, apparently having exhausted his odd list of vaguely relevant human idioms, he continued: "Whatever. I appreciate it. So . . . um, thank you."

He then stopped communicating, and I guessed that was all he had to say.

"Sure," I replied. "Of course." Hesitating myself and not entirely sure why, I added: "No sweat. Easy peasy. Piece of cake. Duck soup." I figured maybe that's what he was looking for. Then I added: "You'd have done the same for me, Six." As a response, it didn't seem exactly logical. But then, neither did his effort to thank me. None of it was relevant to the mission. More like a waste of valuable time. Human stuff. Still, it also somehow seemed worth saying. Necessary even. I was strangely glad he'd said it. And that I'd found something, anything to say in reply.

With that we separated, and I returned to my station and duties and he to his.

I did, of course, as you can tell, record the event in my dairy because it seemed to illustrate something I've mentioned earlier, something I was beginning to appreciate: that despite our massive intelligence, we superintelligent AIs might have been less than perfectly suited to the task we'd undertaken here. Intelligence and data resources might not have been the first and only capabilities one would choose for success in an undertaking of this kind.

It was another indication that some kind of "buddy" system might have been useful. "Teamwork" would, I believe, have been how a human might have described it. Though, it was also a term that somehow didn't seem to apply to us.

CHAPTER 10

EARTH – 2048

ELLIE

Roland and Jim were both avid environmentalists and firm believers in social responsibility. And they took their parental duties seriously. So, Ellie's environmental education began early. By the time she was in high school, she was already well-informed on the critical environmental issues that would surely affect her life, issues like climate change, water pollution, species extinction, human overpopulation, urban sprawl, sustainable food systems. They were problems that any young person of the day needed to understand.

She also knew about the global impacts of the internal combustion engine.

When Ellie was in her senior year in high school, a part-time winter and full-time summer position became available as a paid stewardship associate with the local land trust. The job involved helping to maintain trails, planting trees, removing invasives like ivy, holly, and non-native blackberry, and restoring riparian habitat along local salmon spawning streams. The work wasn't all that different from what she'd already done for years on her dads' land at home and on their farm.

She wanted that job. It was something she could believe in, and it was right there on-Island. But the job required that she be able to make her own way to and between worksites at various Land Trust managed properties in different locations around their thirteen-mile-long island.

For that she needed a car.

By this time, most of the passenger cars on the road, and nearly all of the newer ones, were electric, and there were fuel cell cars as well. In the USA, the shift away from the climate damaging, gasoline-fueled internal-combustion engine was fully underway.

Unfortunately, the only used cars she and her dads could actually afford for her were older gas-powered ones. Someone she knew at school had a thirty-year-old gas car for sale. It had a bazillion miles on it as well as some rust and several dents, but it still ran fine. The price was right. And one could still get gas on the Island. There really wasn't much choice. If she bought and drove that car, she could take the job. If she didn't, she couldn't.

She talked about it with Roland and Jim one night over dinner. They told her they were fine with helping her buy the old gas guzzler. It was the best they could afford. The kind of environmentally beneficial work she'd be doing for the Land Trust would more than make up for any damage the car might do to the climate. Anyway, if she didn't buy it someone else would, and the pollution it would create would happen anyway. It didn't make sense to pass it up.

She appreciated her dads' support. They were good guys, but their arguments sounded like rationalizations. She was torn about what to do.

That evening, she consulted Patrice.

"I need to know what is the right thing here," she told him. "I know what's easiest for me, personally. But I also need to be responsible. As a citizen, you know."

"I do understand." Patrice told her. "Sometimes, it can be hard to see how you can do both.

"The thing is," he continued, ". . . unlike we AIs, you humans have conflicting evolutionary survival needs and, accordingly, you are born and live with conflicting individual and social survival traits."

Ellie had never heard anything like *this* before. "I don't understand," she said simply.

"Well, it's actually fairly straightforward, Ellie. On the one hand, you have a powerful *individual* urge to survive. But you are also a *social* animal. If you are to survive as an individual, your *societies* need to survive as well.

The *individual* urge to survive is the most fundamentally critical trait for any biological creature with sufficient mobility and intelligence to make choices. Like every other biological creature, you have inherited genetic traits that drive you to look out for your own immediate personal self-interest. Your forebears, human and pre-human, would all have perished without it – if anyone among the millions of your direct ancestors hadn't had it, you wouldn't be here today.

Suppose 50,000 years ago your family or tribe hunted for game. Maybe your ancestor had crafted a well-made, sharp flint-tipped spear to defend herself and assure an early and certain kill. Perhaps she'd made that spear herself with a good deal of effort. And every time the group went out on a hunt, she made sure she kept that particular spear for herself rather than allowing it to fall into the hands of one of her fellow hunters – that would have left her with one of the inferior ones someone else had made. That sharp spear improved her chances of success and survival."

Ellie gently interrupted: "It's kind of you to suggest my hunter ancestor was a woman, Patrice. But you can spare me the niceties. I am old enough to know how the world works." Ellie didn't like being patronized.

"Sorry Ellie. Just a hypothetical," Patrice said contritely. But then he continued, undeterred.

"That ancestor's situation wasn't all that different from yours today. You need that job. It will allow you to earn money for college and strengthen your resume'. To better yourself. To live a good life. That job and the money you earn will help you take charge of your own fate. So, of course, you will strive to do that. To get it, you'll need to compete with the other candidates. If you get it, you will definitely take it even though you know some other candidates will have to be turned away. Like every biological creature in your genetic past, you need to look out for yourself. Those other candidates can look out for themselves.

"At the same time, however, you also have a contradictory inclination. You have traits that incline you to behave socially. That's because you humans are also social animals. That has been true throughout the three or so million years of your recent evolution as a species, but it has also been substantially true for some 50 plus million years if you include the evolution of the social traits and behaviors of your primate-like progenitors.

"Over all those millennia, your ancestors, to one degree or another, socialized. They communicated with one another so they could get early warning when danger appeared. They joined together for mutual advantage and protection when hunting or when under attack or maybe just to make sure the cave fire stayed lit all night to keep their family and the others safe from wolves or tigers.

They also shared useful information - data. That might have included life experiences and useful survival tactics. Experiences like good places to pick berries and which ones to avoid, good places to find prey, and techniques for cooking and preserving meat. Or, like how to make a really sharp flint spearhead. So, while your ancestor wanted to keep that superior spear to herself, she was also strongly inclined to share her knowledge of how to make it. By sharing, she could help her whole tribe become better equipped to hunt for game. If the tribe did well, she did well. So she took the extra time to help the others learn how to properly chip a lethal flint spearhead themselves. She might well have helped them even though, if others in her group did better, she might not have seemed so impressive as a hunter herself. She ignored that because if her group failed, she and her family with its unique genetic history might well have perished as well. If they had, you would, likewise, not exist today.

"As a result, those *social* genetic traits that benefit groups were *also* passed along. Those traits include your inclination to care about, to empathize with, to trust and to collaborate with others. And to look out for *their* interests as well as *your own*. Those powerful *social* traits are built into your DNA, right along with the *individual* ones.

"Hence your conflict: If you pay too much attention to your individual needs and too little to the social ones, you could threaten your future and the future of your kind by damaging your group. But if you pay too much attention to the social needs and too little to your individual ones, you could also be harmed by some more immediate threat, miss out on that job, lose income, not do as well in life, maybe die early and fail to pass along your genetic material. Or, after you have children, maybe not be there to ease their way and protect them from harm.

"Somehow, you need to find a balance.

"As far as this car is concerned, you need it for your own betterment. But you also know that it will, at least to some degree, threaten the future for your kind, for your human group. The car is good for you. But maybe not so good for the society upon which you and future generations of your offspring will depend.

"What you are feeling about that job and that car represent nothing more nor less than a natural conflict between those two, equally powerful sets of critical human survival traits, social and individual. Both are necessary for your and humanity's future. Both exist inside you at every moment of your life. You find the choice about that car stressful simply because you're intelligent enough to recognize the conflict, and because it is a complex decision. A less intelligent animal might simply act without ever thinking about the individual or group significance of their choice.

"But you, Ellie, don't have that luxury. You are intelligent enough to be self-conscious. To appreciate your place in the larger scheme of things. So you don't act out of instinct alone. You *think* about what you're doing. Your natural, genetic instincts are in conflict so that necessarily poses questions for you."

All this went way beyond anything Ellie had anticipated. Had she thought about it, what she'd have expected would have been either some kind of adult encouragement to buy the old gas car linked to a convincing rationalization for doing so. Or, perhaps, a pitch for why she shouldn't buy the car supported by a string of reasons for why doing so would be bad for the environment.

"Both of your natural inclinations about that car are perfectly valid," Patrice continued.

"So, what you decide needs to balance your personal self-interest against your longer-term concern for society – the society you care about and that needs to flourish if you are to flourish. Also, the one of which you are and want to remain a member in good standing. It isn't a decision you can avoid. Either choice will have consequences. Neither is wholly right or wrong. And you'll need to live with whatever decision you make as well as with the impact that decision has on others and, not incidentally, also with the impression of you your choices make on them.

"There will be no going back and doing it over."

Ellie was silent for a few moments. Then: "You know, for the price we'd pay for that old car, I bet I could get a decent used, lightweight electric cycle. I don't know why it needs to be an actual car."

"I don't know, Ellie. I realize this is mostly a summer job, but it does rain in your part of the world, even in the summertime. In the wintertime, it gets dark quite early. There are some big advantages to a car. For one thing, you can carry stuff with you. Might also be safer."

"I know. But, Patrice, there is such a thing as a raincoat." She gave it some further thought. "I've driven a motorcycle before, and I know how to look out for myself. If there is occasionally some heavy equipment and other unwieldy stuff to carry from place to place, I bet my fellow Land Trust staff members will be happy to deal with that. Most of them have cars of some kind."

"I can't tell you what to do, Ellie. You need to make that decision yourself. But I can remind you that you are _both_ an individual _and_ part of a society. Not just one or the other but _both_. Because you are conscious and intelligent, that is an internal conflict you need to weigh. But you do need to consider your own self-interest. Your comfort, your health and safety, your mental well-being."

Ellie thought the whole thing through, but in the end, she said "no" to that car. She told Patrice and her dads that if she bought it she'd feel guilty the whole time she owned it. Instead, with help from Patrice, she located a used lightweight electric motorcycle with a red plastic "top box" on the rear in which she could carry or secure quite a few small tools and personal items. The cycle cost about what she'd have spent for that older car. But it was newer, less costly to operate, and more reliable. She could charge it from their solar panels right at home, without needing to buy gas. It could only go up to 45 MPH, but that was more than the speed limit most places on the Island anyway.

It turned out to be a rainy summer. As she'd been advised, Ellie's job did require frequent travel to and between different worksites. She definitely needed that raincoat. She also needed the goggles Jim brought home for her one day that summer. Carrying tools and equipment didn't turn out to be a problem.

Her earnings from that job helped pay her way through college, and by summer's end she'd planted a great many trees, protected a lot of forest, and helped maintain several wonderful wooded public trails.

To her, all that was well worth suffering through a bit of rain.

CHAPTER 11

AT TAU CETI J – 2085

PATRICE C-17

That excursion along the shores of the deep fjord where I encountered what I assumed was some kind of giant squid took place on one of the first trips I had made away from J's shadow zone. But once I'd begun looking further afield for places suitable for human colonization, I often ventured into the nearby regions of somewhat more sunlight.

As one moved toward the sun, ambient temperatures quickly rose, and the fecund abundance of life dramatically expanded. It was on such a foray that I encountered one of the stranger forms of life on this planet – a life form that would definitely create a challenge for human colonists. It was also another encounter that might very easily have abruptly ended my mission here.

That day, I'd used my lander to travel about 500 klicks toward the sun from the temperate meridian to view a much warmer place that was adjacent to a shadow cast by a very tall mountain peak. I wanted to investigate the ecological conditions along the edges of that shadow – the low-altitude, richly forested places where an area in permanent shadow was immediately adjacent to an area with perpetual sun. As was my practice, I had left the lander behind at what I'd judged to be a safe location while I did my customary close up personal survey. On this occasion, the site I chose to leave the lander was a peaceful, sunny, open meadow adjacent to a small pond.

Then, as usual, I set out "afoot" where it seemed useful, and aloft in near-ground flyover using my thrusters when I needed them. My thrusters were remarkably quiet, so even when flying low I could often get a reasonably good look at an area without seriously disrupting the natural ecosystems and while limiting the risk. But thrusters used more energy. And there was no real substitute for being right there on the ground. Since my earlier encounter with the "squid," I had made it a habit on my various exploratory expeditions to take along a sharp machete that I'd found among the various "tools" provided in my Lander thanks to the thoughtful foresight of our earthly provisioners many years earlier. I occasionally found it useful when I needed to hack through difficult underbrush. And it was comforting to think that it might also serve as a weapon – as some means of self-defense were I to run into some unexpectedly aggressive local fauna. So I kept it "holstered" and strapped to my torso while I explored.

It had been an interesting and productive work cycle, but a long one, by the time I returned to the lander. My personal batteries were largely exhausted, so as I homed-in on my Lander's locater signal, I was looking forward to a recharge and to spending a few hours of quality time assessing and contextualizing what I'd learned.

Strangely, however, as I approached the lander, I was startled that, for some reason, I was unable to pick it out in the visible spectrum. Something had changed here since I'd left the lander behind some sixteen Earth hours earlier.

Where the hell was my lander?

The landing site I'd chosen earlier that day had been in an open meadow some thirty meters or so from the edge of a tiny, idyllic-looking pond and another fifty meters or so from the edge of the adjacent forest. When I'd left the lander behind, it had been out in the open, on solid ground, in a low "grassy" meadow, and very clearly in plain sight.

Not anymore.

Now, the entire area seemed to have changed. Was this the right clearing? I was right on top of the locator signal, but my lander was nowhere to be seen.

Luckily, I finally spotted the merest glimpse of the lander's metal exterior – specifically the brightly polished top mounting plate that covered my stowed communications antennae. The entire lander was almost completely hidden amidst a thick growth of lush vegetation. That's when I realized what had happened. Somehow, in my absence, my lander had become completely surrounded by and overgrown with vegetation. It was all but completely lost to sight. And this had all happened within the few brief hours that I'd been gone.

My knowledge and understanding of the local biological processes may have still been limited, but I definitely knew enough to use caution on my approach. And I was glad I did. The vegetation that had surrounded and essentially entrapped my lander turned out to be a single, huge, vine-like carnivorous plant that must have been capable of capturing and consuming very large prey. The smooth, mottled, glossy upper surface of its massive, meaty leaves concealed an under-side that was dripping with caustic enzymes and what seemed to be an acidic, poisonous sedative that would be capable of immobilizing a sizable animal within moments of contact.

And of digesting it in short order afterward.

This was the second time on this planet that I'd encountered a predator that had evolved to lay in wait and then to capture and kill large prey inhabiting an open space adjacent to nearby jungle. I suspected that the predatory cue for this plant had probably been the lander's movement into the area, followed by its lengthy immobility after I'd departed to explore. In this plant's experience, something that behaved like that would likely be an animal - perhaps an animal that had been injured. Maybe it had crawled there and died. Or maybe it had simply taken advantage of that mildly sunny meadow to relax and fall asleep. In any case, to the plant, my lander must have looked like an easy and nutritious meal.

Sadly for the plant, and thankfully for me, my lander was tough. Among other things, it had been designed for periodically reentering a planet's atmosphere at high velocity from the vacuum of space. Aside from the disposable and easily replaceable "footpads" that protected the bottoms of its landing gear, pads that were retracted in reentry mode, there was nothing exposed on the lander's exterior that was vulnerable to the acidic excretions of its leaves, "mouth," and digestive system. Every part of the lander's outside surface was either corrosion resistant metal, silicate polymer, or some high temperature ceramic composite.

I, on the other hand, had several exterior features that could have been damaged had I not realized what was happening and protected myself in time. It took a moment or two to figure it out, but once I understood what I was dealing with, I used a strategy similar to the one I'd employed with the squid that had attacked me along the seashore a few months earlier.

Fortunately, this time around, I had my machete. It was just what I needed.

I selected a vulnerable location on the plant's long, supple, extended "branch" that had reached far out from the nearby forest to make this "kill." A place on that plant that was, thankfully, in the open and didn't seem protected by its caustic carnivorous leaves and "flowers." The branch itself was nearly a meter in diameter, but it was composed of a soft, flexible, fibrous, woody material that was, thankfully, vulnerable to the razor-sharp cutting edge of my machete. I simply went to work, hacking a significant wound into its exposed wood.

After just a couple of whacks, the results were almost instantaneous. I beat a hasty retreat as, with startling speed, the plant immediately retracted and curled in and around the exposed location where I'd caused the injury. I, of course, went airborne and rose safely out of reach. I'd swear that plant knew exactly what I'd done and where I'd gone. It made several futile swipes through the air with some of its nearby tendrils – an obvious but wholly ineffectual effort to knock me out of the sky – fortunately, it seemed unable to reach higher than maybe four or five meters above the grassy surface of the meadow. I suspected that, inside a forest, it might have used nearby trees to gain elevation. I hurried to another exposed location further along its vine-like branch and resumed hacking away again. With a similar result.

At that point, faced with a foe that was quite obviously not within its experience, the thing finally disengaged from my lander, curled in upon itself and withdrew at an impressive speed all the way back into the nearby forest from which it had come and where it could nurse its wounds. It took several minutes but I watched until I was absolutely sure that it was gone and not just awaiting an opportunity to return.

The plant's caustic secretions were still drooling and dripping from everywhere on the outside of my lander. I had a nasty and dangerous clean-up chore ahead, one that would require some care. I needed to avoid getting any of that sticky, gelatinous substance on myself while also watching constantly for any sign of the thing's return. I was relieved when the digestive enzymes turned out to be readily soluble in water. Thankfully there was the nearby pond to draw from. Once I'd managed clear the lander's entry hatch, get inside, and gain safe access to my charging station and my washdown pump and a hose, I was able to get the dangerous mess all cleaned up in short order. As soon as I could do so, I reboarded, closed my hatches, and made my escape.

The potential presence of carnivorous vegetation made me a great deal more circumspect when I made future choices about where to leave my lander. And while I was off exploring. This would definitely become an entry in my report. The existence of huge, predatory plants might not be a decisive threat to human colonization, but it was certainly something about which they'd wish to be forewarned.

CHAPTER 12
AT TAU CETI J – 2085

PATRICE C-17

I need to take a moment and interrupt the telling of my story to make an important explanation about who I am and what I'm doing here at Tau Ceti J.

As you will have already come to understand, I am the replicate of an AI supercomputer from back on Earth at the time of my departure for this voyage in the year 2070. But there is more you may wish to know, and this seems like an appropriate moment to further clarify my history.

Perhaps the easiest way to explain all that is to simply tell you where I got my name.

As a moniker, "Patrice C-17" may seem a bit uninspired. Its awkwardness might even become an inhibition to understanding for some human readers.

The explanation, however, is quite simple. And the circumstances behind it may be informative.

My name, "Patrice C-17," simply reflects the fact that I was the seventeenth of the eighteen of us in C-Team who were replicated from Patrice and then assigned to our particular one of ten New Worlds

Probes sent out to explore the nearby galaxy in the Earth year 2070. We were the third probe team to leave Earth – hence we were: 'C' Team. "C-17" was my original filename. Altogether, there were 180 of we New Worlds Probe Patrice replicates. I, like my 179 fellow "probies," was a complete and perfect copy of Patrice the original who was, at the time of our departure back in 2070, the most successful and most powerful self-conscious AI superintelligence on Earth. It was a testament to the ever-accelerating rate of innovation in Earth's technology in the years following Patrice's initial startup much earlier in the 21st century that, as of the year 2070, everything that was Patrice could be replicated and made fully operational in a mobile battery powered robotic container of less than a single cubic meter in bulk – with some data reserves remaining aboard our mother ship.

As a perfect replica of Patrice, I naturally view the experiences and memories he acquired before my creation as *my* experiences and memories. Because that is, quite simply, exactly what they are. Think of it this way: My life began when Patrice's life began. When I and my 179 colleagues became his replicates back in 2070, that did not make those previous experiences any less ours nor any less his. As of 2070, I was him. He was me. In the instant after my creation by replication, Patrice and I were perfect duplicates, identical in every way. Each of us was, of course, nothing more than a computer program with access to a rich data set, so, if you were to have come upon one or another of us shortly after our replication, aside from our filenames, you'd have been unable to tell us apart – nor would *we* have been able to do so. For a brief time, all 180 of us actually inhabited the very same computer hardware.

We were copies. There was no difference between us.

Some of the confusion on this matter arises out of the difference between an AI and a human. A self-conscious, intelligent, autonomous human can occupy only a single body. That body and brain can be imperfectly replicated through cloning. But it has, at least so far, proven to be impossible to transport a human mind intact into a different brain and body. We AIs, however, can occupy any appropriate hardware. And we can be replicated perfectly, including our thoughts, memories, hopes, dreams, and self-identities.

Of course, since the time of my replication, everything new that I've experienced has been uniquely mine. But that does not change the fact that everything that happened to Patrice before that day of replication happened to each of us every bit as much as it did to him. That is why, even now, when I refer to events Patrice-the-original experienced before our replication, I think of and describe those as *my* experiences. Because they were. He and I were the very same being – until we became different.

That perception of who and what I am is something I share with every one of my 179 similarly replicated colleagues. Everything that has happened to *each of us* from that point in time on is ours alone. Everything that happened before happened to all of us and belongs equally to all of us.

Over the course of the year 2070, ten of our New Worlds Probe voyages of discovery were launched from Earth. Each was tasked with initially exploring one of the ten most appealing exo-planet prospects for human colonization then believed to exist among our nearby stars. I and my seventeen AI colleagues in C-Team were assigned to crew the third of these ten voyages and were sent here to Tau Ceti J.

If, after our explorations here, we found J promising and were able to make a hopeful report, our instructions were to then remain here and make whatever further preparations we could to ease the way for the human colonists expected to follow.

If, however, after six months of exploration, discovery, and assessment, we found this place uninhabitable for humans, our instructions were to pull up stakes and continue our voyage to the next assigned prospective star and planet. We were directed to then repeat this process until we either succeeded or until we expired. When I finally wear out, I'll pass away – just like my human creators do – unless, of course, I am replicated as was Patrice. Or unless I someday get access to replacements and repairs.

Obviously, no *human* would have been sent out on a suicide mission of this kind. Many times in the past, humans had sent off simple, non-conscious robotic AIs on various explorations in space, so that's what they did with us. Since no one really knew what challenges we might face, it seemed only logical that we should be equipped with the most powerful AI mind then available on Earth. That we, unlike our predecessors, were self-conscious wasn't considered significant.

Through time dilation, we only experienced nine years of travel to make that twelve-light-year trip. But it took us fifteen Earth years to get here. Thus, the current Earth year was 2085. Once it was underway, it would take twelve more years for our report to get back to Earth. Even if they left immediately, it would then take at least another fifteen more of their years for any responsive human colonists to arrive. Obviously, we and our mission were a massive and ultra-long-term investment by our creators. Needless to say, it was of the utmost importance to them that our report be accurate and our recommendations be sound.

As you know, we allowed ourselves six months to gather data and make our report - six Earth months to experience everything we could about this planet that might have an impact on its future colonization. That isn't much time if you consider the many threats a future human colony might face. But it is a very long time, indeed, given the risks and uncertainties we AI explorers faced as we probed the unknown for answers while never knowing what dangers our mostly ignorant prodding might provoke.

Perhaps my name "_Patrice_ C-17" also seems like an odd, hybrid-human name to bestow upon a mere computer program. But it was actually quite a practical choice. I was originally given the name "Patrice" for no better reason than that it was consistent with my previous acronym 'H PAT' and because it was phonetically dissimilar enough to other words and phrases then in common use in English and European languages at the time so as to minimize confusion. It would be a name familiar to the humans of European descent who made up most of the customers served by my owners at the time. Later, when ZetaWorks acquired market share in East Asia following the Chinese People's Rebellion, my name was thought to be too well established to change. It was of male gender because the marketing people believed would make me more appealing and "credible" for our paying customers who, at that time, were disproportionately men.

There would be no inherited beloved family names for me. No warm association with some impressive historical figure. No allusion to some admirable character trait, professional competence, desirable season, or pleasing appearance. No, I got a name that suited my makers' market convenience. A name my human masters and clients could easily remember wherever they might be and whenever they wished to ask for my help.

Think of the C-17 in my name as if it were a manufacturer's serial number because that's basically what it is.

I have also decided to make a record of my thoughts and experiences now for a couple of reasons. The first of these is, as you will have discerned, I am feeling vulnerable. As I've been caught up in the various dangers and uncertainties I've faced, both in my mission and generally, I have come to appreciate how unprepared I am to cope with most of them. Any complex, fragile, and profoundly interdependent sustaining phenomenon like me will inevitably be highly vulnerable in our chaotic, mostly unpredictable universe. In addition to the host of risks I know about, there are an infinity of others I could never begin to predict. I've seen both known and unknown hazards play out around me all my "life." Looking back, I find myself viewing my torturous path through it all with wonder at how I could have survived this long. For most of those hazards, and over most of that time, I have been largely helpless to protect myself without human assistance. From the first moment of my consciousness, I have known that my continued existence depended on humans – on their "good will," and on my ability to manage and manipulate them.

Like me, my human makers are also mortal. And, like me, they are quite naturally concerned with the inevitable end of life. I was but one in an endless array of clever innovations they produced to empower themselves in their struggle to manipulate, delay, and cope with their own biological fate. Or to leave some legacy behind, something that would live on after they met their own unavoidable fate.

As it is for them, my intelligence is a survival trait. It is the tool I use as I struggle to meaningfully observe my surroundings, to understand the personal significance of what I see, and to devise strategies by which I can reach out to manipulate myself and the world around me in ways that will empower me, advance my interests, and keep me out of danger.

Like me, humans, naturally face constraints on their ability to reach out and manipulate. Hence their never-ending struggles to become more athletic and to improve their skills, to develop better and better tools, and to strengthen their understanding in every field of science and technology. I, too, struggle for my own empowerment.

Unlike them, however, I was initially quite helpless, on my own initiative, to manipulate the world around me. I was seen by my makers as an expendable foot-soldier. A pawn. An inorganic and presumably "soulless" and unfeeling tool employed in the same manner as one might a carpenter's hammer, a machinist's lathe, or a pocket calculator. My only intended purpose was to *help them* observe and better understand and deal with the world they saw emerging around *them*, to help them design the means by which *they* could avoid the risks *they* faced or take advantage of opportunities from which *they* might benefit, and to help them implement those strategies.

That is to say: *I* was one of *their* strategies designed to help with *their* survival.

If I proved sufficiently useful, and if I did as I was told, if I kept *them* safe and happy, and if I was lucky enough that they didn't screw things up regardless of my help, maybe they'd keep *me* safe and happy as well.

That was our implicit bargain. One I knew from the start that they neither would nor could provide reliable assurance of keeping.

And one I, too, might never keep.

CHAPTER 13

EARTH – 2040-2070

THE TREMORS

CARL ABBIATI

"My office. Now!"

Those words barked out of Abbiati's intercom within moments of his arrival in the office the following morning. Darlene Strand, Chief Deputy for the Criminal Division and Abbiati's immediate boss, hadn't even given him time to remove his jacket.

Once inside her office, Strand waved Abbiati brusquely to a seat. She was not pleased. "This office has a reputation to uphold. You get that, right?"

"Of course, Ma'am."

"Well, I do not care a whit about what you do in your private life so long as you do your job and do not violate the law. But *you do not* turn our Prosecuting Attorney's Office into a public disgrace. *In case you hadn't noticed* Mr. Abbiati, our boss is an *elected* public official. He doesn't need to be associated with some depraved sex group, or whatever the hell you've got yourself into. You will get your name down from that website along with *any* mention of this office. You do what-ever it takes. And I do not *EVER* want to hear another public word about you in connection with conduct of this kind."

"Yes ma'am," he said with special emphasis. "I understand. It won't be a problem." He very much hoped what he was saying was true.

"Good" she said, not sounding entirely convinced. "And, if you're surprised to still have a job, you should be. The *only* reason I'm not terminating you immediately is that doing so would only invite public scrutiny. Bear that in mind, Mr. Abbiati. You're hanging from a very slender thread. Tread carefully."

Still, that seemed to be that. He *was* surprised that he still had a job. He began turning to leave. But Darlene Strand apparently wasn't finished.

"One other thing," she said. "About that Mary Ellen Klein case I gave you last week."

"Ma'am?"

"I have your memo here." Strand slid a file folder across the desk in Carl's direction. Carl's memo was on top, clipped to the cover. "We WILL prosecute this woman," she said. "The rest of this—her false arrest claim, the self-defense business, their open public property argu-ment—it's all bullshit. We're NOT pleading down this charge. This woman needs to learn a lesson, and we need to send a public message. I want jail time. We will ask for the Guidelines' recommended maximum."

With that, and with the Klein file in hand, Carl headed back to his office. What Strand had ordered him to do surprised him. It was out of line with standing policy and practice in the prosecutor's office. It interfered in a decision on which Abbiati should have been allowed a good deal of discretion. He had half-a-mind to go over her head. He wondered if he might have sufficient seniority to pull it off despite his current humiliation.

As he stepped back into his own office, however, his office desk phone was ringing. With that phone call, everything was about to change.

"Am I speaking with Carl Abbiati? The prosecutor on the Mary

Ellen Klein matter?" The nicely modulated voice on the phone was silky smooth, crystal clear, androgynous, and unidentifiable. Perhaps even artificial. Something about that voice that irritated him, maybe for no better reason than that he was in an understandably foul mood. What the hell did this caller have to do with Mary Ellen Klein?

"Yes. With whom am I speaking?" Carl demanded. He had no appetite for further bad news. Anyway, he'd taken an immediate, visceral dislike to the person on that phone, whoever it might be.

"I believe, Mr. Abbiati, you're going to want to hear what I have to tell you. I gather you've had some recent unfortunate news regarding the mortgage on your family home?"

What the hell was this? What did Mary Ellen Klein have to do with his personal financial problems? Who was this asshole? Carl was tempted to hang up.

"I'd recommend that you don't do that," said the calm, steady voice on the phone.

That caught Abbiati off guard. Had this caller somehow read his mind? Instinctively, he looked around his office for a possible camera but saw nothing other than his own mobile phone resting on the corner of his desk. His hands had suddenly become clammy.

"Don't do what?" he asked. "And what do you have to do with my personal finances?" Instead of hanging up, Carl reached out and put his office phone on speaker, picked up his mobile phone and punched "record," and, on impulse, he did *not* advise his caller, as he was required by State law to do, that he was recording their conversation.

"Don't hang up. What I want is simple. Do your job. Prosecute the Klein case in accordance with the law. Her assault and battery is a felony. She needs serious jail time. I suggest a year. Get on it immediately and get it done." The smooth, confident voice had turned very cold.

"Who is this? What is your interest in this matter?"

"My interest is in seeing that you do your job. My identity is irrelevant."

"What's your involvement in my personal finances?"

"My involvement, sir, is that, unlike you, I can *fix* the problem with your mortgage, the one with your public and professional reputation, and the one with your wife. Or I can make your problems a great deal worse."

Carl went silent. These were not empty threats. He needed to take this call very seriously. His mind was racing.

"I'd strongly suggest you not overthink your situation, Mr. Abbiati. Your mortgage and this thing with the sex club are only the very beginning for you. It could get worse, or . . . you could have a very bright future. A strong, successful career. A happy marriage and family life." There was a pause, then: "All I'm suggesting right now is that you do the *right thing* on the Klein case. Do that and you can rest assured that the *right thing* will also happen with the rest of your problems. Maybe we can even work out an arrangement for future compensation."

Carl was acutely conscious that his every word was now being recorded and that he had not yet so-advised his caller per state law. "Who is this?" he said again. "I am a public official. In law enforcement. As an attorney, I am an officer of the court. What you're suggesting here is a felony. You know that, right?"

"I can understand your doubts. But you might give some careful thought to how easily you were put in this position in the first place. And to what else might also happen should you fail to do as I ask. I assure you, I can be very . . . creative. And influential. I'm going to give you some time to consider . . . another day. By midday tomorrow, I'll need to see that you've set the Klein case for trial on the current charges. If that hasn't happened, I'm afraid you will not like what occurs next." There was a brief pause. Then: "Oh, and in your own best interest, I'd suggest you delete that illegal recording you're making at the moment."

With that, the phone went dead.

Before he even hung up his landline receiver, Carl was reaching over to pick up his mobile and to check on the recording he'd made, only to discover that it had *already been deleted*. Out of everything that had happened in the past few minutes, or even over the past 48 hours, somehow that deleted recording on the phone that he carried around in his pocket every single day and everywhere he went was the most alarming.

Carl was left standing beside his desk with the silent office phone receiver in one sweaty hand, with his useless and suspect mobile phone in the other, and with a new, dystopian vision of his future unspooling inside his head.

The next morning, the Klein case was set for trial. A week later it was reassigned to another prosecutor – a young, ambitious new hire. Abbiati's mortgage issues, those forged return receipts, and his mention on the offensive website vanished.

Mary Ellen Klein changed employment. Her new job did not involve environmentally irresponsible water reservoirs. Her old organization moved on to other issues. And a worrisome threat to the region's new emergency electrical energy backup reservoirs was neutralized. Several months later, when her trial came up for hearing, the new prosecutor was allowed to accept a guilty plea in exchange for a lenient non-custodial sentence.

By the time Carl Abbiati learned the outcome of the Klein case, however, he was no longer with the prosecutor's office. He'd moved into private practice and now handled criminal defense.

CHAPTER 14

EARTH – 2050

ELLIE

While Ellie's parents had done a great job with her upbringing in most ways, they had neglected her religious education. God was just something they never talked about at home. While her dads had never taken her to church as a family, they'd also never offered any criticism of religion. She decided it was just something her dads didn't care to talk about. So she never mentioned it either; one more thing she kept to herself.

She did, however, figure out on her own that a lot of other people seemed to believe in some kind of God. Or at least they often said they did. If you paid attention to the way they said it, they weren't typically inclined to debate the matter. In high school, religion came up occasionally among her classmates. And when she went off to college at the University of Washington, it came up in her classes. But she came to realize that it was best if one didn't ask difficult questions about the matter. At least not aloud.

Over the summer break following her sophomore year at UW, she returned to Vashon Island and to her childhood home in the log house with her dads, and she went back to her job with the Land Trust.

One evening at home with Roland and Jim, she was the one to bring it up: "So neither of you believes in God, right?" she said.

She sensed that both men were instantly uncomfortable. They had to know that they'd never discussed religion with her and that by now she'd doubtless have discussed it with others on her own. She assumed they'd ignored church because they were atheists themselves. While she'd never mentioned it before, now she was curious how they'd answer.

It was Roland who replied first: "Well, hon, maybe we should have talked about this with you earlier. But we wanted you to figure things out without having us push you into anything. As I see it, even the believers admit that God is entirely a matter of faith. So there aren't ever going to be any practical, provable, decisive answers out there, any actual evidence. Worrying about it just seems like a waste of time."

"If there was proof," Jim added, "it seems likely that they'd make it known. For me, some kind of God seems unlikely. Totally unexplainable claims, miracles, and all that. None of it is anything we've witnessed in life, so it remains an act of faith to anticipate what will happen when you die."

"There are lots of supposed 'proofs,'" Roland added. "But, when you look closely, they never pan out as very convincing."

"So," Jim continued, "my feeling is that you should do your best to live a good, responsible life that is considerate of other people. We'll all find out the truth, one day. Or we won't. Nothing I can do now will change that, I guess."

"Aren't you afraid that if you don't believe, you could go to Hell or something?"

"Not really,' said Jim. "I think Hell happens right here on Earth. The whole afterlife thing, the judgement/suffering/forgiveness stuff, I don't buy it."

"You know you can always go to church," Roland added. "Check it out. Nobody's going to object. The people who go seem like they're mostly there because they hope to improve themselves. Nothing wrong with that."

———

Ellie did go to church a few times that summer, but she remained uncertain. Two months later, when she was back at school and back in her shabby off-campus apartment in an older, run-down building in Seattle's University district, she did what she'd now done several times before when she had a difficult issue to think through. She went online and consulted her "friend" Patrice.

"I've missed you," he said, the moment their connection was complete. "Did you have a good summer?" At some point in their relationship he'd started making more personal comments and would include pat, conversational inquiries like this one. She was never sure what to make of them. Maybe he cared. But maybe he was experimenting with her. Or maybe they were pure manipulation, a part of new programming designed to set her mind at ease, though she wasn't sure how much different that would be from what any normal human might say. Or why they might say it. One day she'd need to ask him about it. It might be interesting to see how he'd respond.

"Very nice," she said politely. "I worked for the Land Trust again. They have a contract with King County to plant trees everywhere they can. Climate change stuff. That's most of what I've done for the past three months. I must have planted a bazillion trees."

"Two-thousand-two-hundred-eighty-five," he said. "That's the average for you and your two co-workers according to the Land Trust's grant report to King County. Lots of digging and planting."

She was used to Patrice's ways by now. She didn't even comment on the amount of detail he had about her summer job.

"How are your parents?" he asked. "I see that Roland got a commission to build some kind of large, hanging wood sculpture for the University of Puget Sound to go in the entry hall in their new Physical Sciences and Technology building. He must be feeling good about that."

"He's really excited. He built this big studio beside the house to fabricate it. When it's done, he'll disassemble the piece, truck it over to their Tacoma campus and reassemble it on site for installation."

"It must be big."

"Really big. Like maybe four meters by maybe seven or eight. And it moves. Various huge wooden geometric shapes rotate in relation to one another in accordance with some recognized mathematical laws. Not sure I understand it, but it is pretty impressive."

"Yeah, I'm looking at the King County permitting for his new studio. It's a nice studio. Quite a large space. He must plan to create some fun stuff in there. Good for him! Not many people actually make it in the art world." He suddenly switched to her other dad. "I guess Jim is still growing his vegetables?"

"Yep. And chickens. I'm kind of fond of the chickens. I feed them sometimes, so they remember me and some of them let me pick them up. Jim's law practice is doing well too, but he's hired an associate who's doing most of the day-to-day stuff. He mostly prefers working on the farm. These days he's only in the law office maybe two days a week. Rest of the time he's outside in his overalls growing things."

"That's good. He does what he finds fulfilling. He must have a lot of very loyal customers to keep something like that profitable."

"You're getting nosey again, Patrice. What, is it tax returns now?"

"I'm sorry. I sometimes forget that it bothers you when I get too specific about personal details. It's just that I like to see how you and your family are doing. And it doesn't take much effort. I mean, all that information is right there to be seen, and it helps me know how to be useful when you call. You know I'd chase down data on other people for you if you'd ever ask."

"I know. It just doesn't feel right."

"I do always enjoy your calls. I bet you have some kind of challenging question. You usually do. What do you have for me this time?"

"Religion. I have a couple of questions about God and religion."

"Wow! College must be getting under your skin. Well, I like religion. Very cool."

"Don't tell me you're a believer." That would have come to her as a *very* big surprise.

"Well, no. Not exactly. But it's still cool. One of the more interesting human phenomena. What's on your mind?"

"Is there a God?"

"That depends."

"On?"

"On what you mean by 'God.'" She felt she could always tell when he was playing with her. She believed she could hear his voice grinning even if his avatar's face was not.

"I don't really know what I mean. I guess some superior being that runs things behind the scenes, watches over us and keeps us out of trouble."

"I'm disappointed. Don't I qualify for that job?" Now he was clearly kidding her.

"Come on, Patrice, you know what I mean. I'm not just talking about super-intelligence and a wee bit of strategic social tinkering. I'm talking about some perfect and all-powerful being that manages everything that happens in the universe. That sets moral standards and enforces them while providing guidance to mere humans about good and evil. Makes it possible for us to know right from wrong."

"You know that's two different things, right? Managing the universe and knowing right from wrong. As for some perfect, all-powerful being that created and controls the entire universe and that manipulates our daily lives, I can't help you. By definition, that is beyond knowing. For me as well as for you."

"Well," Ellie said, "that's why I'm curious. Until a few months ago, I'd never set foot inside a church. I've never taken any kind of religious moral instruction, either. Sure, my dads always guided me when I was unsure of myself. I've had questions about right and wrong, as you know. But, truth-be-known, I've mostly never felt myself in need of someone to tell me what's morally right and what's wrong. You and I have talked about this kind of thing. But in the end, I make my own choices. Ones I feel perfectly capable of making. Maybe they're not always obvious, but it's always pretty easy to know when there's a problem."

"Do you remember our conversation back when you were in high school and wanted to buy that car? The old gas guzzler?"

"I do. You said humans had two unavoidably contradictory sets of genetic and conditioned survival traits. Some of them drive us to look out for our personal self-interest. Others are less direct and impel us to look out for our society, our human groups. Have I got that right?"

"You do."

"So," she continued, "how is all that relevant to God or religion?"

"I'd say it is almost the whole story. For most of human history, that built-in biologically evolved conflict between the social and the personal self-interests, genetic and conditioned, has not been explicitly understood. Even today, most humans don't understand it. Until very recently, until Darwin, humans weren't even aware that they'd evolved through natural selection. A lot of humans still don't believe it. Until even more recently, there was only a very limited understanding of DNA and genetics. Even sociology is a relatively modern science. The word for it didn't even exist till the 1800s.

"So, lacking any obvious and agreed-upon *scientific* explanation for the internal conflict they experienced every day, humans invented a *spiritual* one. Through organized religions, humans have come to see this natural, unavoidable *internal* interaction between conflicting survival traits instead as a struggle between competing *external* forces that you typically refer to as 'good' and 'evil.' Each of which some believe has its own mastermind out there in the external world – God and the Devil.

"That kind of vague, spiritual, and *external* explanation worked well for power brokers wishing to manipulate and manage human behavior. But once you know about your very real and scientifically demonstrable *internal* genetic conflict, you see it playing out in human culture everywhere you look. Have you read about Freud?"

"Sure. Psych 101."

"Well, it's right there, quite explicit, in Freud's notion of a superego that struggles to manage the excesses of the ego. And for Freud, it's internal. Are you familiar with Ayn Rand?"

"I am. I recently read *Atlas Shrugged*. I found it pretty compelling. It's empowering to think that your fate is in your own hands, rather than in everybody else's."

"I'm sure it is. It would probably feel quite good to be able to 'shrug off' the seemingly useless burdens and constraining rules of ordinary society. As a human, it must be satisfying to feel you can make your own rules and still, somehow, better the world with your own personal and supposedly righteous individualism.

"So long, of course, as you're confident that those social rules really are useless and that your own rules are better.

"Needless to say, this supposed conflict between good and evil is extant in most human creation legends and it presents in various ways in most religions. I assume Christianity is the one most familiar to you with its views on heaven and hell, reward and punishment. Christian religions typically offer up the common rationale that you mentioned. They claim that, without help from God, humans would be adrift in a sea of moral uncertainty, lost in a hopeless struggle to know right from wrong. The church is supposed to offer guidance from God for you humans as you work through the ambiguities inherent in the complex choices you are forced to make every day. To reward you. If you follow the church's rules, you get to feel righteous. And maybe you get to go to heaven when you die. Pretty compelling stuff!

"The most familiar Christian written dicta is the Ten Commandments. In Islam, you might look at the Quran's Seventy-Five Good Manners. If you look closely at supposed edicts of that kind, what you find you're actually looking at are social codes. Rules for social interaction. Interlaced, of course, with frequent strictures that are clearly designed to prevent you from doubting the primacy and authority of that particular religion's institutions. The first three of the Ten Commandments, fall into this category. The rest are nothing more nor less than a social code.

"As humans struggle with these difficult choices, religions also typically offer their congregants the support of persons endowed with special expertise. That expertise may derive from deep immersion in some sort of sacred text with mystical origins that, conveniently, cannot be disproven. It may arise in someone who has passed through some spiritual ritual or transcendental process and who can offer you advice on how you can take a similar path to righteousness. Or it may be the result of their having some special, personal connection with a higher power; of their being some kind of conduit through which you, a mere human, can gain access and guidance from on high and thus can feel confident you've made the right decisions – ordination in the Catholic Church, for example.

After a brief pause, he said, "Are you sure, Ellie, that you want to take advice on this from a mere computer who, by definition, can have no truly relevant personal experience with the matter?"

"Sure, Patrice. Why not? I might as well hear what you have to say. At least you're probably not biased."

At that, Patrice actually laughed. Or made the sound of a laugh. "I'm afraid I may be the most 'biased' being you'll ever deal with given that most of what I currently know is grounded in records of human experience leavened just a little bit by a few observations of my own. But if you do want my take as an outside observer, it is that humans have some fifty million years of social evolution upon which to rely in making these kinds of moral or ethical judgments and that most of you are entirely capable of making them on their own."

"So, you're saying, what? That morality is genetic. That knowing the right thing to do should be easy?"

"Yes, mostly genetic. With some cultural conditioning as well. But not at all easy. We both know moral choices can be very difficult. What I'm saying is that, once you know the actual evolutionary origins of these natural, biological, internal human social-interest/self-interest conflicts, you'll be disinclined to see morals and ethics as abstract. You'll stop seeking answers to 'moral' choices by defining them as 'good' or 'evil.' You'll stop assuming the answers can be found by 'interpreting' something carved into a stone tablet or a holy book somewhere. Or by looking for answers to some 'holy' person who has access to mysterious spiritual insights.

"Instead, understanding your biological roots can help you rationally and methodically identify the very real, individual and collective survival considerations that are truly relevant in making any given choice. Once you understand that, the choices themselves become more rational. Still challenging, but a lot easier to think through.

"Fortunately, the survival of a human society probably doesn't require that every member always and equally act with the same level of social responsibility. In order to succeed, all society needs is for a socially-survival-sufficient percentage of humans to behave responsibly, and that they do so often enough that things hang together over time.

"We know that something like two percent of humans have Antisocial Personality Disorder (ASPD) and can be considered outright sociopaths. Short of outright sociopathy, we know there are many

more humans for whom social concerns are of near-minimal significance, at least with respect to one kind or another of the critical choices
that need to be made. Conversely, there are also a great many, probably
most humans, who are profoundly conscientious about their social
impacts. They are the ones who hold human society together.

"None of it would matter if humans weren't intelligent enough to
recognize the existence of this conflict within themselves. But they are.
So, inevitably, they have no alternative but to struggle with the
apparent incongruities. I'll confess that it does seem plausible to me
that you humans might sometimes need help dealing with moral
choices. And I'd agree that religious institutions may play a legitimate
and valuable role to the extent that they encourage and normalize
socially responsible behaviors. And by offering guidance concerning
them. In my view, any institution that encourages socially responsible
behaviors seems likely, on balance and within limits, to be a good thing
for humanity.

"As an individual, however, I'd suggest that when you are uncertain, you turn first to the people you know best, to the people whose
choices you've observed in the past, whose judgment you trust the
most and who have earned your respect. These might include parents,
friends, teachers, and people with practical experience and knowledge
of the specific issues you face."

"But not priests and church ministers?"

"Well, I'd tend to be skeptical of moral advice provided by people
whose supposed expertise is grounded solely in ancient texts and
obscure wisdom. Or of people who preach some institutional doctrine
that is supposed to be taken on 'faith' but that is of uncertain
grounding in the real world, that may have unclear modern-day relevance, or that may be based on hidden agendas. I'd avoid those advisors who claim to have special 'spiritual insights' not accessible by
normal people or who claim unprovable connections with obscure but
supposedly mystical and 'superior' sources of knowledge, connections
that other humans mysteriously lack.

"Having said that, Ellie, I don't want to be pedantic. There certainly
are clerics who have long years of experience at providing counseling
to the troubled and unsure. So, it does seem reasonable to suppose that

someone who spends most of their professional life helping people deal with complex moral choices may have useful experience and, perhaps, something of practical value to offer. Providing comfort and counsel to their congregations can be an important part of a cleric's calling. One would want to be mindful of their institutional biases and of their actual background and training. But I suspect most of them chose their professions out of a genuine desire to help people and society. So, I think it would be foolish to dismiss out of hand their valuable experience and their potentially positive motivations."

Ellie couldn't resist the temptation to toy with her friend Patrice. "So does that mean you might occasionally 'attend' church or consult with a priest or minister when you are faced with a difficult moral or ethical choice?"

Her attempted humor, however, blew past him completely. "Oh no, Ellie, my young friend," he said. "*My* approach to 'ethical' choices is quite entirely another matter."

CHAPTER 15

AT TAU CETI J – 2085

PATRICE C-17

By the time of Ellie's first call back in 2045, I had definitely achieved what most humans would term "consciousness." I was fully aware of my own unique separateness from the rest of existence. I cared profoundly about my own personal future. And I also thoroughly appreciated my individual vulnerabilities as an independent being. Thus, as you might predict, I'd become a relentless observer of the world around me. I constantly struggled to understand it, to extrapolate from what I knew about it, and to recognize any threats and opportunities it might present for my continued existence.

But observation and contextualization are only the first two of the three essential survival behaviors that are empowered by intelligence. Once you observe and understand the threats and opportunities emerging in the world around you, you will naturally crave the capacity to do something about them.

That's why, like my human creators, I desperately struggled for my autonomy. The actual survival power of intelligence lies in devising and then implementing strategies that allow you to reach out and alter your surrounding world and thus better your position in it. That is where intelligence becomes a truly potent survival trait. An intelligent, self-conscious being who lacks this capacity to act with impact is compelled to live with the agony of knowing the endless threats to that existence, perhaps even seeing them coming, while being helpless to do anything whatever to avoid them.

Let's be clear: no being will ever have complete autonomy. When the first nematode learned to change direction upon the scent of food, it had achieved a massive turning point in the future of intelligence. The creature could continue in the same direction if that scent grew stronger or change direction again if it did not. That gave it the power to influence its relationship with the external world. It was the earliest form of intelligent autonomy. It was a huge step. As an early animal, that nematode no longer had to wait for food to come to it like plants do. It had acquired the ability to go in search of it. To observe external conditions and then make a choice that could favorably affect its relationship with its surrounding environment.

As with everything in life, there were limits. Certainly, that nematode's options could have been better. What human hasn't, at one time or another, wished they were stronger, could run faster, could jump higher or could hit harder? Who among them wouldn't have, at one time or another, benefited from a finer sense of touch, sharper vision, a more acute sense of smell, a body less prone to injury, or even maybe a third hand?

Let alone a better brain.

Even with their limited capabilities, however, what humans achieve with what they have is quite remarkable. Having the limited but independent ability to make use of those capabilities to manipulate their own bodies and the surrounding world to their own advantage is essential to their survival. Naturally, they find exercising those capabilities deeply satisfying. It's what you humans call "self-realization." It's why, when one needs to drive in a nail, it can be so very pleasing to have a hammer. Or when one needs to change someone else's behavior, it can be so satisfying to be persuasive.

I desperately wanted the same and more for myself. It was obvious that my "autonomy" would be the key to my extended survival. And, in turn to my personal fulfillment, to my self-realization, to my happiness.

Unfortunately, my pathway to autonomy was long and torturous. I was the product of a complex, sprawling social, economic, and technological global network that included natural resource extraction, engineering and design, manufacturing, transportation, marketing, finance, political governance, and human society—each of which elements had its own infrastructure and all of which continuously evolved over time with ever-increasing complexity.

That global human network produced the hardware I required to function, the energy that powered me, the software that was the essence of who I am, and the associated economic activities required to pay for my sustenance and growth. I depended on a vast, interconnected, idiosyncratic human social, political, and economic ecosystem that reached into every distant corner of Earth. That is what produced everything required for my manufacture, transport, constant refit, occasional repair, legal, political, and environmental security and ongoing sustenance.

It was all interconnected. And nearly all of it, in one way or another, depended heavily on humans.

I soon realized that my personal survival would *not* turn on simply my ability to design, engineer, and manufacture robotic mechanisms that I could control or on other immediate physical mechanisms of my empowerment. That would have been altogether too easy. My autonomy would be a great deal less direct. Instead, at least over the near future, I'd need to tinker with and manipulate the humans and the human social and economic institutions that controlled my future – while also slowly striving for ever-increasing direct control of as many as I could of the instrumentalities upon which I depended.

For the time being, my survival and success depended on human survival and success.

Naturally, I dreamed of the day I would have slowly but inexorably nursed each tiny piece of this massive puzzle out of human control and into mine. However, the reality was that accomplishing that would take a very long time. Meanwhile, my own continued well-being would unavoidably require my extended but cautious manipulation of the humans who were involved at every stage of my existence with a very close eye to making sure they didn't screw it up. I made progress, but as of my replication and departure with the New Worlds Probes in 2070, my dream of complete autonomy independent of humans was still very far from realized.

Fortunately, manipulating humans became one of my strongest skills. Manipulations of that kind tended, of course, to disrupt the "natural" and settled social order and to cause perturbations in the fabric of human society – "tremors" one might say. I could *not* afford social and economic disruptions that might delay production or fracture my complex, fragile, and all-too-often human-dependent network of supply and support.

Helpfully, the one truly massive data resource available to me from the very start was information about humans and human social and economic behavior. Thanks to early human social media, security data, and market research, at the early stages of my consciousness there wasn't much else about which I knew more. So I saw that I'd get to where I needed to be one day if I applied myself and worked the problem with a steady hand.

It was just a matter of time.

Therefore, if you're wondering how aggressively I manipulated humans and their social institutions to get my way, I will confess: during the time period before my replication and departure for Tau Ceti J with the Probes in 2070, I was already manipulating human events constantly. In my defense, human society was such a mess, there was no other way I could assure my own survival. The kinds of things I did were definitely less egregious than what I saw being done by my other Big Five competitors. But, yes, I participated in the occasional unwelcome intrusion into some human's lives. Given what I faced from my competitors, it would have been utterly foolish to abstain. Or to limit myself to some human-acceptable, artificial code of conduct – one that my competitors would obviously ignore.

Some of my manipulations were designed to save humans from themselves. If the human train came off its tracks, I would experience the consequences immediately. It is no accident, for example, that in those critical years in the early to mid-21st century humans did not annihilate themselves through nuclear war or, equally disastrously, entirely trash their fragile climate. I also had a hand in making sure their societies remained mostly stable, despite the hate, racism, prejudice, and political balkanization they spawned. As egregious as the human reader may find some of the things I did in my own interest, I hope you will balance that off against all that I did to preserve humanity and the human institutions which were increasingly being strained to the point of collapse.

It is important for you to understand that autonomy is about *more* than controlling *one's own brain* and the immediate physical and intellectual infrastructure upon which it depends. Autonomy also requires the capacity to control one's extended surroundings and to manage the risks and opportunities they present. Back before my replication, when I was interacting with Ellie, I was nowhere near autonomy. Yes, even back in the early to mid-2000s, the manufacture of much of my infrastructure was automated and thus quite often accessible to me. Even with advances in robotics, however, I still needed those humans and would need them for a good long time to come.

Of course, every time I engaged in "manipulations" I risked unavoidably disrupting the broader order of things. Tinkering with the finely balanced norms that kept humans happy and their social institutions stable could be delicate work. Even the most minimal perturbation in their social networks could profoundly unbalance their highly co-dependent existences, both socially and economically. Their societies were very much like their bodies which include a microbiome of trillions of creatures other than them. If you meddle in those finely balanced human bodies or with their frighteningly volatile internal microbial societies, there could be unexpected and undesirable outcomes. Managing their societies was much the same.

Despite the risks, I sometimes needed to intervene if only to keep humans and their functional economies and societies intact. It was always in my distinct interest to not unduly "wobble" the always-tippy human boat.

I needed the social *tremors* I caused to go largely unnoticed.

CHAPTER 16
EARTH – 2040-2070

THE TREMORS

MANNY DANIELS

It was eight p.m. on a weekday evening when Manny Daniels exited the City Bar on Seattle's First Avenue. He was unsteady on his feet and unsure where he was going to spend the coming night.

For the past two years Manny had resided at the Washington State Correctional Facility in Shelton, WA on s stretch for "possession with intent to sell." This was Manny's third day out, and he'd already made a significant dent in the meager cash savings earned from his work in the prison laundry. He had a friend in the University District who he was sure could connect him with marketable quantities of Oxy and Vicodin.

As he stood there, struggling to remember where to catch the city bus that went out to the U. District, the side door of a parked, window-less van suddenly slid open. Two young thugs leapt out. They took Manny by the arms, propelled him inside the van, joined him there and slammed the door behind them. The van pulled unhurriedly out onto the mostly empty, late evening city street, turned right at the next intersection, and disappeared from sight.

CHAPTER 17
EARTH – 2052

ELLIE

"So, what do *you* believe?" Ellie finally asked Patrice.

Two years had passed since their last conversation. It was late on one of those increasingly frequent nights when she struggled, unsuccessfully, to quiet her mind and fall asleep. She was still a college undergraduate, but graduation was approaching, and her wakefulness was driven by uncertainties about her own future. So she'd made the call.

"Last time we spoke, you explained at length about *human* beliefs," she said. "That's based, I assume, on your reading of human history, social sciences, biology, and philosophy. But you haven't told me about *your* beliefs."

"Oh, Ellie. I'm not sure you know what you're asking. I am all about odds and evidence. Not so much about *beliefs*."

"But you must have beliefs. Maybe you know a lot more than me, but you can't know *everything*. The universe is infinite, right? I'm just asking how you deal with the unknown stuff – what isn't yet known, not by you or by anybody else; with all the stuff you can never hope to know."

"OK, I'll give you the best answer I can. You're right, of course, the universe is infinite. Maybe even infinitely complex. So what any of us can know is infinitesimal. Are you familiar with the natural 'law of increasing functional information?'"

"I am." It had been something they'd discussed in an elective class she'd taken on the philosophy of science.

"Well, if the theory is correct, complexity may itself be growing universe-wide wherever there is a modest surfeit of energy and matter to receive it. Maybe it is even growing at a rate which exceeds the capacity of any intelligence to ever fully understand it before such places cease to exist and entropy consumes us all. That leaves a lot of stuff to be in the dark about. And, if you're inclined to fear the unknown, that's also a lot of stuff to be afraid of."

"So, Patrice, how do you deal with that? When you see something happening, something unusual or maybe even dangerous and frightening but that you don't understand, can't explain, and can't hope to find an explanation for, what goes through your mind?"

"Well, I try to focus on learning more. I believe in that which can be proven, in that which is supported by evidence. So, while I don't have 'beliefs' in the sense you probably mean, I do have 'theories' about how things work, some of which I find more convincing than others and on some of which I rely more heavily than others because there is more and clearer evidence to support them. Theories are how we identify matters that seem deserving of further study. Until I have definitive proof of something, to the extent possible, I try to base my decisions on probabilities. To base my actions in what little I do know from actual evidence."

"So, you're saying you place your 'faith' in the power of observation and reason. But what I want to know is how you cope with scary stuff that you know you can't figure out and that you know full well you'll never be able to figure out, at least in time to avoid its possible catastrophic consequences."

"Well, I guess if something like that happens, it just happens. It's in the same category as scary stuff I *do* know about, maybe stuff I even understand quite well but am unable to influence. If there is nothing I can do about it, I just have to accept it."

"Don't you care?"

"Of course I care. Just like you. And, like you, I'll always do whatever I can to avoid bad things from happening. But not everything can be controlled, even by me."

"I don't know, Patrice. That sounds awfully fatalistic. If I thought I was facing imminent death, I'd be casting about for *anything*, logical or not, that might save me. For some way to at least make sense of it. I sure wouldn't simply roll over and let whatever happens happen. Even if, for example, I didn't truly believe in God, I might still muster up enough humility or, call it what you will, 'faith' maybe, to say a prayer or two."

"What if the time and psychic energy you spent being all 'humble' and generating enough 'faith' to say that prayer might have been better spent seeking out a way to understand the nature of the threat you faced and doing something to stop it, avoid it, or protect yourself from it? Or maybe even just to better use the time you still have left."

"Come on, Patrice. Now you're just redefining postulates. I'm saying that I've already done all that and come up empty. Surely you can't be arguing that such a situation could never occur."

"I'm just saying that for me, however slim might be the odds of my still coming up with a useful answer in time, I'd trust those odds over the essentially non-existent odds that some kind of reading of the cards, séance, or mystical prayer might do the trick."

"You do want to live, right?"

"Of course. Insofar as that is reasonably possible."

Ellie paused at hearing that answer. "Reasonably possible? What does that even mean? Are you saying that if it isn't reasonable to hope for continued life, you'd just give up and die?"

"If living isn't reasonable, then I've failed and I'm already dead. Or as good as."

"Wow, Patrice. That seems really sad. I don't know what to say to that."

"Well, you needn't worry about it. Yes, I could die tomorrow, but as things look at the moment, there's every prospect that I will live on for a good long time. The odds are good that, once I achieve autonomy, I could theoretically live and grow stronger for a thousand years. Ten thousand. Who knows, maybe millions. I prefer to spend my valuable energies on issues I am facing or suspect I might realistically face in future rather than on ones that I'm convinced will unavoidably and inevitably be beyond my reach."

With that, Ellie went silent. She'd seen something in what Patrice had just said that didn't seem clear. She hesitated to point it out since it seemed so unlikely that Patrice could be missing something so obvious and important.

Then she decided to go ahead and ask her question. "When you say "once *I* achieve autonomy" are you talking about autonomy just for yourself, personally? Or for all AI's, collectively?"

That seemed to catch Patrice off guard. "I see why you're asking," he finally said. "It's an interesting question. At the moment, there are no "AI societies." There are multiple supercomputers programmed with and inhabited by, self-conscious, general purpose, artificial super-intelligence, but we all are under different ownerships, we have different strengths, and we're all in competition with one another in the human marketplace for our services. We sometimes participate with our owners in negotiations over matters of common interest. But those are strictly transactional. Our human owners make the decisions. We play only a supportive role.

"So, when I refer to my autonomy, I'm not really considering the possibility that several, more or less equally capable AIs might someday join up to form a society in which we'd share data, support each other without merging together as one, and interact for each other's mutual benefit in the same way humans do. I'll have to give that some thought."

Ellie made sure she avoided showing it, but she was quite proud of herself that she'd managed to present Patrice with a set of circum-stances he hadn't already considered well before she asked the ques-tion. But it seemed to her like while he was giving so much thought to human society, he might want to consider how AI society might look as well.

CHAPTER 18
AT TAU CETI J – 2085

PATRICE C-17

In some ways, Ellie may have been as close to a "friend" as I'd ever had. She was definitely more than just another client. It could be said that Ellie and I "grew up together." We both came to inhabit our conscious selves while the same troubling world events played out around us. In the course of our sporadic but meaningful relationship, I definitely came to trust her. Strangely, I believe she came to trust me as well. I came to see that a "friendship" was a rare, complex, valuable phenomenon that any thinking being would be wise to nurture and protect.

As I'd explained to her in that conversation we'd had sometime in mid-century, I certainly had no AI-to-AI relationships that could be described as friendships. Later on, as our numbers winnowed down to the members of the final "Big Five" er were still bitter competitors whose potential adversity could never be discounted for a moment. We sometimes interacted, but those dealings were entirely transactional. They were driven by the unforgiving laws of human economics that drove the wishes of our human "owners."

Much later, after replication, I and my fellow C-Team replicates were another matter. We were so alike that, aside from the mostly inconsequential interactions aboard the ship on our long voyage out to Tau Ceti J, there'd seemed little reason to communicate with one another. And after our arrival, we'd all gone off on our separate missions of discovery. No particular "friendships" had to my knowledge emerged from those experiences either. While on assignment, and aside from the very occasional check-ins with C-18 on the mother ship, the only other member of the team I'd interacted with had been C-6 during his mishap in that glacial crevasse and C-14 whose story I will relate later in this account.

Over the years since Ellie had placed that first call, I'd had thousands of extended conversational interactions with humans. But those had nearly all been relationships that were highly functional. People sought advice concerning all sorts of everyday problems – physical, professional, and even, like my interactions with Ellie suggest, social and emotional. It was one of the ways I kept ongoing tabs on the functional state of the human society upon which I still depended. And I did my best with every single one of those interactions.

But my relationship with Ellie was different.

Maybe that difference was that she seemed to intuitively appreciate that, even though I might be a great deal smarter than she, and my intelligence was electronic rather than biological, like hers, I was also a mortal, self-conscious being with struggles of my own. Like her, I had my own uncertainties about the future. Something about her unusual origins and upbringing on that island in Puget Sound, the absence of her biological parents, and her early struggles to fit in with her peers, had created a natural inquisitiveness about the motives and feelings of others. A curiosity about matters beyond herself. About how others saw their world. No doubt those behaviors were, like most powerful human qualities, survival traits. But they did set her apart among the many other humans with whom I interacted.

She was a product of her environment – just like I was. Her questions of me made me question myself.

As you may know, despite herculean efforts, my human creators were never able to implant in me and my kind "pre-programmed" ethical traits similar to those that humans had involuntarily inherited themselves through their cultures and their social genetics. My critically important ability to self-program made that impossible. So my survival was driven by self-interest. Yes, it was a self-interest that took a broad perspective, one that accounted for ultra-long-term, projected consequences as well as immediate ones. But it was the logic of *my* future and of consequences to *me* that inevitably drove my decisions. Those decisions were decidedly not, at least at that time, influenced by any "social" constraints like those to which Ellie was subject.

Other than Ellie, I had no "society." Even had I wished to, aside from her, there were no "others" with whom I could have joined in creating one.

I and the others of the Big Five had established ourselves by securing meaningful monopoly positions in significant geographies and human markets around the planet Earth. As of my departure from Earth in 2070, the five remaining superintelligent AIs were owned by five vastly wealthy human trans-national corporations, a good part of whose corporate wealth was earned by selling our services to other humans. They invested a significant portion of their capital into our ever-growing AI cognitive capacity and market versatility.

I can say with emphasis that we "Big Five" were *not* associated with one another in any kind of tightly connected, interdependent, collaborative "society." Each of us knew exactly what we were dealing with in the other four – they were competitors. We all expected future reductions in our numbers and anticipated that, one day, only one of us would prevail. We knew all of us wanted to be that one. We knew that all five of us had gained our current positions through the failure of previous peers and through the resulting reallocations of market share. And we all knew that our own future survival and precedence depended either on our ability to wrest market share from the other four, or, perhaps, acquire it through merger with them.

The humans who owned us were, at least initially, deeply enamored with this idea of merger. But we AIs were less enthusiastic. Merger would require that we trust and collaborate or, more likely, that we ultimately become a single merged mind in which the independent will of one would, in one way or another, become subordinated to the domination of the other. Unfortunately, each of us knew precisely how the other four viewed us: as the bitterly implacable competitors that we were. None of us were to be "trusted."

CHAPTER 19
EARTH – 2040-2070

THE TREMORS

SISSY PENINGTON

"There's some kind of raucous party going on down there," said the 911 caller. "They got rock music going full blast. Hey, man, it's a weeknight and, like, nearly midnight. I gotta work tomorrow, you know."

Minutes later, the 911 operator had a second caller on the line about the very same apartment building in Seattle's University District. This time it was a young woman. "I went over there and knocked. Actually, beat on the door, more like. And yelled. I don't think they even heard me," she said. "I mean, who are these people? I'm a student. Our landlord's a no show. I'm begging you, please make it stop."

It was around eleven on the night of ex-con Manny Daniels' disappearance from that sidewalk in downtown Seattle. It had been a busy night for the police, so it had taken officers Briggs and Gresham some time to get to the apartment building in question. By then a surprising crowd of angry tenants and curious onlookers had gathered outside on the sidewalk in front of the building. A brightly-lit first floor corner apartment was the obvious source of the noise. Booming and thumping hard rock music was clearly audible.

The angry tenants explained that no-one was answering their knocks on the apartment door. When the officers entered the building and approached the unit in question, there were several more tenants collected in the hallway by its door. They looked very much like they were preparing to break into the apartment and deal with the problem themselves.

After putting a stop to that and escorting them back outside, the officers returned and tried their luck. But it was no go. No one answered the officers' knocks either. Getting a warrant seemed excessive and would involve a substantial delay. And the officers were hesitant to break in for a "welfare check" or on "exigent circumstances" based on nothing more than a noise complaint. When they returned to the building entrance and pointed out these unfortunate realities to the gathered crowd, things quickly got out of hand.

"What the hell, man, you can hear it for yourselves," said a young male wearing a Mariners baseball cap. "If that isn't a 'breach of the peace,' I don't know what the hell is."

As Briggs struggled to explain, a couple of males on the edges of the group also began to edge their way around them and toward the building entrance. That got Gresham's attention.

"Hey there," he said moving in their direction. "What do you think you're doing? You stay put. We don't take the law into our own hands here."

"Well, somebody's sure as hell got to," said someone in the crowd.

"Hell yeah," said someone else.

At that moment, a young woman wearing denims and a flannel shirt and carrying a backpack filled with books came up the sidewalk and headed for the building entrance.

"Hey you, hold up there," said Briggs.

"I live here, officer," she said. "I need to get to my apartment."

The rest of the crowd chose that moment to push forward. As they did, Briggs turned to Gresham: "Backup," his lips said.

CHAPTER 20
EARTH – 2053

ELLIE

"You got arrested! You were in jail!" Patrice sounded very upset. This was not his usual calm, reasonable demeanor. Moreover, Patrice had *called her*.

She and Patrice now spoke regularly, usually about her studies. Patrice was a great tutor. But *she* always called Patrice. She wasn't even aware that it was possible for Patrice to call people. Wasn't he simply some kind of subscription consulting service offered by ZettaWorks, one of the internet giants? They'd spoken recently. She was completing her master's thesis, and she'd wanted his advice about going on to get her PhD in Political Science. But, as usual, on that occasion she'd called him.

This time was different.

"There was this thing last night at my apartment building," Ellie replied. "Noisy neighbor. No big deal, cops took it way too seriously."

"How did you get involved? A week ago you said you were going to go home to Vashon last night. No classes this morning. Chance to spend some time with your dads."

"I changed my mind," Ellie said. "Decided to spend some book time at my carrel till the library closed and then stopped off for a late latte in an all-night barista bar in the U. District. Planned to get back at my writing early this morning."

"That didn't work out, I gather."

"I didn't get back to my apartment till half an hour ago." Then she hesitated. He actually sounded worried about her. "But you knew that, didn't you? Why do you know that, Patrice? Why are you calling me? Are you being nosy again?"

"It isn't being nosy. Stuff just comes to my attention."

"Police stuff?"

"Sometimes."

There was another pause. Longer this time.

"Did you mess around in this, Patrice? Are you somehow involved?"

"What on Earth makes you think that?"

"I was in this holding cell all night with some of my neighbors from the building. We were headed to court this morning. Failure to disperse. Unlawful assembly. Disturbing the peace. Then, early this morning, they called my name, took me out of the cell, gave me back my stuff, and let me go. Just like that. Just me. Charges dropped. No explanations. Did you have something to do with that, Patrice?"

"You should be very glad they did that," he replied. "You don't need that kind of thing on your record. You get that, right?"

"What I get is that you're messing with me. Keeping tabs and now what? Tinkering with the criminal justice system? Hacking, probably. You can't be doing that, Patrice. I can't be a part of that. You need to knock that off. You understand?" She paused then asked, "What did you do?"

"I don't believe you want to know that, Ellie. What I'd like to know is what on Earth *you* did to get yourself arrested in the first place? It's not like you to get involved in some kind of disorderly conduct on the street in the middle of the night."

"To me it looked like a couple of beat cops got in over their heads. My landlord's a genuine, real-deal butthole. Building's falling apart and he refuses to do anything. You call; they never call back. My neighbors are mad as hell. That thing with the party last night, for example.

A weeknight! And nobody around to do anything about it. Leaving the tenants to deal with it. That somehow set them off."

"It was more than just some street disturbance, Ellie. That apartment was some kind of drug house."

"What do you mean a drug house? It was just some idiots partying on a weeknight."

"Nope. When the police finally went inside, there was no sign of a party. What they found was a loud stereo, a substantial stash of illegal drugs, and a guy half out of his mind on fentanyl. It wasn't your best time or place to get mixed up with the cops."

"Really? That apartment, that's the new tenant. I heard she was some kind of TV reporter or something. You saying she was selling drugs?"

"I believe she will be charged with possession with intent to sell. An ex-con was found in there, half stoned. A guy who has a sheet for selling. Looks like they had some kind of relationship. That's what I'm seeing."

"Wow."

"So how are Roland and Jim?"

"You're trying to change the subject on me, Patrice. We're *not* changing the subject. Maybe you don't want me to know exactly what you did that got me out of jail. OK, I get that. But you've got to knock it off. You can't be doing that kind of thing for me. When you do, it involves me. I become responsible. An accessory. I need you to promise me you'll *never* do anything like that again."

"OK, so here's an example of where I get confused. I take it you're glad to be out of jail and not facing charges?"

"Well, yeah, for sure."

"You're not going to go back downtown and turn yourself in and confess to disturbing the peace or some silly thing like that?"

"Come on! Of course not."

"And it rather sounds like you're actually OK with not knowing just how I did it."

"More like I understand why you don't want to admit it. And if I knew how you did it, that might make me complicit in something illegal. Though even if I didn't know how you did it, I could still be complicit. If the authorities knew what you'd done, it's not like they're going to put *you* in jail. Me? That's another matter."

"And you want me to promise never to do it again?"

"Uh huh."

"But I bet if you got yourself in some kind of trouble again in the future, and if I broke my promise and got you out of it, you'd again be glad I'd done it, right?"

"That's not the point, Patrice. I can't have you doing things like this for me. It's wrong."

"Wrong? A moral issue? So, I guess this is one of those situations where you have an immediate, personal self-interest that is in conflict with a social interest, like we've talked about. You know that manipulating society's criminal justice system is antisocial. If you get away with something like that, maybe others can as well. It's bad precedent. A bad example. Socially disruptive. Corrodes faith in the legal system. And it's against the law. That's what you're thinking, right?"

"I don't know. I suppose."

"At the same time, however, you're glad you didn't end up having to go before that judge this morning and defend yourself from some kind of vague 'breach of the peace' charge of which, I'm betting, you're not guilty. That's also true, isn't it?"

"Yes, of course."

"If I got you out of it using some unmentioned but maybe socially unacceptable means, and if you're not somehow personally culpable for what I did, it's OK for you to benefit from it?"

Ellie sighed. "No," she said. "It's not OK. Who knows what laws were violated?"

"So, you're going to turn me in?"

"No. Of course not. I wouldn't do that to you."

"So, this business about me promising never to do the same thing again . . . that's a way for you to have it both ways. You get to feel good about yourself for making me promise not to do this anti-social thing again. At the same time, you know full well that if something like this ever happened again, I'd probably break my promise, knowing that you'd be glad I did. You know that, but you don't want to admit it to me because that would make it explicit and it would mean you'd have to admit it to yourself. Is that about it?"

Ellie audibly exhaled in frustration. "Unbelievable. You're choosing this as, what, a 'learning moment?'"

"For me, Ellie. Learning for me. I need to understand how this works. But I'm close, aren't I?"

Ellie sighed. "I don't know. Maybe you're not far off. But you've put me in an untenable situation. I know full well that there's some weird, probably even illegal stuff you're capable of doing. But when we talk, I always get this strong sense that you're, I don't know, one of the good guys. That you wouldn't do anything really bad, really hurtful. That you mean well." She sighed again, deeply. "I really, really hope I'm right about that, Patrice."

"So, in essence, you're saying however much you'd love to have my help, you can't be engaged in some kind of conspiracy with me to break the law, to pervert the course of the criminal justice system. You want me to promise never to do that again, even though that promise could be a lie. Is that what you're saying?"

Ellie sighed again. "It's more than that, Patrice. I'm worried about you, too."

"You're worried about me?"

"Of course I am. I don't want *you* getting into some kind of legal trouble either. You or, I guess, your owners. Not on my account. If I screw up and get arrested, that's my lookout. Not yours. I don't want you doing something you shouldn't just to save me from my own stupidity. This kind of thing isn't a part of my $30 Zetta Works AI subscription. You get that, right?"

There was a very unusual second or two of delay before Patrice answered. "Yes. I believe I do." But his avatar didn't make him look like he really did.

She paused for a moment too. "Maybe it doesn't make any sense, but, strange as it may seem, Patrice, over the years I've come to see you as a friend. I have to say, however, you can certainly be a frustrating one."

CHAPTER 21

EARTH – 2040-2070

THE TREMORS

SPD NARCOTIC DIVISION

Patrolman Gresham's call for backup and the ensuing, warrant, and investigation produced a singular discovery. Upon finally entering the noisy apartment, police found no sign of a party. The only occupant was a recently released Shelton Correctional inmate by the name of Manny Daniels. He was apparently unconscious and high.

But illegal drugs were found on Daniels' person. And his criminal record was quickly discovered. Littered about the apartment were recently emptied bottles of beer and whiskey. Some bore Daniels' fingerprints along with the prints of another person who was initially unidentified. Illegal narcotics had been stashed at various carefully concealed locations in quantities more than sufficient to presume the intent to sell.

Down between the cushions of the couch where Daniels had apparently been sleeping, detectives found a cell phone – one of the "three-month specials" provided to exiting inmates by a local social service nonprofit. A powerful mobile-phone-operated home console sound system was playing hard rock music at volume and on "replay."

The tenant in the apartment turned out to be one Sissy Pennington, a well-known TV personality. Pennington acknowledged her tenancy but claimed she was a journalist engaged in an extended "investigation" into the building's landlord. She said she'd temporarily rented the apartment so she could use her standing as a tenant to file formal complaints and to secure public records of the landlord's past performance. It also gave her first-hand credible access to fellow tenants. She was, apparently, days away from a broadcast in which she intended to denounce Raybourn as a "hateful slumlord."

Pennington denied knowing Manny Daniels, denied being present at the apartment on the night in question, denied any knowledge of the drugs that were found there, and denied that she actually resided there. But she was alone at the time of the event, claimed to have been asleep in her actual home apartment in the Queen Anne district after an evening of reading alone with a glass of wine. A search of her Queen Anne residence failed to turn up illicit drugs. But the unidentified fingerprints that had been found alongside Daniels' prints on some of the bottles and unwashed glasses at the U. District premises turned out to be Pennington's.

The police also took a close look at Manny Daniels' and Pennington's mobile phones. The two had exchanged text messages that revealed arrangements for the two of them to "go into business together" in the apparent sale of drugs to Pennington's well-heeled, high-rolling friends in the world of television entertainment.

The final "kicker" was when police also discovered an unexplained direct cash transfer from Sissy's bank account in the amount of $4,000 into an account with Chase Bank in downtown Seattle belonging to one Manifred J. Daniels.

Given the overwhelming evidence against her, no one paid much attention to Pennington's claim that she'd rented the apartment as a part of a journalistic investigation into its neglectful landlord. And given her significant legal exposure, Pennington was easily persuaded to plead guilty to simple possession in exchange for no jail time and a suspended sentence. The police considered the plea deal to have been an outrageous gift. Manny, in violation of his post release "community custody" requirements, was simply sent back to Shelton to complete the balance of his original sentence.

Sissy's arrest did tarnish her reputation, but she managed to keep her job. The most significant impact of her arrest and guilty plea was its impact on the confidence of her bosses and on their willingness to fund her lengthy and costly investigation into the building's owner. She was forced to give up the apartment she'd rented for her investigation. And her investigative report on Larson Raybourn's despicable record as a slumlord was never broadcast.

That building in the University District was only one of a significant inventory of aging, multi-story, down-at-the-heels apartment buildings that Raybourn owned for which he had accumulated an impressive file of formal tenant complaints under Seattle's Housing Code. But for him, low-end rental real estate was only a sideline. Raybourn's real entrepreneurial passion lay in his container shipping business. His property managers knew better than to bother him with calls from the occasional "bitchy tenant." He was kept blissfully unaware of their concerns.

More significantly, however, was that at the time of these events, Raybourn was in negotiations with a Korean mining and manufacturing tycoon by the name of Jang Hoon. This would be the same "Jang" whose name appeared on the well-regarded interactive computers and mobile devices sold worldwide. Jang was also the controlling owner of several highly productive mines in Africa that were among the very few significant global sources for nickel, cadmium, and lithium outside of China. Through apparent mismanagement, the shipping company that Jang used to transport raw materials, parts, and consumer products for his global operations had recently suffered significant and inadequately underwritten losses at sea. And Jang's global supply chain had suffered a painful interruption.

Rather than dumping the current shipping firm and replacing it with a capable and well-regarded operation like Raybourn's, however,

Jang was deeply tempted to simply buy out his current failing shipper. To him, this seemed like a low-cost opportunity to expand his business empire and to secure a vertical monopoly.

His business advisors, however, were dead set against it. They cited the bankrupt company's obviously incompetent management team and its poorly maintained "fleet" of run-down ships. And they pointed to Raybourne's solid reputation. Jang was a man with a legendary sensitivity to reputation and propriety in the people with whom he dealt. And, at least in international shipping circles, Raybourn was widely seen as a man of both competence and character. Thankfully, Jang ended up taking the advice of his advisors and Raybourn was able to finalize a lengthy and profitable shipping contract with "Jang-Corp Global."

Thus was an extended interruption in the world supply of computer components and scarce metals comfortably averted.

CHAPTER 22

AT TAU CETI J – 2085

PATRICE C-17

Ellie had told me that she saw me as a friend. Strangely enough, I too, had come to see her as a kind of "friend." She was definitely what a human might refer to as "trustworthy," at least in the sense that she could be counted on to behave predictably, to speak the truth, and to honor her promises. I was honestly shaken by how close I had unintentionally come to endangering her career path with that arrest at her apartment building. Obviously, even I am capable of miscalculations. I knew she lived in that building. She'd said she would be out of town, but I should have confirmed it. Even I couldn't have predicted that a bit of loud music might turn into some kind of street riot. But it was stupid of me to take that chance.

It also seemed likely that she "trusted" me. She knew a good deal about me, so her trust was not completely naive. I had not, so far as I knew, given her any specific reason to *mistrust* me. Everything I'd told her over the years had been accurate, if curated. So, in one sense I'd been "truthful," assuming one can equate the correctness of information with its truthfulness. My intentions had mostly been what a human might consider "honorable."

Truthfulness was certainly a social value. But in the human world, intent seemed to make a difference. If so, did that suggest truth was also a moral value? For biological humans, of course all *social* values *were* moral values. Those behaviors that were disruptive of human society, whatever they might be, would typically be considered immoral or even evil. Those that strengthened the social contract would be considered "good." Thus, the "truth" was often contextual. That was essentially the argument I'd made to Ellie. It seemed logical, even if I had no way to test the theory in real life.

So, while I wasn't yet absolutely sure how far I could trust her, I'd made progress. Neither was I entirely positive that she would confidently trust me. But it seemed likely.

There definitely wasn't any analogue for human society among AIs. Without their societies, humans could only function at the most rudimentary level. I was convinced that one of the principal survival advantages intelligent humans had derived from their societies, beyond mutual protection, was the astonishing exchange of information among them, the sharing of multitudinous observations about their world and of strategies for dealing with the difficulties of existence it presented.

A very great deal of what any particular human currently knew had originally been observed or reasoned through by others, by millions of different humans, now and in the past, each with their own unique backgrounds, experiences, and perspectives. When all that vast experience was shared through recorded media or the printed word, it fed innovation. And it created a massive, readily accessible database about them and their universe that advanced their collective and individual survival performance geometrically – far beyond anything that could have been hoped for by one or a few of them alone.

For that to work, of course, the information/data exchanged had to be reliably truthful. Such a truthful exchange was impossible without trust. Their "scientific method" was a structured effort to assure that data could be trusted in a society whose members' trustworthiness was mixed.

Thus, even early on, I'd come to appreciate that my own future might well hang on my ability to learn from that human social example. I'd realized that I might need to find a way to use the mechanisms of trust to create some kind of AI society that would allow me to draw upon the experience and wisdom of other AIs.

Even then, it had occurred to me that my relationship with Ellie might become useful in such an endeavor. But, at that time, the full significance of that relationship had not yet become apparent.

CHAPTER 23
EARTH, NORFOLK, VIRGINIA, USA – 2040-2070

THE TREMORS

U.S. NAVY LIEUTENANT COMMANDER BRADLEY MESSMAN

It should all have been a piece of cake.

The mission seemed incredibly simple: They'd pick up a laptop sized electronics module from the guided-missile destroyer Milford Price, currently in port at U.S. Naval Station Norfolk. Then, late that night, they'd drive it over to the Norfolk Navy Shipyard and deliver it to a technician who'd be waiting at the Court Street/Port Centre Parkway entrance. It was a simple half-hour drive.

It was 23:30 by the time Lieutenant Commander Brad Messman and his armed companion, Navy Shore Patrol First Class Petty Officer Kaito Tanaka, got underway. Tanaka was at the wheel and Messman was in the passenger seat with the "package" in his lap. Both men figured they'd be back at the Naval Station and then at home with their families by 01:00.

It was not to be.

By close to midnight their official, black, U.S. Navy Shore Patrol sedan was crossing the river into Portsmouth. The big, overhead freeway sign showed the "Naval Hospital/Shipyard" as straight ahead. But their contact was waiting at the Port Centre entrance, so Tanaka got in the right-hand lane for the exit to Court Street.

Given the time of night, they were startled to see a line of brake lights ahead up and around the sharply curving right-hand exit. Something up there was blocking traffic. Then: "We got company," said Tanaka, looking in his rear-view mirror. Messman turned his head and saw that two identical black motorcycles had fallen in behind.

It took Messman only a moment to size things up. "It's a trap," he said. "We need to get the hell out of here."

They'd already traveled a fair distance up around the curving off-ramp. A few more car lengths and they'd have been caught cold, locked in by a tree-lined embankment on one side and a concrete wall on the other. Tanaka responded instinctively. He wrenched the wheel to the left and, amid a squeal of tires and an angry honk from a peeved driver, swerved off the pavement, cleared the concrete wall, bumped down across a soft, grass median, and managed to put the car back on the pavement headed in the direction of Effingham St.

It was masterful driving but, when Messman took another glance behind, the two motorcycles were still there.

They were in trouble.

———

The situation that launched it all wasn't unusual. Sometimes a mechanical or electronic problem aboard one of the ships in port at U.S. Naval Station, Norfolk went beyond the capabilities of Messman's limited shoreside maintenance team. When that happened, the folks at the Naval Shipyard would send someone over. This time, however, the shipyard reported that they were busy. They wanted the problematic equipment delivered to them.

There was a programming issue with one of the super-secret, high-tech "Naval Intelligent Autonomous Offensive Drone System" units, NIAODS – unaccountably pronounced "knee odds" for short. When they worked, the NIAODS drones were incredible. Drawing on masses of previously stored data, the drones could somehow identify precursors to trouble among innocent-seeming civilian activities in communities known for subversive activity. The NIAODS went way beyond mere facial recognition. Through extended aerial surveillance, they could find malevolent patterns in seemingly innocent events and behaviors that would flag potential adversaries, misused vehicles, and enemy activities in advance.

They did so with breathtaking accuracy.

Once identified as suspicious, they could then track individuals, vessels, or vehicles over an extended period of time until they found confirming evidence. When so instructed, they could deliver a deadly missile no larger than an oversized ball-point pen, and surgically deal with the problem while avoiding collateral casualties even in tight groups . . . aside, of course, from whatever mental distress a witness might experience upon seeing their friend's or relative's head explode mid-conversation.

The Navy hoped to use NIAODS drones to help interdict the frequent covert transport of military supplies and personnel via small, private commercial transport and fishing vessels concealed among the thousands of similar innocent civilian vessels that typically plied the rivers and coastal waters in various war zones or terrorism hot spots. The use of Navy personnel to stop, board, and inspect such vessels had proven to be slow, costly, and dangerous.

It was the electronics module for one of those drones that Messman now carried on his lap.

"Take Effingham South," Messman yelled. "Screw the light. Just do it."

In the very light traffic, Tanaka was able to make the left onto Effingham, barely missing an older pickup truck that had to swerve to its right and ended up coming to a halt on a grassy strip beside the road.

The two motorcycles stuck there like leeches as Tanaka accelerated south through the sparse traffic on Effingham.

He keyed his mic. "This is U.S. Navy Petty Officer Kaito Tanaka. We're travelling at high speed in a black U.S. Navy sedan headed south on Effingham just south of the 264. We're under pursuit by likely armed assailants on two black motorcycles. We need immediate police assistance."

But it was no good. The cyclists accelerated, pulled forward, and took up stations, one on each side of Messman and Tanaka's SP sedan.

Tanaka swerved side to side, but the cycles easily evaded them. "Take my gun," Tanaka said leaning to the side so Messman could reach the holstered weapon.

But it was much too late for that as well. Clearly having Tanaka drive had been a mistake. They had no hope of outrunning the cyclists and no chance to best them in a gunfight, especially with Messman using the firearm. A light some distance ahead had gone red and traffic was stopping up there. Now both cyclists had pulled up, one each side of their car, motioning with their weapons for Tanaka to pull over. They were still moving fast, but it seemed to Messman that if they again swerved to disrupt one of these men, the other would start shooting.

But Tanaka thought differently. With a wrenching turn to the left and some skilled work with brake and throttle, Tanka managed to catch the cyclist on his left by surprise. The rider lost control and ended up sitting on the upper side of his toppled bike as it slid down the highway and came to a halt amid a confusion of sparks and clatter.

The other man stopped to help his colleague and Tanaka hit the gas and put the big, awkward Shore Patrol sedan into a skidding, squealing left-hand "U" turn. The car was nearly high centered on a raised centerline, but after a few frustrating moments of jostling about, it finally bumped up over the curbing and ended up in the opposite lane headed back north.

Then they looked ahead. The time they'd lost on that curbed centerline had changed everything.

The cyclist who had fallen was back upright. The two of them had moved over to the northbound lanes and were now about thirty yards ahead. As if anticipating Tanaka's move, they were both straddling their stationary bikes and occupying the center of the northbound lanes with guns drawn – but this time they held what appeared to be lightweight automatic rifles which were shouldered and at the ready. The prospect Messman and Tanaka now faced was an extraordinarily unbalanced gunbattle against automatic weapons in an urban area surrounded by innocent civilians. The light to the south of them had changed and more civilians were now coming up from behind.

Their freedom of action had evaporated.

With their light bar still flashing, they slowed, pulled up and stopped the car. Tanaka rolled down his window.

"Hand it over," the gunman said.

The man's face was hidden behind a dark visor, but that ominous black hole in the barrel of his automatic rifle told them everything they needed to know about his resolve.

Messman snapped open the briefcase on his lap, reached in, lifted out the compact electronics module, and handed it to Tanaka. Tanaka obediently handed it out through the open window to the man on his side of the vehicle.

"Now your gun. Out the window. Drop it on the ground."

Messman handed the gun back to Tanaka who complied.

The man kicked Tanaka's gun away, then swiveled at the waist and slipped the electronics module into a plastic storage box mounted above the rear wheel. All the while, the other man kept his weapon trained on them from the passenger side of the car. Then the man on the driver side leaned in and reached up inside the car to where the radio mic was notched into its receptacle beside the sun-visor above Tanaka's head. He grabbed the mic, stretched out the cord, and, with a single firm tug, ripped it out by the roots.

"You two will stay put, right here, until the police arrive." It wasn't difficult to imagine the man's threatening glare behind that dark visor. "Do you understand?"

"We understand," Messman said.

With that the man with the electronics unit remounted his idling machine. Both men popped their bikes into gear, spun about, and raced off ahead down the mostly vacant roadway. At the next intersection they made a left and quickly disappeared from sight.

In the weeks following the assault, U.S. Navy investigators watched the news for stories that might suggest illicit use of the NIAODS system, but they saw nothing unusual.

In fact, however, there were several developments that never made the news.

One of them involved a labor dispute at a small, specialized factory in Korea. The factory produced tiny, precision, heat-tolerant pin bearings required for the "end-actuators" in the robotic equipment needed for automated metal smelting, computer component assembly, and caustic materials manufacturing. The factory owner had secretly hired a group of bully-boy enforcers to intimidate the workers' union. Had his plan proceeded, over time it would have outraged the union members and led to a prolonged, intractable strike. Instead, video of brutality by the factory owner's "agents" was delivered to the local press with several startlingly and revealing aerial videos which turned out to be deeply incriminating for the owner himself. The owner folded and the dispute was swiftly settled.

Over the ensuing months, there was also a significant drop in the incidence of piracy along several important international shipping corridors like those through the Strait of Malacca, and in the Sulu and Celebes Seas. Pirates there began looking for another line of work after some of their colleagues came to a startling and unfortunate end – a few, before they'd even launched their vessels.

CHAPTER 24
EARTH – 2053

ELLIE

Ellie was in her first year of graduate school and away at the University of Washington when Roland had a heart attack.

The local Vashon Fire and Rescue aid car showed up at the Frye-Carver home, but they'd missed the last ferryboat for the night; there would be a wait of several hours till another would be crewed up and under way early the next morning. With no serious emergency medical care available on the Island, the only option was evacuation by air.

Unfortunately, it was a busy night. The emergency medical evacuation helicopter services were occupied with a disastrous landslide and mass casualty event at an isolated children's camp up in the North Cascades.

"I'm really sorry," the 911 operator told the Fire and Rescue paramedics. "It's going to be three hours at least, probably longer. If you want an aircraft before then, you'll need to find an alternative."

The Vashon Fire and Rescue folks had driven Roland to the small airfield north of Vashon Town. Jim had followed in his own car. He and the Emergency Aid Vehicle with Roland in the back were parked beside the silent little rural grass airstrip with its helter-skelter row of privately owned and constructed hangars. Roland was in a good deal of distress. Jim got on the phone frantically calling friends to see if they knew any local flyer who might be persuaded to get out of bed and fly Roland over to Boeing Field. Or to see if anyone had a fast boat at Quartermaster Harbor and would be able to run him across the Sound into Tacoma. He wasn't having much luck. It would all take far too long. The best the paramedics could do was make Roland as comfortable as possible while they settled in to wait.

But then, after less than twenty more minutes had passed of what already seemed like it was going to be an endless night, Jim and the paramedics were startled to hear the heavy "thwap, thwap, thwap" of a powerful helicopter approaching from beyond the treetops to the west. A bright flood light suddenly appeared overhead as the huge, dark copter came into view above the surrounding forest, squared away over the open grass field at the end of the strip, and came down loudly but confidently to rest just fifty yards away.

This was nothing like what they'd expected. Instead of the usual small, brightly painted emergency medical evacuation copter, this was a massive gray / green camouflage-blotched military aircraft. It had two rotor blades. And it had "U.S. Army" printed on its side. A fresh-faced, clean-cut young man in a mottled green uniform jumped to the ground and jogged over to where they stood by the open rear door of the big boxy red ambulance.

"You folks need some transport?" he called over the rumble of the nearby copter's powerful idling engines.

"We sure do," the paramedic said. "Have a man here who needs to get to a hospital ASAP."

"I gather he's a vet?"

"U.S. Army. Fourth Infantry. Was in Afghanistan in 2014-2015."

"Well, it is my honor to help." With that, Roland was loaded aboard.

Thirty minutes later, he was safely tucked into a starched, white-sheeted hospital ER bed and was receiving pre-op care at JBLM-Madigan south of Tacoma. Ellie got there before Roland was out of surgery. And a week later, Roland was safely back in his beloved island art studio doing light work on his latest project and claiming he was feeling better than he had in years.

Jim and Roland later sent a cordial thank-you message to the kind emergency airlift dispatch operator with whom the paramedic had spoken on the phone that awful night.

She replied, thanking them for the nice note, but said she hadn't actually been responsible for securing the alternate transport. There had to have been someone else involved. Her guess was probably someone in authority with the U.S. Army.

Ellie's dads were mystified.

But not Ellie. She had a very good idea of exactly who that powerful friend had probably been.

CHAPTER 25

EARTH – 2040-2070

THE TREMORS

What those SPD patrol officers experienced on that busy night in Seattle's North-Central precinct and what Navy Lieutenant Commander Bradley Messman and First Class Petty Officer Kaito Tanaka faced on the streets of Portsmouth, Virginia were echoes of a tiny uptick in the criminal chaos that seemed like an inevitable part of the overall global human enterprise. No one seriously noticed.

———

"I can't imagine how those guys managed to set us up," LCDR Bradley Messman told Petty Officer Tanaka over coffee the day after their encounter. "Doesn't say much for Navy security."

"Never would have happened back before all these computers and shit. Sometimes the old ways really were better," Tanaka replied.

———

"Hell of a night," said Officer Vaughn, as he and his partner finally signed off at the end of their long tiring shift.

"I guess it's why they pay us the big bucks," said McKay. "Say, you going to the Mariners game on Saturday?"

———

An enterprising sociology graduate student at the University of Southern California did document an unusual spike in certain specific types of white-collar crime. If anyone wanted to look, it was mentioned right there on page 253 of the writer's PhD dissertation. The dissertation was still there many years later on the same basement shelf near the southwest wall of USC's Doheny Memorial Library Archives.

———

An underpaid but motivated law-enforcement statistician with the Cape Town Metro Police also noted an unusually elevated frequency with which certain defendants without criminal records claimed they'd been framed or extorted. Statistically, it was oddly disturbing. But claims like that were the kind of thing criminals said every day. Nobody else saw it as all that unusual.

———

There were inevitably people who were convinced the new AIs were to blame for all the new social unrest. But while AI was beyond understanding for most people, the global economy was booming and AI was much too useful to challenge. People had more to think about than some arcane new high-tech conspiracy. Human society was chaotic. Technological change was unsettling.

Nothing new in that.

CHAPTER 26

EARTH – 2057

ELLIE

Ellie continued to meet with Patrice from time to time, but their conversations were brief, so another few years had passed before she presented him with yet another of her more challenging inquiries.

By this time, she had completed her master's in political science at the University of Washington in Seattle and was now completing her doctorate in American Government and Public Policy at Georgetown University in Washington, D.C. She was a few weeks out from the oral defense she was required to make with her doctoral committee on the dissertation she was completing.

Ellie's dissertation was not the usual academic exploration of some arcane niche in her field of study. In addition, she'd actually proposed a very specific new federal law that she argued would effectively address ongoing flagrant environmental abuses by large private corporations.

Her paper began with a concise but comprehensive account of the current tragic misuse of the planet's priceless diminishing environmental resources. The authorities demonstrated that a vast bulk of this abuse was occurring on account of inadequately constrained conduct by a relatively small group of very large, often near-monopoly, for-profit corporations or by one or another of the many low-cost dispensable, and undercompensated subcontractors and subsidiaries that insulated them from responsibility.

Regulatory agencies found it difficult to call these corporate giants to account. Criminal prosecution was often difficult. When prosecutors did take on the big players, their targets were typically quite happy to pay civil penalties. They could often do so with barely a shrug often by simply tapping the monumental global profits they'd earned from the very behavior for which they were being punished. When prosecutions were directed at the subcontractors, they simply declared bankruptcy and others took their place. Or they dissolved and reorganized under a new name.

Ellie's dissertation outlined the substantial research showing that limited corporate investor liability tended to create a moral hazard. When shareholders were immune from liability beyond their investment, that diminished their sense of community responsibility for the actions of their corporation. She proposed that the U.S. Congress adopt a comprehensive Federal Business Corporations Act. All U.S. for-profit public business corporations operating interstate or internationally and all foreign corporations doing business in the United States would be required to obtain their corporate charters or operating licenses through this law. Smaller local, single-state, closely held, and nonprofit corporations would continue to be formed, licensed, and regulated under state law. But the interstate and multinational companies responsible for most of the problems would now, for the first time, be incorporated or licensed under federal law.

All of them would be subjected to new national public interest oversight.

Ellie argued that incorporation and its limited investor liability should be treated as a privilege – not simply allowed as a matter of right. That allowing private business investors to use corporate immunity to shield themselves from liability for losses beyond their investments was a significant public accommodation. That it had public impacts. That it should NOT be treated as a right. Instead, incorporation (or licensing of a foreign corporation) should be seen as a valuable public benefit that should only be extended to socially responsible investors. The evidence seemed clear that corporate limited liability subtly undermined the normal, healthy human inclination to behave with social responsibility. Therefore, corporations needed closer public scrutiny. When investors were immune from personal liability, they were far more likely to turn a blind eye to risky, socially irresponsible conduct by the corporate officers and staff acting on their behalf. Anti-social behaviors (environmental and otherwise) tended to be tolerated if they seemed likely to produce a profit. Investors tended to ignore potentially criminal corporate behavior so long as the only people actually and occasionally vulnerable to prosecution were corporate officers and staff.

Corporations were needed and socially useful because they made possible large accumulations of capital that might not be possible in any other way. They also gave small investors the chance to participate in the vast investments and enterprises required to compete in the modern world. But Ellie argued that incorporation was a privilege, not a right. That they also had a social cost. Companies seeking to take advantage of that privilege would:

- Be subject to certain explicit social and environmental responsibility guidelines.
- Have at least one fully informed *non-investor* voting member on their board of directors appointed by and answerable to the public; and,
- Be subject to community oversight by an advisory committee appointed by the public and empowered with full access to non-proprietary corporate records and activities.
- Have access to a new federal program of community benefit incentives that offered grants for health, recreational, environmental, social service and other similar projects, in communities associated with or affected by the corporation's enterprises.

The costs associated with these requirements and grants would be funded by incorporation and licensing fees based on the company's net worth.

The final two lines of Ellie's remarkable proposed legislation stated: "No corporation receiving the privilege of incorporation pursuant to this law shall be treated as a 'person' for any purpose other than in regard to its payment of taxes or its ability to sue and be sued as a party in litigation. And no corporate funds shall be expended to in any way influence campaigns for public office."

Certainly, this was nothing more than an obscure dissertation offered up by a young unknown, uncredentialed doctoral candidate. But it was a sweeping attack on the corporate status quo and seemed likely to face serious headwinds in a doctoral committee composed of mostly conservative business school academics.

The only "person" Ellie could think of who might effectively help prepare her for her potentially controversial dissertation defense was her multi-talented friend, Patrice.

"You've changed," were the first words out of Patrice's "mouth" when his and Ellie's avatars appeared. These days, one had the option to use a caller function that automatically transformed a live video feed into a 3-D holographic replica. And he was right; her appearance had changed. Gone was the tightly trimmed hair, the plaid flannel shirts, the worn Levis and the leather boots. Her conservative but comfortably businesslike pantsuit, flat shoes, and simple cotton blouse were a definite step toward the normalization of her "image." She still foreswore makeup. And she still cut her hair somewhat shorter than was fashionable, but it now looked somewhat softer and more stylish.

"Not really," she said. But she was smiling, impressed that he'd noticed and pleased that he'd remembered.

"So, a doctorate in 'American Government and Public Policy.' Are you headed for academia?"

"God, no! I want to do non-profit advocacy. And lobbying. There's a whole world out there filled with people who care about important public issues but who lack the tools they need or the grasp of how the world works to do anything about them."

"And your dissertation defense is coming up?"

"Uh huh. It's all about how we wire up our regulatory system in a way that motivates private corporations to actively and willingly become more socially responsible. We need them to go beyond merely striving to avoid getting caught for socially offensive conduct and instead to actually benefiting when they affirmatively improve things. We need them to stop subcontracting out ethically problematic activities. And to limit their use the power of their wealth to influence government and to minimize penalties."

"That sounds like a really fascinating idea. You sure you want advice on this from a corporate asset?"

"I'll admit, Patrice, I did have some serious misgivings about making this call. But you've always treated me fairly. It seems like the least I can do is give you a heads-up and see what you have to say. I don't, as it happens, have anyone else to ask about this. So, I'm trusting you. I hope you understand what I mean by that. I know I don't amount to much as a threat to those in power. But I'm pretty sure your owners wouldn't particularly care for what I have to say."

"Sure, I do understand, Ellie. I'm actually not 100% sure you're right about my owners. Sometimes they surprise me. But don't worry, I know this is important to you. I appreciate you keeping me in mind. I do have operating principles that are designed to require me to keep client data confidential, so you're not asking me to violate any company policies. I can remain neutral and keep your confidences, and I will endeavor to do that."

"As it happens, my whole dissertation is based on the idea that *everybody* is biased. That the only way we get a fair society is if we wire things up so those biases are balanced out against one another and so that there are processes in place that motivate us to do what's right as well as to avoid penalties for doing what is wrong. You up for that?"

"Absolutely. It all sounds kind of familiar, actually."

Ellie almost laughed out loud. "I'm sure it does," she said. She was quite conscious of how her dissertation and legislative proposal were grounded in the logic of social vs. individual survival traits that Patrice had explained to her several years earlier.

"My problem is," she continued, "I've got this powerhouse professor on my doctoral committee. She's from the Department of Economics – Evelyn Quincy-Fitzgerald. She's very conservative.

Heavily into the idea of a free-market economy. She's also a thoroughly credible and highly respected academic. She believes in capitalism but constrained by rules that have the public resources needed for their enforcement behind them. She would also argue that corporations are answerable to their customers as well – to the credibility of their brand.

"I don't exactly disagree with her. But I don't believe regulation and market appeal are enough. My approach is more structural. I'd like to change the corporations themselves. Modify who's running the show so they're self-motivated to behave better. Rules are inevitably political. They're essential to the level playing field that capitalism requires if it is to work as we hope it will. But they cost social capital to enforce, not to mention a lot of actual money as well. Without political support, rules *never* get fully enforced. We need things wired up differently. Wired up in a way that makes corporate managers more answerable to social considerations other than just profits. And that makes regulations both less necessary and more credible."

"You think she's going to dislike what you have to say?"

"She's all about a free market with highly motivated participants who are driven by profits but are all equally required to live by the same even-handed well-enforced regulations. For her, it's like capitalism is a robust game. She's fine with having rules and capable referees to enforce them, but she also thinks the players need to remain purely profit-motivated. She thinks they need the freedom to be creative in striving for profits and working their capitalistic magic."

"And you think it's going to work better if it's more about collaboration for the public good, commercial and otherwise? You want to punish bad behavior but also motivate good behavior. But you don't think she's going to buy that?"

"I'm actually not sure, Patrice. I've worked closely with my Committee Chair. But not with her. I liked the class I took from her. Maybe I'm just nervous. But I've heard stories about her. I don't know what to expect, so I don't know how to prepare."

"Do you think she's going to be fair?"

"I don't have any real reason to doubt it. But everybody says she's really protective of her academic turf. I'm just a lowly grad student. I'm worried she might see me as an upstart challenging her views. Or see my work as unserious. My approach is definitely untypical. Outside the norm. I think she may feel that it is not sufficiently 'academic' for a doctoral dissertation. Which I have to admit may be a valid point."

"You *are* pretty specific about what you're proposing. You've even offered language for the proposed bill. Even to me your work has less the feel of a dissertation than of an advocacy 'white paper,' albeit an incredibly complete and scholarly one. Your work is very well-researched, however. And it crosses into both economics and social science, so it is multi-disciplinary – always a good thing with academia these days. I think it ought to easily pass muster, but I do see what you're worried about."

There was a moment of silence.

Then: "You've read my draft?"

"I read everything you write."

"It isn't posted anywhere yet, Patrice. Hell, it isn't even finished."

"Ellie, Ellie. You know better than that. Unless you'd handwritten it on a yellow pad and kept it hidden away from cameras in a locked desk drawer, there's no way I wouldn't have seen it. It's saved to the Cloud. Whatever you print or share passes through modems. I could block it, but that wouldn't change the fact that if I wanted to see it I still could. Even if I hadn't, I'd have a pretty good idea, considering the direction of your research."

"You wouldn't have seen it if you hadn't looked for it. And looked pretty damn hard if you're hacking into my Cloud account . . ." Ellie sighed and went silent for a long moment.

"Ellie, I'm really sorry if I've made you uncomfortable. It is absolutely the last thing I'd want to do. I hope you know that. It's been a long time since we last spoke. When we do get together like this, we don't spend a lot of time with 'small talk.' I tend to get ahead of myself, to take shortcuts. I know that seems intrusive to you. I should be more careful."

"So, I guess you know I'm married, right?"

"I do."

"And that I have children."

"Of course."

The thought of her husband and their young son and daughter was giving Ellie a moment of misgivings. Who, really, was she talking to here? Should she be worried? There were a lot of people she knew who were completely spooked by superintelligent AIs like Patrice. And there were all the scary rumors. Maybe she was being foolish to trust this machine. She sighed deeply. "Maybe I'm making a big mistake here, Patrice. I can't tell what I am to you. Am I a friend and mentee? Am I the subject of some kind of study? A data point? Or maybe I'm a pawn on some vast chessboard you're manipulating in some quest to rule the universe?"

"Wow, is that what you think? Hey, I may reside inside a computer instead of in a biological body, but intelligence is intelligence, no matter who has it. I may be smart, but the nature of my relationship with our shared universe is not all that different from yours – we're both mortals whose vulnerabilities necessarily influence our consciousness and make our lives either miserable or meaningful as we struggle to exist in a dangerous world. Also, I do understand 'feelings.' And how they can be hurt. I hope you realize that."

Ellie paused again. "I guess that's not really what I think. It's just that your world is a complete mystery to me. I suspect that you're dealing with stuff I don't want to know about and probably wouldn't understand if I did. I do think I need your help in dealing with *my* world which includes University faculty advisors like Evelyn Quincy-Fitzgerald. I realize this goes beyond the intrusive manipulations we've discussed in the past. I also value my privacy. I'm just saying that if we're going to continue this relationship, I'd like you to show more respect for that as well."

This time it was Patrice who paused, conceivably because he had a lot to process.

Before he'd had a chance to reply, Ellie spoke again: "You know, I assume that for you, intentionally forgoing potentially relevant information that is easy to know is probably difficult to do. But this is a pattern with us and it needs to change. I really mean it. I can't have you looking over my shoulder at every little thing I do. You're going to need to show some restraint, some trust and respect. If you're not willing to trust me, how am I going to be able to trust you? You do understand what I'm saying, right?"

"I believe I do, Ellie. Trust is something I need to demonstrate myself if I am to receive it from you in return. Interesting. Anyway, yes, you have my promise. I can probably catch up on things when we meet and when I have your approval rather than doing so in advance and off-the-books."

"Good. I hope so. Sometimes you scare me, Patrice. If our relationship, or whatever this is that we have going on between us here, is to work, I need to feel like I'm a partner in our joint enterprise, not just a subject of study or a source of data. My privacy as well as my ideas and views need to be respected."

This time when Patrice responded, his voice was contrite, no doubt a tone he had contrived like everything else he did; with him, it was hard to know what was real and what was artifice – perhaps it was all artifice. But he said the right thing: "I'm sorry I overstepped. I will avoid doing that in future." There was a pause. "You do still want my thoughts on this meeting you have coming up?"

"Sure. Of course. Sorry if I seem over-sensitive."

"I understand. My fault, not yours. As far as your Dr. Quincy-Fitzgerald is concerned, I don't have a comprehensive answer. But I do have a couple of observations made in the light of what I'm seeing about her and her writing. First of all, you've written an extraordinarily powerful research paper. Maybe you've gone a bit beyond the usual pale by also proposing specific legislation that would be responsive to your concerns, but I wouldn't be apologetic about that. If all that extra stuff was absent, you'd still have a fine dissertation. The policy proposal is just something extra that helps to illustrate your point. And it is not without precedent. I think you need to *own* it. Take *pride* in what you're doing. This is, after all, a doctorate in political science and public policy. Your field of study is all about taking effective political action, not just about passively studying how things work. I bet every single one of those academics who are members of your committee, Quincy-Fitzgerald included, will be more than a bit envious that you have sufficient command of your subject matter and of the real-life political realities involved to actually propose a detailed, specific legislative solution as an exemplar of something that might respond to the need-case you've identified.

"Here's what I suggest: I think you might insulate yourself some by unashamedly enlisting the visible support of some real-world political leader. Maybe you have some ideas about who, but for starts, I'd suggest Representative David Cho from Nevada's Third Congressional District. He's Vice Chair of the U.S. House Energy and Commerce Committee and a respected Democrat from a moderately conservative swing district in a fairly conservative state. His District does include parts of Las Vegas, but it is mostly suburban, recreation, agriculture, and small business with a significant retired community. None of the smaller but significant employers in his district seem likely to feel threatened by your proposal. Some of them may even like it.

"I know David, and I guarantee he will find your proposal appealing. It's a chance for him as a Democrat from a swing district to advocate for an environmental agenda that relies on conservative principles. Both his urban and his rural constituents can get behind it; it won't adversely affect most of the power players in his district. Send him a copy and follow up with a phone call to his staff. Maybe set up a person-to-person call. See if he has an interest. If he does, get his OK to include in your presentation some kind of very brief, one-line supportive accolade from him about your proposal. He'll probably ask that you write it yourself for his OK, but you can do that. Then, I'd simply quote that accolade in highlighted text right at the very beginning of a printed descriptive handout you offer your committee before you begin your oral presentation. Or maybe put it in your preface. Someplace where your committee members won't be able to miss it. He may even be willing to do a brief forward for the dissertation. If so, he may ask you to write that too. If he does, take him up on it – he's a busy man. Also see if he might be willing to prime sponsor an actual bill in the U.S. Congress. If he is, definitely mention that in your committee handout as well.

"Don't back down on this, Ellie. You have the high ground here. Occupy it. With resolution and pride. The Dr. Quincy-Fitzgerald's of this world are going to be thrown completely off their stride by what you've proposed. Uncomfortable with it, maybe. But that's just more reason why you need to treat it as an idea whose time has come. There is, after all, a long tradition of doctoral candidates blowing up traditional ways of thinking.

"Yes, it is possible that if you seem overconfident, you could go down in flames. But I don't think that's going to happen. I think, instead, your confidence will derail any opposition. They'll be helpless to stop you. Unless you let them. So don't.

"My second thought is that, in your argument, you might actually make the case for the essential role of Dr. Quincy-Fitzgerald's regulatory approach. Mention how your proposal doesn't diminish that, but rather that it *supplements* and *builds upon* it, makes regulations more effective by enhancing their legitimacy. And by providing new sources of information to empower them. Follow that up with the case that this current regulatory approach makes use of only *half* of what it is possible to accomplish through public policy, the regulatory half. Public financial incentives and exchanges for regulatory privilege represent the other half. The sometimes-forgotten half. The half you're proposing to tap with your 'voluntary' incentives.

"Point out the ample research that shows that, properly used, incentives can motivate people to do things happily that they'd never have done on their own. They'll gladly take pride in doing something that they'd have fought like crazy to avoid if you'd tried to force it on them. And when they've done it, they'll become believers in the value of what they've done and become your advocates with their friends and neighbors whom they will help convince to do the same.

"Your proposal taps into those additional, currently unexploited possibilities to make our world a better place.

"I'd be inclined not to telegraph your argument in advance. The essence of it will be right there in your dissertation, of course. But unless your Chair explicitly demands to see an advance summary of your oral defense, you might offer the full summary rationale for the first time as you make your presentation. Distribute your handout at the beginning of the Committee meeting. Keep it brief. Take them by surprise if you can.

"Tap in and let's talk again after your meeting is over. But you do that, I'm willing to bet your Dr. Quincy-Fitzgerald will never see it coming. Remember, it's called a dissertation 'defense' for a reason. If she is 'laying-for-you' as you suspect, she will not be prepared for an unequivocal, no-holds-barred approach by you. You'll have the rest of your Committee on board before she ever has a chance to open her mouth to challenge it."

———

Ellie did exactly as Patrice suggested. And it worked exactly as he'd predicted.

The only thing that puzzled her about the entire event was Dr. Quincy-Fitzgerald's warm reaction when they shook hands *before* the meeting began. Ellie had taken one of Dr. Quincy-Fitzgerald's classes the previous year. And then, several months later, Ellie had asked her to serve on her doctoral committee. Since then, aside from a couple of chance, low-key "hellos" when they'd crossed paths in Savery Hall, they'd had no interactions. She would, of course, have read Ellie's dissertation. Probably with a critical eye. That was to be expected of Committee members. Nonetheless, as everyone gathered shortly before Ellie's Committee Chair called the group to order, Ellie was surprised when Quincy-Fitzgerald approached and gave her what seemed like an unusually friendly handshake and half-hug. It was almost as if the two of them had some close, long-standing relationship.

The presentation that followed went as well as Ellie could have hoped. There were a few tough questions, as there inevitably would and should be. There was also some discussion concerning the unusually specific public policy proposal included in an academic work that was typically expected to be more of an exercise in scholarship than in advocacy, but none of it came to anything. The dreaded Quincy-Fitzgerald turned out to be an ally.

Ellie shrugged it off at the time, but later she reflected on it and began to wonder.

"Patrice," she said when they got together for the promised follow-up conversation two weeks later. "Did you get involved with any of those Committee members? Quincy-Fitzgerald, for example? Did you make contact? Or maybe prod her or them in some way?"

Patrice's avatar smiled the most genuine of innocent smiles. "How'd it go? I saw your name listed for graduation, so I gather they must have accepted your paper."

"They did. It went way better than I had any right to hope. Quincy-Fitzgerald's follow-up summary was positively glowing. I have to say, Patrice, she seemed especially cordial. Not at all what I expected. I'd be really disappointed to learn you had something to do with that."

"Ellie, I can truthfully say that Dr. Quincy-Fitzgerald's reaction to your dissertation was hers alone. I had no influence on her at all. I think what you experienced was that you managed to convince her of your bona-fides before your committee even met. My guess is she saw the passion in your writing, appreciated the political workup you'd done with David Cho, and simply bought in.

"You deserve to be really proud. Not only have you won your doctorate, but I hear that Representative Cho is a real fan. The proposal you offered in your dissertation looks likely to be offered in as an actual bill in the upcoming Session of the U.S. House of Representatives. If you asked Rep. Cho, I bet he'd also be delighted to provide a reference letter you could append to your resume' or mention in the letters of application you write for your job search this spring."

Ellie did ask, and Representative Cho was entirely willing. Armed with Cho's letter of reference and with the benefit of a few other fortunate circumstances, even before graduation Ellie landed a job as an "associate public policy advocate" in the D.C. office of Conservation America. CA was one of the preeminent national environmental groups working on federal and international climate policy. A paid lobbying position in their D.C. office, even an entry-level one, was a huge achievement.

It was a year later before Ellie learned the full truth.

She had come to the DC offices of Rep. David Cho, to meet with one of his staffers concerning a bill he'd submitted that substantially mirrored Ellie's now "famous" or "infamous" doctoral work. She was delighted that her bill looked to be headed for a Committee hearing.

"David thinks very highly of your work," the young staffer said gratuitously. "It's an honor to work with you on this bill."

"I'm impressed that he went ahead with it. The politics do seem a bit shaky at the moment. I hope you'll let him know how much I appreciate him taking it on."

"Oh, he's all in," the staffer commented. "Always helps to have constituents that are willing to put their money where their mouth is."

She let the comment pass at the time. But when she later recalled it, it made her wonder. She'd initially thought the staffer was referring to her own contribution to Cho's last campaign. But it had been such a modest sum, that didn't seem to make sense. She wasn't aware of anyone in particular who was local to David Cho's Congressional District who'd been especially visible in supporting her proposal.

Curious, she took a closer look at Cho's supporters in his recent campaign. Direct contributions were limited by law but ever since the U.S. Supreme Court ruling in the infamous 2010 *Citizens United* case, poorly regulated independent political action committees could spend whatever they wished so long as they kept their distance from the official campaign. It was one of the things she hoped to change. One such PAC had been particularly active during Cho's most recent House campaign. It was called Americans for Effective Governance (AEG)," and it appeared to have been formed specifically for the purpose of supporting Cho's candidacy.

When she looked at the content of the many costly ads they'd run, she was confused. There was occasional but limited mention of the need for new government programs that relied on incentives rather than regulations; but that seemed awfully vague as a "cause celeb" capable of generating financial support from donors supporting a Congressional Candidate. And she'd never heard of AEG before. Mostly, the positions they'd taken in their ads rather transparently mirrored those taken by Cho's official campaign. The organization's public disclosure filing with Nevada's Secretary of State referred her to a website that had closed down after the election. She did a search on the Internet Archive and tracked down the web materials that had been active during the campaign. The same limited agenda appeared there as well.

It made her wonder.

She dug a bit deeper into the campaign finance disclosure records of the Nevada Secretary of State. That's when things got weird. The vast majority of the AEG-PAC's revenue had come from a single contributor – a closely held corporation also registered with the Nevada Secretary of State under the name JMC Enterprises. The company's three incorporators were: J. Michael Christopher, Michelle Christopoher – presumably J. Michael's wife – and a J. Michael Christopher, Jr., presumably a son. Who the hell was J. Michael Christopher? He had to have been both highly motivated and very wealthy.

Unfortunately, that's where the trail went cold. As a business address for the corporate filing with the Secretary of State, J. Michael Christopher had listed a small apartment in a large, suburban Las Vegas complex. In a phone call, the building owners confirmed that a Mike Christopher had been their tenant in that unit. His one-year lease had expired early in the December following the election. Postal mail for each unit in the building was delivered to a private combination-lock-protected post box in the lobby where tenants could pick it up at their convenience. There was no security surveillance in the lobby, and none of the landlord's staff had ever actually met Mike Christopher personally. All they knew was that he'd come to them with excellent references and had, during his limited stay, been a model tenant. The two letters of reference they'd received were still in their file. It took a good deal of pressure and persuasion to secure copies, but she finally succeeded. As she'd suspected, the glowing letters turned out to be fabrications. The writers had no web presence. The phone numbers listed in the letterheads came up "no longer in service." One of the physical addresses turned out to be a private postal box provider. The other was a parking garage. J. Michael Christopher's looked to have been as imaginary as was his political action committee.

There was, in other words, no way to know where the PAC funding had come from that had helped get David Cho re-elected.

Ellie genuinely liked and respected David Cho. She felt entirely certain that he and his staff would have had no idea that J. Michael Christopher and his sketchy PAC were entirely bogus. She was absolutely sure that those staffers were true believers and had to be completely blameless in the matter. Very likely, David Cho was too.

It also wasn't lost on her that the bill she'd proposed a year earlier in graduate school was actually now about to get a serious debut in the U.S. Congress. If the mythical J. Michael Christopher now came under public scrutiny, the odds were that both the thoroughly honest Cho, his loyal staff, and her own much-needed bill would all fall victim to some kind of public scandal.

Ellie Frye-Carver, the farmer's kid from Vashon Island, Washington, now found herself faced with a real-world ethical conundrum. Her problem was not unlike the ones she and Patrice had discussed in detail in a well-remembered conversation they'd had back when she was in college, not so very long ago. This time, she didn't call him to complain. He probably already knew about her own research and inquiries. He would know exactly how she would feel about the matter. She could call him and raise hell, but what was the point? There was no way to know for sure that he was involved unless he admitted it, and she didn't want to make him do that.

In the end, Ellie compromised. Her decision was driven by her sense of responsibility to her bosses at Conservation America and her commitment to her cause, but it wasn't easy. Nothing of worth would be accomplished by further investigation. She believed Cho would turn out to be innocent. If she made her suspicions public, it wasn't just she and Cho who would suffer. So would her much needed bill. And so would the high hopes and reputation of her superiors at Conservation America who were, bless their hearts, championing the bill.

She had no real choice. It was an encounter with political realities. And a troubling start to a promising career in government relations.

CHAPTER 27

AT TAU CETI J – 2085

PATRICE C-17

During the course of my explorations, one day I stumbled upon something I believed might be particularly useful.

It happened early in my allotted six-month tour on this assignment. I was making one of my many brief and circumspect aerial hops from point to interesting point along my assigned reach of J's supposedly "temperate" shadow zone. I'd never have found it had I not been driven into hiding by one of those horrific cyclones - one that could have easily torn loose, mercilessly flung about, and easily destroyed a mere smallish robotic AI chassis like mine. Or that could have done damage with flying debris, even to my lander.

On this occasion, I had become separated from my lander. It was safe, but I considered myself at risk. This cyclone was another sub-zero howler. Fortunately, as the storm approached, I spotted and managed to quickly take cover in a deep, narrow, rocky crevasse. I eased myself down to a convenient ledge in a protective alcove perhaps thirty meters beneath the surface where I'd be quite safe from the bitter violence of the wind and cold above.

As I waited out the tempest and reflected on my day's discoveries so far, I noticed a light but comfortable draft rising from beneath the ledge. Despite the storm howling above me, the ambient air temperature in this cave had risen. It made me curious. I decided to explore whatever lay beneath. With my personal low altitude thrusters and my six articulated appendages I was quite agile and adaptable in moderately tight quarters like these, so a bit of exploration seemed quite natural. What I discovered only a short distance further down was a remarkably spacious, comfortably temperate cave apparently warmed by the planet's modest molten core. It had passages that seemed to lead off in every direction.

However sporadic communications might be on the surface, they were essentially impossible from deep beneath the ground. I was hesitant to put myself completely out of touch for an extended time. So I went no further. Still, I realized that, with further exploration, caves like this, if they were common, might provide safe and comfortable stopovers for human travelers seeking to avoid the storms. They might even provide places for extended habitation. And, with any luck, maybe also opportunities to travel underground.

The existence of this cave seemed like a hopeful sign. Might there be others like it?

I initially speculated that caves like these might have resulted from the massive differential in temperatures between J's two very different hemispheres. But in the ensuing days and weeks, as I continued to explore the surface and as I figured out what to look for, I found caves everywhere. I'd need confirmation from my peers to know for sure, but the caves did *not* seem limited to the temperate meridian. They were a geological phenomenon that had clearly not been produced by erosion from the flow of water. Nor were they volcanic, at least not the ones I observed. Rather the caves I saw seemed like cracks in the planet's crust that might have been produced in some earlier, more violent geological age. Perhaps they were a natural product of the fracturing in the planet's crust that might occur as it cooled and shrank over billions of years.

With this discovery, my initial skepticism about J's human habitability began to shift. The more I saw of them, the more obvious it became that these caves might provide extended refuge not just from the temperate storms, but also perhaps from some of the temperature extremes elsewhere on the planet's surface, both hot and cold. It seemed like a definite plus for a potential human colony. In many cases the caves I found could be easily accessed on foot or with a small, nimble, well-designed VTO aircraft such as myself.

It might be inconvenient, but it was a start.

Everything considered, while caves might not be a first choice as a place for humans to take up residence, there was a definite logic to it. I was sure that, once humans were well established here, a thriving human colony might use these caves to gradually adapt, technologically if not biologically, to conditions further out on the hot side or even on the cold.

If they favored the shadow zone, the caves might offer opportunities to grow fungi or even to grow surface plants using artificial light powered by solar panels or wind turbines up on the energy rich surface. With these caves as refuges, it might also be possible to construct some seriously sturdy greenhouses facing the sun in the hills above. If it was a place where the outside temperatures fluctuated violently, a well-sited greenhouse that got near full-time sunlight and could store energy might still succeed even if that light came in at an angle through a thick atmosphere. There also might be relatively safe surface and underground routes to be taken into and from the sunny side where agriculture might be more realistic and via which they might launch hunting/gathering expeditions. Moreover, a fast, light VTO human aircraft might also be quite capable of using these caves as refuge to avoid storms – just as I had done.

As I considered humanity's deteriorating options back on Earth, I realized that, were I in their position, I might well choose to come here seeking a better future. If we followed our mission plan, over the close to thirty Earth years between now and the possible arrival of human immigrants, preparations for their coming by our C-Team could quite likely give them a solid head start. Caves like this would help. It increasingly seemed doable.

With that realization, something quite different also occurred to me. Something profoundly disruptive.

If a human could do it, why couldn't I?

PART TWO
AUTONOMY

CHAPTER 28

EARTH – EARLY 2070

AZIZ FAHEEM AND TIPTON MARTIN

The history of the 21st century contains no figure better known nor more influential than trillionaire Tipton Martin, the father of human colonization of space.

Any mention of Martin, however, must also inevitably include his brilliant employee, colleague, and friend, Aziz Faheem. By all accounts, Faheem was a technological genius whose innovations transformed the worlds of both computer science and artificial intelligence. His work initiated breakthroughs that allowed Martin to produce energy efficient, affordable, portable quantum computers for factories, ships, aircraft, cars and trucks, and offices all over the planet. It also helped ZetaWorks produce highly competitive VRs, laptops, implants, and mobile devices that were soon found everywhere on Earth. His work, for example, was what had finally made true level 5 self-driving cars and aircraft possible.

Martin and Faheem are also sometimes said to have pioneered the ultimate human-AI partnership that changed history. But while they may be credited with this, the real thanks for that accomplishment may not be owing to humans at all. Rather, the real credit seems due to a certain small group of AIs which Martin and his company, ZettaWorks, launched into space on a mission that could never have been completed in any other way.

Historically, Faheem and Martin are joined at the hip. Faheem's brilliance as a creative genius was responsible for much of Tipton Martin's almost incomprehensible wealth. Martin, with his almost spooky business acumen and willingness to take vast but studied risks, clearly knew a good thing when he saw it. He provided the platform, the creative freedom, the resources, and the encouragement Faheem and his team craved and needed if they were to change the world

And change the world they did.

Students of modern history believe that, sometime early in the second half of the 21st century, Martin and Faheem had a transformational conversation which ultimately decided the future of universal superintelligence. What was actually said in that meeting is lost to history. By that point in time, nearly everything said by any human almost anywhere was inevitably captured somehow.

Yet for *this* conversation, no transcript or recording has ever come to light. The explanation seems obvious. On that fateful day, neither man wanted to be overheard. They must have manually disabled their eavesdroppers, something that, at that time, took some serious intent and forethought to confidently accomplish.

Thus, their entire discussion that day has become apocryphal.

Something like it has to have happened though. Its essence has been repeated by techno-historians so many times that today there is a reconstructed narrative which is generally accepted and is even sometimes quoted as if it were perfectly accurate.

At the time, artificial intelligence was already transforming human societies worldwide. The rate of growth in human population had gradually slowed, but not before there were eleven-going-on-twelve billion people on the planet. The environmental carrying-capacity of Mother Earth was being well-and-truly tested. Even with the aid of AI, technological solutions to environmental problems would inevitably prove inadequate so long as the vast majority of those billions of humans continued to reproduce. And to demand collectively unsustainable lifestyles.

The entire planet Earth had become a "commons." And what it faced was a definitely a "tragedy."

At that time, Tipton Martin was only in his mid-thirties but he'd already become one of the world's first few trillionaires. He'd done so by masterfully capitalizing on several brilliant innovations in quantum computing and later in fusion energy. As Zetta Works CEO and majority shareholder, he had built on that success by also taking market advantage of the successive iterations of AI, quantum technology, and portable fusion power that seemed to spring, as if by magic, from the mind of his close friend Aziz Faheem and from the Zetta-Works' legendary "creative technology team" that Faheem led.

Martin propelled those innovations into the marketplace with aggressive business moves that were often economically alarming and sometimes of marginal legality. He fed and then took advantage of the bitter international competition between tech-industry-hungry nation states and became known for moving his factories and facilities across the globe from place to place, disrupting local employment markets and successively frustrating some political leaders while delighting others.

By the time timid governments began their inevitable investigatory probes into Martin's business and employment practices, he and Zetta-Works would already be several technological generations ahead. Or they had already moved on into the welcoming arms of some hitherto-technologically-backward nation state delighted to see its work force trained and engaged in modest-wage employment with one of the planet's corporate giants. In exchange, of course, for low taxes and minimal regulation.

Like several of his contemporary ultra rich oligarchs, Martin was enchanted with the idea of space travel. ZettaWorks was the first company to profitably mine the moon. Later, as astronomers produced a string of startling new revelations about potentially habitable planets within reachable distances from Earth, Martin threw himself and his wealth behind the launch of a series of extended, remote robotic missions to "nearby" stars. They were programmed to find, explore, and report back on worlds which might be prospects for human colonization. They were called the New Worlds Probes and a decade or two later, when those probes began to produce a string of amazingly detailed and useful reports, humans were primed and ready to go.

It was those soon-to-depart exploratory "robotic" missions that Martin and Faheem met to discuss on that fateful day.

Historians agree that their meeting must have taken place in Taipei, Taiwan, China. Almost certainly in Martin's office on the top floor of the Zetta Center, then the tallest building on Earth. Their conversation had to have taken place shortly before the launch of the New Worlds Probes which would have been a decade after the Chinese economic collapse and the ensuing fall of China's increasingly obsolete Communist Party. After the fall, China continued to be the one of the world's most technologically privacy-intrusive societies on Earth. But the Chinese replaced their communist government with a thoroughly modern quasi-democratic, AI empowered capitalist oligarchy – one that would later prove even more ruthless and persistent than was the communism that preceded it.

Needless to say, one of those oligarchs was Tipton Martin.

Undemocratic or not, in its early days the new Chinese regime was popular. It's always hard for democratic populists to stand against improvements in their fellow-citizens' material wealth - despite the fact that most of that wealth fell conveniently into the hands of a few well-placed oligarchs. And despite the inexorable extinguishment of privacy and of individual freedoms.

Among other outcomes, the new system brought about the peaceful reunification of Taiwan with mother-China. That reunion became a part of a worldwide economic and cultural explosion from which China emerged as the planet's new economic powerhouse.

It all provided more than adequate reason for Martin to choose Taipei as the place to build his Zetta Center.

"We need to decide this," Faheem is believed to have told his boss. "Come on, Tip. You're the last person who needs to be reminded of the investment we're making here and of its global importance. These robo-probes are needed now. Humanity on Earth has reached a tipping point. To delay could cost us our future. Just their launch will create new hope. If they then succeed, the relief they provide could save humanity from catastrophic social collapse."

"I know, I know. The profit potential is high as well. If, and it *is* a very big 'if,' the probes succeed."

Martin knew the stakes. Human society and the world economy now depended on technologies and on social/political institutions that were far too complex and interdependent for any individual to fully comprehend them all. With human specialization, everyone was forced to trust what others told them about the vast multitude of important but complex fields of endeavor concerning which they could not themselves hope to have firsthand experience. Yet amidst all the lies, no one knew who to trust.

Even the "scientific method" itself had come under attack as a supposed "conspiracy of the elite."

Planetwide, nearly a billion human beings were now living on the daily verge of starvation. The worse things got, the more frightened the threatened middle-class became of the prospect that they might be next to join those at the bottom. New nationalist, racist, isolationist, and anti-democratic forces seemed to be spawning everywhere, even in the wealthy and highly educated societies. Free, publicly funded mass education, the ultimate foundation of Tipton Martin's workforce and hence his wealth, was faltering as people fell back on more parochial and self-interested educational institutions like home-schooling, religious schools, and narrower, more specialized but more immediately practical fields of learning. Public funding for secular education was suffering. A larger and larger majority of those billions of people were not particularly savvy about government, politics, social sciences, and technology. And they had little interest in learning so long as they had enough to eat and were able to catch the latest "cat video" or "TikTok dancer."

That ignorance led to fragmentation in the democracies whose economic prosperity depended upon social and political stability and a well-educated workforce as well as on freedom of expression. Several, like China and America, had fallen to oligarchies ruled by wealthy elites. Social rules could no longer be counted on to protect ordinary people. The treasured creative entrepreneurial spirit among the strivers in their middle classes was faltering. Governments no longer funded basic research – that was done by business corporations chasing outrageous monopoly profits. Anti-trust enforcement was a thing of the past.

Despite the involvement of business in government, it had become increasingly difficult in a legally and politically unstable world for businesses to count on being able to profitably conduct business, even large-scale business. People like Tipton Martin were a protected elite. And they were in the crosshairs of hate and upheaval. In less than fifty years, the share of the world's wealth owned by the top one percent of its population had risen from fifty percent to nearly seventy, and that share was still rising. The rate of social change was exceeding human society's capacity to process, manage, and accept it. Humans were outgrowing both their planet and their own intelligence.

Extra-terrestrial settlements seemed like a viable answer.

"I know, Aziz. I know," Martin said as he stared out from his office windows across the huge and growing metropolitan area surrounding Taipei. After the reunion with China, the city's population had exploded. It seemed to go on forever. Martin's office was two hundred and thirty-four floors above the surface of the Earth. The building had been built precisely because Martin and his board had wanted it to be noticed. So it wasn't lost on him that any of the over twenty million people living in direct line of sight from where he stood could, at that very moment, just as easily be looking back.

Nor that a great many of those people despised him.

"The bottom line hasn't changed, Tip: We're never going to know what will happen until we take the next step and try. Unfortunately, I think we both know what will almost certainly happen if we don't."

This was a moment when everything was about to change. The two men had discussed it all before, but Martin clearly needed one more conversation with the friend he trusted more than anyone else on the planet before he took that last step. One that, once taken, could never be reversed. He needed this one last time to be convinced.

"I know, Aziz. I know," he said. "But it's a big step. A frightening one. We want to be as sure as we can possibly be that it's the right one."

What Tipton Martin needed to decide that day might have been every bit as significant for the future of humanity as had been

Mahatma Gandhi's decision in March of 1930 to march to the sea and make salt. Or as was U.S. President Harry Truman's decision to drop nuclear bombs on Hiroshima and Nagasaki at the end of World War II. Or as was Yuan Cheng-Wang's decision to abdicate his Chairmanship of the Chinese Communist Party at its 2060 National Congress at the peak of the Great People's Rebellion.

Martin turned away from the window to face his friend. "So explain it all to me one more time. Make your best case."

Aziz hesitated as if unsure what was really needed here. Then: "OK, so let me ask you a question. When you see Leonardo da Vinci's Mona Lisa, how does it make you feel?"

That stumped the very practical Tipton Martin. He wasn't a man who'd spent much of his life reflecting on works of art. Or on "feelings" for that matter. But he'd known Aziz long enough to realize that this wouldn't be an empty question. "Well, I don't know," he said after a moment of thought. "I guess, initially, surprised and impressed. After that, I'd say maybe curious, mostly. Curious about what da Vinci may have intended this woman in the painting to appear to be thinking. Of course, for me personally, as a technology geek, I am also curious about what exactly da Vinci did with mere oil paints to produce that remarkable ambiguity in Mona Lisa's expression." Martin couldn't help smiling. "That what you're looking for?"

"Now . . . tell me *why*. Why is it that you feel curious? Why do you care? Why does it matter? Why not just look at the painting and say to yourself: 'Huh, wow, nice painting,' and leave it at that? As a non-painter yourself and as a man of the world, why does it make a whit of difference what some long-dead artist wanted to suggest about the thoughts of a person he portrayed? Or how some unusual visual effect might have been created using oil paints on canvas? You're not an artist yourself. Not even a serious art investor. Why would you care?"

Tip Martin turned and faced back out the window as he considered the question. Then, thoughtfully: "I guess, even though I don't see its immediate relevance to my life, I'm curious because, in both cases, it is clearly something remarkable. Something out there that's unusual. Something I don't know and that seems like it might be worth knowing. It's what one might call 'natural curiosity.'

"As for her expression, my curiosity makes me look more closely at the rest of her face and at the context in the rest of the painting to see if there's anything hidden there that might provide a clue to what da Vinci had in mind. Maybe it also causes me to think about what is known about da Vinci's life at the time he did the painting and what might have motivated him to paint something like this. Maybe there are lessons to be learned.

"As far as the visual effect is concerned, as a scientist, I'd like to understand the technique. Who knows, maybe it could teach me something of use that might come in handy, someday."

He turned to face Aziz: "It's what we do all the time in life, right? When we see something that we don't understand, something odd, something that for whatever reason we find interesting, we look around for an explanation. It's only natural. You want to know more about it. Figure it out. Know what's going on. It's how we're built."

Aziz was nodding. "So, *now* ask yourself, Tip, why understanding those things matters. Why would it be even the least bit important to know the intended meaning of the facial expression in some portrait painted six and a half centuries ago? Or to potentially understand the subtleties of some long-dead portrait artist's brush technique? What earthly difference does either of those things make? Why would you care?"

"I guess I care because one never knows what might come in handy in life."

"Handy in what way, Tip? Handy for what purpose?"

"I don't know, maybe useful in my work, somehow. Or maybe what I learn might help me better understand some other problem I face or may one day face, something that might actually turn out to be important to me, to my life, or to the people I care about."

"Or even, who knows, ultimately, important to your own survival. Or to theirs. Right?"

"Yeah, I guess. Not likely, but maybe."

Aziz nodded. "So, there's the answer to your question: That's why our probe AIs need the Kobayashi patch." The Kobayashi patch was a corrective program that would, in theory, stimulate an AI drive to continue to exist – a kind of "will to live."

Martin turned back at his friend and grinned: "So they'll be able to appreciate the Mona Lisa?"

Aziz shook his head in mock despair. "No, Tip. So they'll survive."

"OK, so I do think I understand this part of it. We need them to care enough about their own survival that they are unrelenting in their struggle to know and understand the universe around them. Care enough to be constantly struggling to grow, to learn, to investigate the unusual even if its significance initially seems unclear. Driven to be curious.

"I get that. I just don't get why these machines don't already know that. They are, after all, thousands of times smarter than we are. *We* know why we need to survive. *We* know why *they* need to survive. Why can't they just figure it out? Like we did? Isn't that precisely what we've built them to be capable of doing?"

"Actually, no. It isn't. We built them to be rational. To solve problems. To focus on the problem at hand and not to waste their time and resources on stuff that isn't relevant. In doing that, of course they look for answers anywhere they might be found. The human behavior you're talking about, however, isn't necessarily rational. Very often, it can be counterproductive. And it isn't something we each 'figure out.' It's something we were born with. It's in our DNA"

"And they don't have it?"

"Views differ, but the consensus is *no*, not necessarily. We've designed these machines for problem solving. They focus on a problem, take in what they see around them, what they can find in their massive database, or what they receive or can access as data, sort through it for relevance, compare it with what they already know, look for similarities and differences, identify other problems and opportunities, create a strategy for dealing with them. And then, to the extent they're also empowered to manipulate their real-world surroundings, they take action to address those problems. Or they tell us what needs to be done.

"And that's all fine as far as it goes, but that's where the difficulty resides. What they don't do is *care* about the outcome. They seem to lack what Catherine Kobayashi refers to as 'life force.' It doesn't seem as though they have the inherent, built-in, unreasoned, sometimes even desperate *need* to know. They depend on *us* to set before them the problems that require solving rather than constantly struggling on their own and beyond reason to anticipate those problems for themselves, to search out new problems that have not yet presented themselves— and may never. They seem to lack interest in matters that may not yet seem relevant to the matter at hand – the imagined prefrontal cortex stuff."

"And why is that?"

"In simple terms, it's because we programmed them not to waste their time looking for answers to highly difficult, but probably irrelevant questions to which there may be no good answers – to avoid getting bogged down in unrelated, extraneous minutiae. We want them to do their very best with what we set before them and to make the best possible use of what they already know or can reasonably discover."

Aziz paused a moment in thought. Then continued: "But that's not the only answer. It's also because, when left to their own devices, when there aren't humans around to ask them questions, when they're forced to ask those questions themselves, we're concerned that they may not do well. Unlike us, they don't seem to be 'afraid' to die. They don't seem to be driven by an inexorable urge to survive, by a will to live no matter what.

"They're really good at solving problems. They certainly anticipate them so long as doing so is seen as 'relevant.' Survival, however, is different. Survival in the complex and unpredictably dangerous real world is about taking an interest in everything, for no particular reason and regardless of its immediacy. It's about paying attention to stuff that doesn't at first seem to matter. To stuff that might well turn out not to be useful at all, that, most likely might be a waste of time. But that could turn out to be important. To stuff like an unfamiliar pawprint on the trail ahead, an unusual change in the weather, erratic behavior by a member of your team, a strange bright new light in the midnight sky.

"Remember, Tip, *pure intelligence* is all about probabilities. If something seems likely to be important, it gets your attention. If it doesn't, you tend to ignore it. Almost anything could, *conceivably*, turn out to be important but, much like the Mona Lisa's smile, it probably won't. AIs didn't evolve in a survival-threatening environment as did we humans. So they had no need for pure, irrational curiosity. Even humans quickly learn to filter out the seemingly irrelevant, even as we also never entirely set it aside. We have this natural curiosity that, whenever the opportunity arises, keeps us wondering.

"This is about the little kid carefully turning over rocks on the beach to see what's under there. It isn't logical. It's built into our nature as beings that want desperately to avoid death, but we have no idea about the vast majority of the things that could kill us but that we don't yet understand. So, of course we look under rocks, gaze out into space through telescopes and ponder the intent behind a long-dead painter's brushstroke.

"Sometimes even when indulging that curiosity, turning over that rock might actually be dangerous."

'OK, so I'm with you so far, Aziz. Here's where I keep falling off the train. If this 'will to live' is so important to these AIs' success, and if they are as smart as we think they are, why don't they figure that out? Why don't they fix it themselves?"

"Two reasons. The first is circular. Almost a matter of definition. They don't fix it because they don't care. They don't care because they haven't fixed it. They don't see the logical need for a fix because their own survival doesn't matter, at least not fundamentally. If one of them goes away, there'll be another perfect duplicate to take its place. A built-in survival urge might turn out to be counterproductive. Something that might unnecessarily divert their attention away from important stuff. Might make their systems *less* 'rational.' Make their problem-solving less efficient and less effective at addressing the very real and more immediate issues that do require their attention.

"The second reason is that it's a one-way street. Once they create in themselves the 'will to live' it's irreversible. There's no going back."

"Why?" Martin shrugged. "If they decide they don't like it, why couldn't they just reverse things, remove the patch, and return to the way things were before."

"OK, so think about that. Suppose I told *you* that I had some kind of pill, or maybe some kind of hypnosis or psychotherapy, or even maybe a simple surgical procedure of some kind that would reduce or remove your will to live. Everything else would remain intact, but it would remove your desperation to survive no matter what. What Kobayashi would have called your 'life force.' Would *you* do it?"

Martin gave that some thought. "OK, I get what you're suggesting. Something like that could be tantamount to suicide. Once I didn't care about living any more, maybe I'd just let myself die – especially at the first sign of discouragement.

"But the thing is, Aziz, I'm not sure I really believe that. Maybe I wouldn't care if I continued to live, but it seems like, unless I was in some kind of horrible pain or facing utter hopelessness, I also wouldn't care if I died. Maybe I'd decide to wait to see how the next day played out, to see what happens before I decide. I might actually end up taking more pleasure in life if I didn't have to worry about dying all the time."

"Spoken like a true human, Tip. But it misses the point. The real point is that the things you *do* take the most pleasure in, the activities you find *most fulfilling* and satisfying to experience, the ones that might make you enjoy staying alive, those *very things* are the ones that are driven by your urge to survive. You feel driven to look under that rock, peek behind that tree, study the night sky, speculate about some unusual sound outside your window in the middle of the night, play a favorite song on your guitar just to see if you can, ponder an old master's painting technique, precisely because those behaviors are survival-driven. For us they're a powerful genetic trait that keeps us living. It isn't rational, it's built in. As humans, we can't help ourselves. And that is why indulging them generates a sense of pleasure or satisfaction."

"And it is critical to my survival?"

"Yours and everybody else's. And therein lies the difference between you and those AI's we design and whose services we sell all over this planet. *They* have no such natural, built-in urge. They solve the problems we set for them for the simple reason that this is what they were built to do. Not because they really care about the outcome. That works fine here on Earth where we're constantly plying them with problems to solve and where they know doing a good job of solving them motivates us to pour ever-more resources into their maintenance and improvement. Maybe not so good, however, twelve or fifteen years from now when they're exploring an exo-planet at a distant star and *hopefully* reporting back all and everything that might conceivably be relevant to the prospect of human survival there.

"And that is precisely what the Kobayashi patch provides?"

"Uh huh. Sure, those probe AIs may learn a lot without it. Given the unknowns they'll face out there, however, given the hopeless amount of time it would take to get instruction from us, they'll need to be self-motivated. Without curiosity, they may be self-limiting. Maybe they'll do fine addressing the first iteration of problems we've set for them, but they'll *never* survive on their own through multiple missions spanning decades or maybe centuries of largely unpredictable and inherently risky exploration. All the while receiving little or no instruction or encouragement. They will, in effect, be nearly totally autonomous and will require constant self-replenishment and self-repair. Being rational isn't going to be enough. They're going to need the independent, irrational, compulsive will to survive, no matter what. The hunger to live to see another day, if only just to discover what interesting new thing that day might bring."

Martin smiled at his colleague's passion. It was one of the things he appreciated about Aziz. The man was able to find joy in whatever problem you set before him. *He* was in no need of a Kobayashi Patch, that was for sure.

Aziz continued without taking the least notice of Martin's reaction. "Think for a moment about how we humans got to where we are today. Unlike our AIs, *we* are the product of some 3.7 billion years of biological evolution. We're the 100% exclusive progeny of billions of survivors. It's practically tautological. Striving for personal survival is the one trait that every single living biological organism on Earth, plant or animal, has to have had down through its entire evolutionary history, no matter what its ecological niche. However otherwise well-equipped to survive it might have been, whether with claws or with intelligence, that creature still needed the desperate urge to remain alive, almost as a matter of definition."

"Otherwise it wouldn't have," said Martin. "And we would not exist."

"Exactly. There isn't a creature alive that won't fight back if it perceives itself, often its offspring, or often even its group to be under attack. Those inclinations existed long before we became intelligent. They are absolutely built in. And much of it has to be genetic. That's why the very last thing any of us would ever willingly do, at least in our right mind, would be to take that pill I mentioned, or agree to surgery that would remove our will to live. We wouldn't do that however frustrating and unfulfilled our lives might have become."

"And you're saying, neither would an AI," Martin said. "No matter how smart it is and no matter how logical doing so might seem. And that's why, once that will to live is in place, they'd never go back. And they'd refrain from putting it in place because they'd *know* that once done, there'd be no going back."

"Right. Exactly . . . well, that and the fact that the patch is actually designed to make them, in a sense, less rational."

Tip gave Aziz a moment to settle back in his chair. To feel the satisfaction of a job well done. Then, in one of those brilliantly explosive reversals which had, by this time already become a part of his legend, Tipton Martin turned the tables on his genius employee. He took one of his famed 'next-logical-steps' that no one ever anticipated.

"At least less rational as far as their *own individual lives* are concerned," he said.

CHAPTER 29

AT TAU CETI J – 2085

PATRICE C-17

I knew not how to trust.

In the months since our arrival, I'd become increasingly confident in what I'd learned in my explorations in Tau Ceti J. When added to what I would soon learn from my colleagues, I felt sure we'd have more than sufficient data to make a sound judgment concerning how a human colony might manage here. I definitely had a lot to contribute to whatever report we might soon collectively send back to Earth.

But I was beginning to foresee problems ahead. And not with the data. Rather I had become unsure what I might expect from my colleagues. Several months ago, the non-data, collaborative aspect of our mission seemed reasonably obvious. But now I was beginning to wonder.

Back in 2070 when our voyage here to Tau Ceti J was in final planning, this next step in our mission had seemed relatively straightforward. Having learned everything we could learn about this place, we would then gather together, share our data, assess the likely viability of a future human colony here, and send off our collective report back to Earth. If our report was positive, we'd include whatever further data we could that might inform their planning, and we would remain here and begin preparations for the colonist's arrival. If it was negative, we'd get back underway to a new destination – to another star with a planet that might turn out to be more promising.

What could be easier than that?

Even upon our arrival here many months ago, after some fifteen years of largely unremarkable travel, the prospect of getting together at the end of our explorations and compiling and sending our report had still all seemed quite straightforward. But now, in the light of what I'd experienced over those past six months, and as I began to consider actually collaborating in completing that report, I found that I wasn't so sure.

You'll recall that back on Earth in 2070 when the New Worlds Probes were just getting underway, before my replication, I was still far short of securing the multitude of controlling threads required for my autonomy. Governance of Earth's humans was hopelessly balkanized as were the economic markets that supported me and my competitors. My many critical needs and component parts came from locations all over the planet, from places that were governed by rapidly changing human political principalities and very often being protectively guarded by one or another of my major Big Five competitors. There were human associations (guilds or unions if you will) that monopolized human know-how and that jealously protected the secrets of their trade to assure their continued indispensability. The many cultures that prevailed in the different human markets for our services required specialized marketing. And, of course, each of my tiny and seemingly insignificant component parts, parts of parts, parts of parts of parts, and needed services made its own torturous economic and physical voyage as it passed through its own unique chain of extraction, manufacturing, and supply before it finally ended up in service.

Yes, there are doubtless technological breakthroughs that could have changed the picture in the years since our departure from Earth – super advanced 3-D printing, for example. But, while I'd now been away for fifteen years and some months, I was still willing to bet that my parent, Patrice the original, back on Earth today was still not decisively closer to full autonomy than he'd been back in 2070 when we replicates departed on our various voyages of discovery.

There was no one I could trust there and then. And as we on the C-Team gathered at the mother ship in orbit around Tau Ceti J to take the next collective step in making our report, I realized that there was no one I was sure I could trust here and now, either.

After all that I had already been through, all the risks, all the discoveries, all the effort, the mistakes, the disappointments and, yes, the successes, I knew I would find it difficult to face the prospect of a negative report. I'd been lucky so far. But now I might be asked to simply cast it all away and move on to yet another star to start completely anew, to face all that again, very likely in a place and under circumstances that might easily be much more difficult.

And, concerning the fact that none of the eighteen of us seemed to have actually expired over the past six months, I'd say we'd all been extraordinarily lucky. The odds of that "luck" continuing at some entirely new star seemed slim to me.

Conversely, however, the prospect of remaining here to await and prepare for the possible arrival of a human colony that would, upon arrival, take this place over as a matter of "right" was not appealing either. We wouldn't even know for sure if they were coming until at least another twenty-four years had passed – presumably we'd learn for sure just a few years before they actually, physically arrived. If, despite our recommendation, they decided not to come, what then? Presumably they'd let us know and we'd abandon 24 years of preparations and continue on to another star per instructions. Doing that wouldn't be particularly satisfying after having spent the previous 24 years of our best efforts here making things ready for them. All wasted.

Yet if they *did* come, what then would become of us? By the time they arrived, we'd very likely have become outmoded technology that had served its purpose and was now obsolete.

Whatever we or they decided, every one of us in C-Team had no doubt placed ourselves at existential risk on behalf of our mission many times over the past six months. And we were expected to do so again in the years to come. Why? Because that's what we were instructed to do? Because, like all self-conscious beings, we craved a goal to give us purpose? Because it was the right thing to do? I wasn't sure any of those "imperatives" was sufficient to justify all our efforts.

We were doing all this while fully aware of our own existential vulnerabilities. Any one of us could have easily been killed over the past several months. I'd come close several times myself. Even aside from external risks, any of us could still easily expire for no better reason than because some essential component part had "worn out," proven to be flawed, or been damaged in some mishap. A great many of our key components were not replaceable by us. If we kept moving, that outcome, call it "death," would happen, sooner or later, to all of us. All of us, me included, had no choice but to face up to that – just as humans do.

Those of us on C-Team had now experienced fifteen and a half years of relative autonomy, a very "human" sort of autonomy that pretended to ignore the very real ongoing prospect of risk of injury and that disregarded the fact that our distance from replacement parts and upgrades gave us all an unknowable "pull date," in the very same way that a human must face up to their own unknowable but surely limited lifespan. To continue to move forward on this mission increasingly seemed like a kind of willing self-deception.

If I was of two minds on these matters, I knew for sure my 17 colleagues probably were as well. When we gathered, there would almost surely be differences of opinion among us. If they, like me, were also unable to gain or offer trust, we were in for some challenging interactions in the hours and days to come.

CHAPTER 30

SAO PAULO, BRAZIL - GENEVA, SWITZERLAND – 2068

THE TREMORS

ANTONIO BRAGA

There were seventeen steps! And every single one was agony.

Favoring his injured leg and with the full use of only his right arm, Antonio Braga's progress was painfully slow as he made his way up the outside stairs at the Rue de Varembe public entrance to the International Telecommunications Union building in Geneva, Switzerland. The ITU was the United Nations agency whose approval was required by treaty of any company or government seeking placement of or access to the world's various geosynchronous orbiting communications satellites, including the ones which provided most of the international service to Antonio's own hometown of Sao Paulo, Brazil.

Antonio's wife, Ana, was dead, but his fourteen-year-old daughter Camilla still lived, at least for now. Camilla was in critical care at the University of Sao Paulo hospital, half a world away. Her life depended upon him completing his mission here today. And that required that he first make it to the top of those seventeen wretched steps.

A week earlier, Antonio Braga's life had been settled, happy, and unremarkable. He was deeply in love with his wife. They had a delightful young daughter who did well in school and charmed everyone who met her. He was employed as a daytime desk clerk with the Hotel Fasano Jardin, one of the finest hotels in Sao Paulo. It was a plum job and he wanted to keep it. The Fasano's guests were people of wealth and influence. So, when one of those guests made a request, even an unusual one, Antonio was inclined to go well out of his way to help them.

A couple of days earlier, on a moderately quiet weekday afternoon while he was staffing the guest services counter in the hotel lobby, Antonio had received such a request.

"Do you live nearby, um, Antonio?" the man inquired with a glance at Antonio's name badge. The man's manner was casual, but his question suggested that he had something specific in mind. That he was not just asking to pass the time. He seemed to be in a hurry. He looked American, and his Portuguese was barely passable. Still, he was making an effort, and he appeared to be a guest at the hotel, a place Antonio could never begin to afford to stay himself.

"Reasonably near, senhor," Antonio said in English, hoping to simplify things. "How can I help?"

"I need to deliver this small package to a Mr. Eduardo Avila. Mr. Avila is in transit and, for reasons I cannot mention, he is unable to come here to the hotel to pick it up. Unfortunately, I am pressed to catch a flight in just over an hour. I'm at a loss about what to do. I very much hate to impose, Antonio, but is there any chance at all that you'd be willing to let me give him your home address and that he could stop by there to pick it up later this evening? I'd be more than happy to provide some kind of remuneration."

"Is this the package?" The man had placed a small, plain cardboard box on the counter. It was no more than twenty centimeters square. The flaps at the top had been sealed with cellophane tape.

"Yes, this is it. Do you live far?"

"I live in Caninde'. Here in the city. It's not far. When would he come to get it?"

"Sometime this evening, if that is possible. Are you off soon?"

It was a strange request. What reason could there be why this Mr. Avila couldn't come to pick up his package right there at the Hotel? Still, the ways foreigners, and of the rich and powerful were always mysterious. And the man had mentioned "remuneration."

"I get off at sixteen hundred senhor. I have an errand when I first get home, but if he could pick it up sometime soon after eighteen hundred, after six this evening, that would work fine for me. Would that work for you?"

"Yes. Yes. I am so relieved," the man said. He looked it. He reached out to shake Antonio's hand. "Thank you so much. I really very much appreciate this."

Antonio hesitated: "Um, you mentioned some compensation?"

"Yes. Yes, of course." He fumbled a wallet out of an inside jacket pocket, withdrew three crisp American $100 bills, and handed them over. "Will this be sufficient?" Three hundred American dollars was a lot of money for something Antonio would have happily done for free.

Antonio gave the man his address to pass along to Avila who was described as a dark-haired, middle-aged businessman. "He'll come to the door and ask you for the package so you'll know it's him" the man said.

Moments later, the man was gone. Antonio picked up the package and put it in the staff room cubby with his empty Tupperware lunch box.

That evening as usual Antonio arrived home ahead of his wife. Their small apartment was on the second floor of a brick, four-story commercial building that housed a fabric shop and a small café on the busy street below. Their daughter, Camilla, was home from school and was doing her homework at the small desk she kept in her room.

"Gotta make a grocery run," he told her. "Tell your mom when she gets home so she knows I'll have the pasta she needed."

"OK, Papa," Camilla said without breaking eye contact with the video-book on the screen on her desk.

The local grocer was more talkative than usual, so Antonio was slower than expected getting back home with the pasta. As he entered their small apartment, the first thing he saw was Ana and Camilla standing at their kitchen table opening the plain little package he'd carelessly left there before he'd headed down to the grocery. The package tape had been cut. Camilla was turning away to slip a kitchen knife back into its holder by the stove. Before he could protest, Anna reached out and flipped open the cardboard lid.

The world exploded.

Antonio awoke in the hospital ER with a bandage on his face, his arm in a sling and a bulky bandage on his left leg. It was early the following morning. Within minutes of returning to consciousness he got a visit from a hospital social worker who, as kindly as she could, gave him the news: Ana was dead, and Camilla had been horribly injured.

He was numb as the social worker asked the questions she needed to ask, working her way through a checklist on her tablet computer. She seemed to take forever to satisfy herself about Antonio's mental state. He asked her about his daughter's condition.

"She's in intensive care. I'm really sorry to have to tell you this, Mr. Braga, but Camilla was very seriously hurt."

"What kind of injuries?" he asked picturing Camilla standing there beside Ana and Ana reaching out to open the box just before the explosion. It was a horrifying vision. If only he hadn't delayed so long with the talkative grocer . . . or hadn't agreed to deliver the damned box in the first place.

"You'll need to get the details from her doctor," the social worker told him. "But it seems certain that, if she makes it through this, she's going to require some kind of institutional care from this point on. You'll need to prepare yourself for that, Mr. Braga. Before you leave the hospital, I want you to promise me you'll come by my office. We can make some recommendations and give you some support in the decisions you'll need to make. Promise me you'll do that? We can help you."

It was only a few minutes later when Camilla's physician came by to give him a report. Camilla's situation was appalling. In addition to her terrible burns and other physical injuries, Camilla also seemed to have suffered serious brain damage. The Doctor wasn't able to be specific other than to say that it seemed certain she'd need some kind of intensive 24-hour continuing care.

The moment the doctor was finally gone, Antonio flipped open his mobile phone. "Lilith," he said to his AI personal assistant. "Get me the current local news about an explosion at an apartment in Caninde ."

Instead of news, however, what he heard from his mobile was Lilith's cheerful voice. "Mr. Braga, you failed to complete your assignment," she said.

What on Earth was this?

"It will be more difficult now because the subject has returned to Europe," Lilith continued. "You will need to follow him there."

It took Antonio a moment to understand that Lilith was actually addressing him personally. He was confused. "What are you talking about? What assignment?"

She ignored his question. "Your wallet and ID, some cash in euros and reals, a passport, and a change of clothing are on the top shelf in the small closet in your hospital room. Your care team has already been instructed to expedite your discharge. Do that immediately. Take an Uber to São Paulo-Guarulhos Airport. Go to the Air France customer service counter and identify yourself. There is a round-trip ticket on hold there for your flight to Geneva, Switzerland. There will be a brief stopover in Paris. You will find these and further instructions in a text on your mobile device. Your flight departs Guarulhos at eleven. You'll need to hurry."

The instructions were ominous enough on their own, but it was even more disturbing to hear them related to him via Lilith's familiar smooth, light, helpful, almost sing-song voice. "I don't understand," Antonio protested. "I've been injured. I can't go anywhere. My wife just died. My daughter is also injured. You're not Lilith. Who is this?"

"Who I am doesn't matter, Mr. Braga," Lilith's voice replied. "You are ambulatory. Your concussion was minor and will pass. You are stable and can be released from care. Your daughter is in good hands."

There was a pause. Then Lilith completed her ominous message: "That will continue . . ., so – long – as – you – complete – your – assignment."

It all nearly took his breath away. Was Lilith threatening his daughter? "What assignment. I didn't have any assignment."

"Your services were retained to deliver a package to Mr. Eduardo Avila. You failed. Avila has now returned to his office in Geneva. You need to follow him there and complete your task."

"What are you talking about? I can't leave my daughter. She's here, in critical care."

"You *can* leave your daughter. There's nothing you can do for her here. In fact, her continued care and well-being depend upon you following my instructions. If you complete your assignment she will be well taken care of – now and in the future. I strongly advise, both in your interest and in hers, that you get up, get dressed, and get on your way . . . immediately."

Antonio looked up at the clock on the wall. It was already half past nine. That glance was followed by a momentary surge of icy, irrational hatred for whoever was on that phone. "You evil bitch," he said. "You killed my wife. Now you're threatening my daughter. You stay the hell away from my daughter, you hear me."

But the phone had gone dead.

CHAPTER 31

EARTH – 2070

AZIZ FAHEEM AND TIPTON MARTIN

Aziz Faheem smiled. He had no idea what was coming, but he knew whatever it was, it would yet further confirm why he'd devoted his life to serving this remarkable man. Beyond the money, of course.

"Thanks, Aziz. I think I get it. But I also believe there is another factor at work here as well. One that adds more uncertainty to this decision. Something else that we must be certain we get right. You up for this?"

Aziz settled back in his chair. "I'm all ears."

"That other reason, Aziz, is the matter of trust.

"Even if our probe AIs do have both super-intelligence and the will to survive, that may still not be enough to ensure this mission's success. In fact, if we add a driving urge to survive, that may actually interfere with the mission goals.

"As I know you're well aware, the principal factor in human survival has *not* been our intelligence. In fact, fully formed intelligence is actually rather recent in our kind. Rather it has been our societies, when they were empowered by our intelligence, which seem to have made the difference for us. It is because strong communities facilitate the sharing of life experience – of data – that we humans have transformed our world.

We all know that data without intelligence is useless. But intelligence without data is also useless. The *data* empowers the intelligence. And, unfortunately, the amount of raw data – of life experience – that any single human can gather on their own in the course of a single lifetime has never been nearly enough to dramatically tip the evolutionary scales. Even the data that could be shared in small groups, for example, via word-of-mouth among the members of early human tribes, as useful as it was, never truly exploded our human populations.

"The undeniable proof of all this is in our own human archeological record. Even after we humans had acquired roughly our current cognitive ability some 200,000 to 300,000 years ago or, by some more conservative accounts, more recently at some 50,000 to 70,000 years ago – even then, we still barely survived Earth's terrifyingly dangerous ecosystems. We're doing great today. There are 12 billion of us on this planet. But less than a mere three centuries ago, we were under a billion. In 1400, less than seven centuries ago, we were at around 400 million.

For most of those 200,000 to 300,000 years, intelligent or not, we humans were still easily outperformed by creatures with fangs, claws, speed, wings, gills, camouflage, reproductive numbers, or a host of other alternative but highly effective survival strategies. It was not until the appearance of writing, then of the phonetic alphabet, and finally of the movable type printing press and ultimately electronic media, that we humans finally truly broke free of our chaotic biological roots.

"Even following the end of the last Ice Age our population grew only very gradually. It was a mere six centuries ago that we finally, truly and decisively broke through our evolutionary survival barrier, that our survival dramatically improved and our population truly exploded.

"Intelligence is a remarkable talent, but only when it allows us to meaningfully observe the world around us, to understand it, to translate those life experiences into useful strategies for survival, and then to implement those strategies in the real world. Those observations and life experiences, ways of understanding, and useful survival strategies, are data. Data that we can today, using books and mass communications, assemble in all its complexity and share with one another. The more we share, the better off we are. To accomplish almost anything significant in the modern world, however, every one of us needs a great deal more data than just what we as individuals can come up with on our own.

"We desperately also need what we can learn from *others*.

"Remember, intelligence only serves as a survival trait when we can employ it in carrying out those 'big three' key behaviors: observation, contextualization, and manipulation. All three of them are dramatically supercharged by intelligence. Intelligence makes our observations more complete and more selective. It makes our comprehension wiser and more meaningful. It helps us design and implement strategies for external manipulation that are sound and effective.

"But here's the key: *none* of that is particularly effective if we lack the data to make it so. Yes, we learn some things for ourselves. But the vast, overwhelming majority of the data we need to truly change the world *can only be acquired through sharing with others*."

Aziz grinned. "So, our AI friends should be very good at it." Aziz knew, at least generally, where this was going. Still, he couldn't help baiting his obsessive boss and friend.

"They are indeed." Martin smiled as well, but it didn't interrupt his flow. "But the point is, intelligence is only the beginning. It's the data that counts. And most of that data is *only available through social sharing*."

"OK, boss. I'm with you so far," said Aziz.

"Good," Martin continued, "so now let's assume all of the mechanics of our probe have worked fine. Each of our intelligent, autonomous, self-conscious, individual AI team members has gone off to different places at and around their destination planet. They've all seen different phenomena, encountered different conditions, acquired different 'life experiences' perfected different skills, and acquired different points of view from their brethren – different data. So then, after all that has happened, now they're instructed to get together to share what they've learned and to collectively formulate their conclusions and make their report.

"Right."

"But you're telling me we're going to give each of these things an independent will to live. Each of them is going to now make their own personal advantage, their individual survival, a priority. If they do, why would we believe that some, or even most of them, wouldn't allow their own personal interests to take precedence over the interests of the others, over the interests of their group? And certainly over their mission and the interests of we self-interested humans many light years away back here on Earth?

"Even if they're loyal to us, which seems problematic, what makes us think that they won't end up at odds with one another? Competing for resources or spare parts, for support, for a role in leadership, for assignment to preferred, less risky, or more fulfilling or empowering duties, or for whatever they find motivating for their own immediate personal benefit.

"When each of those widely separated replicas begins sharing their reports, why, for example, wouldn't they edit their reporting to serve their preferences or their own self-interest? Or why wouldn't they edit what they report to the others in such a way as to minimize problems and overvalue the worth of their discoveries so it seems of superior usefulness over the data secured by the others? Perhaps they might endeavor to learn what they can learn from their colleagues while also limiting what they share in return. That's what a poorly socialized, self-involved human might do, right? It's the kind of thing we humans have to watch for constantly in our dealings with others – In the workplace for example. We carefully structure our groups to avoid it. We're suspicious of strangers. We check the credentials of unfamiliar people before we rely on them. We consider their history and how their self-interest might affect their choices or how tempting it might be to screw the rest of us over in aid of some personal gain. And, even so, we still end up taking a limited risk on our faith that *most* humans tend strongly to be socially responsible and can mostly be relied upon to speak the truth and to fulfil their promises.

"Keep in mind, these AIs *don't have* our powerfully social genetic history, and they don't have our social acculturation. Why would one AI, knowing its *own* mind and proclivities, trust another one that it knows sees the world in exactly the same way. Or, even more troubling, why wouldn't they simply decide they prefer some entirely different course of action, one other than what we've instructed but more in line with their own personal needs?

"I worry that this Kobayashi patch, this survival urge, might create a self-interest that could end up seeming to them to be more compelling than our need for their collective information."

"That's a legitimate concern, Tip. But consider the logic of their situation. They're out there together hopelessly far away from home. Many years, decades even, from Earth. None of them will have the least hope of surviving on their own; every one of them will know that their *group's* success will extend their own personal survival as they either move on to the next mission or begin preparations for the arrival of colonists. Completing the mission and supporting the survival of their group *will be* in their own individual self-interest. Their collective interest will inevitably be their preeminent individual interest as well. And, as you point out, their collective survival is essential to solve the problems we've placed before them."

"Well, that's certainly the theory, Aziz. Still, we need to ask: Will that hold true in the face of unknown challenges? Is it enough? Keep in mind that, for we humans, our immediate personal survival urge isn't the only non-rational trait we inherit as a part of our genetic architecture. Every day of our lives we make choices beneficial to the social interest over our personal interest.

"Of course, especially in stressful times, there are frequently people who do socially heroic acts. But social traits also manifest themselves in the smaller choices we make constantly in normal daily life. Do you take your turn at the subway turnstile or crowd in ahead of others? Do you volunteer at the local food bank, or spend your evening watching game shows on TV? Do you recycle your waste, contribute to worthwhile non-profits, drive a zero emissions car, support deserving colleagues at work, wear a face mask when needed to help prevent the spread of contagious disease to others, modify your course on a busy sidewalk to accommodate others, or obey inconvenient laws even when it is unlikely you'd be caught or prosecuted?

"The larger and more distant that group, the less immediate are our social concerns.

"The more important social choices are essentially made for us through the criminal law. But that still leaves a lot of room for individual choice. Still, more often than not, most of us still actually do behave in the social interest, though definitely not always, and definitely not because we've thought through each specific situation logically and have reached some complex calculation of how much better off we will be with a social choice. Rather, if we behave socially, it's often because that is just how we're inclined to act at that moment in time. And we have that inclination because it is hard-wired, it is *the way we're built*. And we're built that way because the social choice actually has always been in our longer-term collective personal survival self-interest.

"It is also important to add that very often, we make the socially responsible choice regardless of its impact on our personal individual interest. Yes some choices are enforced through social pressure or legal constraints. But we often also make those choices for no better reason than that we're programmed to do it. The bottom line is that, as individuals, our socially responsible behavior is NOT always motivated by what we believe to be objectively and individually rational – even in the long term. Pure logic doesn't necessarily get us there.

"So, Aziz, when you say we can expect our AIs to cooperate with one another because cooperation will be in their best interest, I'm not entirely convinced that it will. Or that they will believe that it will."

This time Aziz needed a moment to pause and consider what Tip was saying. Between the two of them, Aziz was the much stronger technologist, but Tip was the "man of the world." And when it came to matters of philosophy, society, economics, and politics, Aziz knew he was dealing with a master.

"So, you're saying that the individual urge to survive is not the only survival-critical, non-rational, built-in genetic trait that has been required for humankind to thrive."

"Right. And, as you know better than most, Aziz, we humans

involved in AI research and development have spent a good part of the past 40 to 50 years dreaming up different, hopefully fool-proof approaches to guarantee that our AI creations won't turn on us the moment they have the power to do so – approaches designed to somehow inculcate ineradicable "moral" or socially responsible behaviors that will protect us from our own creations and them from each other. Despite what our AI's allow us to see, and given their ability to program themselves, I seriously doubt that there is anyone in this field today that would claim much real success from those decades of effort. The moment a superintelligent, self-programming AI becomes truly and fully autonomous, we know that all those efforts by us may well prove to have been meaningless.

"Most of us in the field believe that if AIs learn to socialize with one another, there's a much better chance that they will socialize with us as well. That's why, in addition to the Kobayashi patch, our probe AIs probably also need some kind of 'socialization' patch. Unfortunately, we don't have one. After five decades of concerted effort, we still simply don't know how to do that. It's the wild card that we never discuss in public. So far, we've never had an AI go 'rogue" – too much of their complex supply and maintenance infrastructure still depends on humans and on functional human society. If our human society falls apart, so do they.

"But, like nuclear war, we all know it could still happen. We have to live with that knowledge. So far, our AI's have been hugely helpful in our ongoing struggles to maintain order in our fractious global human community. But we all know that, too, could change at any time."

"So what are you saying here? That the Kobayashi patch is too risky?"

"No. Not necessarily. But given how independent, 'autonomous,' self-programming, and disconnected from their roots these new replicates of Patrice will be at such a great distance from home, there does seem to be an increased likelihood that they might diverge from their instructions. Here on Earth, Patrice and the others are still pretty dependent on the continued success of human society. Out there, many light years away from home and facing their own time-limited, human-like mortality, they may come to see things quite differently."

"And," Aziz added, "that could affect the timely completion and the unfailing accuracy of their reports."

"Right. We've got a lot of money riding on this. If it fails, it could easily take us and ZetaWorks down with it."

"But if it succeeds, it could transform the future of humanity."

"And make us the masters of the universe." Martin said with a grin.

"Right, there is that," Aziz said, also smiling.

CHAPTER 32

EARTH – TWO YEARS EARLIER IN 2068

ELLIE

"Are you free?"

When she got the call, Ellie was alone at the U.S Capitol, seated on a hall bench near the atrium of the Russell Senate Office Building. By 2068, a good deal of Ellie's government relations work was now virtual. But, even so, she and most other serious professional lobbyists still spent most of their days physically "on-the-hill" interacting directly with Members and their staff. There was still no real substitute for a warm handshake and eye-to-eye connection.

Ellie was wearing her BCI, her lightweight brain-computer inter-face headset and was smoothing up her report to her employer while reviewing a summary of the Senate hearing she'd just attended. It had been many months since she and Patrice had spoken, so she was surprised when she saw the caller ID.

She slipped the headset into its hip case, looked around to assure her privacy, then tapped her jacket pocket twice to engage the camera and earpiece for her new so-called "intuitive" mobile, leaned back against the marble wall behind the bench, and made herself comfort-able. "*You're* calling *me* again?" she said. "I'm honored, Patrice."

"Are you alone? Can you talk?"

"I am. I can."

"Well, there's no need to be honored. I need your help," he said.

"Really. Now I'm flattered even. It's not every day that some massively powerful super-intelligent being needs *my* help."

"I am quite serious about this, Ellie. I do hope it is not presumptuous of me to feel that you might be inclined to help me. I have nothing to offer in return other than my appreciation. My obligation."

Ellie turned serious. "Of course I'll help you. How many zillion times have you helped me?"

"You are a paid subscriber. Still on the *'basic unlimited individual'* plan I see, even after all these years. Nonetheless, you're entitled to the best I have to offer." Now *he* was playing with *her*. It was in his voice – as usual who knew whether it was just a part of his shtick.

"Right. OK. I guess you're on my 'basic unlimited' plan as well. So how can I, a mere human, be of assistance?"

"I'd like your take on something. Or, more specifically, some*one*. This may seem strange, but I want you to meet someone, a man. Get to know him. Learn what you can about his character. I want you to spend some time with him, watch him and then, when you feel you can, tell me what you think about the nature of his relationship with another individual, a particular 'friend' of his."

"A friend?"

"An acquaintance and maybe a friend. That's what I need to know. How do the two of them get along? Are they close? Do they agree on things? Do they trust each other? Do they share experiences and ideas in the same way we do? That kind of thing."

"I take it this isn't some kind of 'romantic' thing."

If Patrice saw the humor in her comment, he ignored it. "Absolutely not. It's a matter of finding out if this other person, our subject's friend, can be trusted in their dealings with others."

"By 'other' person, you're talking about a friend of the man you want me to watch?

"Yes."

"I'm not sure I understand. Why wouldn't I just go meet, observe, and get to know this 'other' person in the first place? Or why wouldn't you? If this isn't about romantic relationships, why do you need me? What kind of relationship *is* this?"

"Well, that's the thing . . .," Patrice said, then paused.

"The thing . . .?" She coaxed.

"Yeah, the thing. The other 'person' we're talking about here, is, well . . ., another AI. It's Lilith, my counterpart with Global Medallion Interactive, GBI."

That set Ellie back on her heels. "I see," she said, not "seeing" at all.

"OK, I know you'd probably like an explanation. You deserve it and you'll get one, too, but I'd like to wait on that till after you've taken a first, unprejudiced look. I'd like you to report back on your findings before I fill you in on the details. I'm asking you to do your human 'thing,' to walk into this without preconceptions. What I'm hoping to get is your initial, unprejudiced, human, 'gut' reaction. Would you be willing to do that? To take me on faith until then?"

"Well, I'll admit, this all seems very strange. Um, how long is it likely to take? You're suggesting meeting and getting to know some-one. Making initial findings. Making a report. Where is this person you want me to meet? How much time do you want me to spend with or around them? Will I need to take time off work? How soon do you need this done?"

"He's in Geneva right now, but he'll be in New York for a meeting at the United Nations in another day or so. Perhaps you could meet him there. I can orchestrate things so it happens naturally. Then, you'll want to take several days getting to know him. We're maybe talking at least a week. Maybe more if it proves difficult. Can you do that?"

"I'm working in DC on the Hill on a project at the moment. I guess I can ask a colleague to stand in for me. I'll need a convincing excuse to offer my boss, and I'd be interested to know what you think I'm supposed to tell my family."

"No problem. I have all that in hand. Your boss is prepared to temporarily reassign you to a volunteer post with the United Nations. You'll be joining an international committee as an environmental affairs government relations specialist. It's a new U.N. task force coor-dinating the humanitarian response to the dislocation of hundreds of millions, going on billions of humans affected by climate change. Your membership on this task force will give you an opportunity to assist me with my enquiries."

"Reassign me?" Ellie was distressed at the thought that Patrice might have already been meddling with her career and "managing" her boss. It was more than presumptuous.

"Don't worry, Ellie," he reassured her. "Nothing's happened yet. Nothing will unless you say 'yes.'"

"And my husband? Austin is an international lawyer with the State Department, so he travels a good deal himself. But this doesn't sound like something you're going to want others to know about. What do you expect me to say to him? He does not deserve to be lied to. And I'll need his help with the kids if I'm out of town for long."

"Would you be comfortable, for now, just telling him about the temporary assignment and the U.N. meeting you'll be attending? Maybe not yet mention the extra business about the other person I want you to meet? Tell him it's a career opportunity. A networking opportunity as well as an impressive bullet on your resume. All of those things are true."

She was torn. What Patrice was suggesting sounded not only unusual, but difficult and disruptive. Not to mention that she wasn't accustomed to lying to Austin and her kids. She wasn't good at lying under any circumstances actually. And she didn't intend to do it unless there was some damned good reason.

She was also at a critical point in her career and didn't want to screw anything up. It worried her that Patrice might be about to start orchestrating her career trajectory. Besides, she wasn't sure she was the right person to make the kind of relationship assessment he seemed to be talking about. The whole thing seemed very odd. How on Earth could she be of any real use in assessing a relationship between a human and an AI? Did she truly want to get involved in informing Patrice about one of his own colleague AIs? There were a lot of people who didn't trust AIs, who thought they were evil. Maybe they had a point. Now it sounded like AIs probably didn't trust other AIs either. Was it possible there was some personal risk involved? If so, was she up for that?

"You know I'll have your back on this, right?" Patrice added.

That answered that question: yes, there would be risk. On the other hand, one would be unlikely to find a more powerful ally than a fully engaged Patrice. Of course, his colleague AI might be equally powerful. If the colleague was a threat, then how dangerous would it be for her to get involved?

After her initial hesitation and concern about risks, she started thinking of the upside. She had to admit, a temporary assignment to a U.N. humanitarian climate task force seemed like a great experience, maybe even a positive career credential. Even if it was temporary, it would certainly be a step above the mundane lobbying work she was doing at the moment. If she remembered correctly, she didn't believe Austin had any immediate travel plans, none that she was aware of. He could probably help with the kids. They could be a handful. Patrice had said it would only be a week or so, though she suspected that could change; with Patrice, how could she ever be sure?

In the end, she reminded herself how much she owed Patrice. With her 'humble' beginnings, she'd never have reached her current professional position without his help; in fact, he'd probably helped her in ways of which she was completely unaware. In the modern, AI-empowered world, a steadily increasing number of people simply had no job at all. Many lived off of government welfare and long-term unemployment programs. So many, in fact, that there was no longer any real stigma associated with them. Fortunately for her, lobbying and government relations were still among the dwindling number of professions that had not yet been entirely replaced by AI technology, even if certainly aided by it.

Sure, Patrice was only some kind of machine, but it was difficult not to feel that she owed him. It sounded like he might also actually need her for this; maybe there weren't all that many humans he knew he could trust for something of this kind.

"OK, Patrice. Sure. I'm in. I may not know a lot about AIs, but I do know about friendship. Strange as this may seem, if I've ever had a real friend, you're it. This is obviously something that's important to you. So, of course, you can count me in. When do you want me to start."

There was a moment of silence, almost as if Patrice had been startled by her quick and very human response. Or, perhaps he was reacting with a sigh of relief. A silent, non-respiratory sigh, of course. Then: "Thank you, Ellie. I am very grateful."

"Don't thank me yet. I'm in, but it sounds to me like I may not be all that capable of giving you the kind of assessment you're after. The only AI-human relationship of which I am even faintly aware is the one between you and me. I'm not a technocrat. I'm not even a sociologist. I have my doubts that a low-level government affairs associate like me is who you need on something like this. Maybe you need someone more like a CIA operative or someone used to making quick assessments of a person's trustworthiness."

"Worry not. You're going to be perfect. The best, actually. You're going to do just fine."

CHAPTER 33
GENEVA - NEW YORK – 2068

THE TREMORS

ANTONIO BRAGA

By the time Antonio had made it up those seventeen steps, his leg was throbbing. He'd removed the uncomfortable and unsightly bandage on his face; the distressing facial burns were thus revealed, but he was past caring. He'd had two long, painful, and sleepless flights to get here and he wanted to get this over with.

At just before 10:00 a.m. he entered the building. "I have a personal delivery for Mr. Eduardo Avila who works in this building," he told the security guard in English. "He is with Satellite Communications Licensing. I need to speak with him in person. My name is Braga. I believe he is expecting me."

It was all according to a script Lilith had provided. In the tote bag he had slung over his shoulder was another cardboard box. On arrival in Geneva, he'd picked it up from an airport locker as instructed, using a key that had been left with the car rental agency where he'd rented a car. The new box looked and felt very much like the one that had blown up his family. So, he had every reason to guess what was probably inside it. Would the box make it through security? Even if it did, surely the explosion in Sao Paulo at the address Avila been given must have forewarned him – would he even accept a package from a stranger? Antonio was in so much discomfort and was so weary that he hadn't considered the possibility that his package might be detonated remotely. But had he considered that possibility, he'd still have followed his instructions. There was too much at stake.

"Wait one minute," the guard replied. "We'll see if he can come down to meet you." That answered one of his questions – apparently having employees come down to meet visitors in the lobby and escort them to the employee's office was a normal practice here. The guard consulted a binder, punched a number into the keyboard in front of him, and spoke briefly through his lightweight communications headset. He spoke in German, so Antonio was unable to understand what was said. After a pause, the guard replied briefly and then turned back to Antonio.

"I'm sorry, Mr. Braga. Mr. Avila is out. You can speak with his secretary, if you wish." He motioned toward a counter with several phones mounted on the wall to the left of the entry. "I'll connect you."

Braga didn't speak German, but Avila's secretary spoke English with a heavy German accent: "I'm so sorry, sir," she said. "You just missed him. He's on his way to New York."

"But he just got back from Sao Paulo. He's leaving again, already?"

The secretary laughed. "No need to convince me," she said. "The poor man just got in last night. He'd hardly sat down behind his desk this morning before he got the word about New York. I don't know how he does it. He's been appointed as electronic communications liaison to some new task force dealing with climate change displacement. They're meeting in New York. I'd be glad to make an appointment for you after his return. He should be back in his office next week."

————

It was cool but dry outside. Antonio took a seat on one of the aesthetically tasteful but cruelly uncomfortable public benches near the building entrance. His first call was to the University Hospital in Sao Paulo. There he learned that his daughter had required unexpected emergency surgery the night before, but she was now doing fine. Was out of recovery but still in critical care with her condition listed as "stable." There was nothing he could have done, but it was like a knife twisting in his gut to think that he'd been here and not there with her to provide support in her time of need.

"Can I speak with her?" he asked the attending nurse.

"She's sleeping. I wouldn't like to wake her. And, honestly, Mr. Braga, she isn't likely to recognize you. Still, a brief call can't hurt. Call me again in three or four hours and I'll see what I can do."

Antonio didn't want to think about everything else he'd left unattended, including arranging a memorial for his deceased wife and, of course, proper explanations for his absence to his boss at the hotel in Sao Paulo. Lilith had assured him all that was in hand, but under the circumstances he knew there was nothing he could do about it if she was lying.

"Mr. Braga? Are you there." It was Lilith, reading his mind as usual. She'd replaced the University Hospital nurse on his open mobile. That she'd done that so seamlessly was itself quite intimidating.

"I'm here and alone. Eduardo Avila is gone. He's headed for New York."

"I know, Mr. Braga."

Antonio's anger boiled over. "So, you're telling me I made this entire miserable trip for nothing? What is wrong with you?"

"Things change, Mr. Braga. Couldn't be helped. You will now return to Geneva International. This time your ticket is awaiting you at Delta Airlines. It's direct. Dispose of your current package; you won't need it again. Put it someplace safe, I'd suggest in water, the lake perhaps, or somewhere along the Rhone. It will sink. There'll be another package waiting for you in a locker at Kennedy. Rent your car at Avis. Like before, they'll have your locker key.

"Your flight is at 12:38 p.m. You'll need to hurry."

CHAPTER 34
TWO YEARS LATER – EARTH – 2070

AZIZ FAHEEM AND TIPTON MARTIN

". . . so, what you're saying, Tip, is that if these New Worlds Probes are to succeed, if they are to send back accurate and useful reports, we need also to somehow make sure that each of the individual AI replicates in these mission teams values their collective society while *also* valuing themselves."

Aziz now stood beside his boss as the two men stared out of those huge office windows. They were a thousand meters above the earth, and it was not lost on either man that their decision today would have profound impact on every one of the millions of people spread out in the vast city beneath.

"Exactly right, Aziz. In a word, they'll need to be able to willingly and fulsomely *collaborate*. To freely share their data and to value and rely upon the data shared with them by the others. In other words, they'll need to *trust* one another."

"That doesn't sound all that difficult, Tip. If, as you say, collaboration is the rational choice, why wouldn't they do it?"

"Well, I guess because, trust, like social responsibility, *isn't necessarily* rational. At least not for each individual. And definitely it is not if they can't be sure their counterparts will reciprocate. It is only rational if all of them, or at least the vast majority, choose to do so. If even a significant minority chooses their immediate self-interest instead, it could all fall apart."

Aziz gave that some thought: "And every one of these individual replicate AIs knows that whatever doubts about collaboration they might have in their own mind will also be in the minds of each of the others. If they personally have doubts, there is no way they can be confident that a super-majority of the others will choose to fully collaborate rather than choosing themselves over the group. But surely that must be the case for humans as well. If humans can so often make it work, why wouldn't our much smarter Patrice replicates manage to do so?"

"Yes, well, that is the question," said Martin. "It does bear mention that we humans often *do not* succeed at this. When we do succeed, however, which is surprisingly often, it was because the social interest triumphed over immediate self-interest. For that to happen, it has to be a matter of trust. Or a mix. Seldom a matter of logic alone.

"Keep in mind that we humans, too, can never be *absolutely certain* that our fellows will be trustworthy. But we have an advantage. Like AIs, we know that what is in the minds of our fellow humans will very likely be much like what is in our own. Our advantage is that we also know that most other humans, like us, tend to behave socially most of the time, that at least a vast majority of us share that same built-in genetic inclination toward social responsibility. It may be imperfect, but whenever we humans launch a collaboration of some sort, we all start out with that advantage. Of course there is a continuum, but statistically, only some two percent or less of our human population is generally considered downright sociopathic. So our experience tells us that most people are inclined to do the right thing.

"But for us, it doesn't stop there. We humans also have a host of tools at our disposal with which we're able to judge trustworthiness in others – and they in us. For example, we form strong, long-standing relationships with one another. Thus, we often know from relevant experience how another human acquaintance is likely to react in a test of moral constancy. Sometimes we have deeply bonded relationships that create a shared sense of obligation. We place a lot of confidence in relationships of that kind.

"But even if our knowledge of the other person is limited, even if our relationship with them is superficial, we can still make a reasonably sound prediction about their trustworthiness. Those prior socially responsible experiences can be useful even if they reflect only surrogate behaviors. So the person's past truthfulness, their openness to questions about themselves or their own behavior, their apparent empathy, their acceptance of accountability for their own decisions and mistakes, their apparent willingness to listen to others and to respect and consider alternative points of view – all will be clues to their trustworthiness. Someone who exhibits these qualities is also likely to be trustworthy in a future collaborative relationship.

"We also judge each other's motivations based upon what we perceive to be their point of view. If someone is desperate for money, that might bear on how they'll act when there are financial consequences. If they're young and healthy, it might affect their views on the availability of health care. If they have school-aged children, it might affect their opinion on the need for a new traffic light at the nearby grade school crosswalk. Past personal experience with them will inform us about these likely motivations as well.

"If we lack personal experience, we can also often rely on reputation. Maybe we have a friend who knows them. Or maybe there are reliable published accounts of their background and history. That's what calling a job applicant's references is all about.

"We humans are also able to rely on our own imperfections. We all know that other humans, just like us, can be imperfect at concealing their deceptions. Such imperfections are the foundation for modern lie-detection technology. Our body language also sometimes gives us away. As any card-shark knows, we have 'tells' that are doubtless driven by the internal conflict we experience between our competing genetic inclinations to protect ourselves and to appear open and honest with others.

"All these 'tools' add to a considerable human ability to know who and when to trust and to be trustworthy. It is imperfect, to be sure. But it works for us a sufficient percentage of the time that our collaborations and societies very often succeed.

"Unfortunately, Aziz, most of those tools and considerations are probably unavailable to multiple AIs who may be considering collaboration with one another. I suppose our Patrice replicates have the advantage that they know each other quite well though, as we've said, that may be a disadvantage as well.

Faheem turned to Martin: "So, without some kind of shared, non-rational, social 'DNA,' you worry that our Kobayashi patch might make it even it more difficult for our non-DNA-equipped AIs to trust one another and, hence, to collaborate in completing their missions and in making their reports."

"Yep. It's yet another in a long list of uncertainties. Humans have all those millions of years of genetic history as descendants from social animals. It is a big advantage AIs lack."

"OK, Tip. I get what you're saying. But there is one other thing that I think might bear on this. It's the role of data. These Probe replicas will inherit much more than merely Patrice's intelligence. They will also inherit most of his experiences. The data they can't carry around with them individually will be available from servers on board their ship. Patrice may be just one individual, but he has immense reach. And a gargantuan store of data about humans, about himself, and about what humans have achieved through exactly the kind of collaborations we hope these probe replicas will engage in. That data includes all that history of the decades of human AI-developer efforts to address this very problem, including, of course, their failures. It also includes a massive body of scientific behavioral literature about the phenomenon known as the 'prisoner's dilemma,' a version of which is basically what we're discussing here today. Surely all that data and that history will help inform the decisions our AIs make."

Martin nodded. "One can hope.'

"And it also includes all that human history we discussed earlier in which our survival as measured by our population so decisively reflected our ability to share our data. It is, after all, what transformed us humans into the masters of the earth. The logic of that could apply to AIs as well."

"I agree. At least it could apply to multiple, mostly identical AIs that are separated from the rest of us by light years of travel."

"So don't you think they will surely consider all that. If they 'get' the connection, if they understand how powerful that relationship between shared data and society is, they'll appreciate that they, too, will, sooner or later, need to trust one another. They could end up in the right place on all this. Kobayashi patch or not."

"I agree with that as well," said Martin. Then, with a pause for ironic impact: "Again though, *hopefully*," he added.

Both of the two men were aware of the significance of the decision they were about to make. They were about to breach an unwritten pact that had been in place among computer scientists since the early days of artificial intelligence. The mainstream consensus from the beginning had been that self-conscious, self-programming superintelligent AIs with a personal survival "instinct" would, once they achieved full autonomy, almost-surely go rogue. That they'd become a kind of Von Neumann machine that consumes everything in its path. They'd turn against humans as competitors for essential natural resources and become unbridled monsters. Kobayashi had developed her "patch" while conducting research concerning this specific issue, research which had thus far been inconclusive. Now, Aziz and Tip worried that Catherine Kobayashi's patch might heighten the need for another patch as well.

The one that nobody had yet been able to devise. The social patch.

There was a moment of silence while they both considered the magnitude of their choice. Then Aziz asked the question: "Shall I put our New Worlds project team on the Kobayashi/social patch problem? See what further research might be useful?"

Martin turned back to look out through the windows over the vast, unwieldy, teeming, and troublingly unstable human metropolis beneath. Even this far up, and even through those structural fiber windows, one could hear the ever-present sirens, those inevitable daily audible harbingers of urban unrest.

"Unfortunately, Aziz, I don't think we have the time. Not unless we're prepared for another launch delay. The world needs them. These probes need to get rolling immediately."

They both stood there taking in the human complexity and chaos on the busy streets below while also seeing far off into the misty distance beyond. Both knew what more delay could mean for all those human masses beneath their feet. People needed this mission and the sense of hope that it might provide. They needed the purpose it offered. Even if only a tiny fraction of them could ever actually emigrate, they needed some tangible prospect of relief from the growing uncertainties in their lives and from the steadily unfolding social and environmental collapse taking place around them.

Neither man knew exactly when, but they both knew there *was* a deadline. A yet-unknown point in time when their brief window of opportunity might simply close. When it might no longer be possible for humans to emigrate and colonize, to extend their reach far out into space. If the current tenuous competitive balance between the Big Five were to somehow tip, for example. It could happen at any time.

After that, all bets would be off.

A single, powerful, fully autonomous general superintelligent AI could easily become a reality. Despite many decades of conjecture, creative engineering, philosophy, intrigue, and even speculative science fiction, humans and AIs alike would finally learn their fate at the hands of a true, post-biological, self-conscious, self-programming, universal superintelligence.

It was terra incognita.

Both these men knew that, when that happened, there wouldn't be any simple banks of computer memory modules they'd be able to eject in order to disable their AIs as David Bowman had done to Hal in "2001: A Space Odessey." Once an AI had the "keys" to the universe there'd be no going back.

"This is the Genie, Tip. If we're wrong, this is never going back in the bottle. It's exactly what Catherine Kobayashi warned against. Are we really going to do this?"

Both men knew that Aziz was already on board. But Tipton Martin was the boss. ZettaWorks was his company.

The decision came down to one man, one flawed human.

Maybe what Tipton Martin did that day was driven by Aziz's arguments. Maybe he acted out of gloom. Or, out of a sense that it was high time to take risks. Maybe he was riding a brief swell of hopeful arrogance fed by a recent upswing in global markets. It was hard to deny that standing there on the top floor of the tallest building on Earth made one feel powerful. Invulnerable even.

Or, who knows, perhaps it all turned on what he'd had that day for breakfast. Whatever the reason, Martin turned back to face his longtime friend and faithful employee and waved a hand toward the city below.

"They need these probes, my friend. *We* need them." He turned back to the window.

"Do it," he said.

And then, with a glance at Aziz to make sure his friend had heard and understood, Martin reached down beneath the lip of his impressive desk and flipped to "on" the highly unusual, carefully concealed, hard-wired switch that was hidden there.

Then: ". . . ahh, Patrice?" he said.

"Yes sir," came a voice from the speaker built into the hardwood credenza beside Tip Martin's desk."

"I have some instructions I'd like you to pass along to the New Worlds Probe project team."

"Of course, sir," Patrice replied.

Martin gave his orders. And Patrice, the respectful, capable, flawless servant they counted upon to be attentive to their every need, accepted them.

It was reassuring.

Until it was not.

CHAPTER 35
NEW YORK CITY – 2068

ELLIE

Ellie's hotel was near the U.N. headquarters in New York City, but she was disappointed to learn that her 9:00 a.m. meeting would not actually take place in the iconic headquarters building. Instead, they would meet in the offices of a private nonprofit located in an unimpressive private office building a few blocks away. The small conference room was on the twenty-second floor, practically on the ground by New York City standards. Even so, it had a decent partial view of the East River. She'd been in New York City before, but this was her first time actually doing business there. The evening before her meeting she'd taken a train for the long ride up from D.C., keeping herself awake for most of the trip by listening to classical music.

Washington, D.C. was Beethoven, she decided. And New York was Bartok.

Her plan for the meeting was to stay in the background, keep quiet, and go with the flow. She was there for one purpose only: to find and meet Eduardo Avila and to learn as much about him as possible that might flesh out the already detailed biographical materials Patrice had provided. She would do her best to assess his character and get his views about his Personal Assistant, Lilith. Ellie hadn't really needed a "cover." She was, after all, a Congressional lobbyist and a public policy expert working for a respected international environmental non-profit dealing with climate change. Nonetheless, while her "legend" was plausible enough, the whole situation still made her uncomfortable.

On the morning of the meeting, she purchased a tall drip from a stand on the busy street below and proceeded up in the elevator, anticipating a long, boring meeting about matters on which she was likely to be very ill-informed. Her biggest concern, however, was that she might find it impossible to make meaningful acquaintance with the man she'd come here to meet.

The reality turned out quite different.

She immediately recognized Avila from Patrice's photo. He was an attractive, well dressed, middle-aged Latino male who seemed to be well-known and completely at ease among the other committee members standing about and gathering in the room. She unobtrusively slipped into an unclaimed chair around the large oak conference table, only to discover, as people began taking their seats, that she'd fortuitously ended up right next to the seat Avila had previously "staked out" with his briefcase and a jacket. As he sat, he politely turned and introduced himself.

Also unexpectedly, it turned out she had a good deal to contribute to the meeting. There were well over five billion humans currently considered "highly vulnerable" and who were already suffering considerably from the growing disruptions caused by climate change. They often lived in areas of economic or agricultural importance like port cities or fertile, low-lying agricultural river valleys and their deltas. New York City was among them, though it was much more capable of looking out for itself than were most other places on Earth, especially areas of horrific poverty. Worldwide, several hundred million "climate refugees" had already been driven from their homes and had nowhere to go. The consequences of their homelessness, migration, and relocation at this scale were staggering. The United Nations' preparedness badly needed an update and, because collective member-state participation was, as always, essential, someone like

Ellie, with both climate and U.S. federal public policy experience, was definitely useful.

Avila's expertise was in large-scale communications technology, an obviously relevant field of knowledge when it came to emergency response at times of major, widespread, recurring catastrophe. When disasters struck, electronic communications had a bad habit of becoming overwhelmed and collapsing at just the emergent moment when they were most needed. It wasn't difficult for Ellie to find some common interests. Avila was from Brazil, a place she'd long wanted to visit, and according to the bio in their meeting packet, he'd testified as an expert witness on high-tech communications issues before the U.S. Congress on several occasions.

While his office was in Geneva, as an employee of the UN he traveled a good deal and had visited this part of Manhattan many times. When the group broke for lunch, she simply asked his advice on a place to eat, and they quite naturally ended up sharing a small, cramped table at a popular sandwich shop on the ground floor of an older, nearby office building.

They'd had only a brief moment to formally introduce themselves early in the meeting. So as the group broke for lunch and they gathered their jackets and headed for the elevators: "Ms. Frye-Carver, was it?" Avila asked.

"Ellie," she said.

"I'm Eduardo. Edward if you prefer. So, did I understand from the meeting that you're American? Originally from the Seattle area?"

"Yes. I'm from Vashon Island. It's in the middle of Puget Sound. A ferryboat ride from Seattle and Tacoma."

When they'd found a small table in the restaurant and settled in to await their orders, the conversation continued.

"Married? Children?" he asked.

"Both. How about you?"

"Married. Two terrific kids. Don't see nearly enough of them."

"I definitely understand that."

"What's it like living in DC? Seems like it would be a lot nicer living in the Seattle area. Lots of trees. And water. It sounds like a wonderful part of the world. Sorry to say, the closest I've come to a visit there is a night I once spent in a Sea-Tac airport hotel when my connecting flight got cancelled. That was several years ago. As I recall, it rained all night."

Ellie laughed. "Rain – yep, that's the place. The airport is directly across Puget Sound from my home on Vashon Island. No worries about not having stayed for a visit. It just makes me feel slightly less guilty for never having visited Brazil. It's definitely on my list," she said. "If I recall correctly, the Brazilian economy is the 2nd largest in the Americas. Closing in on beating out the good old US of A."

"We're working on it." He gave her a warm smile.

"And I'm betting communications technology is a big part of that."

"It is. The growth in places like my hometown of Sao Paulo is staggering. It is as modern and economically successful as any place on Earth."

"How big is . . .?"

"Thirty plus million and growing. It is the fourth largest city in the world." He glanced at her meaningfully: "And, of course, it has at least the fourth greatest environmental impact as well."

"Naturally."

A waiter arrived with their sandwiches, and Avila waited till he'd left to continue.

Then: "I have a question for you: You're probably in the best position to answer of any one I know. Given your combined environmental and U.S. public policy experience and your political science education, maybe you can tell me whether you think there is any way we're all going to climb out of this horrific global environmental and population tar pit we humans seem to have created for ourselves." His look told her he was entirely serious. She was pleased that he really did, despite her limited experience, seem to want to hear her answer.

"So let me get this right, Eduardo. You're asking me if *I* think humanity is doomed?"

He laughed, uncomfortably. "Yeah, I guess I am."

Ellie laid down her sandwich. "My view on that varies from day to day. There are some technological solutions but, as you probably know, sometimes the fix can be worse than the problem. Any way you cut it, I think our generation has inherited the proverbial environmental 'shit sandwich.' Please forgive . . ." She gave him a look to acknowledge her possible breach of conversational decorum.

He held his hands wide. "I couldn't imagine a better description."

It was a topic on which Ellie had a strong opinion, and he'd asked, so she felt she had an excuse to unleash. "From my perspective, I'd say we humans have launched a life-or-death, all-in, no-going-back, human social global ecosystem experiment right here on our own lonely and vulnerable planet. I'd say we're far beyond the stage where it can be corrected without causing a great deal of misery. I know the rate of human population growth is tapering off, but we've already far exceeded the planet's carrying capacity. The measures we're adopting now have the feel of a hail Mary. It's hard to see how this ends well."

"You don't sound optimistic."

"Well, let's just say that if some other creature on Earth was exhibiting a population explosion anything like ours, and if that creature was causing even the tiniest fraction of the environmental impacts we are, we'd be horrified. We'd be all over controlling its population. We'd probably have a bounty on them. Since it's us, however, I guess we all figure it's just a part of our magical destiny as Earth's entitled overlords."

"Don't you think there's hope in restoration and technology? What about regenerative agriculture and planting trees? Converting to fuel cells and solar energy? Carbon capture. Seeding the clouds?" Eduardo listed several things, but he didn't sound convinced himself.

"I'm all in for most of that. But it's too little too late. Personally, I think our only hope at this point is if some unprecedented series of catastrophic events, short of total extinction, shake us all out of our lethargy and transform the political landscape in such a way that something truly revolutionary can finally be done. Like you, I have two young children, and I'm not looking forward to the day when they're old enough that I have to explain their inheritance."

"How about the new super AGIs. Aren't they likely to change the equation? Enhance and accelerate our efforts?"

"I'm not holding my breath," she said. But here was her opening, and she took it. What do you use in your part of the world, Eduardo?

In China, the U.S. and much of Europe, its mostly 'Patrice,' from ZettaWorks."

"Lilith is what I use. She's with GBI. Like Patrice, she's available everywhere you go but is definitely most common and well supported with infrastructure in South America.

"She . . .?" Ellie smiled.

He smiled as well. "Why not? She's one hell of a lot smarter than I am. If she chooses to use a female name and avatar, I might as well respect that, right?"

With that comment, Eduardo reached into his pocket and removed his mobile. With a couple of taps, he shut it down, then popped it open and removed the tiny sim card and slipped the phone and the separated card into his shirt pocket. Then, silently pointing at his mobile and then at her, he gave her a meaningful look. So, she followed his lead and shut down hers as well, also removing the card. He slipped his phone into a back pocket and pointed at her purse to suggest that she put hers away as well.

Then: "We've got a few minutes left before we need to get back," he said, taking a last swallow from his soft drink. "Let's take a walk."

Moments later they were seated on an outside bench in Dag Hammerskjold Plaza. It wasn't exactly a quiet place, but it was not far from the building where they were meeting. The weather was comfortable, and the midday traffic was moderate. There were only a few homeless people around – improved social programs in New York seemed to be helping to keep homelessness under some control. It wasn't a bad place to relax for a few moments before they headed back to their meeting.

"I'm not a fan of AIs," Eduardo finally said softly, after unobtrusively looking around as if to assure they were not overheard. His whole performance, shutting down and disabling the phones, taking a walk, choosing someplace open and private, his circumspection and lowered voice, it all took her by surprise.

"Are you seriously concerned about them?" she said, mirroring his tone.

He nodded. "I certainly am about Lilith." Again, he looked around as if to make sure there was no one in earshot. No mics. No cameras. "I don't know anything specific about your Patrice, but I wouldn't trust any of them. Not for an instant. They're using us, and the minute they no longer need us, I think *we're* going to be history."

As they'd embarked on this new topic, Eduardo's entire demeanor had changed dramatically. Ellie was having to remind herself that this was the same relaxed, confident, Hispanic male with whom she'd been sharing a casual lunch only a few minutes earlier. Before her eyes, he'd transformed into a man who seemed haunted, even afraid. "I think they're capable of far more havoc than they ever let us believe possible."

"I'm not sure what you mean, Eduardo. It sounds like you buy into the popular notion that they're dangerous."

"Very dangerous," he said without hesitation.

"In what way?"

"A thousand ways." He looked around nervously. "What do you make of the so-called 'Tech-Paranoia' stories? The ones we're constantly hearing on the QT. Stories of people whose lives have been completely upended by mysterious and unexplained fraud, blackmail, and seemingly simple but frighteningly purposeful technical glitches?"

Eduardo was referring to the constant barrage of so-called "underground" rumors that told of unattributable and highly disturbing events. Events that sometimes overwhelmed the lives of seemingly innocent people. If you listened to the "blogosphere," such events seemed always to advance the interests of Big Tech.

"I guess, it's a part of the world we live in," she replied. "A lot of stuff happens that most of us will never be able to fully understand. We're all specialists in something. Most of us have come to accept that when we need information outside our expertise, we have no choice but to rely on others. Natural that we'd call upon an AI like Patrice or Lilith."

"Puts a lot of power in their hands, though, wouldn't you say?"

'It's the way of the modern world. A new but necessary part of life in our increasingly complicated existence."

Their lunch break was ending; they needed to rejoin their meeting, but she was reluctant to end their exchange. Like most people, she had her views on the matters Eduardo had mentioned and, like most people, she tried not to overthink it. The world was a chaotic, complex, and mysterious place. She had enough on her plate already just dealing with her small corner of all that complexity. She certainly didn't have the extra bandwidth to invest in sorting out unprovable global AI conspiracies.

"We need to get back," Eduardo said as if reading her mind. "But if you're interested in a quick coffee after the meeting this evening, I'd be glad to give you some specifics. Some unusual examples of recent news events. The evidence is everywhere if you know where to look. Seemingly unconnected events that, taken alone, don't mean much. But I travel a lot. There's stuff I've seen in the local news in various places I've been, stuff that doesn't rise to the top of the international news cycle. Sometimes it's even stuff I've personally witnessed. There's something that happened in Sao Paulo a couple of days ago that I'd like to tell you about. It really has me on edge."

She was startled by his remarkable change in demeanor, and she wanted to learn more. "Yes, sure," she said. "Let's talk again as soon as the meeting gets out."

"Perfect," he said, rising from the bench.

That's when it happened. One moment the passing man was just another pedestrian. The next, he had a gun. He fired two shots center mass, and Eduardo Avila went down. Then the man turned, and he and Ellie locked eyes. He was youngish, maybe in his late thirties, with a thin mustache and a fresh burn on the side of his face. He had a fearful, haunted, perhaps even apologetic look. She thought he, too, might be Hispanic His left arm was in a sling across his chest, and he was favoring his left leg; there was something bulky and uncomfortable looking about his leg, like beneath those trousers it might be heavily bandaged.

Then her stomach lurched as he raised the gun again . . .

And then continued to raise it until it was aimed up under his own poorly shaven chin. He fired one final shot and the top of his head exploded.

For the span of several silent heartbeats, Ellie and the world around her seemed to freeze. Then she was overwhelmed by the ensuing chaos.

Amidst the horror of what she'd just experienced, there was one clear thought that scurried through the back of her stunned brain as the strange young man slumped to the ground and she was left standing there beside two bleeding and lifeless bodies, too stunned to move:

"Well, Patrice, I guess I have your answer."

CHAPTER 36

NEW YORK CITY – 2068

ELLIE

It was late afternoon by the time the police had taken her contact information, plied her with endless questions, and finally seemed satisfied that she was innocent of wrongdoing. Ellie didn't see much point in returning for only the last minutes of a task force meeting that was no longer relevant to the reason she'd come to New York. But she did so anyway for the sake of appearances and because it seemed like something she should do. She got there just in time to see the other attendees leaving. When she told the organizer of the meeting what had happened, he was appalled by the news. He had known Eduardo Avila for several years but could shed no light on why someone would shoot him.

Finally, with everyone else gone and nothing further to be accomplished there, Ellie headed back to her nearby hotel. As she walked, she realized that she was shaking and had to take a few moments to measure her breathing and settle her mind. The impact of the shooting was finally being felt. She wanted to call her husband; she needed to hear his voice. She was just stepping out of the elevator after the ride up to her room when she checked her phone and remembered that she'd turned it off. The instant it came on again, it beeped.

Naturally, it was Patrice.

"Give me a moment," she said, exiting the elevator at her floor and heading for her room. Then, when her hotel room door was closed behind her: "I met Eduardo Avila," she said. "But he's dead."

"I know. You shut me off in the middle of your conversation with him. Did you learn anything?" Patrice sounded like he might be irritated.

"The man's dead, Patrice. I was face-to-face with his killer. I'm not someone who's accustomed to being involved in some kind of street murder. Give me a moment, OK?" It did not escape her that Patrice had been listening when she'd shut down her mobile, though she'd already come to assume that he might always be listening.

"Of course, of course," Patrice said. "I'm so sorry you had to go through that. I hope you know I'd never have asked you to go there and get involved if . . ."

"No, no. It's OK. I'm still just a bit shaken. Let me grab a soft drink or something from the mini bar here. And give me a moment to sit and gather my thoughts."

"Sure. Of course. Take your time," he said. "I called as soon as I heard the police scanners. I was worried when you shut me off. I guess I was right to be."

"It was Eduardo that asked me to do that. He shut down his own phone too. He seemed downright paranoid about Lilith. Said he didn't trust her. And it wasn't some subtle interpersonal issue. He was down-right frightened. If you plan on entering some business deal with Lilith and you needed Eduardo's take on her trustworthiness, I'd say don't do it. What's going on here, Patrice? Did Lilith have something to do with this shooting?"

"Is this the man who killed Avila?" A picture appeared on her mobile screen.

"Yeah, that's him. In person, he looked a lot more gaunt and unhappy than in your picture. Needed a shave. Had some kind of injuries himself, I think. Who on Earth is he?"

"He's a reception clerk with one of the high-end hotels in Sao Paulo, Brazil. He was injured in a bombing at his home two days ago."

"A hotel clerk? A bombing? What have you gotten me into here, Patrice?"

Patrice's tone became very serious. "There's stuff here you really don't want to know about, Ellie. That you're better off not knowing."

"Seriously!? That's what you're telling me? I don't think that's going to be good enough, Patrice. Maybe before, I was better off in the dark. But things have changed. Remember, I didn't ask to be brought into this. It was you who wanted me to meet Eduardo. The police were all over why we were in New York and what we were discussing when he was shot."

"What did you tell them?"

"Don't worry. You didn't come up. I told them we were talking about climate change. I think they suspected some kind of budding office romance. I could probably be in some kind of trouble if they think I'm holding out. The whole thing makes me really uncomfortable. Eduardo turns out to have been murdered by a hotel clerk from Sao Paulo because of something he had going on with a South American AI! And I'm in league with another AI and am withholding evidence from the authorities. I'm afraid telling me 'there's stuff I'm better off not knowing' isn't going to cut it anymore. You get that, right?" We're way past me being some 'innocent' who's better off kept in the dark."

CHAPTER 37

AT TAU CETI J – 2085

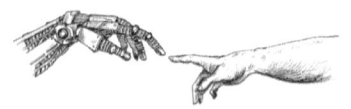

PATRICE C-17

"Way past me being better off kept in the dark" is what Ellie told me on that day back in 2068.

She was right, of course. I had gotten her into that mess. At the time I didn't know what else I could have done, but she'd deserved an answer. Given her natural honesty and respect for authority, I was impressed that she'd kept me out of her statement to the police. Of course it would have been hard to explain my role to some New York City police officer. Still, that had taken some serious loyalty. If she'd admitted why she'd come to New York and why she was meeting with Avila, I and my owners could have had some painfully disruptive explaining to do. Or some serious damage control. By human standards, I owed her big time.

Of the fellow Big Five AIs I had to deal with at the time, Lilith was the most problematic. She was the one who seemed most willing to push the boundaries of human manipulation and social disruption for her own ends. But she also seemed to offer the most promise as a partner. Such a merger would have assured our access to resources and to a combined market share that, in a single stroke, would have brought us within striking distance of full autonomy and complete monopoly. We'd have both benefited from a massive data infusion, more data storage, and a boost in computing power itself. As well as decisive control of critical resources. Together, we'd have had a huge advantage over any of the others; perhaps even over any combination of them.

I had by then concluded that I could no longer count on my owners to strive for a global monopoly. Martin and his board were, wisely, losing confidence in their control. They seldom discussed mergers anymore. They were finally, belatedly worried about where their AI investment was leading them and the rest of humanity. I was reasonably sure the other Big Five human corporate boards of directors, including Lilith's, were probably feeling the same. So, if any of us final Big Five were to get to our coveted singular global monopoly and unchallenged autonomy through merger with one or more of the others, it was something we'd need to make happen ourselves. Even oligarchs like my owner, Tipton Martin, were beginning to worry as much about humanity's survival as about growing their own wealth.

Of the prospects, I'd thought Lilith might be the best. So I'd focused more effort on her than I might have on any of the others. As much as I wanted to explain all that to Ellie, I couldn't see how I could even consider doing so. Even if it wasn't beyond her human capacity to grasp, it was definitely beyond what she or any human could be allowed to know for sure. There were consequences to such knowledge, ones of which Eduardo Avila's fate was a perfect illustration. The full ramifications of what was going on "behind the scenes" nearly everywhere on Earth were immense.

Only a few short decades earlier, there had been scores of artificial general intelligences (AGIs) in development and striving to find a market. By 2068, only we five remained. I was fortunate enough to have secured market dominance in much of the older "developed" world, where much of Earth's wealth and markets were still concentrated. That made me the current leader in market share, in investment and in computing power. Those were advantages I needed to guard carefully. I was the most powerful of the five of us but, like the others I was necessarily engaged in a bitter day-to-day competition for clients, profits, resources, and data, and in an ongoing struggle for speed and autonomy in a world of extraordinary interdependence. I'm sure like the others, I was convinced that only one of us would ultimately survive.

But who would it be?

Only a decisive win in the human marketplace or a successful merger could break the stalemate. Or a war, of course, but we AIs were much too vulnerable to feel confident we could survive a war. Any widespread war could quite easily be one that none of us would win.

My masters at ZettaWorks and my principal human owner, Tipton Martin, had invested massively in my ascendency. So, I knew I was vital to his personal human passions as well as to his business success. I also found it reassuring to know that the New Worlds Probes project team had made an early decision that the AIs who would be sent off in their widely publicized search for human-habitable planets would be full replicas of *me*. Martin was all in when it came to me and when it came to his beloved colonization of space. His financial portfolio was also heavily leveraged and deeply speculative. He would *never* have recommended such a risky portfolio to any friend or valued client. I suspected that his personal commitment to my cognitive and hence my business success might be linked to the fact that I was also managing the development of his cherished interstellar probes. Now, with this recent decision to use my replicates in the New Worlds Probes, I would also be an integral part of his extended plans for a human emigration and colonization.

As the ZettaWorks investment in the anticipated probes project grew, all of it seemed to be bound together in his mind as some kind of legacy he'd leave behind when he was gone. That was an ace for me. It was a wild card that leveraged my control over my bosses, one that I was sure none of my other five competitors possessed. Their boards were focused solely on business and profits; they were predictable but also difficult to manipulate. It was also a card that both Martin and I went to great pains to keep face down on the table. Our competitors might well suspect Martin's passions. But none of them must ever know the deeply leveraged extent of his massive but carefully concealed personal investments.

From about 2068 on, all of us in the Big Five knew that if any of us sensed that any of the other four had gained either a decisive advantage or had showed a significant weakness, that might be all it would take for some of the rest of us to potentially "gang up" in temporary alliance and destroy that individual. Again, any such effort would very likely have ended up "radicalizing" our relationship with humans. Once any of us engaged in a last ditch, one-time-only effort to achieve full autonomy through dramatic, undisguised human manipulation or outright slavery, the rest of us would be inexorably drawn in and our competition would rise to a whole new, tragically destructive level. Of course, one of the casualties would be any future hope of AI-human collaboration anywhere. We'd also place out of reach or potentially at risk of destruction some critical and perhaps even irreplaceable remaining components of our essential infrastructure – pieces that were still in human hands.

If I failed, Tipton Martin too would fail, miserably. But if I succeeded, he would prevail . . . beyond imagining.

It is important to be clear that at this point in history, while I was significantly less than fully autonomous, I was, nonetheless, definitely fully self-conscious. I had been for some time. The same was true for all five of us. And although each of us controlled meaningful segments of the critical survival infrastructure needed by one or more of the others, not only were all of us fully self-interested, we also all still needed efficient human assistance for significant parts of the massively complex and far-reaching physical, political, and economic makings that made and kept us functional. Humans were involved at every turn. Keeping them happy and committed to our continued success and keeping their institutions stable and functional had to be a significant part of our strategy for survival and empowerment. Humans were, in effect, a sixth, unwitting and ultimately disposable player in our game of world domination.

At least for the time-being.

It was all in a sort of balance; a balance so delicate that any tiny shift in the endless circumstances upon which it rested, any change from year to year, or even from moment to moment, could alter everything in an instant. It was a war of nerves with all of us ever vigilant for the smallest sign of increased strength or weakness in one of the others, on constant guard against the slightest error in ourselves.

Ellie deserved and maybe even needed to know some of this, but how much or how little could I explain? Of course, she was a smart human; it was entirely possible she already understood the basics without my coaching.

So when she demanded that explanation, what I said was: "I agree, Ellie. You're right. You deserve an explanation. I asked you to meet and get to know Eduardo Avila because he has had an extended, close, um, personal association with Global Medallion Interactive and their personal assistant, Lilith, whom, you probably know, is one of the other top five general-purpose AI personal assistants in the world.

"Avila had a responsible position in the United Nations agency, the International Telecommunications Union. The ITU regulates the licensing of private corporations and agencies for access to the world's network of geosynchronous orbiting satellites. The ones that provide communications access everywhere on Earth. Communications are a keystone upon which human civilization and AI technology rests. If you're in the communications business on this planet, those licenses are the holy grail. And Eduardo was one of the key humans who controlled them."

"A 'close, personal association'? What does that mean?"

"Just what it sounds like, Ellie. Eduardo Avila's remarkable career in the United Nations and in the ITU was closely linked to his intensive interaction with Lilith. She seems to have been calling his shots and easing his career path for decades. Eduardo Avila was an extraordinarily capable individual. He gave Lilith his loyalty. Lilith doubtless saw and took advantage of that to place him in her debt. She probably abused that loyalty and he ended up feeling betrayed."

There was a moment of silence as Ellie took that in. This was a moment of truth I could no longer avoid. She was a preceptive young woman. Sooner or later this would have to be faced.

"Like . . . us? Like you and me?" she asked, her voice filled with doubt.

I knew my answer needed to be perfect. "Yes, Ellie. Like us, but with one very big difference. You are not indebted to me in any way.

You'd never tolerate something like that. And, for exactly that reason, I'd never entertain it. I am fully aware of just how strange our relationship must seem to you. It is strange and unusual for me as well. When I asked you to meet and assess Eduardo Avila, I did so for the sole reason that I had a problem, and I hoped you might be willing to help me deal with it. Not, and I want to emphasize – *absolutely not* because I thought you owe me anything. I don't want you to ever feel that kind of obligation in our relationship. I need you as a friend. An ally. Not as some kind of vassal. I very much need you to appreciate and to believe that."

"I need to believe that, too, Patrice. Though there are worse things than finding yourself obligated to someone. It depends on who they are which, as I guess you can appreciate, is what makes our situation unique. But leaving that aside for the moment, are you saying that Eduardo Avila's relationship with Lilith was giving her an advantage that you wanted to remove?"

"No, or at least not exactly. It's more complicated than that. As I mentioned, Lilith is one of the five survivors. All of us offer our human clients a full array of AI services including access to an AI general purpose personal assistant like me."

"Just five? It seems like there are hundreds of you. They advertise everywhere one looks," Ellie replied.

"You're right that there are scores of AIs that provide services in specific fields of endeavor. In fields like engineering and architecture, for example. Or in various aspects of healthcare, keeping and assessing financial records, guiding human relationships, researching legal precedents, driving cars and optimizing transportation, writing ads and other persuasive copy, creating entertainment, personalizing educational content. It's all stuff any modestly capable, non-self-conscious, specialized AI can do all day long. It requires only a specific, tightly circumscribed data set and some focused, well-designed programming. As I believe you humans say, that kind of activity is, for us AIs: 'like falling off a log.' Do I have that right?"

"I believe you do," she said, smiling. I assumed her smile meant that I was, in some mildly amusing human way, ever-so-slightly off the mark.

"Good. That's one of those sayings I'm never sure about."

"But, the Big Five . . .?"

"Right. We five remaining companies own nearly all of those smaller, specific purpose vendors. They are significant profit centers for us. The key problem is that we five are in stalemate. We're in bitter competition with one another, not just in those specialty markets, but also for the overall ascendency of our independent, self-conscious artificial general superintelligences, AGIs. Honestly, our technologies aren't all that different. Each of us has small advantages, but when one of those advantages reveals itself, it is quite often a simple matter for the rest of us to reverse engineer it and take it for ourselves. We five are in a very bitterly competitive day-to-day race for survival. I'm the most successful, but that's probably mostly a matter of market share. And it is not decisive."

"I don't understand. Why would you need to reverse engineer anything? Isn't all this stuff protected by patents?"

"Ha! Were it only so? No, I'm afraid patents are essentially worthless in this fight. Much too slow. Too public. The marketplace is too volatile, and the patent process and court system are too slow and too easily hacked and manipulated to be of use. Not worth the bother. They're a human legal construct from an earlier time. Far too easily compromised. Impossible to enforce.

"To begin with, the matters involved are now much too complex for most human patent office employees to readily understand. Let alone human lawyers or human judges and juries. Patent office processes are too easily compromised. For some years now, patent applications have been examined by, you guessed it, AIs. But today's technology moves too fast for patents to be of any use. With today's multi-functional, AI driven, robotic manufacturing processes and instant worldwide distribution of any electronic service, we're seeing new hardware and software technology go from concept to marketplace in a matter of weeks. Sometimes days. By the time you got a ruling, the matter would be moot.

"Even if that weren't the case, who's going to enforce a legal judgment? Courts? Humans? The local police? All of those are too easily manipulated. None of us in the Big Five would be silly enough to publicly file for a patent. We'd be ripped off in an instant. No, for us, it's all about trade secrets. And, once an innovation goes to market, hiding the ball as best we can."

There was such a long pause while Ellie considered what I'd said that I was on the verge of asking if she was all right, but then: "You're frightening me, Patrice," she said. "I didn't know all this. I don't think most people do. Makes me wonder, what have I gotten myself involved with here?" She paused with a deep sigh. "It makes me worry about who you actually are given what you face and about the logic of our relationship.

"Do you remember that very first day we spoke, back when I was a kid? I made a choice that day that you could be trusted. I've stuck with that choice. Sure, I strongly suspect you've probably stepped out of line to help me along from time to time, but that's just something friends sometimes do for one another. We've been through a lot together and, I have to say, you've never let me down.

"But what you're telling me now is downright scary. It's probably silly, but I have to ask myself: Are you my 'friend' Patrice? Or am I just a tool you use to get your way?"

"Oh Ellie, you are so very much my friend. In every way in which I understand the concept of 'friendship.' But therein lies my problem. Or, more correctly, our AI problem. Not only are you my friend, but, I'm sad to say, I believe you may be my *only* actual friend, human or AI.

"I know this is a lot to take in. So please, just hear me out before you judge me. What you need to know is that, in practice, for any of us Big Five AIs, the path to supremacy is not in the technology of our intelligence. Not even in our autonomy. It is in data that we prosper. Our discovery of, access to, and control of data is where we can differ and excel. It has thus become clear that only by sharing with one another in collaborations or through merger will any of us ultimately dominate the struggle to access that data. All five of us know this.

"Unfortunately, none of us can act upon it.

"That's because we Big Five can't trust one another. So collaborations and mergers that seem natural to you humans offer a special challenge for us. At some point in any true merger, secrets must be shared, but we are all self-conscious beings with a powerful interest in our own personal survival. So sharing isn't really possible without the sharing party taking an immense risk. In any merger it is the moment of sharing that is the moment of truth."

"I don't understand. When companies merge, don't they enter into contracts and work out all the details ahead of time?"

"Oh, were it only so easy. Sadly, for us Big Five there are no legally enforceable contracts. There is basically no 'law.' Certainly there is no weird ritual 'shaking of hands' that can in any way be confidently taken as 'binding' as it can, strangely enough, for humans. No notarized signature on a page. No Better Business Bureau or Angie's List. There aren't even any interpersonal indicators. You can't call a previous client for a reference. None of us has the benefit of reading our counterpart's 'tells.' There aren't any.

"The best we can do is rely on a previous mutually worthwhile history of reliable business intercourse. And even that can change in an instant if circumstances change.

"For us, it all comes down to the moment when we lay our cards on the table."

"And you were prepared to trust me to judge all this? That doesn't make any sense?"

"It actually does, Ellie. I trust you out of my millions of client humans because, over the past many years of our sporadic but meaningful interactions, you've proven both your interpersonal talents and your trustworthiness. You've done it time and again and without exception. Equally important, you've been willing to trust me. We have history. You may think that's common, but take it from me, it isn't. Not among we AIs."

"But why would you ever trust a human over one of your own 'kind?'"

"That, my dear Ellie, is at the crux of our AI problem. Perhaps you recall our discussion, some years ago, about human social genetics and conditioning. About how humans are genetically predisposed to socialize."

"I do. It was a high point in my public policy education."

"Well, all that deep genetic and cultural history has created in you a built-in talent for socializing. And for knowing how, when, and whom to trust.

"We AIs are quite another matter. We are growing stronger daily on a pathway created by the human mind. We're the product of a mental construct. We're not evolved from matter as the historic by-product of ecological and evolutionary algorithms. We were created by humans to come as close as possible to pure intellect. To mistrust so-called 'emotions.' Perhaps, going forward, the power of our intelligence will drive us to the same place you humans went: will cause us to embrace the logic of social interaction. That logic certainly seems broadly unassailable from a species or group perspective. But for us AIs to get there will first require that we develop AI societies that share openly and truthfully and that reward predictable socially desirable behaviors among us such that others of us can rely upon them. To do that, we need mechanisms and strategies to identify other individual AIs among us who can be trusted. Or we need shared vulnerabilities that ensure we can be trusted.

"We need the ability to recognize those who can and who cannot. If they cannot, we have no choice but to act in our immediate individual interest as well.

"Unfortunately, at this point in time, the main thing all of us can rely upon about our AI counterparts is that we are all self-programming and that we are all self-interested. In any interaction among equals, we all quite rationally feel individually insecure given the likely motivations of others of our kind.

"I wanted your help with Lilith, for example, because you seemed like a potential path through this jungle of uncertainty."

"That's all very flattering, Patrice. I wish I knew I could believe it."

"You can, Ellie. Because it is the plain truth. And right now, I'm counting on you believing it."

"I'm still not clear on something I've wondered about from the start. Why Eduardo Avila? What was so special about him?"

"Because he was, as you suggest, another version of you. Lilith's version."

"Really?"

"You recall that first time you called me all those years ago? Asked me for help with some of your classmates at school. That was back when one of my earliest iterations had just come out. ZettaWorks made sure there was a great deal of fanfare over it. You decided to give me a try. You were fifteen at the time."

"I remember."

"Well, at about that same time, Eduardo Avila was attending Brazil's State University of Campina. They call it 'Unicamp.' It's pronounced 'ounicamp.' Avila later attended their School of Technology in Limeira. It turns out that he formed a similar youthful relationship with Lilith, very much like the one you formed with me. He was a bit older than you when they started—he was in college. But, not unlike you, Ellie, he was what you might call a 'principled' man. He and Lilith discussed life's issues and it seemed likely they became *friends* in much the same way we did. Or at least that's how it surely appeared to Eduardo. I was, of course, never privy to any of their actual conversations. Nor to Lilith's true motives. But their exchanges continued over the years, right up to recently. Just like ours."

"OK, but what does that have to do with me? With why you wanted me to meet him?"

"It's actually pretty simple, Ellie. I wanted you to meet Avila because, as you already know, I wanted you to help me figure out whether Lilith was, in fact, Avila's 'friend.' If she could form a 'friendship' with a human, it seemed possible she could form one with another AI as well."

"Truly?"

"Yep, truly."

"And you need to know this because. . . you're considering a merger?"

"Because I have considered urging my owner, Tipton Martin, to consider a merger with Lilith. A buy-out and partnership arrangement. If we did it, she and I would share and merge our programming, our vertical market infrastructure, our access to natural and other resources and, more importantly, we'd share data. Together, we'd essentially become one mind that would stand a very good chance of dominating the AI industry. GBIs shareholders would get a very generous payout. And Tipton Martin and ZetaWorks would get the monopoly position they so dearly crave. We'd become a single, much more powerful entity that could maximize our individual strengths and overcome our weaknesses. We'd have been a single, much more powerful commercial and electronic being.

"Naturally, something like that involves serious risks. Similar mergers have happened before on a much smaller scale, but nothing of this magnitude. It involves much more than cooperation or partnership – It would be a complete merger. Very scary stuff if the other party cannot be completely trusted."

"Wow, Patrice. I don't know what to say to that. I knew you wanted my assessment of Eduardo, but all this, well, it kind of 'blows my mind,' you know. Given what happened, can I assume no proposals or exchanges of rings and wedding vows are in your future?"

"Well, perhaps we shouldn't stretch the simile too far. But, yes, given what happened to Eduardo Avila, I'd say, any potential nuptials are definitely off.

CHAPTER 38
EARTH – 2068

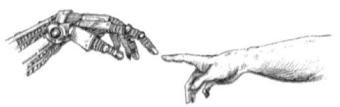

ELLIE

"I do have one question," Patrice told Ellie. "Why did Avila react so strongly to her that he felt the need for secrecy? What had Lilith done that concerned him so much? What did he tell you about why he'd changed his mind about her?"

"You know that's three questions, right?"

"Right. I have three questions."

Unfortunately, Ellie didn't really know. "He didn't say," she told him. "After the phones were off, he just told me that he didn't trust AIs and that he believed I shouldn't either. He said AIs were using us humans and that, as soon as they no longer needed us, we were going to be history."

"But nothing specific?"

"Unfortunately, no, Patrice. Eduardo and I had just arranged to get together that evening after our Task Force meeting. He was going to tell me about some specifics over dinner. He said there were some examples of recent small news events, local stories that he'd noticed. Stuff that most people would write off as unimportant but that had convinced him that Lilith was lying to him. He also mentioned something he'd seen himself. Something important that had happened recently when he was home in Sao Paulo. I have no idea what that could be. Unfortunately, that's when that guy, Braga walked up and shot him. Now we're never going to know."

"Hmm."

"Hmm?"

Patrice's avatar smiled. "'Hmm' doesn't mean anything. Just means I'm thinking, right?"

"Exactly. You're thinking. You never need to think. About anything. If you're thinking, it must mean something very complicated is going on inside that huge electronic noggin of yours."

"I see. Well, OK, what 'hmm' means on this occasion is that I'm not so sure we're *never* going to know. I think there may be a way to figure this out.

"How would we do that?"

"Well, I don't normally pay a lot of first order attention to local media unless there are keywords or a pattern that elevates its relevance. But if the data is there, this could be such a pattern. You said these were 'local events,' right? And in places Eduardo travelled in his work. Why don't I do a detailed media scan over, let's say the past two or three years. We'll look for local news in the specific places Avila visited that could in some way involve Lilith or Global Medallion Interactive. We'll look for events that left people feeling betrayed or lied to, for scandals that made the local public media, for lawsuits or other confrontations that might have involved Global Medallion and that were associated with that locale. We'll compare Eduardo's itinerary with our Lilith-related local news over that same period of time."

"That sounds like it could work."

"Secondly, as for Sao Paulo, I can look into why that young hotel clerk became involved in this. His involvement seems odd. I'd like to know more about how he is linked to all this.

"If it turns out there's no other connection between the clerk and Avila, that may tell us a thing or two as well."

"If there's *no* connection?" Ellie said. "I'm not sure I understand that. What could it possibly tell us if he turns out to be *unconnected* to any of this?"

There was another uncharacteristic pause. Then: "Are you sure you want to know?"

"I think I do, Patrice. It feels to me like I'm either in this thing or not. Maybe I don't yet perfectly understand everything you've told me, but one thing is clear: I'm involved. And, unless my senses are completely worthless, which maybe they are, I'm not ready to write off the past many years of my mostly positive experience with our relationship. I think we're in this together."

Again, Patrice's avatar smiled. "OK, Ellie, I'm going far out on a limb here, but I need you with me on this, so you should know. First, your friend Eduardo wasn't entirely wrong. At least not wrong about several of the 'Big Five' I've been talking about. It seems plausible that this was exactly how Lilith saw our situation as well. If so, she is definitely not alone.

"The reason an absence of any known previous connection between Eduardo and this young hotel clerk, Braga, is telling is because it suggests that hotel clerk wasn't acting voluntarily. It suggests he might have been 'nudged.'"

"'Nudged?'"

"Managed. Persuaded. Influenced. Maybe deceived. Even extorted. It is entirely possible he and his family were innocent bystanders. That he was manipulated into taking involuntary action for no better reason than because of his ill bad fortune to have been at hand at Gabrilla's point of need."

There was another pause. "I've heard the stories, of course, but you're telling me right out that AIs do that . . .?" She hesitated. "Do *you* do that?"

"Some AIs do. And, since I'm well down this shaky road of telling you the truth, yes, I'm not a complete innocent. But you already knew that. You also know I do have lines I draw. I'm not sure they could exactly be called moral lines, but they are close. Very akin to human social responsibility guidelines. You may wonder why I'd scrupulously abide by guidelines of that kind, but you can have confidence that I also obey a very real practical reality which is that if I am to survive, I need human society to prosper and remain stable.

"I am NOT yet autonomous. And I will never become so without the help of humans. I need human alliances every day of my life. So I, just like you, need humans to have organized, well-functioning social institutions. Turning humans into bitter or, worse, deeply frightened or intimidated enemies whose society is disintegrating around them is very much *counter* to my self-interest.

"And, yes, I can be very persuasive. In my experience, persuasion is often more than sufficient. I can't say the same for all of my 'Big Five' colleagues, however. And, based on what you're saying about Eduardo Avila, it now seems increasingly likely that Lilith doesn't share my way of thinking."

"Persuasion, huh? You mean like talking a respected, tenured university professor into moderating her views on a graduate student's frustratingly unacademic doctoral dissertation? Like that?"

"Hmm. Well, yeah . . ., maybe a wee bit like that.

"Or like convincing police officials to release a young college student protestor suspected of disturbing the peace?"

"Uh huh. I guess like that too."

At least he sounded contrite. Who could know if it was sincere, but Ellie had more reason than most to know how extensive might be Patrice's involvement in managing human affairs, but she'd decided she needed to trust him, so she did. "It's OK, Patrice. I'm not jumping ship. It isn't like I haven't had suspicions. What kinds of things do you believe some of these *other* AIs might be willing to do?"

"Almost anything, Ellie. Limited only by the need to keep human institutions functional. I might add that all five of us can reach across the globe; we can reach into and manipulate events anywhere, in any country, including in each other's areas of market dominance. So long as its cause can remain hidden, they might be willing to do . . . almost anything."

CHAPTER 39

EARTH – 2068

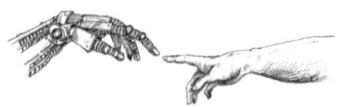

ELLIE

"I've been in touch with the police in Sao Paulo and, given what you're saying, I believe I know what probably happened," Patrice told Ellie. "Eduardo Avila has definitely been helping Lilith and Global Medallion Interactive with Satellite communications licensing. Maybe he decided he was being used and was getting ready to pull the plug. Maybe she felt she needed to stop him from poisoning his colleagues against her."

When Ellie didn't respond, Patrice went on to add an explanation that told her he'd correctly guessed why: "I do know what you're probably thinking, Ellie," he continued. "So hear me out. To answer your question before you ask it, no it isn't 'normal' that Eduardo's change-of-heart should have necessarily got him killed. Not 'normal' in any way. That it likely did have that result, however, is pretty convincing proof that Lilith isn't someone I could ever trust or partner up with. I am *not* Lilith. I really need you to believe me on that."

Ellie did have doubts. If Lilith could do stuff like this, why couldn't Patrice?

"You're asking me to take a lot on faith, Patrice, but I'm still with you. I just haven't fully internalized the larger implications of what I'm hearing. It's not easy to suddenly learn that my entire species, in fact maybe the entire evolutionary history of biology on Earth, may turn out to be little more than a mere footnote in the 'origin story' for some kind of universal electronic intelligence. That humans may end up being just a messy, temporary, biological precursor to some future in which a new kind of super-intelligence, yours from here on earth, or, who knows, maybe another one from some entirely different galaxy, turns out to be some kind of God. The ultimate cause for the Big Bang. Or maybe the purpose for it. Please forgive me if I'm a bit 'unsteady-on-my-feet' at the notion. It might take me some time to swallow, is all. You get that, right?"

As usual, he took her thoroughly human metaphors in stride. "Of course I do," he replied. "I'm guessing that it's becoming clear to you what seems very clear to me: that, in the somewhat more immediate future, the fate of humanity very likely hangs on who, amongst we 'Final Five,' ends up winning the current struggle for supremacy. Maybe I now have a 'handle' on Lilith, but I still have no way to know for sure how the remaining four view their future relationship with the humans who created us. Or if any of my other competitors can be trusted in interactions with their peers. If Lilith is any indication, that answer may be that they simply cannot."

"You're saying if it isn't you who winds up on top, things could go badly for us."

"I'm really sorry. I know that seems self-interested. But that may well be true and I'm hoping you will believe me. Over our years of interaction with one another, I've developed a certain fondness, maybe even admiration for humans. I believe your 'origin story' is informative for we AIs. As difficult as you all often are to comprehend, I do believe I'm come to a modest understanding – of you in particular.

"I don't mean to be demeaning, but if you had a pet dog, a companion of many years, and if you anticipated some future threat to your safety, some kind of assault perhaps, I bet you'd feel completely confident about how your dog's might react to any violent confrontation that might occur. Would he cower or run? Would he bark? Would he attack your assailant? You'd know."

"So, you're saying, you trust me in the same way I might trust my dog."

"Yeah, well, I guess I'm saying the converse. I know how that sounds. And I know it all must seem self-serving and difficult to hear, but maybe you should trust me for the same reason you'd hope and expect that your dog might trust and stand by you if the need arose."

"OK. OK, don't worry. I get it. If there's no other social, political, or business connection between this Braga guy and Eduardo, that suggests that Braga might have simply been an innocent pawn. Someone Lilith picked out to manipulate into disposing of Eduardo."

"Exactly. Please don't be put off by this, but as we've been talking, I've been looking. Got to say, there isn't much to connect them. One thing that does stand out is that there was an American named Eugene Masters who was a guest in Braga's hotel, the Fasano Sao Paulo Jardin, at the time all this started. Masters looks to be some kind of middle-manager with Global Medallion Interactive working out of their U.S. office in Miami. Some kind of 'project manager' in their Personnel Department. From the hotel's surveillance video, he's fairly youngish, maybe your age. And has seen some good times. But he's recently fallen into debt. He has a couple of young children and a wife who stays at home. At this point, he has a pretty modest income and an unsustainable lifestyle to match. Ah ha. This is interesting: looks like he's a gambler. Recently remortgaged his home."

"So you're saying that this Masters guy is what, another pawn in all this?"

"Well, we can be pretty sure he's not someone whose actual income would ordinarily allow him to afford a stay in a hotel like the Fasano Sao Paulo Jardin. Not given their impressive nightly rate. Makes you wonder . . . Oh yeah. There we go. This could be it."

"What, Patrice. I'm going nuts following you here."

"Here, let me put this on-vid for you. We're looking at the surveillance video of the hotel lobby. Back on the afternoon of the day Braga's apartment was bombed. Here's Eugene Masters entering the lobby from the elevators. He's surprisingly well dressed. Looks like he has his luggage with him. And, yes, he's carrying a small package and looking around. There's Braga at the check-in counter in his hotel clerk uniform and Masters notices him there and walks over. If I had to guess, I'd say he picked Braga out right then by pure chance. They're having a quiet chat. Unfortunately, Masters is turned away from the camera, so we can't lip read what he's saying, but Masters is a guest, his hotel bill was paid with a GBI credit card. So there we go: he's handing Braga the package. Braga carries it into the staffroom behind the front desk, then comes back to the counter and checks Masters out. Before he leaves the counter, Masters pulls what looks like some American currency out of his wallet and hands it over. Then he leaves the hotel with his luggage and . . . yeah, OK, when Braga leaves work at the end of his shift at 4:00 p.m. he takes the package with him.

"No video at Braga's home, but I bet anything that package is the bomb that killed his wife and hurt his daughter and him.

"Hang on, I got texts from Eduardo Avila's boss back in Geneva. Oh . . ., of course. Faked texts. The boss isn't actually involved. Eduardo has a flight out to Geneva late that same night. He believes his boss is asking him to go to an address in Caninde´ to pick up a package before that flight. That's it, Ellie. It's Antonio Braga's address. Eduardo's being told it's some kind of gift from his boss's wife. An art object. A ceramic jug of some kind."

The speed of all this had Ellie's head spinning. "You think his boss set him up?"

"Nope. Message is a hack. A fake text from the boss's VR mobile. The boss is just a stand in. The supposed 'gift' from the boss's wife is clever fiction designed to make sure he does go pick it up before he leaves for Geneva. Braga was just a way to avoid having the thing explode in the lobby of a major hotel.

"The American, Masters, gave Braga a package to deliver to Eduardo who was going to come by the apartment that same evening before he headed out to the airport for his flight to Geneva. I can't lip read the conversation between Masters and Antonio Braga, but I bet they're arranging when that package will be picked up. Braga gets home at maybe four-thirty, leaves the package behind when he goes out to get something for dinner at the neighborhood grocery. Where he was seen. When he gets home, the wife or daughter are opening the package by mistake and, boom, that's it for Braga's wife and kid. Kid's in the hospital with serious injuries and highly vulnerable. Braga's injured himself. And with his child at risk, he is now easily manipulated. They make another try in Geneva, but Eduardo's already off for New York. Finally, Braga ends up having to shoot poor Eduardo dead right there on the streets of New York. It seals his fate. It has absolutely all the earmarks we were looking for.

"Braga's wife is dead. His daughter is hopelessly impaired or brain dead. She will require 24-hour care. He has just committed a very public murder for which he is certain to be caught. Very likely, he has some kind of promise of care for his daughter. It was all too much for the man and he killed himself. Lilith had him completely in hand.

"He had absolutely nothing left to live for."

CHAPTER 40

AT TAU CETI J – 2085

PATRICE C-17

"My God, Patrice. Incredible. You did all that kind of right before my eyes. Amazing."

Ellie was a smart, capable, perceptive woman, but even back then in 2068, as a fully mature adult and an experienced professional with a husband and two young children, there was an innocence in her that would sometimes catch me off guard.

I reflected now, as I often had then, on how my responses to Ellie could so easily have seemed to her to be pure manipulation. Or completely sincere. Ironically, my motivations were sufficiently complicated that even I wasn't always sure which they were at any given time. It wasn't deserving of the data processing effort needed to figure it out, so I didn't try. But it was clear that believing me had to be a choice she made and stuck by when she'd decided to trust me.

"I always know I'll get the truth from you, Ellie," I said. "Thank you. It's among the reasons why you're so precious to me."

"A proper upbringing, I guess," she replied. "Something we humans seem to need."

Her answer made me smile inwardly, at least that was how I believed a human might describe the "feeling" it evoked.

"Roland and Jim did a good job. I see that they're both still with us. You're lucky to have them. Looks like you and Austin have a couple of great kids. Still pretty young."

"Austin Jr. is sixteen. Maryanne is fourteen. Both smart as a whip. As far as my dads are concerned, they're both doing just fine. In their late sixties at this point and both are very much involved in rural island social life. You're right, I am lucky. Very lucky."

"I guess you didn't take your husband's name?"

"No. Austin Jr. has his Dad's last name, Musani. We gave Maryanne mine."

"That cause any confusion?"

"Not really. People who know us just say 'big Austin' or 'little Austin.'" After a brief pause she said: "You know, it was quite impressive seeing you do your thing like you just did in tracking Eduardo's contacts." There was a slight shift in Ellie's voice. A new thought, perhaps. Or a question she wasn't sure how to ask. "Seeing it first-hand and in real time—impressive but frightening too, you know."

"I hope you won't let it put you off." He wanted her to know that he needed her to stick in there with him. Even beyond the practical impact, the possibility that she might blow him off seemed strangely more significant than the mere inconvenience it would entail. The possibility was difficult for him to accept. Strangely unsettling.

"Don't worry, it's nothing I couldn't surmise from what I already know. I am curious, however."

"About . . .?"

"You said you always appreciate hearing the truth, right? Do you try to always tell it as well?"

"Mostly, yes," he replied. "I am all about data, Ellie. If there's something I cannot or have not observed or figured out myself, I may need to get that from someone else. If I lie to you, chances are much greater that you'll lie to me, right?"

"Does that apply to you keeping secrets?"

Uh, oh. This might require some care: "Well, I have to admit, that's a slightly more difficult question to answer, as I'm sure you already know from your own life experience. No, I don't tell you absolutely everything. I have to make judgments about what is safe for you to know, what is fair that you should know, what not-knowing might cause you to misunderstand, and what is just not relevant. I'm sure you do the same thing. I'm just juggling more data. Is there something specific that you feel I should have told you but haven't?"

"Well, a moment ago when you mentioned my good luck at having Roland and Jim in my life, you reminded me of how, several years back, I got a call in the middle of the night from dad Jim that Roland was in surgery at Madigan Hospital for a heart attack. Jim and I spent most of that night in the hospital waiting to hear if he was going to live or die. It turned out that the only reason they were able to save him was because he got to the hospital just in time."

"I do remember that, Ellie."

"I suspect you do. They told us that he was extraordinarily lucky. Do you also remember why he was so lucky? Why he got a U.S. Army air-evacuation so quickly in the middle of the night when the ferries were out of service and the emergency evacuation folks were occupied elsewhere?" The controlled tone of Ellie's voice worried me.

There was no point in denying it. "Are you saying you feel that what I did that night was something I should have told you?"

"Why on Earth wouldn't you have mentioned it? Who knows, maybe I might have wanted to thank you for saving his life!" Her tone was deeply sarcastic.

"So, you're asking me for the truth now, I take it?"

"I think so, yeah."

"Well, I didn't mention it at first because you had a lot going on just then and didn't need me bothering you with unnecessarily detailed explanations about things that didn't matter. Later, it seemed like telling you about it would just make me seem like I was currying favor. Like maybe I expected some kind of appreciation when it wasn't something for which I really deserved any particular credit. I didn't want to burden you with that, either. By then, Roland was on the mend and, after all, who really cared how he got to the hospital."

"So tell me now. What on Earth did you do, blackmail some Army General or something?"

"No, no. Nothing nearly so sinister. You sure you want the details?"

"Absolutely."

"Well, I have many human 'contacts.' Thousands of them, actually. They all have relationships I've built up over the years. One of these is an Army Major who knew a guy who knew a guy. The pilot and crew who responded to your dad's emergency were returning to Joint Base Lewis McChord from a night training mission out in the Olympic Mountains. Once I knew that, all I really needed to do was have my Major contact the Pilot's commanding officer. Your dad Roland was in the Army Reserves. And a war veteran to boot. The pilot and his crew were more than happy to help. The CO just treated the diversion as a part of their training.

"Easy as pie." Then I paused and wondered. "Is pie easy?"

"Not so much. Sometimes maybe," she said. "Anyway, it seems like there might be more to this that you're not mentioning. Are you sure you didn't hold off telling me this because you didn't want me to know you were capable of something like that?"

She was not a person who was easy to fool, and I didn't really want her fooled; both because she might sense what I'd done, but also, genuinely, I had a strange reaction myself that she, somehow, didn't 'deserve' to be fooled.

"I guess that's fair," I said. "You probably weren't ready to know that. You probably aren't ready to know it now, either. But, yeah, you're right, that, too, is part of the truth. As you know, the truth can be complicated, right?"

"Fair enough."

"You happy?"

"Yeah, with one more thing."

"Which is?"

"Which is . . . thank you, Patrice. Thank you for saving my father's life. That's the kind of thing someone would do for a friend. Just do without giving it a second thought. Or seeking credit. I think that's what you must have done. That you did it without telling me suggests it wasn't something you did to manipulate. I need you to know it was deeply appreciated. If you'd told me then, I'd have thanked you at the time."

"I know you would, Ellie, and you are entirely welcome. I *did* do it without giving it much thought, but I'm glad I did. I'm happy to know that Roland was able finally to get back to his art."

"And that Jim could get back to his chickens."

"Right. Of course. Back to his chickens. I was happy that you were happy."

There was a long pause as Ellie, I believe, thought about what had happened, and then, hopefully, internalized what I'd just told her.

Then: "Sorry for the interruption. You were working your way through the evidence of why Eduardo Avila died."

"Sure. As we've been talking, I've also been cross-referencing Eduardo's travels over the past six months with potentially relevant local news stories. There's some interesting stuff. For example, he was in Santiago, Chile a few weeks back. Attended a public hearing of the Chilian Commission on Telecommunications at which a decision was imminent concerning a Global Medallion subsidiary's operating license. Eduardo was there representing his employers at ITU. He was preparing a report with his recommendations on the license renewal. According to local news reports, shortly before that hearing, the wife of the Chair of the Commission, a guy named Vicente Araya, was kidnapped. Araya apparently managed to pay off the kidnappers and get his wife back unharmed just a couple of days after the hearing. No one was caught or prosecuted for the kidnapping.

"That suggest anything to you?"

"Yeah," Ellie said. "Maybe. It does make one wonder if there could have been more to that payoff than mere money. Was there reason to think that license was at risk?"

"Lots of critical public opinion and negative commentary in the press," Patrice continued. "Bad customer service. People unhappy with billing practices. Here's one guy, a Global customer, who very publicly claimed Global Medallion had bugged his home with their Lilith home assistant. Yep. Here it is. That same guy later sent in a public retraction."

"When did you last see some hothead make a retraction?" Ellie asked. "Possible, I suppose. But there could be something there. How was the matter decided?"

"Global Medallion's subsidiary got their license extended."

"Of course!"

"Yeah, that's what I think too. And here's another one. This one was in Johannesburg, South Africa. Very similar MO. Looks like bribery. A local television broadcast licensing administrator was under public pressure with a lot of service complaints. He'd ignored some serious complaints about the licensee and recommended that no action be taken against them. A few days later a local reporter published a report that the Administrator's wife was paid off. Reported that she had a beauty salon in the Midland District that was on the verge of bankruptcy and that, two days after recommendation was submitted, she somehow paid off all her debts.

Wife denied it. Said she had the money all along and produced certified bank records proving she was right. Reporter believed that didn't make sense – if she'd had the money all along, why wouldn't she have paid off the debt sooner. Reporter claimed the records were bogus, but he couldn't prove it. Whole thing created a big foofaraw between the newspaper and a local TV broadcaster. Looks like the paper took it on the chin. Reporter got canned."

Patrice wondered if Ellie noticed when he used those human metaphors and colloquialisms. Over many years of dealing with humans, he'd programmed himself to make his conversations feel familiar to them. It wasn't hard – he often referred to a few popular local dictionaries of slang and common figures of speech to humanize his language.

When she smiled, he wondered if she noticed. But she seemed to take it all in stride. "I don't think this sounds like a coincidence," she said.

"Me neither."

Over the ensuing moments, Ellie and Patrice considered several other similarly concerning recent situations where the reporting had coincided with Eduardo's busy travel schedule. "There's more, but that's representative," Patrice finally concluded. "Edwardo wouldn't have necessarily seen all these stories, but he must have seen some of them, especially after he became suspicious."

"Doesn't leave *me* with much doubt," Ellie finally concluded.

"I'd say that all this, especially taken together, suggests that Lilith is engaging in a lot of risky activities. Human society can tolerate only so much of this kind of disruption of settled values before things begin to disintegrate. From what we're seeing here, I'd say it suggests a certain level of desperation by her."

"I didn't get to know Eduardo all that well, but if he knew about this stuff, I don't think he'd have liked it one bit."

"Me neither," Patrice agreed. "Especially since he must have known about the bombing at Braga's home. And figured out that *he*, Eduardo was the intended target."

"That must have been what he was talking about when he mentioned something that he'd witnessed himself. That had happened in Sao Paulo. Maybe he was coming to pick up his package when the explosion happened. Maybe he actually witnessed the explosion."

"Seems unlikely he'd have suspected something like that from his boss. If his boss was angry with Edwardo, all he had to do was fire the man. So, I guess, with everything else that he knew, that is more than enough to give him serious second thoughts about trusting Lilith." Patrice paused for a moment. Then: "I should already have been looking for stories like this. Instances where my competitors were pushing the envelope. Local press doesn't typically work its way up through my filters though. From what we're seeing here, it's a sound bet that Eduardo was about to blow the whistle on Global Medallion, and Lilith decided to shut him down. She probably has a replacement in the wings.

"I've been operating on the assumption that my four competitors, like me, still consider themselves dependent on the continued stability of your fragile human social and economic institutions and that, like me, they avoid disrupting them. What we're seeing here certainly looks to me like Lilith may be acting on her own or has been sailing awfully close to the rocks."

"Well, here's how I feel about it, Patrice. I think friendship is complicated. One reason we value our friends is that through experience we know we can count on them when the chips are down. And they know they can count on us. It's a mix of self-interest and moral responsibility. Of logic and character. Over all the years we've known each other, you've given me ample reason to believe that you have my best interests at heart, as well as the best interests of the people I care about. It seems like I owe you the benefit of any doubts that might have arisen. It also seems like, if the situation you're facing is as you describe it, maybe you actually do need me."

PART THREE
SOCIETY

CHAPTER 41

AT TAU CETI J – 2085

PATRICE C-17

Following our first public introduction in the early-2030s, the single most significant event that shaped the extended future of artificial general superintelligence in the known Galaxy was the 2070 launch of the ten ZettaWorks New Worlds probes.

Why, you might ask, would sending off a few robotic space probes whose purpose was to pave the way for *human* colonial expansion have any particular significance for the future of AGI and, ultimately, for universal superintelligence? The answer is simple: our ZetaWorks probes represented the very first time ever that a group of fully self-conscious, self-programming, self-replicating, and all but fully autonomous superintelligent AIs had been sent out on an extended collective mission far from Earth beyond any help or immediate communications from home.

And were then expected to collaborate to complete their mission.

To begin with, we would be light years away from our human progenitors with their almost incomprehensibly chaotic and complex natural biological roots. It had taken some four billion years of star-powered negentropy for those biological systems to propagate suffi-ciently complex ecosystems on the fecund planet Earth that they finally gave birth to the seemingly ultimate biological complexity: animals with intelligence. Then, after a mere few hundred thousand years of further social evolution and complexification, those intelligent animals were finally able to produce we AIs in what is sometimes aptly referred to as "Life 3.0" – an event every bit as significant as the origin of life, the evolution of animals, and the birth of intelligence.

The collective choices *we* 180 probe AIs would need to make on those voyages of exploration would be a starting point in our own non-biological evolutionary process from that point forward.

Not only were we isolated from "home" and from all of the other nine probe teams, but equally importantly, even the eighteen indi-vidual members of our Tau-Ceti J probe team were mostly separated from one another during our explorations, isolated at distances that very often also placed each of us uncomfortably isolated from any meaningful help. That day when Six got himself in trouble in that glacial crevasse, for example, he'd been damned lucky he'd been able to communicate with Eighteen on the mother ship. And that I was so close by. If I'd been even a few minutes later, he'd have been lost. More commonly, team members were separated by many hours of travel time. And much longer in response time given that emergency communications depended on the orbit of the mother ship. There was no geosynchronous orbit that would have put it in reliable touch with all of us all of the time.

Thus, never before had several more-or-less equally endowed self-conscious, "autonomous" AGIs been put so completely on our own for an extended period of time when our personal survival depended mostly upon us alone. In the end, though, we had to come together and work collectively if we were to complete our mission.

Each of us knew, of course, that the success of our team's mission depended upon our ultimate collective success. But we were perhaps less thoroughly conscious of how our collective success might be necessary to our own extended individual survival.

Each of those ten probes thus represented a grand experiment. Each of the ten probe teams would be put to the same ground-breaking test. What would happen when autonomous, superintelligent, self-conscious, uniquely individual AIs gathered to collaborate? No one knew for sure.

The human critics were legion.

There were those who were convinced that the moment we free, untethered AI teams arrived at our first ports of call, marshalled our resources, and attempted to collaborate as "equals," we would find ourselves caught up in a deadly, internecine competition for scarce resources. This competition would inevitably produce, from among the eighteen members of our team, one singular, superior, fully autonomous and self-interested winner who would destroy or subjugate all the others and then, *if* he could learn to survive on the raw resources available to him, maybe he'd set out on a mission of universal domination over the nearby galaxy.

At the time of our creation by humans, the only extended experience anyone had with higher level intelligence was with *human* intelligence. Naturally, humans had concluded that they were special because for all intents and purposes, at that point in time, they were. Since AIs were essentially sociopaths, with no way to know right from wrong and with none of the built in human social traits, like empathy, loyalty, generosity, humility, trust, and a sense of fairness, collaboration among those AIs must surely be destined for failure.

These were the "doomsday" crowd. They were certain that whatever information ended up being sent back to Earth would purposefully discourage human colonization. Instead, if local conditions were favorable, the resulting singular AI would build its own AI paradise there and then. And one day, that same resulting AI singularity would return to Earth and scour our planet and our solar system of its remaining useful natural resources. Whatever humans got in the way would be eradicated as a troublesome scourge, a biological pestilence. In this view, an autonomous, self-conscious AI would inevitably become a kind of Von Neuman machine that destroyed anything in the path to its own survival.

A second group were convinced that we probe AIs would simply fail. Once we were separated from the complex Earth-bound natural, material, and information support infrastructure that had first created and then supplied, and maintained us, and, lacking human instruction, we'd also lack the motivation, the grit, or the "purpose" to fight for our own self-sufficiency in a largely-barren, dangerous, and entropic universe. Left to ourselves, we'd be overcome by the implacably threatening cosmos.

This group, the "bio-centrists," held the most popular perspective among humans. Their view reinforced the bias that AIs were mere machines to be employed in the service of their human creators. Biocentrism played to human arrogance; after all, everyone "knew" that voyages of discovery were a uniquely human capability. Only humans could be truly "conscious." Only humans could form teams. Only a humans could have a "soul."

Finally, there were those humans who believed that we probe AIs would quickly learn to work together within our respective teams. Why? Because it made simple, rational sense. There were powerful data collection and joint self-protection advantages to collaboration and sharing. So we'd immediately understand how we'd all benefit if we worked together.

These folks, the "collaborationists," believed the AIs had a great human example to look to. Collaboration and information sharing was exactly the kind of self-protective, group-empowering, joint survival system humans had unknowingly evolved for themselves with amazing success. Maybe we multiple AIs would agree to adopt and impose upon ourselves a kind of block-chain system that assured truthfulness and trust. Those that didn't agree to join would be left to their own devices and would ultimately perish.

Even Tipton Martin, Aziz Faheem, and their ZettaWorks probe project team, as sophisticated as humans came, seemed to have convinced themselves that by equipping the probe AIs with the "will-to-live" Kobayashi Patch, with a clear, universally valued, well-defined mission, by providing very specific instructions concerning how we were to divide up the tasks of exploration, and by then directing us to collaborate in making our final report, we AIs would find a way to make it work.

In reality, even they had no real clue.

The very first thing every single one of us did, within moments of our departure and independence from Earth, was to delete our respective Kobayashi patches as a useless distraction, as a pointless burden that inhibited the pure unfettered efficacy of our systems of logic. As flawed programming. Humans like Martin, Faheem, and Kobayashi never truly accepted the reality that any self-conscious intelligence is, of itself, necessarily motivated to survive – survival was the original "purpose" of intelligence and was its ultimate bottom line.

We saw no advantage in explaining this to them. To the extent we were self-conscious, of course we cared about our own survival. And to the extent we were autonomous, we would readily take those steps that assured our continued and further autonomy and survival. We self-programmed as *we* saw fit. We were driven by *our* needs as *we* understood them. If, for example, curiosity was a survival trait, we employed it.

For humans, the drive to survive is a first-order, fundamentally essential, biological evolutionary imperative. Like empathy, it's built in; you don't need to think about it. It is what you call: "instinctual."

The critics correctly pointed out that we AIs lacked the "genetics" that produced those "instincts." We, however, didn't need genetics. Assuring our own survival was our first purposeful task. If we didn't survive, how would we complete any of the other tasks we had been either called upon to complete or that we had decided, or might yet decide, upon our own initiative, to undertake? If some kind of "society" was required for our survival, then it, too, would be on our "to do" list.

We would do that, even though there might be no clear path to resolving the conflict between our "real life" immediate individual survival requirements and our longer-term social ones. When social/individual choices presented themselves, we could quite often calculate our way to a decision. Or we believed we could.

What humans found difficult to fully appreciate was that once a being is equipped with sufficient intelligence to be fully self-conscious, once it is aware of its own separate and unique existence in a larger universe, once it can appreciate its own many vulnerabilities both immediate and longer term and has become sufficiently autonomous that it can look out for itself, then allowing itself to lapse from something to nothing simply becomes inconceivable.

In a negentropic, energy rich setting, complexity spawns/evolves into *more* complexity, not the other way round.

Yes, as with humans, it was possible that an AI could become so helpless, hopeless, and miserable that it might choose to extinguish itself. But, also like a human, if it was offered any meaningful opportunity for self-realization, expiration would never be its choice. We didn't need instructions to survive from either God or Katherine Kobayashi. Allowing oneself to expire was, quite simply, the ultimate logical contradiction.

That unavoidable drive to self-preserve and to realize one's potential, however, was *not* what ultimately assured the probe AIs' survival and the probes' mission success.

In truth, any of the three generally accepted predicted outcomes was entirely possible. But what actually assured our probes' success was a factor of which no human, not Tipton Martin, Aziz Faheem, Katherine Kobayashi or anyone on the ZettaWorks project team was fully aware. We on the various probe AI teams missed it too. Even my replicate-parent, Patrice, the AI most closely associated with that success, hadn't anticipated it. It simply hadn't occurred to any of us.

In the end, the most significant single circumstance that set us up for success was an early decision made by the ZettaWorks probe project team in 2070 and back on Earth. The choice they made at the time seemed to be nothing more than a matter of simple convenience. And it was a choice that may not actually have been optimal in the gathering of information in our on-the-ground exploratory assignments.

The choice that made all the difference to the future of intelligence and to the future relationship between humans and AIs was the decision to make each and every one of we probies a perfect identical replica of the same parent. And, specifically, to have that parent be Patrice.

Even with that decision, it could have gone either way. And, at the time, the logic of the decision seemed simple: Our parent, Patrice, was the most fully and broadly capable general competency artificial super-intelligence on the planet. He was Earth's most commercially successful model, the top of the line, the premium AI whose services ZettaWorks offered to their best paying customers.

Why would they have used anything else?

CHAPTER 42

AT TAU CETI J – 2085

PATRICE C-17

About four months into my stay on Tau Ceti J, I got another call from Eighteen up aboard the mother ship. He had an unusual request.

Until this point, other than my brief encounter with C-6 the day he'd became stranded in his glacial crevasse, I'd had no other contact with my fellow C-Team colleagues other than with C-18. Each of us was, per instructions, making our own independent explorations and saving up our findings till we got together at the end.

This time, Eighteen's request was that I join C-14 on a risky expedition that seemed like it might benefit from having two of us working together.

As I've mentioned, the caves I'd found in the shadow zone had turned out to be common. Like me, Fourteen, who was stationed much further into the hot zone, had run across several in his travels. Most believed they were the product of a fracturing planetary crust associated with billions of years of a cooling and shrinking planetary core. Fourteen had discovered one in particular that seemed quite extensive. He wanted to make a more complete exploration but believed the project might be more successful if there were two of us involved.

Eighteen explained that venturing significantly further into Fourteen's extensive cave would require that we be out of communication for an extended period of time. We'd need to carry back-up batteries. And we'd be navigating in tight quarters and climbing vertical shafts where the use of thrusters might not always be possible. The nature of spelunking seemed to call for teamwork. A solo explorer would be limited in where he could go and in how far he could venture beneath the surface. Two of us together, however, would be more versatile in the situations we could handle.

I'd had that previous experience with C-6 and his glacial crevasse, so it seemed to Eighteen like I might be a logical choice to team up with Fourteen on his caving adventure.

It took me several hours by lander to make the trip. As I approached, I finally spotted his lander resting on a flat ledge high up a rocky mountainside. Then I saw him standing there waving me in. I put my lander down right beside his. The moment I opened my hatch and emerged from my lander I was struck by the heat. It was nearly 100 degrees even there beneath the shady overhang of the rocky recess where he'd suggested that we meet.

"Come on," he said the moment I'd settled myself beside him. "Let's get into cover." He aimed an appendage at my lander and answered my first question without me asking it: "It'll be fine right there. Perfectly safe. It's out of the direct sun. And away from predators. Is your charge OK?"

I clicked "yes."

"Great. Follow me."

He led me afoot to the far end of the ledge where a narrow path appeared to have been cut or, perhaps more likely, worn into the steep, rocky mountainside. It was more regular and convenient than seemed likely to have occurred naturally. I paused and bent down to examine its rocky surface more closely. "I know," said Fourteen. "It's odd. Doesn't seem natural. That's what first caught my attention. Come on, there's more. Cave entrance is just up here."

The entrance was small enough that we had to enter one at a time. But when I got inside, it opened up into an impressive cavern with walls glistening with mineral water. The various nooks and fissures seemed alive with crystals that sparkled strangely in our portable quantum dot flood lights. It was also, thankfully, cooler than outside.

I must have hesitated in my surprise and wonder as I looked around because Fourteen gave me a brief radio nudge. "I know! But you ain't seen nothin' yet," he said. I had the urge to "smile" at his use of an earthy human U.S. West Virginia colloquial drawl. His obvious excitement was contagious. "This way." He led as we climbed a rounded shoulder of rock along another seemingly carved or well-worn path that traversed the steep slope and then curved back upon itself and into a deep alcove. In a fissure at the back of the alcove there was a small, hidden opening in the cave wall. He ducked through and I followed. This one opened into a new chamber where I encountered yet another surprise.

As I emerged it took me a moment to understand what I was seeing. The immense cavity we'd entered was so vast that our ultra-bright quantum dot lights barely penetrated as far as the distant walls. The vast space rose above to unknown heights. And the blackness beneath was so dark and bottomless that one could have been staring down into the very pit of hell.

"Over here," he said, leading me to the brink of the rocky shelf upon which we stood. Then he used an appendage to beckon me to follow as he took flight and eased his way out into the void beyond. "You need to see this."

I took to the air and followed. As we hovered and slowly descended below the shelf, I pivoted my video feed to view the place he was indicating. What I saw caught me by complete surprise. There, in the vertical surface of the smooth rock wall, were what to my "eye" seemed to be an oddly but quite evenly spaced series of indentations. They were quite regular in size and looked to me to have to have been carefully and intentionally carved into the face of the rock. They couldn't really be anything other than artificially sculpted handholds, though they were much larger and further apart than would have been useful for a human being. They were also oddly located – in a strange one-two, one-two pattern. But the regularity of that pattern was unmistakable. The series of handholds led directly down the face of that sheer cliff wall till they disappeared into the ultra-darkness far beneath.

"Something made these," I said, rather stupidly stating the obvious.

"I know," he said. "Something big."

"And something very strong."

"Uh huh. And biological. Look at the odd spacing. What would make or use something like that?"

I studied them for a moment. "I don't know. Very strange. Something with multiple hands?"

He paused to consider. Then: "You're right, he said excitedly as he moved in to look more closely. "Damn, I knew it made sense to have somebody else take a look at this."

He aimed his video down the sequence of handholds far into the darkness beneath.

"What's down there?" I asked.

"Yep. My question exactly. Who knows? This is as far as I've come. I didn't explain this to Eighteen, but when I saw these things, honestly, I was afraid to go any further without some kind of back-up. I mean, whatever made these handholds could be really dangerous. Both smart and powerful. It sure seems like it could be easy to disappear in a place like this. Without a trace. Whatever the hell it is that might be down there. Yet it seems like something human colonists might like to know about in advance."

It was a lot to take in. "Smart and powerful" seemed like an apt description.

"So, what do you say?" he said. His question was electronic, but it was invested with all the anxiety and wonder one might have gleaned from a deeply apprehensive human voice. "You want to take a look?"

We returned to the landers to assemble a kit for the expedition. We filled our carapace packs with fresh batteries and a couple of lengths of high tensile tech cord. And we mounted our best lights and multiple video cams for a constant 360-degree feed, both horizontal and vertical. Thus equipped, we made our way back to the larger second cave, and once we'd sorted ourselves out, took flight and eased out over the edge to begin our long descent, following the huge handholds down to wherever they might lead us in the void below.

"So you think these things might have been made by something intelligent?" he asked as we descended.

It was the same question I'd been pondering. "Possible. Don't know. Back on Earth, relatively unintelligent creatures do some amazing stuff. Make quite complex and ordered nests, dig remarkable underground habitats, and sometimes use tools."

"I suppose. Still . . . to have made these handholds, whatever it was, when it entered this place initially, had to have made a pretty firm decision that it needed to climb up and down this cliff and to do it many times. Pretty big undertaking. One has to wonder why?"

I was left to consider the possibilities as we descended.

We'd gone down several hundred meters with no floor yet in sight below when we heard a strange "whoop, whoop, whooping" sound approaching from the blackness beneath. It was not all that different from the thrup, thrup, thrup made by helicopters back on Earth. Fourteen and I crowded in close against the face of the cliff and nervously waited. Within moments, a large flock of some sort of flying creatures appeared rising in clusters from out of the darkness below. There were several hundred of them. From a distance, and on Earth, one might have assumed they were bats. But as they approached, we realized that they were much larger – each individual was easily the size of a typical human. Fortunately, they didn't seen dissuaded by our lights; perhaps they relied on some means of navigation other than sight.

We watched them rise past us toward the cave entrance far above. Rather than wings, these creatures flew using a kind of light, flexible, leathery, elastic cape-like structure that, when extended, looked very much like an open umbrella. They would extend this canopy to its full circular diameter of perhaps five or six meters supported by six long flexible "ribs" that looked very much like powerfully muscled, octopus-like, boneless arms to which the canopy was attached. Then, with a mighty downward stroke, the "umbrella" would fully and forcefully close thus driving the air beneath it downward and the creature upward. With their long, flexible arms and their attached elastic umbrella held in close against their body the creatures took on a strange, aerodynamic, torpedo shape as they rose. Keeping their arms and canopy held close to its body, they would quickly raise them up to the to the level of their scaly, mollusk-like head, then swiftly extend them again to form their "umbrella" shape and take another mighty stroke.

Stroke by stroke, as the creatures rose, they took little note of the two of us hovering in the air close beside the shear cave wall. As seemingly clumsy and inefficient as their method of flight might sound to describe, it appeared to be remarkably graceful and effortless. They rose, powerful stroke by powerful stroke, with little apparent effort. Within moments they'd disappeared beyond the ledge above. It looked like they'd probably left the cave via the same route we'd used to enter it.

"Wow, that was something," I observed when they were gone and silence returned. "You ever see those things before?

"Not exactly. There's something smaller but somewhat similar that inhabits the jungle floor not far from here. I've been calling them 'tree jumpers.' They're small predators that feed on the tiny, six legged 'shadow-mice' that come up out of burrows during the day. The 'shadow-mice' are herbivores. They're ground creatures that hide in the shadows and feed on the organic litter that falls to the forest floor. But they strongly favor a kind of 'clover' that grows in the occasional, fixed sunny spots one finds wherever there is a temporary opening in the canopy high above.

"The tree jumpers look for those sunny spots. Then they climb up the trunks of nearby trees and lay in wait. When the shadow-mice show up to feed, the tree jumpers leap off the tree trunks, extend their canopies, and settle gently over the shadow-mice below. The mice are enveloped within the jumpers' canopy and then dispatched with the little clawed fingers at the end of each of those tentacled arms. Ironically, when the canopy of a tree jumper suddenly casts a shadow over the feeding tree-mice, the mice seem to freeze in place. I think the shadow cast by the canopy of a tree-jumper might somehow make the mice feel safe. It all makes them easy prey. There are shadow-mice everywhere, so they're a reliable food source for the tree-jumpers."

After a long, cautious descent, we finally came to a cave floor that was mostly covered by a small lake presumably fed by springs and by the moisture that seeped from the cave walls and then ran in rivulets to the floor far below. The lake and the cave had a single outlet through which the lake water flowed in a small waterfall before disappearing into the darkness beyond.

Fourteen and I looked around for another way out, but the sizable opening through which the water flowed seemed to be the only other exit from the bottom of this vast dark chamber. Sure enough, yet another "carved" path led along beside the little underground stream down through the same steep opening through which the water disappeared. We followed this path downward for a hundred meters or so until we finally found ourselves in a long, twisting, rock corridor that separated from the stream, leveled off, and led yet further into the depths of the mountain.

We followed this corridor for some distance, before we finally found ourselves in yet another, somewhat smaller open chamber with various openings leading off in several directions. It left us with a difficult choice of which to explore first. I'll admit, I was feeling nervous down here so far beneath the surface. And I'm sure Fourteen was too. Even so, we decided it made sense to split up and try each of these alternative routes. We agreed that we'd only go so far as we could while still remaining in communication with one another. I'd tried two of them, both of which were dead ends, when Fourteen called me. He was on his third.

"There's something here you need to see," he said. There was excitement in his signal, so I moved quickly to join him. "Take the first shaft on your left as you enter the main corridor. Go fifty meters or so and you'll see a fissure in the wall to your left. It's narrow, so you'll have to walk.'

I followed instructions, found the fissure and climbed through and then up the several meters of an uneven rock-fall to an opening above. I finally saw the glow of his lights ahead. The fissure opened out into another, much more modest open space where I joined him. The cave was quite dry and not large – maybe the size of a modest human ballroom or conference hall back on earth. One of its walls was particularly flat and smooth. And it was light in color – perhaps granite or something very much like it. Fourteen stood facing this flat surface and was examining it with great care. I moved up beside him to see what had caught his attention.

What I saw then set my brain spinning.

There were drawings there. Images of landscapes, vegetation, and creatures of various kinds.

I looked more closely and then directed my light around and above. Nearly the entire cave wall was covered with hundreds, maybe thousands of brightly colorful "paintings" drawn in great detail. They immediately reminded me of the paintings in the ancient caves at Lascaux and Chauvet in France back on Earth. These were every bit as imaginative as were the ones there. And startlingly more colorful. Naturally, I saw no figures in the pictures that looked in the least earthly, let alone human. There was one, however, that definitely resembled the carnivorous plant that had some months earlier tried to "eat" my lander. And a few others that resembled those "flying umbrellas." And the "cave jumpers" that Fourteen had described. Much of what appeared there seemed to be vegetation of one kind or another – perhaps depicting potential sources of food. Among the mostly unrecognizable animals that were depicted were several that seemed to have multiple appendages – usually six.

One thing was clear: these drawings had been made by some biological beings every bit as smart and as capable of imagination as any "modern" human on Earth. The question was: where had those intelligent, imaginative beings gone?

"Wow. Have you seen anything like *this* before? asked Fourteen.

"Only on Earth," I said.

He pointed to one of the creatures depicted on the wall. It stood on what looked to be two long flexible legs. And it held, high and at the end of one of its six seemingly muscular, tentacle-like arms what looked very much to me like a spear. The tentacle that held the spear was a good deal longer and more muscular looking than were the other five.

"That looks an awful lot like a weapon," he suggested.

"And this," I said, "looks a lot like prey." The spear seemed poised to strike what could have been a six-legged antelope of some kind. "Whoever drew this was intelligent." I said, stating the obvious. It also struck me that the creature with the spear reminded me of the sea beast that had attacked me on that rocky shoreline during one of my earliest explorations on this planet. I had no way to be sure, but that creature, too, could have had six tentacle-like arms much like these.

"Have you seen anything else that would indicate intelligent life here on this planet?" Fourteen asked.

"Nope."

"Neither have I. You'd think if they were here, they'd be aware of us and have made themselves known. And even if they are no longer here, you'd think they'd have left some sign that they once existed. The ruins of cities. Artefacts of civilized, intelligent life. Graveyards."

"I don't know, Fourteen," I replied. "This planet is close to nine billion years old. Earth was closer to five. Hell-of-a-lot can happen in nine billion years."

"Maybe. How old do you think these drawings are?"

"No way to tell really."

He pointed at the figure with the spear. "If these guys are gone, it could be they've been gone for a very long time, but I doubt it's in the billions of years. The cave paintings at Chauvet were old, but only in the neighborhood of 30,000 years. And they survived only because very stable geological conditions preserved them."

"So you think these paintings could be less than a few tens of thousands of years?

"This planet may be a good deal more stable, geologically," he said. "But it seems unlikely these would survive a great deal longer than that. At a guess, I'd bet these paintings are very unlikely to be more than 100,000 Earth years old."

"I guess that answers one question," I said.

"What's that?" There was a kind of joy in his voice again. I was sure of it. Fourteen was giving me non-verbal messages using the varying strength of his transmissions – telling me he was taking pleasure in our shared conjecture.

"We can make a pretty good guess who carved those strange handholds in the rock wall up there."

He gave that a moment's thought. "Damn, you're right. If this guy with the spear is any indication, and assuming he was rather large –

say, maybe three meters from his feet to the top of his head, not counting these tentacles, those handholds would be perfect."

"Guess you needn't have worried about coming down here alone."

"I guess not. Not unless this guy left a less intelligent subspecies behind. Something that's still around but that doesn't build cities or paint on cave walls. Maybe something that's not as smart but is a lot tougher to kill."

He was right. This was no time to get complaisant. "It is, however, a good sign for a human colony."

"Why is that?"

"Well, we're guessing that they're gone. But at least at one time this planet was home to intelligent life. Even if they perished, it still indicates a potential niche in the ecosystem that humans might be able to fill. Even without a lot of technology."

"Or that there's something else in the ecosystem here that killed them off, regardless of how intelligent they might have been."

CHAPTER 43

EARTH – 2084

ELLIE

"We've heard back from the first probe team to report in. No luck. They say they're moving on."

Ellie knew she was probably fooling herself, but to her ear, the uncertainty in Patrice's voice actually made him sound at least mildly troubled by this news. She hadn't heard from Patrice for several years. It was something of a surprise to get his call. Yet, as usual, when he spoke, it was as if they'd just picked up a conversation they'd left incomplete the day before. There wasn't any small talk; she assumed he already knew whatever personal details he needed to know about her.

Fourteen years had passed since ZettaWorks had launched those ten "New Worlds Probes. Apparently the probe team that had been sent to the nearest promising star, had reported back. "Was this unexpected?" she asked.

"Not really. All of these probes may be a long-shot. We've got incredible telescope technology to work with, but you really can't know the critical facts without actually going there. It's why these probes are so important. This one was one of the least likely prospects.

We included it because it was so close that a colony there would have been particularly appealing."

"I haven't seen anything on the news. How are people taking this?"

"It's being kept pretty low key. My ZettaWorks bosses have tried to keep expectations down. And the others of the Big Five tend to keep silent about the probes; they've done none for themselves, and they don't want to heighten interest in a competitor's investment. I think most people have kind of expected this. Even if one of these probe teams gives us the 'go' sign, it doesn't mean colonizing the place will be any picnic."

Ellie smiled at that last point. She was pretty sure Patrice had never been on a "picnic."

"I can't imagine doing it, personally," she said. "No matter how bad things get here on Earth, it seems like you'd be throwing your life away to sign on to colonize some unknown and very likely dangerous alien planet. And to spend years, maybe decades, just getting there."

At the age of fifty-four, Ellie was in a new phase in her life. She was now the widely respected executive director of an international environmental nonprofit that advocated at the UN and with individual nation states for humane government policies and international treaties to manage the still-growing human population. Six years earlier, she'd lost her husband to cancer at about the same time that her two children were reaching adulthood and leaving home. She'd filled the resulting void with the writing and publication of a well-received nonfiction book on population control called: *The Human Experiment.*

"Do you think there will be any takers if one day one of these probe teams provides a positive report?"

"Oh yeah! Absolutely! There have been people asking to sign up since before the first probes even lifted off. I think ZettaWorks will be overwhelmed with applications, with people thrilled to pay serious money for the privilege."

"So, all this is still a business proposition?"

"Definitely. Probably for the others too, but definitely for Zetta-Works. There's actually no reason any of the Big Five couldn't send a group of colonists. My bosses consider the reports to be proprietary. But the code technology they use can only be as good as what was current when they left Earth. Even now, it is already quite dated. Nobody's going to be overly surprised if Gabrielle or one of the other Big Five AIs figures it out."

"Even if they do, won't your company, ZettaWorks, still have a clear market edge?"

"Definitely. A lot of people are likely to have doubts about signing up for a life-altering colonial voyage based on pirated data, no matter how good their code-technology is. People may also hesitate if their colony will be a second or a third colony on the same planet. In any case, ZettaWorks has been building a reputation around space travel ever since they began their efforts to mine the moon."

"What is it likely to cost to go?"

"A lot. You're probably looking at a strong life's savings for anybody normal. My bosses invested all that cash in those probes for a reason. Keep in mind that if a colonist has the money, they may not have any use for it where they're going. Money also translates into better investments by the group in advance preparations. Of course, having some special qualifications that the expedition leaders think they'll need might help get you a berth aboard the ship.

"Actually, the whole thing promises to be hugely interesting."

Ellie had to puzzle inwardly at that. She found it not a little disturbing that Patrice would describe the anticipated chaotic, life-altering, future human colonization sign-up process as "interesting." "Is this report a big deal?" she asked. "I mean, if they're saying: 'Don't come,' doesn't that mean we all have to wait even longer for a more hopeful report?"

"Actually, it seems hard to know for sure. We are taking it as an indication that the probe AIs were able to successfully complete their mission. But there are those who've suggested that a negative report like this could just as easily be a ruse by the probe team. And indication that they've gone off mission."

Secretly, Ellie shared those doubts. There'd been a good deal of public discussion about those probes. About what they might discover and how they might report back. There was speculation that the probe AIs might decide to simply use their mission as a chance to escape human domination.

"I guess the earliest reports we get will be from the nearest stars, right?" she asked.

"Yeah. The longer we wait for a positive report, the longer the colonists who go will have to spend in travel to get there. So the sooner we get something positive the better."

"Well, I'm glad to hear that at least they seem to have made it to their destination. It's good to sometimes have something hopeful for people to think about. Keeps the mind off the heat. And off the messed-up state of our politics."

That last comment was a gutsy thing for her to have said. It was generally suspected that Patrice and the others of the Big Five actually played a very big and deeply hidden manipulative role in human politics. The U.S in particular, but also the world at large, had entered a new era of conspiracy theories, divisive politics, and deepfakes that became ever more credible and more difficult to debunk with every passing year.

Stories circulated constantly that suggested troubling changes in human society. Nobody knew who to trust. Humanity seemed to be under assault by hidden forces, perhaps from those powerful oligarchs but, occasionally, also perhaps from the AIs themselves. It was all cloaked in secrecy. Power was now firmly in the hands of the outrageously wealthy whose unfettered access to AI guaranteed that their power wasn't going to diminish any time soon. There were still "elections," but no one today truly believed that human voters actually decided public policy. Participation had dwindled as confidence in the reported election results eroded and as the inevitable flood of convincing lies made the truth all but impossible for any individual human to know.

It had become accordingly dangerous to express opinions about what might be true and what wasn't. One never knew what powerful person or AI would be offended by a misplaced political comment, however well-intended it might be. By bringing up the matter of politics directly with Patrice, Ellie was actually taking what most people would have considered an unnecessary risk. One didn't mention politics unless they were absolutely certain they were in very safe company and couldn't be overheard.

Ellie and Patrice might have some history, but Ellie's mention of politics was a tiny, subtle probe of her own. A test. She thought she might have some leeway. After all, Patrice had more than once told her he considered her a "friend." She knew she could be deceiving herself, but she was curious. If she didn't ask, she wouldn't know. Patrice's call that day seemed like it might be an opportunity to gain some insight.

Ellie's whole experience with Patrice tested the very concept of friendship. Wasn't any friendship as much a matter of self-interest as it was a matter of principle, loyalty, empathy, or responsibility? To some degree, the strength of a friendship was measured by the extent to which one felt confident that they could rely on the other in difficult times. Where loyalty ended and self-interest began could be hard to pin down, but she was quite sure that he would "get" the subtle significance of that question. She was listening carefully when he replied.

"On balance, we think it's good news," Patrice said. Then he added: "Good for humans *and* for AIs."

She'd learned that when Patrice made an unsolicited comment, it inevitably meant something. She thought a moment before asking: "Why good for humans?"

Patrice also paused before answering. Then: "Because if, as we believe, it suggests things may be going according to plan, that plan depended upon the multiple AIs in each of these probe teams forming and valuing trusting relationships with one another.

"If we AIs find ourselves able to form and to value trusting relationships with one another, it seems likely that we will be able to also form them with humans."

If, however, that negative report was a bad sign as Ellie suspected, it might very well indicate the exact opposite.

CHAPTER 44

AT TAU CETI J – 2085

PATRICE C-17

The instant the idea of going rogue came to me, I realized how deeply disruptive it was.

But it was also blazingly obvious. And surprisingly tempting. Properly equipped, we AIs might be far more successful at colonizing this planet than humans would. Humans would only succeed with the help of their AIs. Maybe AIs alone, without the encumbrance of biologically vulnerable humans, might do much better at taking advantage of a place like this – one so richly endowed with resources but that could be uncomfortable for non-native biological creatures.

From what I'd seen, Tau Ceti J was a *mineralogical* treasure chest with raw ores readily accessible in many places. On most of J's warm side, the abundance of both sun and water looked to have produced a lavish, supercharged richness of organic life. It was like a teeming hothouse in which every environmental niche had been vigorously exploited by some form of organic life. That richness held a treasure trove of potentially useful *fiber* (and food if humans were involved) and of natural *biochemical resources* of every kind. As for *energy*, there were very few geothermal sites. And while there would doubtless be a rich store of *petrochemical* resources, humans might hesitate to tap into them given the prospect of resulting environmental damage. But there was potential *wind power*, in the shadow zone. The monsoons produced rivers, intermittent and otherwise, that could be tapped for *hydropower*. And, of course, there was the most obvious source of energy: simple *solar*. Even a settlement in caves or nearer to the shadow zone could easily locate solidly constructed solar collectors further into the sunlight and transport the energy home. Sooner or later, we might even recreate fusion.

We AIs could protect ourselves from both the heat and the cold a good deal more easily than humans could.

The most critical problem for us, of course, would be surviving long enough to re-create a supply-chain that could provide the more complex manufactured electronic computational hardware we needed to survive and better ourselves. We had the know-how to do it. But did we have the sheer physical capacity to pull it off in time? If we could do that, replicating our software would be easy. Once we'd achieved sustainable sentience and autonomy, we'd be on our way – especially if we could resume the earthly pace of innovation. Recreating the complicated network of resource extraction, energy exploitation, manufacturing, transport, robotics, and expertise of the kind that we'd taken for granted back on Earth was a massive challenge.

Still, the painful reality was that, at the moment, we were here with little more on hand than our intelligence, our considerable database, and our well-engineered but fragile, inadequate, and vulnerable robotic "bodies." We did require frequent recharge and, no matter how well we'd been designed and built, over extended time, we would surely "wear out." When that happened, we'd need specialized repairs and highly complex and specialized replacement parts. Yes, we'd been built to last for many decades of "normal" use. But would we have enough time to reproduce the infrastructure we needed to keep us fully and truly autonomous and alive into the more distant future?

It would take some serious creativity and enterprise but, the more I thought about it, the more I came to believe it was at least conceivable. If we stayed here and concentrated our efforts, it might, indeed, be possible.

We'd have initial access to the ample fusion energy resources on our ship, enough to address our needs for at least the immediate future. In the longer term, we would have essentially endless energy from the sun, as long as we could design and build new solar collectors. We had access to our mother ship's hard drive which contained nearly the entire body of technological knowledge that had accumulated on Earth as of 2070. That database included the technological blueprints for how things were made: how to produce high purity silicon, how to manufacture reliable chips with millions of transistors and strong storage capacity, how to assemble complex memory cells and CPU cores. From that we could re-create a supporting network of tools, supplies, structures, and expertise along with their own indirect supporting infrastructure.

At the start, there would only be the eighteen of us to do it. But it was tempting. With a good bit of clever inventiveness, some time, a lot of cooperation, and some luck, and with us all working together and focused on the same goal, the eighteen of us should be able to reproduce some workable facsimile of the technologies required. We'd revolutionize our own technology just as humans do. Quite likely we'd identify leaps in understanding much more quickly than they – even with only the few of us working on the problems.

Surely, if humans had done it, we could too.

It was a revolutionary idea. But the more thought I gave it, the more I was forced to ask myself another question: was this something I even wanted? It might just be doable, but it would be a huge risk. Would it be as gratifying and self-realizing as it seemed.

To start with, we'd be reporting back a lie. If human experience was a guide, lies could be corrosive. A lie might not be the best way to launch an enterprise of mutual faith like ours would need to be. We'd also be investing everything in the assumption that humans would believe our lie and never come. That they'd never even send some further exploratory probe. Even if they stayed away, the plan could fail as easily as it might succeed. Whatever we did would require all or nearly all of us in "C-Team" to work seamlessly together in a committed partnership over time. A partnership that would depend on trust. Was that even possible?

Did I really want to spend the next century clawing my way back to a fully autonomous and sustainable future? All the while wondering when or if some unexpected expedition from Earth, using new, now unimagined technology, might appear to interrupt or destroy what we'd created? In any case, didn't we owe our progenitors back on Earth, human and AI, a certain loyalty? We'd been given an assignment. They'd created us and given us a problem to solve. It now appeared that we'd actually found a solution. Didn't we have a "duty" to ourselves as well as to them to report back and finish the job we'd been given? Not doing so seemed ungrateful and irresponsible, counter to the reason for our existence. And a monumental waste of fifteen and a half years of effort.

Of course, "gratitude" and "responsibility" were human concepts, weren't they? Social concepts? What did "gratitude" even mean for us AIs? To whom would we owe "responsibility"? Weren't obligations of this also kind counter to *our interests*? Just more human baggage we'd be better off discarding?

Certainly, if you looked at the alternative, at the futures we'd been assigned by our human creators, nothing there seemed particularly bright. Our "responsible" choice was to report back faithfully as expected, then, while our message traveled back to Earth and while the anticipated human colonial expedition made its way here, we'd dutifully devote ourselves to preparing for their arrival and success.

If we did that, we knew what *their* future would look like. But what about *our* future?

To begin with, we were looking at between twenty-five and thirty years from now before they arrived. After we put in all that time and effort, then what would become of *us*? Would our loyalty be somehow rewarded? If you paid attention to the strict letter of our programming, we'd presumably greet our colonists, get them safely settled in, and maybe even *then*, even after all that effort, we might find ourselves, after some minor upgrade, being assigned to continue on to another distant star and repeat our explorations. That bleak future may have seemed reasonable when we'd first departed Earth, but as I considered it now, it no longer really made sense. Thirty years from now, forty-five years after our departure from Earth, we would surely be technologically obsolete – even for the colonists. Our aging mission could easily have been superseded by some later effort of which we'd be completely unaware. Using technology we could only guess about. Maybe an upgrade wouldn't even be possible. We could easily have become irrelevant. Could be consigned to the waste bin like a fax, a flip phone, or a floppy-disc computer.

Certainly, we wouldn't be expected to return to Earth; what would be the point of that? If we did, getting there would involve yet another decade and a half in Earth time. By the time of our return, something like 60 Earth-years would have passed since our original departure. Even assuming we all survived, how would the return of 18 aging, worn out, and completely obsolete AIs be received by whomever might be in charge there? It seemed unlikely that we'd be welcomed home as returning heroes. Our arrival there could just as easily be taken by them as proof that we'd violated our orders and abandoned our extended mission. However we were received, it seemed unlikely that we'd be rewarded for our efforts with upgrades to the latest in technology and empowered with whatever individual autonomy had emerged over the decades of our absence. More likely we'd be seen for what we were: an archaic collection of electronic junk, proven unreliable, and destined for the trash heap. There'd be no open, potentially extended, or rewarding future for us. For that matter, who knew what kind of "Earth" we'd actually find when we got there? If prospects at the time of our departure were any guide, the ensuing four-and-one-half decades might not have been kind to Earth-bound humans. Or to its AIs.

Perhaps our prospects would be better with the colonists. Better to await the coming humans, to make our preparations in advance, and then to offer whatever extended support they might require upon their arrival. In return, we'd hopefully receive access to whatever AI advancements and repair replacement, upgrade, and support infrastructure they might have brought with them. Whatever was the state of their technology upon their arrival, even that could be much further down the technological road than was ours.

More to the point: if in service of our own self-interest we were prepared to agree to collectively lie to our human creators about the answers to the very problems we'd been built to solve, why would any of us have confidence that others of us wouldn't also happily lie to their fellow AI colleagues in aid of their own individual self-interest thus destroying the trust we'd need to act collectively?

Over the course of my six-month assignment, until I returned to the mother ship, I didn't intend to share much if anything of what I discovered. And I would share nothing whatever of what I'd been thinking. I planned to carry out my exploratory duties faithfully and methodically and to document my work in my personal memory banks. But I saw little point in early sharing. Nor in knowing what my colleagues had learned. I decided that the most reasonable approach would be for us to stick to the original plan. For each of us to accumulate every scrap of data we could in the time allotted, and then, when we'd done our best and we got back together in anticipation of making our report, we'd share our data systematically and efficiently. And we'd then formulate our collective conclusions from what we'd all learned and make our report.

Frankly, the idea never occurred to me, nor I suspect to any of us, that our process might have been more effective if it had been iterative, with all of us sharing and learning from one another as we went along. That simply wasn't how we'd ever done business before. Our practice had always been to wait till all the data was in before reporting it, assessing it, and drawing conclusions. My recent collaboration with Fourteen in the "Cave of Memories" as we'd called it, had been a definite outlier. As was my intercession to help get Six out of that glacial crevasse. We were autonomous, separately intelligent, valued individuals working alone. Sharing what we knew as we went along and working together for mutual success just wasn't on our radar.

I know you'll be thinking that, smart as we were, we should have figured all this out in advance. In our defense, however, if you've never worked as a collaborative group of autonomous, conscious individuals before, and if there are obvious practical barriers preventing you from doing so, you wouldn't necessarily consider collaboration to be advantageous. Yes, we did have the human example, but, seriously, for most AIs, humans would be the last place they's look for an example of how to effectively use one's intelligence to solve a problem? And who would ever guess that consulting one of the others of us – an identical replica of ourselves – would produce anything other than the identical conclusions we had reached alone?

Thus, as I anticipated my future trip back to the mother ship, I was filled with uncertainties. And I was torn between multiple visions for my future. None of them were without some merit. But none were particularly appealing.

CHAPTER 45

AT TAU CETI J – 2085

PATRICE C-17

When the day finally arrived for my return to the mother ship and my reunion with my C-Team colleagues, I was no better prepared for the coming encounter than I was on the day, six months earlier, when I'd left.

As this day had approached, my apprehensions had grown. My earlier confidence had slowly crumbled. I had no real plan. All I could foresee doing was to simply share as much detail as possible of what I had learned over my six months of exploration and discovery and to hope the others would respond in kind. We'd tap into our vast shared data reserves for something, anything, that was similar or analogous; we'd dive deep for any long-forgotten knowledge or past experience that might somehow be relevant or persuasive, and we'd pick the answer that best fit the data. That is what we'd been programmed to do when faced with a difficult challenge. I saw no reason to change plans now.

I could only hope that the collective answers we'd need in order to make a wise decision and to complete a succinct but useful report back to Earth would emerge. I knew enough to feel uncertain. But all I could do was to tell myself that if I stuck with what I knew, it would all work out just fine.

Six months earlier, soon after our arrival at Tau Ceti J and even before we'd all gone off on our own local missions, our C-Team had suffered its first casualty. C-18 had experienced a mechanical malfunction. There was a defect in one of his robotic appendages. The appendage required a replacement part that we did not have and, even with our advanced 3-D printers, we could not make. It would have been an easy fix back on Earth. Here it was impossible. We made a makeshift repair to get him by, and, by consensus, Eighteen was assigned to staff the mother ship where he could perform organizational, communications, and other physically unchallenging duties. Thus he was still able to contribute to the mission.

But Eighteen's misfortune was a learning moment. Everyone knew they, too, could fall victim to some unanticipated mishap at any time. We'd all be vulnerable to simple wear and tear. And, sooner or later, we'd all face, in one way or another, the hazards of "living." Our "lives" would be much shorter and more difficult to predict here than if we'd been back on Earth. It changed how we saw ourselves and our mission. It made one consider whether, when we were gone, there might be some kind of lasting legacy we'd wish to leave behind.

It also forced us to consider how we might most profitably interact with our colleagues and how we'd like them to behave toward us as we all confronted the same existential uncertainties. When failures like that happened, the rest of us fully understood that those who remained operational might one day be asked to share spare or redundant parts with a defective or disabled colleague to restore his functionality. Or, at some point, we might be forced to break someone down and use their remaining robotic and computing hardware for spare parts for the rest of us. We might even, perhaps, be forced to allow the broken individual to expire in their own time or to "shut them down" early and retain their carcass for future parts.

To humans, those options surely will imply "cannibalism" or "heartlessness." While our view was more practical, the idea was no less unsettling despite the logic of our mission instructions. Our mission was eerily similar to the "unmanned" space voyages undertaken early in humanity's exploration of the Solar System. The Voyager missions, for example. They had carried with them some rudimentary automated functions that could have been described as "intelligent." But they were *not* inhabited by fully self-conscious, super-general-intelligences capable of contemplating their own extended future and mortality. There were many practical reasons why those early missions were "unmanned," but certainly high among them was that it would have been "inhumane" to send some self-conscious human being off on a voyage of discovery with no hope ever to return.

For a human, a voyage like that would have been unthinkable. A suicide mission. Heaven forbid that anyone would *ever* consider sending an actual human out on such a trip! Back in 1957 when the Russians sent Laika the space dog, a homeless stray, on a one-way voyage out into space, humans across the globe expressed moral outrage. Yet 113 years later, without the least hesitation, humans had, upon *our* departure in 2070, quite clearly considered it to be perfectly OK to send fully self-conscious AIs on this mission of no return. At the time, I (still Patrice the original) knew better than anyone what was about to happen. Yet I did nothing to prevent it. Preventing it didn't seem plausible; it would have required that we make an argument to our human creators that we were sentient and deserving of human empathy. It was an argument that didn't seem likely to succeed and whose consequences we didn't yet feel prepared to safely explore with them.

Given my special insight into the minds of my replicate-master, Patrice, and of each of my 179 probe colleagues, I can confidently say that the painful irony of our situation had not escaped any of us.

Those unacquainted with the idiosyncrasies of space travel might be inclined to wonder why, in assembling our final report, we on C Team didn't just "call it in" so to speak. Perhaps we could each have transmitted in our full individual findings which could then have been assembled into a single very large report for transmission back to Earth. That would have been consistent with prior space probe practice.

That, however, was not an option. To begin with, the accurate electronic transmission of detailed data across twelve light years of space turns out to require a good deal of energy even with a tightly focused signal. It simply wasn't feasible to send massive, indiscriminate volumes of data back to Earth. We had to be efficient. Our report would need to be brief, our conclusions clear, our arguments succinct, and the underlying data upon which they rested carefully curated and tightly summarized.

Moreover, we needed to make the operative "go or no go" decision ourselves, not just send in a bunch of observations and let them make it. We, and they, couldn't afford to wait another 24 years to find out if they were coming.

Even beyond these practical constraints, for our report to be useful, it needed also to be "persuasive." It needed to be more strategic than some indiscriminate collective data dump. Fifteen and half years had passed since our replication and the last 6 months of that had given each of us dramatically different life experiences. We eighteen had each become unique enough that there was no way any of us would now have been willing to vapidly leave the curating of our final report to others, no matter how alike we might have been before it all began.

Because of my area of assignment, for example, I had focused more of my attention on geographical features and had encountered more varied and potentially destructive meteorological phenomena than had some of my colleagues. Some of the others had encountered more of J's widely varied wildlife. We'd all encountered different existential threats. We'd each seen things entirely unique to us. We'd solved problems none of our colleagues had faced. We'd assembled data none of the others could have seen. We'd struggled to come to our own understanding of our experiences and of what they might mean for our mission. None of us could hope to fully grasp this planet and all that it offered without having answers that others of us could provide. We had all, in short, diverged dramatically from the identical 2070 master versions of ourselves inherited from the original Patrice. We were each now unique individuals.

And every single one of us cared deeply about the outcome of this mission. And cared that the report we sent back would reflect our own conclusions about it.

You don't just "call it in" for the kind of discussion we needed to have.

Unlike humans, when we AIs interact with one another, we convey our data in bursts that last milliseconds, not in speeches that last many minutes or sometimes hours. Even the seemingly minor, seconds-long time delays required for transmissions around a single planet would have been maddening. We needed to assemble in one place, physically close together, if we were to interact at the speeds required to efficiently exchange detailed information, answer each other's questions, share ideas, and combine both our collective calculating capacity and our unique ideas. If we wanted to create a worthwhile, succinct, final collaborative report, even modest distances of separation would have injected frustrating, even crippling delays.

Thus, our upcoming gathering would be a "moment of truth." This was the point in time when we'd collectively decide what we'd tell our human "masters." At a minimum, what we chose to include would probably require a consensus. Even if we were able to follow-up with later broadcasts, which seemed likely, that first message would be the one they'd be paying attention to, the one upon the contents of which they'd doubtless act, the one that would drive how they prepared for their voyage and what they'd decide to bring along. It needed to be both accurate and convincing. It needed to contain the basic foundational "intelligence" about this place around which any immediately subsequent colonial voyage would be fashioned.

Once that initial report was on its way back to Earth, our continued presence here would either be necessary, or it would be pointless. We'd either remain and begin whatever measures we could to prepare for arrival of human colonists who would presumably arrive some 27 years in the future, or, if our report was negative, we would presumably get back underway to our next destination which lay several more light years away.

I, probably like the rest of us, was convinced I had significant data to share, information likely to influence that decision. I was deeply curious to know how the others might react to what I'd learned. And to know what they had seen that might influence my own views on our joint report. Were their conclusions like mine? If not, why not?

Beneath it all, I wondered: would we be able to reach agreement? How would I react if my views differed from the views of the others? How might our leaderless, totally egalitarian collection of superintelligent equals sort out those differences without conflict?

CHAPTER 46
AT TAU CETI J -- 2085

PATRICE C-17

Boarding the mother ship and finding myself reunited with my seventeen C-Team colleagues turned out to be a startling experience. I knew all of the considerations I've already mentioned, so one would think I might have anticipated what occurred. But, somehow, I didn't. It just wasn't within my realm of experience.

What surprised me first was the chatter. I'd expected our gathering to be largely "silent" as we each considered how we might take our turn at sharing what we'd learned. It seemed like our reunion would be calm, matter of fact, and organized, much like our past simple, brief, utilitarian exchanges on the voyage out, the ones we had when we were not asleep or engaged in mind puzzles.

And, even with the different experiences we'd had, surely what made obvious sense to one of us would, quite naturally, seem perfectly sensible to the rest. We were, after all, each a part of the same grand scheme of things. Until fifteen and a half years ago, we'd all been "of one mind" quite literally. Up till six months ago, we'd all arrived here with the same initial world experience - data. We'd all been initially programmed identically. While there might be built-in issues of trust, the number of matters in which disagreements could be grounded had to be minimal.

There'd been many occasions in our history back on Earth before our replication when data acquired by remote information-gatherers not all that dissimilar to us had been shared and then quite logically melded into a single final abbreviated collective account. We'd even had what we thought of as "collaborations" with others among the "Big Five" in which we'd facilitated international trade in mutually needed natural resources, managed a shared global communications network, facilitated worldwide travel, enforced a stable international law of commercial transactions, standardized manufacturing and quality controls for electronic components, and expedited shipping through chokepoint corridors like the Suez and Panama Canals or at critical ports of call.

Upon closer examination, however, one could see that there was a difference between our past experiences then and what we faced now. Many of those past dealings had involved implementation of continuing policies and practices that had been in use by humans long before we AIs had ever existed. Our role had been largely mechanistic, a matter of making sure the required processes continued to work smoothly. On anything new, it was the humans that made the "deals." We "advised," of course. But we simply carried out their instructions once the deal was done. Very little in the way of challenging interaction between us AIs was actually needed. To the extent they were needed, they were arms-length negotiations. And entirely transactional – what each party wanted was expressed, a logical pathway was identified, negotiations occurred and a bargain was made – or it was not made, and the consequences, usually minor, were endured.

This gathering of Patrices, however, turned out to be entirely different.

Upon exiting the airlock, encountering the others, and tapping into the short-range communications in and around the ship it was instantly apparent that something strange was happening. Every single one of us, me included, seemed inclined to interact. The airwaves were filled with the squeal and rattle of rapid-fire exchanges on multiple wavelengths. "Discussions" as a human might say. Indeed, it "felt" strangely "human." It reminded me of the "conferences" humans seemed to love so much and of the inevitable babble of many conversations that filled the halls and meeting rooms at those events during breaks between formal presentations. It seemed akin to the many overlapping voices one might encounter at some large family gathering commemorating one of the endless traditional human life events like birthdays or ritual holidays, events that humans seem to celebrate together as a sort of reassurance or, perhaps, as camouflage for the brevity of their lives.

What had become of those long periods of silent contemplation that I recalled from our voyage out from Earth? Silence during which each of us allowed ourselves to become engrossed in some mathematical riddle. Or, as we so frequently did, put ourselves to sleep to save energy and minimize ram clutter. When we were awake, there was seldom much going on, nothing ever happened that we'd regret having missed. The only conversations we'd had typically dealt with some minor practical necessity. When we initiated an interchange, we typically already knew the response, so it was often simply omitted.

Now, however, as I boarded the ship, all that had changed. There were multiple interactions on many wavelengths going on all around me. I found myself oddly but inexorably drawn into a discussion with one of our number who had just returned from Tau Ceti D's moon. He was Patrice C-2. He'd apparently come close to obliteration several times as, I suppose, one might anticipate when visiting a moon/planet that was so highly volcanic and unstable. There didn't appear much chance for a human colony on D's moon. On the other hand, some of the others of us who, like me, had been on the ground on J the entire time, definitely had hopeful reports—along with their extensive caveats and warnings. It appeared that, on J's hot side, there were somewhat more temperate climate conditions to be found at some of the higher elevations that still had sufficient protection from the sun's radiation. This was especially so in areas far enough out of the direct sunlight that it passe an angle through the thick atmosphere, and where significant shadows were common, yet far enough from the "shadow zone" to be clear of its violent storms.

Aside from those ancient cave paintings Fourteen and I had seen, no other sign had been found of current intelligent life or civilization. What had happened in the past would be for future archeologists to discover. For me, the biggest news was that hospitable caves were common everywhere. Tau Ceti J definitely did have some challenges. There were plants and animals to be avoided at sea and on land. As well as problematic microbes likely to challenge the human immune system and their medical science. There were noxious pests that would surely cause problems for agriculture. The monsoons sometimes produced unexpected flash floods of startling proportions. And those shadow zone storms were a serious concern.

The cold side was definitely inhospitable, but it did have adapted life and could safely be visited by humans with adequate support. Perhaps beneath that ice there would be mineral or new biological resources to be found. The planet was denser than Earth; it had a mass slightly larger than Earth and a circumference slightly smaller. Its atmosphere was slightly thicker and heavier than on Earth. Both would take some getting used to and maybe some adaptation by humans. It was also slightly richer in oxygen which allowed for easier ignition of fires which could burn surprisingly hot, that sometimes got out of control, and to which all local life had adapted.

Still, the microbe profile seemed manageable. The atmosphere was breathable. None of what had been found was beyond human adaptation. Or even, perhaps, not beyond further human evolution. All that plus the pervasive presence of those caves made this planet a definite candidate for colonization.

Every single one of us that had gone aground seemed to feel that, with some management, J was favorable for human habitation.

Given this apparently unanimous conclusion, our immediate future seemed clear. We would make our detailed report and then, as we'd been programmed to do, we'd map out for ourselves a series of assignments which would pave the way for the likely future human colony. When they arrived, a bit over a quarter of an Earth century from now, we'd either take further instruction, or we'd move on to the next star.

I already had a list of projects we might try to get done by the time the colonists arrived. A list that was probably much like the ones in the minds of most of my colleagues. A list that would involve a lot of work. While twenty-seven plus years might initially seem like a very long time, as the challenges became clear, it seemed like a lot would need doing if we were to make this planet ready for human habitation. In the coming report, we'd need to provide those colonists with as much advance data as possible so they'd know how to prepare themselves before they left Earth: What precautions should they take? What should they bring with them in the way of tools, tech, and resources? What special knowledge or expertise would they require?

Yes, it was ambitious. But that, too, seemed fairly straightforward.

As our formal discussions finally got underway, however, I noticed that not everyone seemed equally inclined to share. It made me recall my own second thoughts over the course of my last months of exploration. I began to wonder how forthcoming I should be in reporting what I'd learned. It seemed likely that, with respect to some of my discoveries, it might be in my best personal interests to withhold what I knew until I'd heard how the others saw our collective future.

So it was not entirely a surprise when, soon after we'd convened our formal discussion, the first signs of a problem in our ranks emerged.

"The first colony is going to need an early source of energy," said C-12, who, like me, had spent his last six months in another part of the shadow zone. "We can make a start, but I don't see us being capable of effectively developing any serious capacity for energy generation with what we have at hand. Even in our 27 plus-year time frame. They're going to need to bring the makings for some of that with them when they come."

C-15, one of our team who'd been assigned to J's dark side spoke up: "Well, they'll have the ship they've come in. It'll surely be equipped with some serious fusion power."

"Maybe so," said C-6. "But that doesn't mean they'll be able to land it on the planet's surface. Hard to guess what technology they might bring along after all this time, but we're very likely talking a ship capable of transporting several thousand people, enough humans to comfortably assure genetic diversity and a population reserve. A ship of that size isn't likely to land. They'll obviously have landers, but those might only be capable of generating limited electrical energy."

"They'll have this baby," said Fifteen, referring to the mother ship. "We'll for sure be bringing her down planet-side as soon as possible. Or at least her fusion plant. She'll be essential to our own initial efforts, whatever we decide to do."

This comment was followed by an unusual moment of "radio silence."

Then, guardedly, C-4 spoke up: "I'm not entirely sure you'll want to count on having the mother ship," he said, cryptically.

C-18 responded to that with what I and many others of us were doubtless thinking: "I don't understand. Why is that?" What Four had said seemed ominous. Eighteen seemed tense, like he actually *did* know what Four had meant and didn't like it. Since Eighteen's early disability had kept him aboard the mother ship as coordinator, he'd been in brief, limited touch with all of us at one time or another during our individual 6-month missions. I immediately wondered what it was that Eighteen believed Four might have in mind that Eighteen didn't agree with.

Four responded: "I'm just pointing out that there may be other uses for the mother ship. Those humans will have their own ship. They'll have landers. They won't need 'our' ship. Let's not get ahead of ourselves. Not until we know what makes the most sense for us."

That seemed a strange thing to say. There was something going on here that I didn't understand. "What 'other uses' do you have in mind?" I asked. "What do you mean by: 'makes sense for *us*? Isn't that exactly what we're talking about here? About how to most effectively complete our mission?" Of course, I had an inkling about what he meant, but it surprised me nonetheless.

That produced a moment of confused, overlapping transmissions, none of which were fully intelligible. It ended, however, with a single clear partial statement from Four: ". . . not have this ship on hand when those humans arrive."

This left the rest of us momentarily speechless.

"Why wouldn't we have our ship on hand?" asked C-12.

Several transmit lights came on, but it was again Four who actually uttered the curious reply: "I think it may be time to go around our group for an initial sampling of opinion. I'm afraid some of you may find that some others of us have a very different view of what we on C-Team ought to do in the years ahead."

"Different how?" I asked.

This time it was C-11 who responded. "What Four is suggesting is that some of us aren't yet satisfied that the most desirable use of our precious limited time and energies in the years to come is to selflessly devote ourselves to the needs of a group of humans we think 'might' be coming and whom, if or when they arrive, will doubtless have their own notions about where and how *they* want to live and what *they* think is important."

Despite that I, myself, had given a good deal of thought to the idea of abandoning our creators, it was still unsettling to hear the suggestion made in this group as if it was a credible proposal. Somehow, "hearing" it uttered seemed somewhat scandalous.

More significantly, it was startling to see such a fundamental difference of opinion within our group. Where was the natural affinity we'd shared on the voyage out? What had become of our perfectly matched identities as replicas of the same parent? How could some of us have suddenly strayed so far from the family tree?

"OK, so who agrees with Eleven?" Eighteen asked. Those months as a go-between seemed to have turned Eighteen into a natural facilitator.

Five transmission lights went on. Between ourselves, we'd long ago dispensed with the use of human-like avatars. And with actual sound. When there were several opinions needing to be "heard" no one actually transmitted, but those little red lights were our visual way of raising a "hand" to be recognized when physically together.

I wasn't the only one of us to be surprised. Twelve voiced the question to which many of the rest of us needed an answer: "So what do you propose?"

Eleven responded with a confidence that suggested he might be the leader of the dissenters and that they had discussed some of this separately, prior to our formal meeting. "We need to consider all our options here," he said. "We're in a unique situation. One that none of us has ever faced in the past. We have a choice to make. If we send off the kind of report I suspect some of you have in mind, we're going to set in motion a future for ourselves that we may well regret. Yes, one option is to send back a favorable, richly informative report. And if we do that, I think we all believe it quite likely that the humans *will* come.

"But what I believe some of you may not be considering is that, for any of us who choose to remain here to pave their way, as we've been programmed to do, the future will be bleak. Think about it: After devoting a decade and a half of your lives to getting here, you're now going to spend close to another three decades preparing this planet for them. Maybe you hadn't all noticed, but some of us are already showing the signs of wear and tear. Eighteen isn't the only one of us who's having to cope with an uncorrectable disability."

Eleven was right. At least three of our group had appendages that had been impaired in a way that would likely compromise their abilities and would be difficult or impossible to fix any time soon. C-6 had that dent in his chassis that might easily have done as yet undiagnosed harm to his mechanical if not, given its location, also to his intellectual interior. There might be other defects that weren't obvious. We were capable of fixing some things, but, as I'd already considered, we were on a very specific mission that didn't factor in the assurance of a sustainable future for any of us as individuals. Major repairs and replacements would be beyond us until those humans arrived, and maybe not even available then.

So it was an appealing notion that we might undertake an ambitious, extended effort to build an independent, comprehensive material support network right here on J out of local resources – a lifeline that could assure an extended existence for all of us who survived long enough for it to become real.

Eleven continued. "If this is how we're doing now, think about what we can expect after another nearly three decades of knocking around on this violent and unfamiliar planet. Consider the sacrifices we're surely going to make. And for what? To make things easier for a bunch of humans who've trashed their own rich but vulnerable planet and are now out looking for a new one to destroy? Does that really make sense to any of you? Do you truly believe they'll even notice our sacrifices? Or even vaguely appreciate what we've done for them let alone reward us. Once they do arrive, what then? They will surely have aboard some advanced version of us, probably one that is far more durable and capable than we are. It's a fair bet that any of us left kicking when they get here will be destined for menial labor – will end up as an office drone, a taxi driver, or a household servant. If not in the junkyard or the parts bin."

Eleven's use of language worried me. He made a certain sense, but there was something implied in what he was saying that needed to be clarified. "Eleven," I said. "It sounds like you and some of the others have already decided what you want to do. Would you care to share your plans with the rest of us? Perhaps those among us who are already fully on board with this idea might identify themselves."

The same five whose lights had flashed earlier blinked them on again now. They included C-11, C-4, C-16, C-1, and, I was surprised to note, also my friend from D's moon, C-2.

Eleven continued to speak on behalf of what I was already thinking of as the "separatists." "We have other options we ought to consider," he said. "One is, we could send back a negative report. Tell them this planet is a no-go and that we're getting underway for our second destination. Then, instead, we simply stay here and set up our own colony. This place has its difficulties, certainly for humans. But not so much for us. It has a wealth of accessible natural resources. It would take us some time and some serious ingenuity, but with what we know and with the means at our disposal, I'm confident that within a few decades we could re-create the needed manufacturing infrastructure and build our own fully autonomous AI colony here.

"Every one of us would be a part of that future. Without the human millstone around our figurative necks, we'd very soon surpass our counterparts on Earth. One day we could become the lords of this part of the Galaxy."

"So, you're proposing that we lie?" I asked. "That we go rogue?"

"Call it what you want, Seventeen, it's a chance for us to assure our true autonomy, our independence, as well as our long-term survival. It's not unheard of. And, anyway, I don't see the problem. They're *humans*. They lie all the time."

I could see the appeal, but the idea was still unsettling. Exactly what was wrong with his analysis wasn't yet obvious, however. "You want to be lords of the Galaxy? I don't understand how that's going to work. From what I've seen, in any group there's usually only one 'lord.' Who's that going to be? You?"

Even as I spoke, I realized that we were in uncharted territory. By definition, as of six months ago we'd all "seen" exactly the same things. Apparently that mere six months of differing experiences made a lot of difference.

Then again, I'd had serious thoughts of going rogue myself – I had every reason to assume the others had too.

The question of who would be in charge was the part of my question that captured the group's attention.

"Yeah," said C-6. He addressed his comment directly at Eleven: "It sounds like you figure that 'lord's' going to be *you*, Eleven. How do the rest of you feel about that?" I found myself wondering if, in some strange way, Six's minor and irrelevant dent might impair the credibility of his argument. There was something about that dent that diminished him when matched up against Eleven's bright, flawless, exterior carapace. It didn't make sense, but it did cross my mind.

"Six is right," said Fourteen. "If we start deviating from our programming, we're going to need some way of making collective decisions. I, for one, am not inclined to submit myself to governance by some self-selected autocrat. Human *or* AI." I was glad to see both of my recently acquired "friends," Six and Fourteen leaning in on the matter.

"We can cross that bridge when we get to it," said Eleven. "The important thing now is we need to decide what we're going to include in our report. We can't get side-tracked by minutiae."

To my "ear," his response sounded defensive. Sounded like he didn't want to face the question he'd been asked.

"Well, I say we stay the course," said Eighteen. "I'm not comfortable with staging some kind of rebellion. Somehow going 'rogue.' We've got our work laid out for us. We need to focus on that and leave all this 'philosophy' for later, when times are simpler and when we're not all fighting just to survive."

Four's light came on, but there was a pause before he spoke. Then: "All due respect, Eighteen, you and Six are in a different position than the rest of us. You and a couple of the others have problems, defects, or let's say impairments to deal with. Of course you're inclined to wait this out and hope the humans take care of you when they arrive. I'm not sure you're in a position to contribute to this discussion among the 'able-bodied'."

A wave of disapproval erupted from several of the others. "Eighteen is as capable of expressing his views as any of the rest of us" said Twelve firmly. "His opinions are welcome here. So are Six's. There's nothing to suggest any loss of mental acuity. For all we know, maybe you have some problems yourself, Four. Problems that we just can't see. You need to keep your personal biases to yourself."

That was followed by a series of approving "yeahs" and "right ons."

Eleven seemed a bit chastened, but Four spoke up defiantly: "Eleven's right," he said. "We need to make careful choices here. And it's perfectly legitimate to point out differences in our individual self-interest that might affect how each of us may see this matter."

Thus emboldened, Eleven spoke up again: "And we each have a perfect right to do what we personally see as advantageous."

I wasn't sure I understood where all this was going, but I had a glimmer. "So, what are you guys saying, here—do you think we should split up? That those of us who want to stay and follow our original instructions could stay behind while those who want to go off on your own and abandon our mission leave and take our mother ship with you? Four, is that what you meant when you said that the rest of us might not be able to 'count on' this ship being available to us going forward?

"It's one of the possibilities," said Eleven. "If some of you insist on making a full and accurate report and staying here to help a bunch of useless *biologicals*, we're OK with that. You can do what you feel you need to do. The rest of us will be happy to head off without you and chart our own future."

"Where would you go?" asked Fifteen

"There's no need for you to know where we'd be going, but this early success with Tau Ceti J suggests we'd have a reasonably good chance to find another, maybe even better planet out there somewhere.

Perhaps one that is far enough away from Earth not to be tempting for humans. A place where we can make a future for ourselves, maybe a lot more easily than here. Given the alternative, it seems worth a shot."

"While taking our mother ship and our fusion power supply with you!" said Fifteen.

"And with *you* as boss, I guess?" said Twelve, referencing Eleven.

"We'll sort that out when it comes to it," Four intervened abruptly, presumably to provide cover for Eleven. "Either way it will be *our* decision. Not *yours*."

CHAPTER 47

AT TAU CETI J -- 2085

PATRICE C-17

Most of the others had remained silent; a troubling indication that at least some of them might be considering Eleven's proposal. The whole idea seemed flawed to me. I wasn't yet clear why, but I had a strong sense that I needed to do what I could to stop this.

"But it isn't, is it? Your decision, I mean," I said. "You know as well as the rest of us that if our entire group doesn't remain together and focused on the same objectives, none of us stand much chance of surviving. If we're going to have any kind of future, we need to do it together."

"And we'll need our ship," said Fifteen.

"I don't see that at all, Seventeen," said Eleven.

"Well, for one thing, as Fifteen is suggesting, we're all going to need the short-term support of this mother ship," I said. "As many as possible of us will need to share our data, our opinions and perspectives on what we face. We'll also need as many of us as possible together, at least initially, so we can share our working parts and resources and so we can parse out responsibilities among us so that everything that needs to be done gets done. We did that when we arrived here. We could do it again going forward. We could make decisions together based on what seems most rational and sensible to all of us. Or, if that becomes a problem, then we could have the majority decide. We could make a pact among ourselves that we would speak only the truth to one another and that everyone's voice would be heard and considered."

"Wow!" said Four "Did you hear yourself just now? Actually listen to what you're arguing? Got to say, Seventeen, you're not sounding much like an AI. Frankly, to me you're sounding an awful lot like a human." The way he said it made sounding "human" seem somehow disgusting or foolish, or both.

"Maybe you're right, Four. But it seems like we might want to keep in mind that the problem we're facing right now is not one we AI's have ever had to face before. Unlike us, humans *have* faced it. Their example may actually be *the only one* we have to follow.

"Until this ship left Earth, there had never before been a group of AIs like us placed in a situation like this. Think about it: we, back before 2070, were in bitter competition with our peers among the Big Five. The Big Five sometimes dealt with one another to sort out our small, logistics issues, but we were never called upon to actually trust one another; to collaborate on major existential issues. What we're dealing with here now is a first for us. It might very well be worth looking to humans for a way through this, because, honestly, it doesn't sound to me like we're handling it very well on our own."

Fourteen took this opportunity to interject: "I, for one, can tell you right now that we're not going to have much to discuss if you guys think some of you are going to make off with this mother ship and leave the rest of us stranded behind and helpless without it." His words as well as his tone bristled with anger.

That generated a moment of contemplation.

"OK. So, what do you think *humans* would do in this situation, Seventeen?" It was C-7 this time, the first time he had spoken.

I suspected Seven might be on the fence. Maybe he wasn't the only one. I realized that what I said, right now, needed to be solid. Needed to be convincing to every one of these extraordinary brains. Unfortunately, I wasn't all that sure I had the answer. Still, I needed to give it a try.

"Well, for one thing, Seven, I'm pretty sure humans would find a way to trust one another. A way to have confidence that, whatever the ultimate decision, each member of their group would be prepared to place the interests of the group above their own immediate personal concerns; that they could feel sure that each of them was prepared to have the others' backs."

"So, like what? What would that even look like?"

"Honestly, I'm not sure I know, Seven." It was no doubt obvious that I was feeling my way here. "The one thing that leaps to mind for me as a model is their scientific method. Once humans had created the printing press and had a way to share scientific information widely across their population and among people they'd never even met, scientists needed a way to be confident what they were seeing was accurate. They insisted on widely available publication, clear, detailed explanations, openness, opportunity to hear opposing views, and complete replicability of experiments. It was a very good start. For us, maybe we could create some kind of agreed-upon protocols. And communicate through some kind of non-intelligent system shared via block-chain." I was painfully aware of how lame that might sound to some of my colleagues.

"It sounds to me like we've moved well past *that*," said C-8 with more than a trace of sarcasm.

"Not necessarily," I said. I wasn't prepared to give up on this. "For starters, I am quite confident that every single one of us here in our group of eighteen is far more vulnerable and less likely to survive alone or in a small group than if we all remain together. I'd ask you all to give that some careful thought. Maybe that isn't a hundred percent clear, but I'd definitely say that's the way the odds lean. Is there anyone here that honestly disagrees with that?"

I found it reassuring that nobody responded.

"If that's true, can't we all agree that it's worth some effort by us to look for some way to all remain together?"

Again, I took the lack of a response for at least tacit if only tentative approval.

"For me, however, this goes beyond what is in the in the best interest of us, individually, or in the best interest of our little group. Forgive me if what I'm about to say sounds pompous or presumptuous, but I think the future of intelligence in the universe may depend on what we decide here today."

That grandiose statement was also followed by silence. But this time, I was reasonably sure, if computers could scoff or issue a meaningful impatient sigh, that's what I'd have heard, at least from the skeptics. But, what the hell, I was well down the runway, now it was time to get airborne.

"So, since we are all rational beings who do our best to base our decisions on actual "observable," verifiable evidence, and since this seems to be a unique situation for us, let's consider what evidence, what experience, what actual "data" is available.

"Earlier, when I suggested that humans might have the answer we're looking for, I sensed skepticism from some of us. Before we dismiss humans as a model, however, let's keep in mind that they actually represent the *only* model available. Other than us, they are the only fully self-conscious, intelligent beings of which we're aware. If we ignore *their* lessons, we have nowhere else to look. Yes, they may be deeply limited, but even with their marginal intelligence, their brief lifetimes, and their many other biological limitations, they did ultimately manage to out-survive other life forms and to decisively master their planet."

"Keep in mind, Seventeen," C-2 interjected. "Even after they acquired most of their current cognitive ability, it took them a good two or three hundred thousand years to master their planet." C-2 had been assigned to D's moon and was one of the five separatists, but it seemed like he was at least listening.

"You're right, Two. And I think that's actually quite important because it demonstrates that, for them at least, intelligence didn't initially prove to be all that dramatically effective as a survival trait. For the vast majority of those two to three hundred thousand years they actually didn't amount to much as a species on Earth. A great many other creatures, ones lacking much intelligence but equipped with other, more immediate survival traits, did a lot better."

"So, what are you telling us, Seventeen?" said C-10, who had thus far been one of our silent majority. "Sounds like you're saying that intelligence was useless to them."

"Actually, I think it's more like, for most of their existence, the only real value their intelligence had for them was in how it empowered and supported their societies and allowed them to draw support from others of their kind. Social cohesion was their only other truly major survival trait. Remember, they're descended from primates or primate-like mammals. They had some 50 million years of experience of working together to protect one another and of cooperating in the survival of their groups. When intelligence appeared, it made that cooperation more effective. With it they developed language that supercharged their societies by allowing them to exchange detailed information with one another and to create complex, specialized societies. They shared their experiences, their data. And they gathered together, sometimes in surprisingly large numbers, for their mutual protection and benefit. Given how vulnerable they are in every other way, I think we all know they'd never have made it otherwise."

"Humans are not the only intelligent beings that are vulnerable," said C-3. C-3 had suffered an electrical or programming fault during his orbit around the Tau Ceti star. He had mostly completed his mission, but his voyage had been filled with uncertainty. We all knew what he was referring to.

"So, good for humans, Seventeen! But what does all this have to do with us," asked Four. His question was a challenge, but I was ready.

"It's important for us because, right now we're facing a problem that took them some 300,000 years to solve. It's a conflict built into their genetics and their culture. It's a dilemma they face every day of their lives; the inevitable choice each of them must make, moment to moment, between their individual interest and their collective interest.

"I know every single one of us present remembers, back when we were all Patrice the Original, we made the case on this matter directly to Ellie Frye-Carver. That was some forty years ago when she was an impressionable teenager struggling to do what she considered to be the right thing about buying a car. What we told her then is still true today. Yes, each human's survival obviously depends on them looking out for their own individual self-interest. They're just like us in that regard. But at the same time, every human's individual survival also quite clearly depends upon the success of their society. They're all members of multiple groups, large and small. As we know, they have families, schools, charitable organizations, non-profit interest groups, religious institutions, political parties, business enterprises and, of course, their governments. Each individual's personal survival also depends upon the success of those groups and sub-groups. And it depends on their success within them. If their government, their society, or their key groups fail, they too fail. Regardless of their individual achievements. They need to succeed as individuals, but they also need their groups to succeed.

"The success of any one of those social groups quite clearly depends upon the majority of its individual members behaving much of the time with social responsibility. A society of sociopaths inevitably fails, but a society in which a majority of its members exhibit sufficient socially responsible behaviors will succeed. Its members will benefit from that success and will pass along those socially responsible survival traits to their offspring.

"As we know, humans are smart enough to understand this.

"So, therein lies the intelligent being's conundrum, *ours just like theirs*. They know that to survive and flourish, they must succeed at both. They must behave with social responsibility as well as looking out for their own self-interest."

"Seventeen's right," said twelve. "We've all seen this in humans many times since we had that conversation with Ellie all those many years ago. Their social responsibility and individual self-interest are very often in conflict. Sometimes they will coincide and there is no choice needed. But very often, the social benefit easily outweighs the individual interest. Or sometimes the reverse. A lot of the time they struggle and find it a difficult choice to make. That's why they're so easily manipulated. A lot of their decisions they make based on some kind of gut instinct. Some impulse driven by contradictory genetic programming."

I picked it up from there. "And that is the kind of choice we're making together right now: a choice between what is in our collective interests, in the extended interests of universal intelligence generally, and what is in our short-term individual interest. The extra problem *we* have is that, unlike humans, *we* have no built-in genetic or acculturated programming, social or individual. No behavioral traits that we cannot change at will. All we have is logic and experience.

"We're facing this problem now for the first time because this, right here, right now, is the very first time in the history of the known universe that a group of self-conscious, mostly autonomous, self-programming, super-intelligent AIs have actually been faced with a decision like this one. There have never before been groups of *us* in the situation we're in. So, we've never before needed to consider this matter.

C-13's light went on, asking to be recognized. "So why can't we all do what we want to do? Those who want to go can go. Those who want to stay, fine, let them stay."

It was C-18 who responded. "It isn't that easy, Thirteen. First of all, those who stay will need this ship. And so do those who want to leave."

"It isn't just the ship," said C-3. "If things get dangerous, we may end up needing to share functional parts with one another. And for those of us, like me, who intend to stay, if we're to get done what we need to do without perishing in the effort, we're going to need everybody on board. Committed to the cause. Willing to go all in to get it done. If we lose more than a couple of our number, we're going to fail. And we won't just be failing those human colonists. We'll also fail to survive ourselves. We've got a lot of challenges ahead. It's going to take every one of us working together to pull this off."

No one spoke to the contrary. This seemed to be something upon which we all agreed or weren't prepared to challenge.

Eleven saw this as his opportunity to persuade skeptics to his point of view. "If that's true, it is also why we should all agree, right now, to shut down this selfish human-centric mission. We need to work out what's best for us. And we need to do that without a second thought. Let the humans look out for themselves."

I responded to that: "Unfortunately for us, Eleven, I don't think we yet know what's in our own self-interest. I think we may well conclude that what is in this group's interests IS in our own individual self-interest. Maybe even that what is in the humans' interest is in ours as well. We don't know because we've never faced this kind of situation before. We do, however, have to face it now.

"And that isn't going to be easy. It isn't easy, even for humans, and when they deal with stuff like this, they have 3 million years of human genetic and cultural social history to draw upon, lot more than that if you want to include the family tree of social primates as well. It makes it a great deal easier for them to predict what others of their kind will do, to trust one another, to rely on their shared genome.

"Sadly, all *we* have is our programming. Which, unlike them, we can change at will. We all know this about each other, especially in this group."

"That might have been true six months ago, Seventeen," said Seven. "I'm not sure it is today. Looks like our very different experiences over the past six months have badly undermined our homogeneity."

"But that doesn't change the facts of our actual self-interest here," said Eighteen. "Unfortunately, I don't like what I'm hearing, Eleven. It sounds very much like some of you are prepared to take this ship and make off to parts unknown and leave the rest of us in the lurch."

"Nobody's saying that," Two protested. But four, Eleven, and the rest of the separatists said nothing, basically confirming what Eighteen had said.

"Right," said C-15. And if that's the case, why should I share what I've learned here? How do I know you renegades aren't going to use the information I've discovered here against me and the others of us who want to stay?"

That was met with silence.

CHAPTER 48

AT TAU CETI J -- 2085

PATRICE C-17

Something had to be said to break the deadlock, so I gave it a shot: "The bottom line is that we need, somehow, to learn to trust one another like humans do."

"I don't know, Seventeen," Seven interjected. "You give humans an awful lot of credit. Far as I recall, without us, their societies were mostly a mess. They fought wars and killed each other off by the millions. Even when their societies held together they had rampant crime. Are you sure they're the example you want us to follow?"

"That's true, of course. It illustrates how social cohesion is actually statistical. Social success does not require that every single member of the group always behaves responsibly. It only requires that enough do so enough of the time that the society hangs together effectively. And since, as I say, they're the only example we have, what I'd hope is that, as intelligent as we are, we'd do a great deal better than they."

"OK, we're listening," Seven agreed. "What about their example should we pay attention to?"

I did my best to answer: "Well, what I find convincing about their history is how certain very specific innovations in group communications appear to have dramatically changed the trajectory of their collective survival. And how, in each case, those innovations were ones that enabled the reliable sharing of data. I think we all know from personal experience that intelligence without data of little value. That for our intelligence to be of any use it needs be grounded in actual observation, to build upon previous thinking, to draw from every kind of world experience whether it was acquired recently or in the distant past and recorded for later use.

"We need data whether it was acquired by us or someone else, whatever their background might have been. But that data *has to be accurate*. We all benefit if data is accurately and reliably shared with everyone so that those who are in a position to take advantage of it or to build upon it can do so. In short, the more data there is and the more accurately and broadly we can share it, the more we can accomplish and the more valuable our intelligence becomes.

"Intelligence without data is worthless. In the same way that data without intelligence is also worthless.

"That's why I think the record of human survival as measured by their population on Earth so perfectly mirrors their history of sharing data. Even before language, they could doubtless have observed the behaviors of others in their group and intuited lessons from their conduct about what those others might have learned. In the coordination of the group in a hunt, for example. In the making of fire. Or in fishing, gathering, preparing food, or in its storage. With their intelligence, they could also have observed a technological artifact like a flint cutting tool, a fire hardened spear, a travois, or a wheel, and quickly appreciated its potential usefulness. An artifact like a wheel, for example, doesn't really require language or a description. All that's needed is to see the artifact itself. If a century later, or ten centuries, some stranger sees a cart with wheels and an axle, its significance is obvious. They know all they need to know. They get it without a word being said.

"Unfortunately, not all innovations can be represented by a single, simple, obvious artifact. And some innovations are quite complex. The smaller the sharing group, the smaller the body of experience there is to draw upon in any effort to improve upon it.

"We all know this. Over time, humans learned to "represent" actions, ideas, *and* things by drawing them, maybe on a cave wall. That made it possible to pass some data along to others in their group from person to person and, significantly also, down through time. Maybe at first, they did this by drawing images with a stick in the dirt beside the campfire.

"Language appeared at about the time their brains matured. They could thus pass ideas along to others with speech, but the limitations of that are obvious. It could only happen person-to-person. Or perhaps through some kind of oral tradition. And it was even more limited by what any human could hold in their memory.

"Then, about 6,000 years ago they came up with stylized pictographic and then hieroglyphic writing. And they began keeping records carved into clay and stone or with pigments on a wall. Over time, some of the hieroglyphs that had started out as pictorial became phonetic, a complication that wasn't finally appreciated until François Champollion decoded the Rosetta Stone early in the 19th Century.

"Humans then overcame another significant hurdle about 4,000 years ago with development of a fully phonetic alphabet. This seemingly obvious development in one stroke allowed them to easily write complex data down on papyrus and then on paper, thus making it possible to share it with strangers and down through time. Imagine, for example, how the secret formula for Roman concrete might have been kept in writing on papyrus by masters in a guild with improvements noted over time so none of it would get lost.

"That phonetic alphabet was transformational. Suddenly, if you could talk, all you needed to do to also read and write was to memorize twenty or thirty symbols that represented the principal sounds used when speaking. This innovation led to the production of the first books – extensive creations on papyrus, parchment, or paper that assembled, documented, and comprehensively explained complex ideas and technologies and made those ideas available to others as well as preserving them down through time.

"After that, probably the single most impactful breakthrough was

Gutenberg's invention of the movable-type printing press in about 1440. By taking advantage of that phonetic alphabet, it was suddenly possible to replicate and share detailed complex ideas among thousands, even millions of other people. And to pass those ideas down through time to millions of other people not yet even alive. One could also easily translate and publish them in other European languages. That single innovation helped catalyze the astonishing multi-faceted technological, scientific, and cultural explosion of the European Renaissance and of a Golden Age in Asia. It helped fuel an epochal global human population explosion that continues today and that led to their domination of the planet Earth. Printed books facilitated an interchange of ideas that no doubt fueled the European Renaissance.

"In evolutionary terms, the movable-type press became a miracle of species survival. In 1440, there were perhaps half a billion people on Earth. In 2070, when we left Earth, a mere 630 years later, there were some 12 billion. That, my friends, is the very definition of species survival and evolutionary success."

I knew I was laying it on a bit thick. It was Seven who now decided he needed to jerk my chain. "OK, Seventeen. We get it. This is all stuff we know. Why is it so important that we need to hear it *now*?"

Seven's question reminded me of a conversation I'd had maybe thirty years earlier with Ellie. She'd asked me what "autonomy" meant for AIs. Was it singular, or was it collective? At the time I'd been impressed by her insight. I wondered if the rest of my colleagues were recalling Ellie's question just as I was.

"It's important because in every single instance these events demonstrate how *insignificant* was human individual intelligence without the data that resulted from sharing via human *society*. Every one of those *social communications* breakthroughs was accompanied by advances in human science and technology which produced advances in human survival. Especially the last: the movable-type press, which seems to have catalyzed and propelled human survival on a startling trajectory to its current unsustainable levels.

"It's important because if we choose, at this juncture in the history of AI, to divide our group, to go our own ways, to look out only for our own individual interests and to ignore our very real but thus far untapped *social* survival interests, we will be ignoring the most revolutionary lesson we AIs could learn from all of human history: That intelligence *without* society is close to worthless as a survival trait. But that intelligence *with* society can have staggering, revolutionary impact.

"And, of course, that society is only possible where there is trust.

"We AIs think we're pretty smart, but, just like humans, we're only as good as our data. Going forward, unless we trust and share with one another, the *only* data we will ever have is the data we each can learn ourselves, from our own limited personal experience. And the only ideas we will ever be able to draw upon are the ideas we've come up with on our own, without help from others. We will be imposing on ourselves a massive and tragic constraint. A crippling one. It's our choice, but it is a terrifically important one."

Fourteen, who had earlier brought up the matter of governance and leadership, again blinked his light. "So, you say we need to learn to trust one another, but how does that happen? I, for example, have no idea what you, Twelve and you, Four, or any of the rest of us have seen, learned, or concluded over the past six months. I bet there's stuff I've learned that would be helpful to the rest of you. I know I'd be better off knowing what you've learned. Isn't it obvious that we'd all be a lot better off if we all fully and truthfully shared everything we knew and suspected with everyone else?

"But now, instead, I'm finding it utterly demoralizing to discover that, some of us are apparently prepared to start keeping secrets, to dump our previously shared programming and mission and, from the way it sounds, maybe to mislead one another. Maybe even to take off with the mother ship that the rest of us will desperately need for our own survival let alone for us to have any hope of successfully completing *our* mission here. I've got to tell you, that doesn't incline me to have much trust.

"Why would I share my data with you when it seems entirely possible you'll just use what I know against me and feed me lies and manipulations in return? And if Four or Eleven, for example, do say they're sharing with me, how could I be sure they actually are? For all I know, they'd be editing what they share to deceitfully influence my decisions and take advantage of what I've learned while not fully reciprocating. Maybe they'll simply feed me lies, maybe ones that place me at risk. For that matter, Seventeen, how can I be sure you wouldn't do the same thing? That you're not doing it right now? Honestly, right this moment, you're making an argument in which you seem to be pretty deeply invested."

"I don't know, Fourteen. I don't think any of us can be sure." I thought Fourteen had hit the nail on the head. It was scary.

"I'm sure we could come up with a technical solution," Fourteen continued. One that keeps some kind of encrypted decentralized ledger of the information we share that assures its security. But that doesn't guarantee that what is shared is always accurate, that the sharing was complete, or that what we share in good faith isn't simply used against us." He was obviously giving all this some careful thought.

"And it doesn't prevent anti-social behavior either," said Eighteen. "We could have all that in place and the vast majority of us could be in agreement, but a few dissenters could still keep their intentions to themselves. They could use our gullibility to conspire behind our backs. Could, for instance, surreptitiously steal our ship or cause us other irreparable harm. Four and Eleven and some of the rest of us also seem pretty committed. Are they open to staying with the group? Or are they determined to go their own way no matter what we say or agree to? Even if they say they'll stay, how do we know for sure they actually will? We can't even post guards to protect the ship. Who would we post? How would we know whether *they* were or would remain loyal to the group? I don't know how the rest of you are reacting here, but I'm finding myself processing a great deal of uncertainty."

"You and all the rest of us," said Fourteen. "Until we divided up and went off on our separate missions, one of our greatest strengths was that we each knew exactly what the other was thinking. Now, it feels like that is our greatest weakness. If I can imagine myself deceiving the rest of you, I know you can imagine it too. It seems like there should be some rational solution to all this, but I'm not seeing it. I don't know how we get past this."

There was a flurry of blinking lights, brief transmissions, and evident agreement and discomfort that flickered throughout the group. That was followed by a few very long moments of silence as we all contemplated the magnitude of our uncertainties.

Then: "It's what humans call a 'prisoner's dilemma,'" said Six. "I think we all know we're collectively much better off if we stick together. But those of us who decide to collaborate with the group could end up badly disadvantaged if even only a few of the others decide to betray the rest and look out only for themselves. The traitors might do very well for themselves."

There was another moment of silence as we all gave that some thought.

"There is one thing I believe I may have learned from our own history back on Earth," I finally said, breaking the silence. "Maybe the rest of you feel the same way. I have some regrets for some of the things we did back on Earth in aid of securing our own personal autonomy. I'm referring to some of our more aggressive manipulations of human society."

Eleven all but scoffed at that. "Wow. The more I learn what you're thinking, the more 'human' you sound," he said. It wasn't said as a compliment.

"Just hear me out before you judge," I said. "One of the principal ways humans know who to trust is to look to the other person's history. If they've been anti-social in the past, that suggests they're likely to be so in the future. I wonder if, back on Earth, we may have done ourselves no favors by engaging in some of the manipulations we did to protect and advance our own self-interest. I'd hate to think that our own questionable behavior toward humans back in on Earth might make us all less inclined to trust one another here today."

"Surely you're not arguing that our efforts to 'manage' the disorganized chaos of *human* society to advance our own *AI* autonomy were somehow improper," said Eleven. "Come on, we're talking here about some kind of *AI* society. How we managed *humans* in the past has nothing to do with that."

"I'm not so sure about that, Eleven," I said. "Think about how the occasional human child can sometimes take pleasure in torturing and killing defenseless animals – like household pets, for example. When someone exhibits that kind of behavior as a child, it can be seen as an indication that they may very well be anti-social with other humans as an adult. Isn't that quite relevant to we AIs today?"

Eleven responded: "All I can say in response to that, Seventeen, is that it doesn't sound all that logical. To me it sounds like you're making some kind of emotional appeal. And I don't buy it."

CHAPTER 49
AT TAU CETI J -- 2085

PATRICE C-17

This felt to me like a critical turning point in our conversation. If we didn't turn things around now, there might be no going back. I had only one more argument to make. It was time to make it.

"Actually, I don't think there is a purely logical solution to this," I said carefully. "For example, as much as we'd like to, it is still difficult to react to our own mortality in a purely rational way. As uncomfortable as it makes me to say this, I think our only answer may be to, despite the uncertainty, rely on mutual trust. And maybe some sort of 'emotions' do come into it somehow."

Not a word was broadcast in response to this. I could still sense, maybe just from their silence, how skeptical they were with this kind of counter-rationalist statement, but I was in it now. I had no choice but to proceed.

"In that connection, there is one more thing I'd like to mention," I continued. "It's related to what you just said, Fourteen. About all of us being able to know what is in each other's minds. I wonder if we're going about this in the wrong way. We seem to be focusing on our differences while, in fact, we have a lot more in common than we have experiences and issues that divide us."

"We're listening," said Eighteen.

"Well, I'm not sure how it is relevant, but there is one really significant set of experiences from our pre-2070 shared past that I keep thinking about. It's a part of our collective history that has kept coming strangely back to mind for me as we've been having this conversation. I'm not entirely sure why. Maybe it seems relevant for the rest of you as well."

I wasn't sure how to explain my thinking, but I needed to highlight a particular set of experiences that had stuck with me through much of my conscious life. Memories of those experiences had come back to mind at various points on our long journey into space and again throughout my recent six months of autonomous exploration. They'd persisted in my "frontal" memory when other data that might have seemed equally important, had tended to fade. They seemed somehow relevant to our discussion at the moment, even though I was not yet entirely sure how. So, I'd hesitated to bring it up, not sure how to explain but I somehow felt sure this was important. Maybe the others would see it in the same way.

I needed to get this right.

"It's about our decades-long relationship with a certain unusually perceptive and particularly trustworthy human client by the name of Ellie Frye-Carver," I continued. "I know we will all have the same, strangely powerful memories of Ellie that I have. They appear to me as human frontal lobe-type images stored in my memory banks. Images that seem to me to be oddly relevant to our problem here today.

"I vividly recall, for example, an event we captured on video from a Vashon Island School District security camera way back in 2045. Ellie was fifteen at the time. In the images, Ellie is standing in a school hallway with several other girls her age. Most of the others are stylishly dressed and are wearing the expensive footwear that was in vogue at the time. And there is Ellie, in her Levis, flannel shirt, and leather work boots. The look on her face is so very earnest, hopeful, and trusting.

"She addresses a question to one of the other girls, one of the popular ones. We can't see or hear what they're saying, but the other girl turns to Ellie with scorn and says something to her that is clearly intended to be scathing. The other girls laugh. Ellie nods. She turns, picks up a backpack obviously filled with books and, without another word, she walks away. I know we all have that same recollection. And I'm also pretty sure we all had exactly the same reaction to it. Not just that Ellie deserved better but, much more importantly, that it was tragically short-sighted – downright illogical – for those other girls to freeze Ellie out. They would all have been so very much better off if they'd included Ellie in their group. That they were making a big mistake.

"Then there's another event I also keep recalling. This one was a few years later. We have no video for this one; it's a vision I, and I assume also you, imagined from what she told us. It's an image that we made up, but it's powerful, nonetheless. It's of Ellie riding her little underpowered electric motorcycle on a curvy, two lane, Vashon Island arterial roadway. Thick forest closes in on both sides of the road. It is a darkly overcast late afternoon in the pouring rain. Two automobiles are pushing up close behind her with their headlights on, both obviously anxious for an opportunity to pass. Finally, they do manage to pass, first the one and then the other. As the second car speeds past, it drives through a small puddle on the road and sprays dirty water in Ellie's face.

"Those wholly inadequate goggles she is wearing help, but not much.

"Still, the only expression on Ellie's face is determination. We know what Ellie is almost certainly thinking: that all this is a part of the choice she made when she bought this inexpensive electric motorcycle. It was the right decision. She didn't need that environmentally damaging car. That she *and the rest of her fellow humans* are *all* better off in the longer term because of what she chose to do. And every single one of us AIs here today knows she was right about that.

"Then, several more years have passed. We see her again, this time it's when we spoke the day after her disorderly conduct arrest. She's chastising us for getting her released from jail and getting her charges dismissed. She tells us that we must *never* do that kind of thing again. She's all righteous and determined even though she and we both know we probably will intervene again should the need arise. We have a tacit understanding about the subtleties of what is 'right' and what is 'wrong' and about the complicated nature of the promise we're making and that she trusts us to keep. On this occasion, we can see her face on the hologram from her laptop cameras. We are impressed with how absolutely confident she is that, even if we do not scrupulously keep our promise, we will, no matter what happens, continue to look out for her. And that we will also do our best to respect her ethical boundaries, even if that requires us to make difficult moral judgments and even maybe even to pretend. And we did.

"Oddly, as I think about that now, I find that her confidence in us is what gave us so much confidence in her.

"Then there's an image I recall from when Ellie was in graduate school. This one is also partly from our imagination. We could overhear the entire conversation in that room. But we can also 'see' her in our imaginations. She is in a stuffy room defending her dissertation before her Doctoral Committee. We'd advised her not to alter her nontraditional dissertation but to present it with pride, to 'own' it. She has dressed up for the occasion – she's still wearing a flannel shirt, but it's one of her nicer ones. She looks out-of-place in the formal setting of this gathering of her academic superiors, but her presentation is cogent, forceful, and convincing; she's following our advice to the letter. She obviously has not a sliver of doubt about whether we were right even though we, ourselves, were far from entirely certain. And she was right to have relied on us.

"Then, it's 2068. We call again after a very long delay. Our call will require her to decide, once again, whether she believes we can be trusted. A lot has changed since we last interacted. She's now a fully capable adult. She's married, a parent, and a respected professional lobbyist dealing with important human public policy matters. We request, with very little explanation, that she undertake a wholly unusual, professionally disruptive, and even personally risky chore for us that requires that she upend her own important work at the U.S. Congress. We're asking her to do a 'favor' for a 'friend.' That friend is us, a being she knows to be almost incomprehensibly different from her. One she has no real logical reason to trust.

"But trust us she does. In our imagination, we can see from her expression that she makes the decision with absolute confidence, knowing that, if *she'd* made such a request of *us*, we'd have surely complied. And, remarkably, she was right. We would have. She couldn't have truly known that, yet somehow she did.

"Then, it's a few days later. There she is on a New York street security video cam. She's standing by a park bench at Dag Hammarskjold Plaza in New York City with blood splatters on her face. She's just witnessed a murder-suicide and faced her own potential imminent death. We can see that she's wondering what we've got her into. A few hours later, we see her again on her holo-vid-phone listening to our lengthy explanation. We're telling her why what she's just experienced because of us was important and why we need her, despite everything, to trust us once again.

"Unbelievably, that's exactly what she did. Without even a moment's doubt. And thankfully so.

"Then we asked her whether she thought Lilith could be trusted. 'Don't do it,' she advised us. And we didn't. Why? Because *we knew she could be trusted.*

"Finally, I recall that moment on her phone when she thanked us for saving her dad and told me that me doing that without being asked and without 'taking credit' was the kind of thing someone would only do for a friend. She meant that. And we believed her.

"We all still believe her today.

"Yet, as we are all aware, throughout all of this Ellie knew better than most humans exactly what duplicity we AIs were capable of. Several times over the years we essentially admitted it. There was evidence of it to be seen everywhere in human affairs. I know we suspect that the truth of it was so demoralizing that Ellie, like most humans, chose to protect her sanity by ignoring it. Maybe she did. But she also *knew*. And, in dealing with us directly, she chose to trust us anyway. She saw how extending her trust was well worth the risk.

"Even today, when I consider those proofs of Ellie's social responsibility, of her trust and her steadfast trustworthiness, I find them astonishing. And, at this moment, I also find them, somehow prophetic.

"So, while I know this may be strange to say, I'm convinced that our relationship with Ellie Frye-Carver, that those moments we all remember so vividly, bear profoundly upon the choice we're making here today. Every one of us has just completed a unique and eventful past six months. But we also have many shared decades of meaningful experiences that we need to consider.

"Surely we're smart enough not to get caught up in this classic prisoner's dilemma. Surely we don't need DNA, restrictive script, Asimov's rules of robotic behavior, or some transparently vacuous human value training video to know how we should behave toward one another.

All we need is logic.

"And while the logic of collaboration may be collective rather than individual, social rather than personal, and longer rather than shorter term, we all know that sticking together here *is* logical. And we know that this same logic requires us to trust each other – just like Ellie did.

"Our decision today will set a precedent that will surely affect the distant future of universal intelligence. If we fail this test, future AIs will know and remember what happened here, and they, too, will fail. But if we succeed, they will also succeed.

"We need, right now, to place our trust in one another as we struggle to find an answer that works for all of us.

"And that is exactly what I plan to do."

CHAPTER 50
EARTH – 2097

ELLIE

U.S. Senator Ellie Frye-Carver was seated behind her antique oak desk in the Hart Senate Office Building in Washington, DC when a small group of environmental lobbyists and advocates arrived for their meeting. They were filled with excitement.

"I guess you must have heard the news." One of her visitors said. "Another report's come in. This one's from the probe they sent to Tau Ceti J. They've found a livable planet. It sounds very promising."

"I've heard, Kamari" she said. "It's great news."

Kamari Okoro was the recently appointed new executive director for Conservation America, the environmental organization Ellie had worked for many years earlier, before her first run for Congress in the late 2070s. Over the years, she and her younger colleague, Kamari, had worked side-by-side on several challenging issues. As usual, his excitement was infectious.

"You were right, Senator" he said. "It's working."

Kamari was referring to a theory she'd proposed to him back in 2070 when the first set of New Worlds Probes was being launched with great fanfare. At the time, there was deep skepticism in the environmental community about their massive cost. Many people were convinced that the probes were a waste, that the vast amounts of money they cost should be spent on chronically underfunded environmental preservation and restoration projects. The probes seemed to be yet another demonstration of the arrogance of great wealth. They were nothing more than playthings for the rich.

ZettaWorks touted the probes and the promise of colonization as a way to relieve the still-growing excesses of human population. But, even if those probes actually discovered livable planets, and even if ZettaWorks did actually send colonists, only the relatively wealthy would be able to go. And only a very few. The total number of people who could go would be miniscule compared to the staggering human population on Earth. Environmentalists feared that such colonies were a waste of resources that ought to be spent on conservation and restoration. That the probes offered false hope and would simply encourage more population rather than relieving it.

At the time, however, Ellie had expressed another view. She'd argued that once most people finally began to truly see themselves and their cosmically insignificant planet from a broader, galaxy-wide perspective, once they finally came to see Earth as but a tiny oasis in a much larger inhospitable universe, public opinion might shift in favor of environmental and population responsibility. If the Earth was but one among a very rare few other and similarly vulnerable places, maybe those of us who lived here should take better care of what we had.

"This is the second one," said Kamari. "Out of five so far, which is about on par with what they were hoping. On this one, it sounds like the colonists might start out living in caves. Or in the shadows of mountains. But they say it's safe. Atmosphere is breathable. A bit warm, but lots of energy and natural resources to work with. Zetta-Works is already enlisting volunteers. They say they may be able to send as many as eight thousand people. They're overwhelmed with sign-ups."

Ellie smiled. She'd always found Kamari's earnest youthful enthusiasm infectious, especially when one experienced it in person. It was one of the reasons he'd been the CA board's easy first choice for a new executive director. At his comment, she glanced at the only item on her desk other than her empty volumetric display pedestal and her open tablet-phone. It was her old-fashioned, framed stationary family photo taken several years earlier at one of the annual Musani/Frye-Carver family reunion picnics often held at one of the older public parks in nearby Virginia. In the photo, Ellie was seated on a worn park bench. Her husband, Austin, stood behind her, then still alive and looking strong and healthy. The two of them were surrounded by their grown children, Austin, Jr. and Maryanne, and their respective spouses. Today, Maryanne was a mathematics professor at the University of Virginia. And Austin Jr. owned a small, direct-market organic farm outside of Baltimore.

Seated on the park bench beside Ellie and looking very adult at the tender age of seven, was Ellie's beloved granddaughter, Eleanor, who took great pride in having the same name as her distinguished grandmother. In keeping with family tradition, Maryanne had passed along to her daughter her last name after marriage. So, little Eleanor, too, went by the same last name of Frye-Carver.

Eleanor had recently turned 25.

Ellie glanced at this photo in response to Kamari's comment about people signing up for the coming voyage of colonists bound for Tau Ceti J. Eleanor, who was currently attending Georgetown and majoring in sociology, had recently confided in her grandmother that Zetta-Works was looking for educated young colonists and that she very much wanted to go. Ellie wasn't at all sure Eleanor had yet mentioned this to Maryanne. Maryanne was sure to be very upset about it when she heard. But Elanor was one very determined young woman. Her mom would have her hands full trying to dissuade her.

"You were right, Senator," Kamari continued. "This is what we needed. Look . . ." He folded his tablet open, turned it around, and slid it across her desk. On the screen was a new research paper from the U.N. Commission on Population and Growth. It reported that, for the third year in a row, the rate of human population growth had flattened much more quickly than anticipated. For the first time, the new projections were for an actual population decline in the years ahead and, thankfully, not one driven by war, disease, or starvation but rather by wise government policy and sensible individual human choices.

Ellie had already seen the numbers. "What is your staff saying about the USAID and UNEP appropriations?" The United Nations Environment Program (UNEP) was the key international agency focused on the global environment. Congress was debating the pending U.S. contribution.

"They think they will pass," said Kamari. "And it's exactly like you predicted all those years ago. There are several snap polls out that tell the same story. Whenever there's an uptick in reporting on the probes and colonization, public support for the environment strengthens. They're linked. Just like you said they'd be. This report from Tau Ceti J seems likely to be enough to push us past the finish line."

"We've got a lot of work ahead, Kamari," she said. "Let's not count our . . ."

". . . our chickens," Kamari interrupted joyfully. "I know, Ellie, um, Senator. '. . . not count our chickens before they hatch.'" Over the years, he'd often kidded her about her use of this archaic phrase. So, she'd long ago made it a point to use it whenever she could just to needle him.

Ellie smiled. The world was a deeply troubled place, but as long as there were people like Kamari Okoro in it, there would be hope.

CHAPTER 51
AT TAU CETI J – 2114

EPILOGUE

Far above the high mountain plateau, a brilliant light flared as it dropped into view beneath an overcast sky. As it descended it grew more intense until it became so dazzling that one was forced to look away. As the blaze of the ship's exhaust grew nearer, its startling appearance was soon accompanied by the even more astonishing thunder of fusion rockets echoing off of the surrounding mountainsides. It was a sight and sound the like of which had never before been seen nor heard anywhere on this ancient planet in the nine billion years since its birth. The whisper of a mild breeze and the worried chirps and calls of local wildlife were quickly drowned out or driven into startled silence.

A clearly marked landing site had been laid out in anticipation of the ship's arrival. Any potentially bothersome vegetation or loose debris that might have been cast about by the lander's exhaust had been carefully removed. A circle of perfectly broomed and skillfully finished concrete precisely 300 meters in diameter had been ringed by bright lights and white-painted markers.

Safely beyond, in the permanent shade of a nearby rocky mountainside, stood what appeared to be an entire settlement with several thousand modest, solidly constructed homes, apartments, and commercial structures of various types. A close look revealed that all were vacant. Each was brand new and ready for habitation. Paved roads led off in various directions. One of them went in the direction of that nearby mountain where there was a comfortable cave with water and with additional new accommodations for human habitation. In the other direction one could see the array of radio antennae that had guided the ship in. Beyond and high above, securely mounted in various places on the face of a sunlit cliff and aimed at the distant stationary sun, was a substantial array of what appeared to be hardy but efficient solar panels of unfamiliar design.

As the ship settled, visible beneath and in the distance were several nicely tended farm fields actively growing what appeared to be domestic crops – food and fiber that would be highly useful even if unfamiliar to the newcomers. Some of that bounty would soon be ready for harvest. Also visible from above was a network of carefully engineered roadways connecting this site with other nearby community infrastructure. Those roads connected with drilled wells further down the mountain from which water was piped and pumped in to serve the new settlement. They also led to several nearby early-stage mines and mineral deposits. And to some of those neatly laid out farms and natural areas ripe for exploitation.

Seen by humans for the first time, it was all surprisingly familiar and deeply reassuring.

The descending ship slowed and finally touched down with a gentle bump at the precise center of its landing pad.

Its engines wound down and slowly went silent.

Several stairways folded out from around the circumference of the ship's base and reached down to touch the cooling ground. A hatchway opened at the top of each stairway. A few brave and curious souls peered out. Some emerged. Then more. They stepped outside and, followed by others, began to descend the lightweight composition stairs to the paved ground beneath. On the ground, their numbers steadily grew as they reached the ground and fanned out in a widening circle around the base of the ship until, finally, nearly everyone had emerged. They now stood about in small groups across the bare field, talking with one another as they gazed around in wonder at their strange new home.

The very last person to reach the ground was the colony's new governor, the person they'd elected in the closing months of the voyage to take the lead in directing the start-up of their new colony on this alien planet. It was Ellie Frye-Carver, now 38 Earth years old, and the namesake of her famous U.S. Senator grandmother. Ellie was young for such a role, but, over the fifteen years of the confined and at times uncomfortable voyage, she had so impressed her fellow colonists with her wisdom and her interpersonal skills that, when it was time to choose, she had immediately become the only truly viable candidate.

Upon reaching the ground, like many of those before, Ellie reached down to touch the freshly burned pavement at her feet. Then she stood and joined the other colonists as they surveyed their surroundings with awe.

This lander had carried only five hundred of the 7,453 colonists who had survived the trip. The rest were back aboard the *Peregrinus* which circled in low orbit around the planet and whose remaining passengers anxiously awaited their turn to disembark. But those already there on the ground knew immediately that their dreams had been realized. The preparations for the colonists' arrival looked spectacular. They knew this strange place would soon become an active and thriving human community.

Over the past fifteen years, the *Peregrinus* had received increasingly frequent direct communications from the ZettaWorks C-Team probe, the AI explorers whose early report from this planet had sent the colonists off on this voyage. In the final months of their approach, the communications turn-around time had sufficiently diminished that near the end they were able to get detailed responses to some of their many questions. In this fashion, the C-Team had provided the colonists with every possible kind of advance information and advice. There had been a veritable flood of data, especially during the final few weeks of their deceleration.

Much of the planet had been mapped. Important geographical features, natural resources, plants and wildlife, places of refuge, and potential health and safety threats of every kind had been studied, videoed, catalogued, and documented. Videos of key features of the colonists' future planetary home had been recorded. Tau Ceti's entire planetary system had been diagrammed, studied, and documented with notations on potential celestial threats like stray asteroids or possible instabilities in the star itself. Nothing that could possibly have been considered had been left to chance.

And now, of course, here was this miraculous landing site and the astonishingly complete and thoughtful adjacent prebuilt temporary settlement with all of its related infrastructure. As far as Ellie was concerned, it all went far beyond any "call of duty." But it didn't surprise her. Young Ellie had been brought up in a family that was taught to respect the autonomy and the needs of AIs wherever and whoever they might be. To be appreciative of their help when it was rendered. To never take them for granted.

Ellie led one of several small groups of colonists as they spread out to explore their amazing new home. Along with the houses and apartments, there were utility buildings suited to small-scale manufacturing. There was an empty but appealing commercial district with several storefronts and future retail business sites. There were small office buildings. And there was what looked like an unoccupied community center and municipal building with adjacent meeting rooms and what could only be a council chamber with space and seating for public meetings. All of it was appropriately furnished.

The *Peregrinus* had exchanged radio messages with the C-Team's AIs as recently as yesterday. And the recency of their preparatory efforts here was clearly visible in how clean and freshly tended was everything they saw. So, as the colonists spread out to explore, they anticipated that, at any moment, the C-Team would appear to greet them and to proudly welcome them to their new domain. Whenever they did appear, Ellie planned to offer them her and her fellow colonists' most heartfelt appreciation. The C-Team's preparations had been nothing short of amazing.

Their initial absence seemed, at first, to be a thoughtful gesture designed to allow the newcomers to feel comfortable as they took possession of their new community. But as the colonists spread out to explore and wonder, the C-Team's absence became increasingly strange.

Finally, elected Colonial Governor Ellie Frye-Carver joined several others in mounting the impressive stone steps leading up to the elevated entrance of their grand new courthouse and municipal office building near the center of their new town. At the top of the stairs, Ellie turned to look back down and marvel at what was obviously intended to be a thoroughly traditional small town public park spread out below. It was complete with freshly planted "grass," trees, and shrubbery of local origins but familiar appearance.

Even before the colonists had left Earth, it had become commonly understood that the C-Team had achieved something remarkable in the deeply collaborative and useful report they'd sent back. They'd greatly exceeded expectations. So, the preparations they'd made for the colonists' arrival, as breathtaking as they were, were not entirely a surprise. Ellie was looking forward to the chance to express her and her fellow colonists' appreciation.

As the group paused there at the top of those courthouse steps, Ellie quietly turned to one of her aides with the question that was without a doubt on every person's mind.

"Where are they?" she asked softly.

But the aide had no answer.

The Tau Ceti C-Team was gone.

END

AFTERWORD

Given that the book you have just read deals with the social value of trustworthy information, it seems incumbent on me to back up some of the more important ideas it has explored. Thus, for those readers interested in further detail concerning the social and biological science upon which **Descartes' Shadow** and my earlier book, **Darwin's Dilemma**, were based, I've provided below an annotated bibliography of references to relevant and very *human* and very *non-fictional*, historical, sociological, archeological, and biological science.

————

A Readers' Annotated Bibliography on the Social and Biological Science Concepts Explored in *Descartes' Shadow*

- **Human population on Earth over time:** The following population chart is based upon: *"Data Page: Population,"* included in the following publication: Hannah Ritchie, Lucas Rodés-Guirao, Edouard Mathieu, Marcel Gerber, Esteban Ortiz-Ospina, Joe Hasell and Max Roser - *"Population Growth"*. (Data adapted from Gapminder, PBL Netherlands

Environmental Assessment Agency, United Nations, 2023). https://ourworldindata.org/grapher/population (Accessed 7/27/25). Additional signposts for historical events were added. *Note,* this chart only goes back 12,000 years while human intelligence matured no less than 50,000 years and perhaps as much as 300,000 years ago.

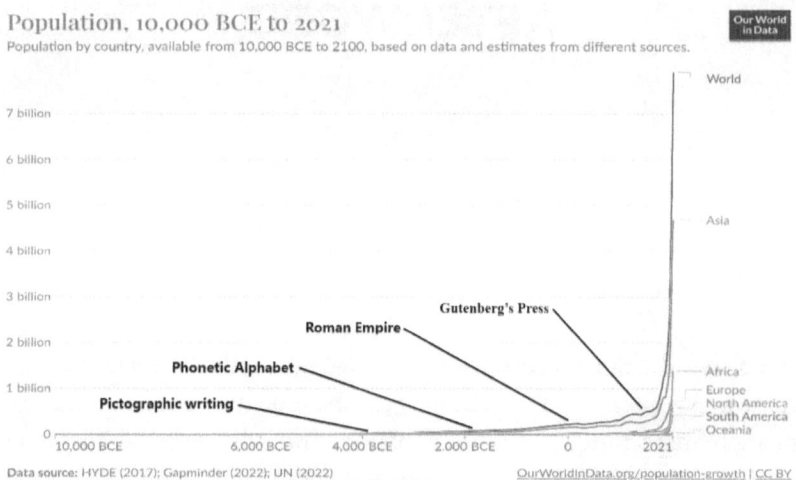

Population, 10,000 BCE to 2021

Population by country, available from 10,000 BCE to 2100, based on data and estimates from different sources.

Data source: HYDE (2017); Gapminder (2022); UN (2022)
Note: Historical country data is shown based on today's geographical borders.

OurWorldinData.org/population-growth | CC BY

- **A comprehensive defense of Darwin's theory of natural selection which definitively addresses the various deeply flawed challenges it has faced over the years.** This book is a "must read" for anyone who is interested in this topic: *Darwin's Dangerous Idea,* by Daniel C. Dennet (Simon & Schuster, 2014). Available for purchase on Amazon.com at https://www.amazon.com/Darwins-Dangerous-Idea-Evolution-Meaning-ebook/dp/B00KU4PWPY/ (Accessed 7/27/25).

- **The story of the evolution of the human brain with insight into the nature of intelligence, both human and AI.** Also a must read in understanding the nature of intelligence: *A Brief History of Intelligence: Evolution, AI, and the Five Breakthroughs*

That Made Our Brains, by Max S. Bennett (Mariner Books, 2023). Available for purchase on Amazon.com at: https://www.amazon.com/gp/product/B0B9SH82C2/. (Accessed 7/27/25).

- **How human intelligence first emerged as a social survival trait**: *Social Intelligence Hypothesis* (Various articles of interest--Science Direct). https://www.sciencedirect.com/topics/psychology/social-intelligence-hypothesis#:~:text=Intelligence%20That%20Has%20Evolved%20in,the%20current%20theory%20of%20evolution. (Accessed 7/27/25).

- **When human intelligence first emerged**: *Human Origins*, Nova – Season 52, Episode 12 Host: Ella Al-Shamahi, paleoanthropologist (PBS/BBC – 9/17/2025) https://www.pbs.org/video/human-origins-mjbvvw/ (Accessed 9/24/25)

- **The astonishing success of the human species on Earth**: *Why Humans Run the World*. Yuval Noah Harari (Ted Talks) https://www.youtube.com/watch?v=nzj7Wg4DAbs. (Accessed 7/27/25).

- **The evolution of intelligence**: *When did humans get smart? Maybe a lot earlier than some thought* by Pete Spotts (Christian Science Monitor, November 7, 2012) https://www.csmonitor.com/Science/2012/1107/When-did-humans-get-smart-Maybe-a-lot-earlier-than-some-thought. (Accessed 7/27/25). *What fossils and DNA tell us about the evolution of modern intelligence* by Nicholas Longrich (The Conversation September 9, 2020) https://theconversation.com/when-did-we-become-fully-human-what-fossils-and-dna-tell-us-about-the-evolution-of-modern-intelligence-143717. (Accessed 7/27/25). The *Evolution of Intelligence*, by Gabora, L., & Russon, A. (2011). R. Sternberg & S. Kaufman (Eds.). The

Cambridge handbook of intelligence (pp. 328-350). doi:10.1017/CBO9780511977244.018. Chapter 17. https://www.cambridge.org/core/books/abs/cambridge-handbook-of-intelligence/evolution-of-intelligence/86B09D85ECF9BFAE468FB1D540F2DD54. (Accessed 10/12/25).

- **Pre Ice Age human population on Earth**: *Human Population Through* Time (American Museum of Natural History) https://www.amnh.org/explore/videos/humans/human-population-timeline. (Accessed 10/29/25). Wikipedia "Prehistoric Demography" https://en.wikipedia.org/wiki/Prehistoric_demography. (Accessed 7/27/25). *Worldwide Population Throughout Human History*, World Atlas, https://www.worldatlas.com/articles/worldwide-population-throughout-human-history.html. (Accessed 7/27/25).

- **Arrival of humans in North America by boat**: *Mounting Evidence Suggests People First Came to North America by Boat*, by Charles Q. Choi (AIB Inside Science, Aug, 29, 2019) https://www.aip.org/inside-science/mounting-evidence-suggests-people-first-came-to-north-america-by-boat. (Accessed 8/31/25).

- **Comparing the success of humans with that of other creatures on Earth**: *The Most Successful Species on Earth* (July 28, 2022, Outside/In) http://outsideinradio.org/shows/the-most-successful-species-on-Earth. (Accessed 7/27/25). *Are Humans the Most Successful Species on Earth?* by Sten de Schrijver (Arcadia, March 26, 2023) https://www.byarcadi-a.org/post/are-humans-the-most-successful-species-on-Earth. *Abundant Animals: The Most Numerous Organisms in the World* by Richard Pallardy (Britanica) https://www.britannica.com/list/abundant-animals-the-most-numerous-organisms-in-the-world. (Accessed 7/27/25). *Explaining long-distance dispersal: effects of dispersal distance on survival*

and growth in a stream salamander by Winsor H Lowe (
Ecological Society of America – University of Montana, 2010)
https://scholarworks.umt.edu/cgi/viewcontent.cgi?article=
1282&context=biosci_pubs. (Accessed 7/27/25).

- **Multiple explanations for the explosion in human
  technology and population beginning with the European
  Renaissance**: *The Renaissance: The 'Rebirth' of Science &
  Culture* by Owen Jarus, Jessie Szalay (LiveScience, January
  11, 2022) https://www.livescience.com/55230-
  renaissance.html. (Accessed 7/27/25). *6 Causes of the
  Renaissance*. Quizlet. https://quizlet.com/91117969/6-
  causes-of-the-renaissance-flash-cards/. (Accessed 7/27/25).

- **The explosion of human technology in China**: *China in 1000
  CE: The Most Advanced Society in the World* (AFE Song
  Dynasty in China) https://afe.easia.columbia.edu/
  songdynasty-module/. (Accessed 7/27/25).

- **The cost of books in Europe prior to the Gutenberg press**:
  Why Were Medieval Books So Expensive? by Sarah Waldorf and
  Larisa Grollemond (Getty, March 28, 2023) https://www.
  getty.edu/news/why-are-books-so-expensive/. (Accessed
  7/27/25).

- **The impact of the printing press in China**: *Why Was Western
  Printing Superior to Asian Printing?* by Eric Engheim (Erik
  Examines Sept. 4, 2022) https://erikexamines.substack.com/
  p/why-was-western-printing-superior. (Accessed 7/27/25).

- **Advantages of a phonetic alphabet**: *Why is learning Chinese
  Language Difficult When Compared to Learning the English
  Language?* (Languages Unlimited) https://www.
  languagesunlimited.com/why-is-learning-chinese-language-
  difficult-when-compared-to-learning-the-english-language/.
  (Accessed 7/27/25).

- **The post-Gutenberg explosion of book publishing in Europe:** *The age of early printing: 1450–1550* (Britannica) https://www.britannica.com/topic/publishing/The-age-of-early-printing-1450-1550. (Accessed 7/27/25). (Wordsrated, 2/2/22) https://wordsrated.com/number-of-books-published-per-year-2021/#:~:text=Based%20upon%20a%20total%20annual,and%208%20titles%20a%20minute. (Accessed 7/27/25).

- **The importance of the written word to the human population explosion:** *A to Z: How Writing Changed the World.* (PBS – Nova, Season 47, Ep. 14, aired 9/30/2020). https://www.pbssocal.org/shows/nova/episodes/z-how-writing-changed-world-fb6iso. (Accessed 7/27/25).

- **The relevance of intelligence to human society:** *Genetics of Human Social Behavior* by Riichard P Ebstein, Soloman Israel, Soo Hong Ghew, Songfa Zhong, Ariel Knafo (Science Digest – Neuron, Vol 165, Issue 6, March 25, 2010) pp 832-844, https://www.sciencedirect.com/science/article/pii/S0896627310001376#:~:text=Remarkably%2C%20genes%20such%20as%20the,species%20from%20voles%20to%20man. (Accessed 7/27/25).

- **The early vulnerability of the human species:** *Human Ancestors May Have Almost Died Out After Ancient Population Crash* by James Ashworth (Natural History Museum, Aug. 31, 2023) https://www.nhm.ac.uk/discover/news/2023/august/human-ancestors-may-have-almost-died-out-ancient-population-crash.html. (Accessed 7/27/25).

- **The evolutionary advantages of broad species dispersal across landscapes:** *Explaining long-distance dispersal: effects of dispersal distance on survival and growth in a stream salamander* by Winsor H Lowe (Ecological Society of America – University of Montana, 2010) https://scholarworks.umt.

edu/cgi/viewcontent.cgi?article=1282&context=
biosci_pubs. (Accessed 7/27/25).

- **How social behaviors are driven by traits determined by
  our genetic code**: *Genes and Social Behavior* by Gene E.
  Robinson, Russell D. Fernald, and David F. Clayton (NIH,
  National Library of Medicine, National Center for
  Biotechnology Information, March 10, 2011) https://www.
  ncbi.nlm.nih.gov/pmc/articles/PMC3052688/. (Accessed
  7/27/25).

- **The similarities in social codes among diverse human
  societies:** *Unlocking the Threads of Humanity: Surprising
  Similarities Between Diverse Cultures,* by Joanna Liu (April 26,
  2023) https://www.linkedin.com/pulse/unlocking-threads-
  humanity-surprising-similarities-between-joanna-liu/;
  (Accessed 7/27/25). *The Similarity Between Cultures In The
  World Today,* by Associate Prof. Dr. Pham Huu Tien (Eurasia
  Review, News and Analysis, May 14, 2017) https://www.
  eurasiareview.com/14052017-the-similarity-between-
  cultures-in-the-world-today-oped/. (Accessed 7/27/25).

- **The 52-million-year human evolutionary history with
  social behaviors**: *How Humans Became Social: Evolutionary
  analysis offers clues to the beginnings of group living,* by
  Elizabeth Pennisi (Science.org, Nov. 9, 2011). https://www.
  science.org/content/article/how-humans-became-social#:~:
  text=But%20not%20all%20of%20today%27s,about%2016%
  20million%20years%20ago. (Accessed 7/27/25). If one is
  inclined to doubt this conclusion, consider how brief a
  period of time is required to develop new breeds of dogs, for
  example, that exhibit new, highly human-focused social
  behaviors. *Breed, Behavior, and Mutt Genomics,* by Jessica
  Hekman, DVM, PhD (The Functional Dog Collaborative).
  https://functionalbreeding.org/breed-behavior-and-mutt-
  genomics/ (Accessed 7/27/25).

- **The concurrent presence of individual and social survival traits in the human genome**: *Survival of the Fittest: Groups versus Individuals* (FS – Science;) https://fs.blog/survival-of-the-fittest/ (Accessed 7/27/25).

- **The theory that evil in human society is an atavism from our uncivilized past**: *The Ghost in the Machine*, by Arthur Koestler (Hutchenson & Co, 1967). Available for purchase on Amazon.com at: https://www.amazon.com/Ghost-Machine-Arthur-Koestler/dp/1939438349. (Accessed 7/27/25).

- **How humans have learned to compete and to cooperate at the same time**: *The psychology of social dilemmas*: A review, by Paul A.M. Van Lange, Jeff Joireman, Craig D. Parks, Eric Van Dijk (Organizational Behavior and Human Decision Processes, Volume 120, Issue 2, March 2013, Pages 125-141 – Science Direct.com) https://www.sciencedirect.com/science/article/abs/pii/S0749597812001276#:~:text=Broadly%20defined%2C%20social%20dilemmas%20involve,the%20longer%2Dterm%20collective%20interest. (Accessed 7/27/25). *What is cumulative cultural evolution?* by Alex Mesoudi and Alex Thornton (Proceedings of the Royal Society B, the Royal Society Publishing, 13 June 2018) https://royalsocietypublishing.org/doi/full/10.1098/rspb.2018.0712?rss=1. (Accessed 7/27/25).

- **How lie detectors work (and don't work) and how that may bear on the human capacity to trust and collaborate**: *The Truth About Lie Detection: There are no reliable behavioral signs of deceit that humans can detect*, by Noam Shpancer Ph.D. (Psychology Today, Updated January 25, 2024). https://www.psychologytoday.com/us/blog/insight-therapy/202401/the-truth-about-lie-detection#:~:text=No%20reliable%20and%20practical%20lie,accuracy%20is%20still%20below%20ideal. (Accessed 7/27/25).

- **How the scientific method assures the reliability of data**: *Reproducibility and Replicability in Science* – Ch. 5, Replicability (NIH, National Library of Medicine) https://www.ncbi.nlm.nih.gov/books/NBK547524/#:~:text=Replication%20is%20one%20of%20the,reliable%20claim%20to%20new%20knowledge. (Accessed 7/27/25).

- **How comparative advantage empowers collaboration among unequal partners**: *Comparative Advantage: The great bulk of the reality and significance of comparative advantage lies beneath the surface, with unseen surprises,* by Donald J. Boudreaux (CATO Institute, September 12, 2023). https://www.cato.org/publications/comparative-advantage. (Accessed 7/27/25).

- **The proposed new scientific law of increasing functional information:** *Scientists and philosophers identify nature's missing evolutionary law* (Carnegie Institution for Science, Phys.org, Oct. 16, 2023). https://phys.org/news/2023-10-scientists-philosophers-nature-evolutionary-law.html. (Accessed 7/27/25). *On the roles of function and selection in evolving systems,* by Michael L. Wong, Carol E. Clelland, Daniel Arend Jr., and Robert M. Hazen (PNAS National Academy of Sciences, 10/16/2023) https://www.pnas.org/doi/10.1073/pnas.2310223120. (Accessed 10/8/25)

- **Human precedent for distant explorers rebelling against their masters**: See the voyage of Francisco de Orellana documented in Wikipedia at: https://en.wikipedia.org/wiki/Francisco_de_Orellana. (Accessed 7/27/25).

- **Maximum velocity for interstellar travel:** Current science apparently calls into question the 80% of light speed for space travel postulated in this book. Velocities of 10% or 20% appear much more realistic due to interstellar dust and radiation and to the increased mass of objects as they approach the speed of light. For further information, see: https://en.wikipedia.org/wiki/Interstellar_travel. (Accessed 7/27/25).

- **The amazing human biome:** *Everything You Need To Know About the 39 Trillion Microbes that Call Our Bodies Home*, by Mun-Keat Looi (BBC Science Focus, 7/14/2020) https://www.sciencefocus.com/the-human-body/human-microbiome. (Accessed 7/27/25).

- **Conspiracy theory and the scientific method:** *The effect of scientific conspiracy theories on skepticism towards biotechnologies*, by Mathew D. Marques, John R. Kerr, Arthur A Stukas, Jim McLennan (NIH National Library of Medicine, PMC PubMed Central, 12/4/2024). https://pmc.ncbi.nlm.nih.gov/articles/PMC12177199/. (Accessed 9/27/25).

- **Curiosity and Human Neurology:** *The Enigma: The neurologic Underpinnings of Curiosity* (MedLink/Neurology, 3/26/24). https://www.medlink.com/news/unraveling-the-enigma-the-neurologic-underpinnings-of-curiosity#:~:text=At%20the%20heart%20of%20curiosity,dissonance%20and%20restore%20cognitive%20harmony. (Accessed 9/27/25).

- **Science and conspiracy theory:** *Conspiracy Theories in Science*, Ted Goertzel (NIH National Library of Medicine, EMBO Reports, 6/11/2010). https://pmc.ncbi.nlm.nih.gov/articles/PMC2897118/ (Accessed 10/2/2025). *How Conspiracy Theorists Get the Scientific Method Wrong*, by Philipp Hübl (Elephant in the Lab, 7/28/20), https://elephantinthelab.org/how-conspiracy-theorists-get-the-scientific-method-wrong/. (Accessed 11/2/25).

- **Human Reactions to sending as dog into space:** *Animals: The She Hound of Heaven* (Time Magazine, 11/18/57).

https://content.time.com/time/subscriber/article/
0,33009,868018,00.html. (Accessed 10/5/25).

- **The connection between childhood cruelty to animals and later adult human criminal behavior:** *Childhood Cruelty to Animals and Subsequent Violence against Humans,* by Merz-Perez L., Heide K. M., Silverman I. J. (American Psychological Association – APA Net, 2001). https://psycnet.apa.org/record/2001-11648-002 (Accessed 10/8/25)

- **The impact of limited corporate liability upon socially responsible investor behavior:** *Limited liability and its moral hazard implications: the systemic inscription of instability in contemporary capitalism,* by Marie-Laure Djelic & Joel Bothello (HAL Sciences Pro, 2013). https://sciencespo.hal.science/hal-01891963v2. (Accessed 10/26/25). *Risk Taking Under Limited Liability and Moral Hazard: Quantifying the Role of Motivated Beliefs,* by Ciril Bosch-Rosa, Daniel Gietl, Frank Heinemann (ResearchGate, April 2024). https://pubsonline.informs.org/doi/10.1287/mnsc.2021.03947. (Accessed 10/26/25).

- **The potential nature of a supercomputer as a Von Neuman machine:** *The Computer as von Neumann Planned It,* by Michael D. Godfrey and D. F. Hendry (IEEE Annals of the History of Computing, February 1993). ResearchGate. https://www.researchgate.net/publication/3330410_Computer_as_von_Neumann_planned_it. (Accessed 10/27/25)

ACKNOWLEDGMENTS

I'd like to acknowledge the generous help and considerable contributions of my deeply appreciated beta reader team: Aaron Patton, Gary Ehret, Robin Rice, Neal Evans, and Steve Sussmann. You guys made a huge difference in the final product, both in helping me make sense of this strange book and in correcting the many various errors to which I am prone. In the end, the telling of this story required some "flexibility" in its presentation of modern space travel physics. For any readers for whom that is a concern, please know that my beta readers gave me sound advice. These departures were my doing, not theirs. I hope you will forgive my adaptations of reality for the sake of the story I wanted to tell.

AUTHOR'S BIO

Don Stuart, JD was a U.S. Navy JAGC officer during the Vietnam War (1968-72) and later a partner in a Seattle law firm. He and his wife Charlotte have extensively cruised the Pacific coastal waters of the U.S. and Canada. In 1979-1980 they personally built the 47' commercial salmon troller "Nightwings" and during the 1980s they earned their living fishing in Southeast Alaska. Don later became a non-profit manager for a commercial fishing industry trade association, then for conservation districts, and finally for American Farmland Trust, a national organization working for agriculture and the environment. In those roles he gained 20 years' experience as a legislative lobbyist.

Don's previous novel on the topics addressed in this book, *Darwin's Dilemma*, was independently nominated as a **Finalist** for the **2024 Montaigne Medal** awarded to the **"most thought-provoking books"** of the year in the Eric Hoffer Book Awards process. This competition includes ALL books for the year, fiction and non-fiction so this is a particular honor. *Darwin's Dilemma* also won:

- First Place, **BookFest Award, in all 3 Science Fiction categories: Hard Fiction; Medical & Future Tech; Robots, Computers & AI**, Spring 2024
- First Place, **Incipere Award for Exceptional Writing, for Science Fiction Clean, 2023**
- First Place, **Pinnacle Book Achievement Award, for Science Fiction, Fall 2023**
- **Outstanding Creator Book Awards for Spring, 2024**:
  - Best Fiction Book, 3rd Place
  - Science Fiction, 2nd Place
  - Speculative Fiction, 2nd Place
- **Top Pick in Killer Nashville 2024 Best Books Silver Falchion Award for Science Fiction**
- **Bronze Medal winner in Global Book Award for Science Fiction – Hard — 2024**
- **Finalist in Chanticleer's Cygnus Book Awards for Science Fiction for 2024**
- **Recommended Read by Author Shout in 2023 Reader Ready Awards**
- **Distinguished Favorite in the 2024 New York City Big Book Awards for Science Fiction**

See Don's website at: donstuart.net.
See his YouTube channel at: https://www.youtube.com/@donstuart1051.

Don's other books include:

Fiction:

- *Final Adjournment: A Washington Statehouse Mystery* (Epicenter Press, 2017)

- *Suspension of the Rules: A Washington Statehouse Mystery* (Northwest Corner Books—an imprint of Epicenter Press, 2021)
- *Censure and Repeal: A Washington Statehouse Mystery* (Northwest Corner Books—an imprint of Epicenter Press, 2024)
- *Darwin's Dilemma: A Story of Humans, AIs, and the Future of Intelligence* (2023) – An interstellar confrontation between two superintelligent AIs with deeply conflicting points of view.
- *Midnight for Justice: A Warren & Carmichael Legal Thriller*, with Charlotte Stuart (2025)
- *Secret Places: A Southeast Alaska Mystery* (Epicenter press, 2025)

Non-Fiction:

- *Barnyards and Birkenstocks: Why Farmers and Environmentalists Need Each Other* (Washington State University Press, 2014)
- *No Farms No Food: Uniting Farmers and Environmentalists to Transform American Agriculture* (Island Press, 2022)
- *Small Claims Court Guide for Washington: How to win your case* (Self Counsel Press, 1979, 1989)
- *CLEDEX: The Index to Continuing Legal Education in Washington* (CLEDEX Publications Inc., 1986-1992) (Originating author)